nish Secret

Emma Burstall studied English at Cambridge University before becoming a journalist and author. *Tremarnock*, the first novel in her series set in a delightful Cornish village, was published in 2015 and became a top ten bestseller.

Also by Emma Burstall

Gym and Slimline
Never Close Your Eyes
The Darling Girls

Tremarnock Series

Tremarnock
The Cornish Guest House
Tremarnock Summer
A Cornish Secret

A Cornish Secret

Emma Burstall

HEAD
ZEUS

First published in the UK in 2018 by Head of Zeus Ltd
This paperback edition published in 2019 by Head of Zeus Ltd

Copyright © Emma Burstall 2018

9 7 5 3 1 2 4 6 8

A catalogue record for this book is available
from the British Library.

ISBN (PB): 9781786698858
ISBN (E): 9781786698834

Typesetting: Divaddict Publishing Solutions Ltd
Map: Amber Anderson

Printed and bound in Great Britain by
CPI Group (UK) Ltd, Croydon CR0 4YY

Head of Zeus Ltd
First Floor East
5–8 Hardwick Street
London EC1R 4RG

WWW.HEADOFZEUS.COM

To Georgia Maguire and Ed Templeton

KEY

1. JACK'S COTTAGE
2. THE VICTORY INN
3. CHILDREN'S PLAY PARK
4. EBB TIDE (TONY AND FELIPE'S PLACE)
5. THE NOOK (PAT'S FORMER PLACE)
6. DOVE COTTAGE (ESME'S PLACE)
7. SHELL COTTAGE
8. BAG END (LIZ AND ROBERT'S PLACE)
9. THE METHODIST CHURCH
10. COPPER COTTAGE
11. DOLLY'S PLACE
12. DYNNARGH (JEAN AND TOM'S PLACE)
13. THE STABLES
14. THE HOLE IN THE WALL PUB
15. THE FISHMONGER
16. THE MARKETPLACE
17. THE BAKERY
18. GENERAL STORE
19. SEASPRAY BOUTIQUE
20. GULL COTTAGE (JENNY AND JOHN'S PLACE)

Chapter One

RAIN SPLATTERED OUTSIDE the apartment window, staining the slate-blue dome of the grand Église Saint-Augustin and turning the Paris pavements murky grey. A woman below in a camel-coloured trench coat reached into her bag and pulled out a black umbrella with white spots and a jaunty frill. Caroline found herself thinking of Renoir's *Les Parapluies*, which always made her smile because the people in it looked so cheerful.

There was nothing jolly about this lady, however, with her head bent low against the wind, her shoulders hunched, pace quickening with each step as she scurried along the Boulevard Malesherbes. Caroline didn't blame her for rushing; she wouldn't choose to be out in this, with or without umbrella, although sometimes the four walls of the apartment felt more like a prison than a haven from the elements.

She turned away from the window back to the sturdy black suitcase on the end of her bed and inspected its contents. Had she packed enough sweaters? The ugly green cagoule would protect her from the rain, but wouldn't keep her cosy. She wasn't bound for le Midi, after all. Where she was going, the weather was entirely unpredictable and it was the tail end of summer now, too. There could be thunderstorms, gales and goodness knew what. On the other hand, it might be warm and balmy. Impossible to tell.

Cornwall. She felt a little shiver of excitement. She'd been there only once with her family when she was a child and even then, they'd stayed just a week. She could vaguely remember narrow cobbled streets, rocky beaches and stopping for a cream tea in a farmer's garden, where her younger brother had been stung by a wasp and had made an appalling racket, much to their mother's mortification.

Other than that, her knowledge of the county was based largely on books, television programmes and magazine articles. She pictured quaint little fishing villages, handmade pasty shops and ruddy-faced locals with drawling burrs, but it might be quite different now: spoiled, its cute image nothing more than a commercial ploy to lure gullible tourists like her.

No matter, she thought, walking over to the chest of drawers against the wall and pulling out another jumper; she wasn't intending to do much sightseeing. The point of the trip was to gain an insight into how it might have felt for the Christian pilgrims who trudged along St Michael's Way in medieval times, right across the peninsula from Lelant, near St Ives, to St Michael's Mount on the opposite coast, before journeying to France and, ultimately, the grand cathedral of Santiago de Compostela in northern Spain. It was here that the bones of the apostle St James were said to lie, and according to legend, if you completed the whole journey on foot you would leave your burdens behind. How glorious!

Would she, like the pilgrims of old, experience a spiritual awakening, an unburdening of the soul? She smiled grimly to herself. Sore feet, more like, and aching shins. But it would be interesting, for sure, and, of course, there was Esme…

She felt her stomach lurch and gave herself a mental shake. No point stressing about that. If they didn't get on, it was only five little days. Anyone could survive five days in another's company, surely? And they weren't exactly strangers; they'd been in touch, albeit loosely, for over forty years.

'I've got the keys to the new house.' Caroline's husband Philip dragged her back to the present.

She looked across the wide, light room to where he stood displaying a small bunch of keys on a steel ring in the palm of his outstretched hand. He was of medium height, his grey hair cut very short in an attempt to disguise the balding patch on the centre of his head, while his eyebrows, still thick and dark, seemed to belong to someone else. He used to be robust and athletic but was thinner now; his pale blue shirt, rolled up at the sleeves, hung limply around his chest and waist. Caroline thought that he seemed diminished, shrunken, almost; half the man he once was, or that she'd thought he'd been.

She was reminded of the fake boiled egg gag that the children used to play. They'd turn the egg upside down in the eggcup as if it hadn't been eaten, then she'd come up and stick her spoon through the shell and exclaim, 'Oh, you tricked me AGAIN!'

Hadn't she always known that the egg was empty? Cracked in places, with bits of sticky yolk clinging to the sides? But she'd put on a good show, for sure. She'd even half-believed it herself.

She glanced back to her suitcase on the spotless cream bedspread and sensed her husband flinch, as if her silence had stung him.

'Won't you cancel your trip and come and see it with me?' he asked at last, standing well back as if he knew better than to encroach on the chilly space that surrounded her; a wartime neutral zone. 'I'll drive. We can spend a few days exploring the area.'

Caroline swallowed. The boyish hesitancy in his voice stirred something deep within – a maternal echo, perhaps, but she batted it away.

'I can't, it's all booked. You go and enjoy it.'

He seemed about to leave, but changed his mind and hovered for a moment as if plucking up courage. 'How long are you going to keep this up, Caro?'

He sounded wounded, as if it was all somehow her fault, and she felt her insides harden, like burned sugar at the bottom of a pan. He watched as she moved over to the cabinet on what used to be her side of the bed; she slept on both sides, now, and sometimes sprawled right across the middle. Then she opened the top drawer and pulled out her passport, travel documents and luggage tags, already filled in.

'I'll be back in a week.'

'I hope you find what you're looking for.' His deep voice seemed to resonate around the walls before he came to an abrupt halt right at her feet.

'Me too.' She swept past him into the hallway towards the cupboard where she'd left her brand-new walking boots, still unopened in their smart white cardboard box.

He followed her just as far as the spare bedroom, then entered it, closing the door softly behind him. She didn't see him again until the next morning, when she was dragging her suitcase into the lift to take down the two flights of stairs to the waiting taxi.

Across the English Channel, in the little seaside village of Tremarnock in south-east Cornwall, Esme Posorsky was pacing around her upstairs flat, checking again that the white shutters were properly closed, electrical sockets turned off and appliances unplugged. She wasn't normally as conscientious, but she'd already dressed, washed, had two cups of tea and zipped up her suitcase. The pot plants had been watered; Rasputin, her fluffy marmalade cat, had been fed and she'd arranged for her friend and neighbour, Liz, to feed him in her absence.

She'd locked up her pottery studio in the neighbouring village and didn't need to go there again. The washing, normally hanging on a wooden airer by the bedroom radiator, had been put away, and there were no stray cups or plates on the draining board. She really couldn't think of anything else, and there was still an hour before she'd need to leave for the railway station. Why did time go so slowly when you wanted it to fly?

She decided that she'd be better off taking a walk than sitting around here twiddling her thumbs, and found herself wishing that she could call on Tabitha. The young woman had only recently moved out of the downstairs flat with her small son, Oscar, and Esme missed them. They hadn't gone far, but Dove Cottage felt a bit lonely now: quieter and colder, because the heat no longer rose up through the floorboards of the old fisherman's cottage. Her gas and electricity bills would rocket this winter, for sure.

She slipped on her green Birkenstock sandals and checked herself in the small oval wall mirror by the door. Like most of the items in the flat, it was an antique of sorts; not worth much but pleasing to look at, with its gilt frame and bevelled edges. It dated back to the thirties and had been left to her by her Polish grandmother, along with various bits of jewellery. Esme tended to the view, like her hero, William Morris, that you should have nothing in the house that you did not know to be useful or believe to be beautiful. To this, though, she would add 'or dear to your heart', because she could be tremendously sentimental.

A strand of her salt-and-pepper hair had escaped from its bun and she fastened it with a hairgrip as she gazed at her reflection: the thin face, pale skin, broad, high forehead, probing little grey eyes and sharp nose. She wasn't vain, because she'd never considered herself beautiful. Down the years she'd heard herself described as 'strong-boned', 'handsome' and 'unusual', which she'd chosen to take as compliments; but she'd never heard anyone call her pretty.

In any case, she liked to think that what she lacked in beauty, she more than made up for in style. She loved colour, and as an art student in London in the seventies, she'd cultivated an eccentric, bohemian air with long, flowing cheesecloth skirts, droopy ethnic tops – usually picked up in flea markets – and outlandish jewellery. It was an image that she'd stuck with because she knew it suited her, and even now, at sixty-one, it gave her some satisfaction to know that she still stood out in a crowd.

That said, today she felt unusually dowdy. The khaki walking trousers, bought just recently, were an odd shape, and her faded, navy cotton top had cat hairs on it. She picked them off, one by one, and checked the clasps at the back of her turquoise stud earrings. She'd have to do.

She was about to switch off the overhead light and grab her bag from the small table beneath the mirror when she heard footsteps clattering up the fire escape that led to her front door. Grateful for the distraction, she hurried to open up and was pleased to find Liz on the step, clutching the hand of her small daughter, Lowenna.

If Esme hadn't known them so well she might have laughed, because the pair were like identical versions of each other in different sizes. Both slightly built, they had straight dark hair tied back in ponytails, pale skin and big, round chocolate-brown eyes that gazed at you from beneath heavy fringes. The main dissimilarity on this particular morning, apart from their heights, was that Liz had a beautiful smile while Lowenna's round face was scrunched up tight, her bottom lip sticking out.

Esme didn't know much about the ways of children and might have ignored the little girl's sulky expression, but Lowenna broke away from her mother and raced past both women into the darkened front room, where she threw herself on her tummy, drummed her small feet on the floorboards and proceeded to shriek.

'What's the matter?' Esme asked, tipping her head to one side and staring at the child as though at a strange creature in a zoo.

'Little Ducklings,' Liz replied grimly. 'She screamed blue murder all the way through.'

'Oh dear.'

Esme had heard about Lowenna's swimming lessons, which were supposed to cure her fear of water but didn't seem to be working too well. The little girl, now two years old, had had a phobia ever since a near-fatal accident the previous September, when Liz's friend Bramble had taken her into the sea to paddle and they'd been caught in a rip tide. Luckily, Bramble's fiancé Matt had arrived just in time to prevent a tragedy.

'Would she like a biscuit?' Esme asked, slightly desperate because the screeching was hurting her ears.

When Liz said yes, the noise stopped, as if by magic.

Lowenna followed Esme to the kitchen and watched her rootle in the biscuit tin. Then, with a chocolate chip cookie in one hand and some wooden salad servers to play with in the other, the child sat happily in front of the fireplace on a rug decorated with strutting peacocks.

Esme opened the shutters again and bright sunlight flooded the room, illuminating the peacocks' vivid blue and green feathers, the jewel-like colour of the cushions on the sofa and the shimmering gold Buddha on the shelf above the TV. Just behind it was a statue of the Virgin Mary in a white gown and royal blue cape, her hands clasped in prayer. Having been brought up a Catholic, Esme still went to Mass once a week, but she'd be the first to admit that these days it was more out of habit than anything else. She was interested in world religions and had studied them a bit; in truth, she found the Buddhist philosophy more palatable, though she'd never seriously considered converting.

'I hope I'm not delaying you?' Liz asked, taking a seat beside her friend on the pinkish-purple sofa. 'Rosie said she'd like to feed Rasputin. I just wanted to check that's OK with you?'

Rosie was Liz's fourteen-year-old daughter by her previous partner, Greg.

'Of course,' said Esme. She'd known the girl since she was small. She and her mother, stepfather and little sister now lived in the cottage several doors down, called Bag End.

Soon the women were nursing homemade lattes in vintage porcelain mugs decorated with English roses. The room was quiet for a moment, save for Lowenna's contented mumblings, the odd screech of a seagull outside and the occasional rumbling of a car driving by.

Liz, who wore flip-flops, jeans and a simple white T-shirt, crossed one leg over another and asked Esme about her forthcoming walking trip. 'You haven't told me who you're going with?'

'Someone I was at school with,' Esme replied, blowing on her drink before taking a sip. 'Caroline. We boarded together at St Hilda's in Canterbury. It was a convent school, run by nuns. She was a couple of years below me and I was her "buddy", which meant it was my job to help her settle in. She only stayed a year and a half but we've kept in touch, though we haven't actually seen each other in all that time. Her husband worked for an international aid agency and they've lived all over the world, most recently in Paris. He's just retired. It'll be quite strange to see her again.'

Liz's eyes widened. 'Goodness! You'll have a lot to catch up on!'

Esme went on to explain that Caroline had made it her mission to walk the entire length of the famous Camino Santiago de Compostela, the ancient pilgrims' route, completing different sections each time. She'd already done part of the French and Spanish sections and when she'd discovered that one leg of the trek started in Cornwall, she'd resolved to do it.

She had mentioned the idea in an email and soon, a plan had been hatched. The women would finally meet after all this time to trudge the route together, along with a tranche of the spectacular South West Coast Path, making it a five-day holiday in total.

'You weren't tempted to visit Caroline before this?' Liz asked.

Esme shook her head. 'We were both too busy. It's a miracle we've managed to find a window now.'

Liz raised her eyebrows, and Esme knew what she was thinking: that her diary wasn't exactly packed. She was single, after all, and self-employed, so she could surely please herself?

'What about you? How's the family?' she asked, changing the subject. 'I haven't seen Robert for ages.'

Liz pulled a face. 'Me neither.'

Her husband, who owned the famous fish restaurant A Winkle in Time in Tremarnock, was in negotiations to buy the Secret Shack, a run-down café on Polrethen beach, and turn it into a thriving eatery serving simple, freshly made food such as seafood chowder, crab sandwiches, lobster and chips and homemade Cornish pasties.

She understood, she said, that it could be a money-spinner but was worried about the work involved.

'His business plan took ages, and now he seems to be spending every spare moment talking to builders and suppliers, and he hasn't even signed on the dotted line yet. I dread to think what it will be like if the deal goes ahead. He'll be working twenty-four/seven. I've told him I think it's a bad idea, but he's obsessed with making money. He says he won't be happy till we're really secure, but I think we're all right as we are. He feels so responsible for everybody – me and the girls, his sister, Sarah, Loveday...' Loveday was Robert's niece who worked as a waitress at his restaurant, along with her boyfriend, Jesse. 'He's hardly getting any sleep and I'm worried he'll make himself ill.' Liz's voice trailed off and she let out a long sigh.

'Maybe he needs a project,' Esme commented, taking another sip of coffee. 'Don't men love a new venture?'

Liz looked doubtful, but the truth was that Esme's mind was on other things. Liz's creamy-brown eyeshadow had reminded her about her makeup bag, which hadn't been packed. Would she really need cosmetics? They were only going walking. Then again, they'd no doubt eat out in the evenings and they'd be sure to linger over a glass of wine or two. Everyone looked better with a bit of eyeshadow and mascara...

'Excuse me.' She put her mug on the shelf beside her and jumped up to run and fetch the bag from the bathroom, and stuff it in the corner of her suitcase.

Liz handed back the wooden salad servers that Lowenna had been playing with. 'It's time we left. We've delayed you long enough. Thanks for the coffee and the biscuit, it worked a treat!'

Esme didn't try to dissuade her; half an hour had gone by, and she'd made up her mind to catch an early bus to the station. She'd rather sit on the platform bench and read her book or do the crossword than risk being late.

'Are you sure you don't want a lift?' asked Liz. 'It would be no trouble.'

She'd already offered on several previous occasions, knowing that Esme's ancient Lexus had broken down and was at the garage being repaired.

'Thank you, but no.' Esme rose herself and closed the shutters once more, so that her visitor could be in no doubt that the conversation was at an end.

Liz had left Lowenna's pushchair at the bottom of the fire escape and once the little girl was strapped in, they made their way down narrow winding South Street towards the marketplace, in search of a loaf of bread. But they didn't get far; as they passed Seaspray Boutique, its owner Audrey came dashing out, waving a copy of the local newspaper, the *Tremarnock Bugle*, above her head.

Audrey, in her fifties, was tall and eye-catching – even more so today, dressed in a bright pink tunic top that had been on one of her shop-window mannequins only days before.

'Have you heard?' she said slightly breathlessly, thrusting the paper into Liz's hands before turning back to lock the door of her shop, which had a CLOSED FOR LUNCH sign on the inside.

Liz stared at the paper as if she wasn't quite sure what to do with it.

'The council's agreed to sell the play park,' Audrey exclaimed. The paper was upside down, so she turned it around and jabbed at an article on the front page with her index finger. 'They approved it last night. Look. It's all here.'

'Wha-at? How *could* they?'

Liz started to scan the report and her mouth dropped open. The issue of the children's playground was hardly new. Developers had been sniffing around the village for months, with their clipboards and smug expressions, and she'd already signed countless petitions and written objection letters.

More active locals, who'd been making a bigger noise, had warned that their concerns seemed to be falling on deaf ears, but she'd never actually believed that developers would get the go-ahead to build one hundred brand-new homes, most of which would be out of the reach of local people's pockets. Yet here it was, in black and white:

COUNCIL APPROVES CONTROVERSIAL TREMARNOCK HOUSING ESTATE

A little further down, she read:

Outline plans were eventually given the go-ahead by a single vote during a tense meeting of the council's district planning committee last night.

Residents had pleaded with councillors to reject the proposals, raising concerns over highway safety and the impact on the countryside and local services. However, chairing the meeting, Lucinda Graham (Lib Dem, Langowan) reminded members that the council had, just one year ago, voted to approve the site for development.

'If we are to refuse this application, I think there are half a dozen applications which will have to be refused. We have a requirement to provide so many houses and there's nothing we can do about it.'

Agreeing, Laurence Nares-Pillow (Con, Porthraden), said, 'If we can't provide those houses, the government's planning inspector will rule on the matter, not where we want to have them but where the inspector wants them.'

Putting the decision to the vote resulted in five votes for and five against the application, with Mrs Graham ultimately casting the deciding vote in favour of the development.

The proposals from Bedminster New Homes will see a mix of three-, four- and five-bedroom homes built on the 0.95 hectare site. The plans also include seventy-five parking spaces and two access points on Fore Street and Cardew Avenue, which would be widened in an effort to improve safety.

Once she'd reached the bottom, Liz exhaled loudly.

Audrey gave a grim nod. 'Shocking, isn't it?' She ran a hand through her dark hair, which was tipped with platinum streaks, cut pixie-short and artfully mussed, before giving Liz a firm push, which sent her and the pushchair bowling slowly down the hill. 'We'll go and find Barbara,' she said bossily. 'She's sure to have some ideas.'

Liz sighed. Barbara, landlady of the Lobster Pot on the seafront, was a tremendous source of information as well as an arch organiser. Liz was very fond of her, but she'd been hoping to grab an hour with her book while Lowenna had an after-lunch snooze. As it was, the little girl would probably drop off in her pushchair and wake up hungry and out of sorts. Still, the playground was a major issue; children adored it and no one wanted an ugly new estate on the doorstep, least of all Liz. If there was a fight to be had then she, for one, was up for it.

They didn't get far when Barbara herself came bustling up the hill in the opposite direction from the Lobster Pot, her dark blonde hair, normally stiff with lacquer, sticking up untidily. She was in black trousers and a low-cut red top that revealed quite a lot of tanned cleavage, and her face was flushed.

'The marketplace,' she said, nodding in the direction of the turning that led to the square, and Liz and Audrey followed obediently. The sound of Barbara's high heels clopping on the cobbles seemed to act like a muezzin's call to prayer, as more and more folk appeared from doors and alleyways and trailed after her.

'It's a scandal,' Liz heard behind her. 'Shouldn't be allowed,' muttered someone else.

Emotions were clearly running high, and she wished that Robert were beside her; but he'd be busy with the lunchtime shift at A Winkle in Time and she didn't want to bother him.

Word travelled fast in Tremarnock. A sizeable crowd had already gathered in the square, which had a stone cenotaph in the middle bearing the names of local men who had died in the Second World War, and was lined with shops. Liz spotted Ryan, the fishmonger, still in his white overalls streaked with blood; Rick Kane, who owned the gift shop, Treasure Trove; and the couple who ran the popular little bakery. Jean the childminder was there, too, with her husband Tom and two toddlers in a double buggy, as well as pensioners Ruby and Victor, and Jenny and John Lambert, who had a fishing tackle store on the seafront.

Someone had thoughtfully placed an upturned crate in front of the cenotaph and Barbara pushed her way through the throng and climbed onto it. Before she had the chance to speak, however, someone else dug Liz in the ribs and she turned to find Robert's niece Loveday grinning at her, with two rather extraordinary buns perched on either side of her head and a glittery blue parting running down the middle. Behind her was her boyfriend, Jesse, and beside him, Liz's friend Tabitha and her boyfriend Danny.

Liz was surprised that Robert had allowed Loveday and Jesse, his sous-chef, to leave the restaurant. She was about to ask what had happened when Barbara cleared her throat and shouted, 'Welcome, all!'

A hush descended.

It was the first week in September, and a welcome spell of blazing sunshine the previous month had given way to overcast skies and intermittent rain. But the temperature was still quite high, and the air damp and humid; most folk were in T-shirts and shorts, skirts and summer dresses, clutching brollies and raincoats just in case.

Barbara proceeded to tell them about the newspaper article, which many had already seen, adding her own observations for good measure. She conjured up a frightening vision of clogged roads and overcrowded GP surgeries and schools, with supermarkets and burger joints springing up on every corner and asthma-inducing traffic fumes. If she were to be believed, the village would rapidly lose its Cornish identity and start to feel like a sprawling London suburb.

'This can't be allowed to happen,' she hollered, banging a fist on her palm for dramatic effect. 'The question is, how are we going to stop it?'

'I say we storm the council buildings and chain 'em up till they change their minds.' Ryan the fishmonger's body had tensed and his eyes flashed dangerously.

There were various mumblings of assent, until Barbara advised that this would be illegal. 'The development will still go ahead and there'll be bugger-all we can do about it if we're behind bars.'

Having seemed all set to take up tongs, fish slices, pliers and whatever other instruments of torture he could lay his hands on, Ryan looked quite crestfallen.

'Let's build an ugly great house in that Lucinda Graham's front garden as she cast the deciding vote. See how she likes it,' grumbled Rick Kane, who sported a bushy grey beard and impressive sideburns.

'That's all very well, but where we going to get the bricks and mortar?' Jean replied crossly. 'And how are we supposed to build it without her knowing?'

Silence descended for a moment as people pondered the wisdom of this observation.

'Why don't we stage a sit-in, like those eco-warriors off the news?' Loveday piped up. 'We can sleep in the trees – there's loads of them around the play park. They can't tear them down if we're in them, can they?'

Liz was surprised. As far as she knew, Robert's niece rarely watched the news, and had certainly never shown an interest in environmental activism. The idea, however, seemed to go down rather well with the mob.

'Excellent plan,' said Tom who, at sixty-odd, seemed a little old to be contemplating kipping in branches.

'We can draw up a rota,' Danny chipped in. He ran the Hole in the Wall pub on Fore Street and he and Tabitha, who had recently moved in together with Oscar, were nuts about each other.

'I'll build us some treehouses,' offered Jesse, whose blond corkscrew curls had frizzed up in the damp, muggy atmosphere. 'I made one in the pear tree in my back garden when I was a kid. It's still there.'

'I think that's asking for trouble,' Audrey said, sniffing. She was standing beside Liz. 'It would give quite the wrong impression. Before you know it, word would be out and we'd have hippies and New Age travellers flocking to the village in their filthy clothes and ghastly old vans and tents.' She shuddered. 'It's the last thing we need.'

'What about nudists? If we're lucky we might get some of those, too!' This came from Tony, who worked in PR and divided his time between here and a flat in London. He and his Brazilian partner, Felipe, had never been that keen on Audrey, and there was a cutting edge to his voice.

Gales of laughter erupted, along with cries of, 'Hear, hear!' and 'Get 'em off!'

Audrey, who was beside Liz, pursed her lips and glowered.

'Erm, Charlie Pearce, *Tremarnock Bugle*.' A female voice rose above the clamour. 'Do you have a name for your direct action group? I mean, is there an official title?'

On tiptoe, Liz spied a young woman with a mop of thick messy auburn hair standing close to the cenotaph, notebook and pen in hand. She was of medium height and quite curvaceous; her small, upturned nose was covered in freckles.

All at once the hubbub ceased and everyone looked confused, including Barbara, who shifted uncomfortably on her temporary podium and glanced around for support. Although the reporter wouldn't have been able to see Liz, she too felt as if there were a spotlight on her face.

'A title? For our direct action protest group? Of course, that's what we are, yes,' Barbara said, rallying. 'We've exhausted all other avenues. What a good idea!' Puffing out her impressive chest, she added, 'Any ideas about what we should call ourselves?'

Some people frowned, while others threw out a host of underwhelming ideas until Rick came up with the most palatable: '*Tremarnock Resists!* It's nice and simple and it does what it says on the tin.'

'Tremarnock Resists,' Barbara repeated, testing the words on her tongue. 'I like it! It's not long or complicated and it's good to have the village name in there. It makes it clear we're all in this together and we mean business – we're a force to be reckoned with.'

There were murmurs of approval. Only one person, Ruby, objected because she said the name sounded aggressive. 'I know feelings are strong, but this isn't the Second World War. We must try to keep things in perspective.'

'What would you prefer – Tremarnock Rolls Over and Surrenders?' chortled Tom, the husband of Jean the childminder. He'd always enjoyed his own jokes.

The crowd erupted again and Ruby, who was rather sensitive, bit her lip and looked close to tears. Barbara quickly proposed putting it to the vote, and in the end the suggestion was passed by a comfortable margin.

They'd been standing in the square for about twenty minutes and a few people were becoming bored and had begun to shuffle away. Barbara looked quite flustered. 'Wait a minute...!' she started to say.

But Charlie-the-reporter interrupted. 'Can I just ask, when's your next meeting?'

The shuffling stopped, and Barbara seemed relieved. 'Thank you,' she replied. Then, raising her voice, she said, 'This is only the first get-together, folks. We've all agreed to act. Now we need to come up with a strategy.'

'Let's have a meeting at the Methodist church hall,' Tony chipped in. 'Felipe will do some leaflets tonight. We'll drop them round the village straight away.'

Tony was good at nominating his partner Felipe for jobs, but if he minded, he didn't let on; he just nodded and smiled in an affable and resigned sort of way.

'Thank you,' Barbara said again. 'We should have the meeting very soon – tomorrow, ideally; there's no time to waste. I'll check with the minister but I expect the hall will be free. Anyone who wants to be on the planning committee, please stay behind and talk to me now.'

Liz hesitated. It was a cause that she really believed in, but she was already doing voluntary work, helping her husband at the restaurant when he needed her and looking after the children. She had enough on her plate. Before she left, however, she wove her way to Barbara through the sea of bodies and assured her that she'd assist as much as she could.

'You're a star,' Barbara said, gratefully accepting Tom's proffered hand as she stepped down from the wobbly crate. 'I'm afraid we've got a bloody big battle on our hands. I'm going to need all the help I can get.'

Chapter Two

ESME LIKED TRAIN journeys; they reminded her of her peripatetic youth. She'd spent the first eight years of her life in Botswana, where she could still remember running around barefoot, playing hide and seek with the local children and 'Suna Baby', their version of dodgeball, using old plastic bags or stockings.

Later, the family had relocated to Egypt, then Turkey, and her parents and younger brother had been based in Islamabad when she'd started boarding school at the age of eleven. From that point, she'd returned home only once or twice a year, often spending shorter holidays with relatives or friends in different parts of the UK.

As a consequence, she'd been forced to become very independent. This in itself hadn't bothered her, though she'd sometimes been troubled by a sense of being different from the other girls, just a little bit odd. Perhaps it was her height – she was always the tallest – or the fact that she hadn't seemed to find quite the same things funny or interesting. She'd had friends, but no one she was particularly close to; not until Caroline had come along, that is, when everything had changed.

After leaving school, Esme had travelled all over the

world on her own, often by rail, picking up books and other artefacts which she'd tried to incorporate in some way into her ceramic creations. She was a good potter, she knew, and today her more conventional bowls and vessels sold for a decent price in local shops and art exhibitions, mainly in the holiday season. Sometimes she'd get lucrative commissions, too.

What she really liked making, however, weren't vases, urns and tableware; her passion was for experimenting with asymmetric shapes and tall narrow forms, along with colour, mixing metallic oxides and other pigments into the clay and leaving her work unglazed. The earthy speckles and bands of coloured clay seemed to bleed and blend together freely, recalling, to her mind, pleasing landscapes and geographical forms that spoke for themselves and had no practical use.

Unfortunately, these creations didn't go down as well with the punters, which frustrated her immensely; she grumbled, usually to herself, that she wasn't put on this earth to make cups, saucers and breakfast bowls. If they wanted those, they should jolly well go to John Lewis.

But she was lucky that despite her unpredictable earnings, she could get by well enough, partly because there was only herself to look after. Furthermore, her father and mother had left her a small nest egg when they'd died, for which she was eternally grateful. In any case, her needs were simple, her main extravagance still being foreign travel, and she had no one to bequeath anything to when she passed away.

There was only one other person on the little station platform when she arrived – a young woman in a red and white stripy T-shirt and jeans who was pacing up and down, as if this would somehow make the train come faster.

Esme settled on a white wooden bench, taking in the neatly tended palm tree in a pot beside her and the old retired railway carriage opposite, which had been painted yellow and was now rented out as a holiday home with a difference. The tubs outside were overflowing with late geraniums, but there were no other signs of human life. Perhaps the carriage was used only during the famous arts festival at the stately home up the road, when the village was packed with visitors from all around the globe.

She fished out her newspaper but barely read a word, listening instead to the gentle cooing and twittering of the birds in the trees overhead, which seemed to calm her overactive brain. A small part of her felt like turning around, walking back up the winding lane and catching the return bus to Tremarnock, but she told herself that she was braver than that. Brave and deeply curious, in a way that no photograph from or chatty correspondence with Caroline could possibly fulfil.

Even so, Esme was almost sorry when she heard the distant rattle of the train and watched it snake around the corner before coming to a halt at her feet. It was nearly always full, public transport around here being relatively scarce, and she wandered along the two carriages looking for a space, relieved to find one at last at the very back, by a window.

The woman in the stripy T-shirt settled down beside her, balancing a large basket on her lap, but Esme avoided eye contact. As they whizzed through the countryside, past flocks of sheep and herds of cows, fields of bright yellow rapeseed and forests of giant firs, she tried to remember how she'd felt all those years ago, when she'd made part of this same journey from her Canterbury school to Truro, to stay with her mother's friend one Easter holiday.

Aunt Margery, as Esme had been told to call her, although they were in no way related, had lived on her own in a white bungalow on the outskirts of the city and Esme had met her only once or twice before. Then aged seventeen, she'd been furious with her father for laying down the law and insisting that she go there, rather than to a better-known cousin in London.

As it had turned out, the stay hadn't been nearly as bad as feared; Aunt Margery had proved to be kind and sensitive, respecting Esme's need at that time for privacy, and interfering little with her day-to-day plans. She had never visited Cornwall before, and spent her time getting to know the area, taking local trains and buses to the beaches of St Agnes and Perranporth, Falmouth and Newquay, wandering around churches and libraries and sometimes just lying on her back in grassy fields and watching the clouds float by.

Something had happened during that four weeks that, she later realised, had changed her for ever; and it wasn't only that the holiday inspired in her a lifelong love of the county that had eventually led to her settling here.

Aunt Margery was a wildlife painter, and watching her at her easel, observing the birds pecking on the seed that she left out in her cottage garden, the flocks of magpies, butterflies landing on bushes and squirrels scurrying up trees, had made Esme realise that it was possible to find contentment in work, far from people with their complex problems and confusing ways. Slowly but surely, her sense of unease had started to lift.

When she'd returned to school in the May, she'd made up her mind to pursue her own interest in art, particularly sculpture and ceramics. The other girls might long for boyfriends and parties, glamour, glitz and, eventually, marriage and children, but she would free herself up to focus on her career; hang what people thought. And although she feared that the kernel of sadness that had lodged in her heart some time before would never truly leave, she had at least begun to make some sort of peace with it.

She took from her bag the ham sandwiches that she'd packed and unwrapped the foil around them. The thick, nutty brown bread, which she'd bought from the bakery in Tremarnock yesterday, was still fresh, and the ham tasted sweet and smoky.

Things really weren't too bad, she thought, staring through the smudged windows, listening to the steady chatter of the folk sitting around her and the hypnotic chug and rattle of the engine. She would be able to tell her friend, hand on heart, that she was content with her lot. Caroline, with her husband and two children, her Bichon Frise called Lulu and sizeable apartment in a smart area of Paris, might raise her eyebrows, but that was her problem; Esme knew the truth.

Stop that right now! She gave herself a mental slap on the wrist. This wasn't a competition, for goodness' sake, and it was ridiculous to feel nervous. If she was going to be silly, she shouldn't have come.

Perhaps when they'd been twenty, thirty or even forty, it was only to be expected that a touch of rivalry had occasionally crept into the women's communications, as if each felt the need to prove to the other that in the great race of life, they were the winner. But neither, surely, had anything left to prove? Esme had made a modest name for herself and Caroline's family were thriving. She, too, still worked as a part-time English language lecturer and seemed to have a host of friends and interests, as well as a successful husband.

Having finished her sandwich, Esme fished a sherbet lemon from her coat pocket and popped it into her mouth. The woman next to her shuffled in her seat and she almost offered her one, then changed her mind, fearing that it might spark a conversation.

In any case, she reflected, peeping in the bag, there were only two left and she might need them. Rick Kane still kept a jar in his Tremarnock shop, Treasure Trove, just for her, because he knew they were her favourites; but she didn't like to go in there more than was absolutely necessary.

Rick. She gave a little shudder. They'd started seeing quite a lot of each last year, and at first she'd enjoyed his company. He was knowledgeable about all sorts of things, especially history, and they were both keen on walks, swimming and nature. But he had become too pushy, wanting to turn their relationship into something it wasn't, so that in the end she'd had to tell him to back off. The whole episode had been rather a nightmare.

So lost was she in her thoughts that she scarcely noticed when they stopped at Liskeard and a gaggle of schoolchildren boarded, talking in high, excited voices and jostling with each other for seats. An inspector in a blue uniform, with a red face and sandy moustache, strolled down the carriage looking left and right, and it was only when he asked her twice for her ticket that she remembered she hadn't yet bought one and reached in her bag for her purse.

'Nice mornin',' he said genially, putting her card into the pay machine, and she accidentally dropped her ticket when he passed it across. Bending down to retrieve it, she noticed that the lady in the stripy T-shirt was wearing bright red shoes. Damn. Esme had forgotten to pack smart shoes for the evening and it was too late to turn back now. She glanced at her own clumpy brown walking boots and frowned. Not a good look with a skirt and floaty top. Perhaps she could pick something up in St Ives.

Caroline was bound not to have forgotten *her* evening shoes, Esme thought glumly. Caroline seemed super-competent and good at just about everything, from icing cakes and repairing her husband's shirts and trousers to dealing with tricky builders, organising elaborate parties and coping with truculent elderly in-laws. In other words, she was an exemplary wife and mother.

More people piled in at Bodmin Parkway and Lostwithiel and by now, it was standing room only. On approaching Par, an announcement told passengers to change for services on the Newquay branch line, and Esme watched a tanned man in bright yellow shorts and flip-flops carry a large surfboard in a protective silver case towards the exit. He was no doubt bound for the beach. Very brave, on a day like today, she mused. It was pleasant, sure, but not exactly hot. There again, surfers liked a good breeze and they did wear wetsuits.

As he vanished out of sight, it crossed her mind that Caroline might have brought one with her, just for swimming in the sea. In fact she'd probably have the right gear for all eventualities. Looking back, the seeds of her efficiency were there from when she'd first arrived at St Hilda's aged eleven, her trunk bulging with neatly ironed knickers, vests and blouses, which she proceeded to place carefully in drawers, wiping out the creases as she did so. Unlike Esme, Caroline never wore socks that didn't match or forgot to brush her hair, and she always had a clean hankie to hand.

The other girls instantly nicknamed her 'Prissy Peters' (Peters was her maiden name) and laughed at her behind her back. But Esme suspected there was something more to the new girl's almost obsessive orderliness, and her heart went out to her.

Caroline was small and slight, with wispy fair hair, big, round frightened blue eyes and a narrow mouth that turned down slightly at the corners, as if she were permanently on the verge of tears. She jumped at the slightest noise, and one look from a teacher could make her shrink. It was as if by keeping her possessions in order, she somehow hoped that she could control her external surroundings, and the more anxious she seemed to be, the more tidy her desk and wardrobe became.

Despite her unpromising start, however, she blossomed at St Hilda's, and Esme liked to think that as her 'buddy' she'd played no small part in that. Within a few weeks, Caroline was no longer escaping to her dorm whenever she could and crying each night for her mother. It soon became clear that she enjoyed arts and crafts, and she and Esme spent their leisure hours painting, drawing and doing crochet and embroidery – encouraged by the nuns who ran the school, who liked to see pupils engaged in what they regarded as suitable feminine pursuits.

But despite appearances, they were by no means goody-goodies. Esme was thrilled to discover that Caroline had a mischievous side which, when unleashed, could lead them both into naughtiness which they generally got away with because no one expected such quiet girls to disobey the rules. They'd had fun, for sure, as well as sad times…

The uniform greyness of St Austell gave way to fields of solar panels and wind turbines, and Esme sat bolt upright when she spotted the familiar spires of Truro cathedral, towering above the houses, shops, factories and car parks. The giant rose window visible from the carriage seemed to glitter, jewel-like, in the watery sunshine, a beacon of hope and austere beauty amid the confusing urban sprawl.

There was a general murmuring and fidgeting as passengers prepared to alight, lifting down suitcases from racks, adjusting dresses and shirts, assembling children and, in some cases, dogs. They seemed to take an age but at last the whistle peeped, the breaks hissed, the engine revved and they were off again, past banks of purple-pink rosebay willowherb, yellow ragwort and lilac buddleia.

Before long, they reached the ugly industrial outskirts of Redruth, and when the train stopped again, Esme watched a girl with waist-length brown hair walk along the platform towards a boy in baseball boots and a back-to-front cap. Soon she was enveloping him in a passionate clinch; then he put an arm around her and led her away.

Esme was strangely touched, thinking that love could thrive even in the most unprepossessing surroundings, like the surprisingly beautiful flowers along the railway banks.

She herself got off at St Erth and crossed the little bridge to the other side, wrinkling her nose as the farmyard smells chased up her nostrils. Once again, she had to jostle with the crowds for a window seat and as the line narrowed to a single track, she forced herself to focus on the spectacular views of the mudflats and saltmarshes of the wide, sweeping Hayle Estuary.

They climbed up, up onto steep cliffs overlooking the mighty Atlantic Ocean, passing the great expanse of Carbis Bay. There were quite a few tiny people on the beach, some with surfboards and canoes, others just standing around chatting, but they were all huddled in one corner beside the cliffs, as if the prospect of being alone in such a vast, empty landscape was simply too much.

Higher they climbed, hugging the cliff edge, until all at once they were rounding the headland and the rooftops, palm trees, Victorian lampposts festooned with hanging baskets and golden sands of St Ives came into sight. There was a distinct holiday feel about the place, even when the sky was filled with clouds: the seagulls on chimneypots, the little wooden station hut with its jolly blue and white awning, the ice-cream wagon, the boats bobbing in the harbour, the colourful flags flying for the brave men and women of the RNLI lifeboat charity – all contributed to an atmosphere of relaxation and gaiety.

It was only when she'd retrieved her bag from the overhead rack and waited for the excited schoolchildren to leave that she alighted herself, pausing in the car park for a moment to dig out her map. The hotel was just half a mile from the station and she had already decided to go on foot, as there was plenty of time. The journey had taken under two hours and Caroline wouldn't arrive until at least three, possibly later.

Esme paused while a turquoise double-decker bus pulled out of the waiting bay, with the words ATLANTIC COASTERS and pictures of white seagulls emblazoned on its side. Then she turned left, away from the narrow, packed streets of the town centre, and started to climb uphill, dragging her small suitcase on wheels behind her, past the beach, putting green and a long row of substantial houses, many painted white, some with the brick left bare. From the neat front gardens it appeared that a lot were occupied, though a few had To LET signs up and their shutters were closed. Others were B&Bs. Posters advertising a forthcoming two-week music and arts festival were pinned on gates and displayed in windows, and Esme was quite pleased to be missing it.

She'd exhibited there herself several times and enjoyed it, but the town was always extra-busy; it was hard to find a table in a café or restaurant, and you had to queue for everything.

A sweet scent filled the air, perhaps from the wild flowers sprouting from walls. Blue and pink hydrangea bushes lined the way and she paused again to remove her navy cardigan. It was close, despite the sea breeze; a woman with a cocker spaniel on a lead a little way ahead stopped to strip off her top layer, too, and tie it around her waist.

The path snaked steeply for a while longer and Esme was beginning to think she'd never arrive until she turned the final corner and spotted signs for her hotel. It was an even steeper climb to the entrance, up stone steps via a shady garden full of giant ferns and palm trees. She had to bump her suitcase up the highest steps and stop again several times to catch her breath.

At last the hotel itself came into view, an imposing ivy-clad nineteenth-century building with fake turrets and extensive grounds. Esme had chosen it carefully, not just because of its location, right by the coast and only fifteen minutes from the station, or for the promised sea views; from the website, it had looked like the sort of place that she guessed Caroline would like: good-quality furnishings and subtle décor, comfortable, solid and just a teeny bit dull.

Perhaps she was misjudging her friend, but she suspected that her tastes were on the conservative side. In any case, Esme had avoided showing Caroline photographs of her more unusual pottery pieces and hadn't mentioned her solo trip to an ashram in India, either.

After carrying her case over the bumpy gravel path, she stepped through the open front door and looked around. To her relief, the hallway was just as she'd hoped: cream walls, a subtle tartan carpet, anodyne prints of seaside scenes and a vague smell of furniture polish. A young woman in a white blouse sitting behind the main desk looked up from her book and smiled as Esme approached.

'Do you need a voucher for the car park?' she asked in a strong Cornish accent when they'd finished the check-in process, but Esme said no, she had come by train.

She was just taking her room key when someone tapped her on the shoulder and she swung around, surprised.

'Esme?' It was a small, slight woman with a neat, carefully highlighted straight blonde bob and a slightly apprehensive smile. 'It is you, isn't it?'

Her cheeks were hollower than Esme remembered, and fine lines fanned outwards from the corners of her eyes. Between her brows were two horizontal grooves, like the number eleven, and her skin appeared fragile, almost translucent. But the eyes themselves were the same – bright cornflower blue and watchful, like a bird's – and she stood straight-backed, chin slightly raised, pretty and brave, just as always.

'Caroline!' Esme replied, swaying slightly. The other woman stepped forward and Esme bent down to kiss her lightly, noticing the softness of her cheek and the faint smell of apple blossom, or perhaps it was pear. 'I didn't think you'd be here yet.'

'I decided to get a taxi from Newquay,' Caroline explained, drawing back. 'A bit extravagant, I know, but it was super-fast. You won't tell, will you?' She wrinkled her nose in amusement, and Esme recalled that it was something she used to do as a girl.

'Word of honour,' she replied, smiling. 'I'll take my bag up, then shall we find a cup of tea?'

The receptionist, who'd clearly been pretending not to watch from behind her desk, pointed towards a lounge area along the corridor. 'We serve tea and cakes till 5.30 p.m. and after that, it's cocktail hour.'

'Let's do both,' said Caroline. 'I bet you're thirsty after your journey. I certainly am!'

Heartened by the ease of their initial greeting, Esme hurried to find her room, which was at the side of the building on the first floor; it was wide and spacious, with views out over the lawn and harbour. Without bothering to unpack, she checked herself in the mirror above the washbasin in the adjoining bathroom, pinned back several wisps of grey-brown hair and hurried downstairs again.

Caroline was already sitting on a brown leather sofa some way along from the reception desk, and there was a tray of tea, with scones, jam and cream, on the glass table in front of her. An elderly couple were side-by-side on an identical sofa but other than that, they were the only guests.

'Come and sit down!' Caroline cried, patting the seat beside her. As she leaned forward to pour the tea, the neckline of her white cotton top gaped a little to reveal the small silver and topaz necklace that Esme had sent for her birthday last year.

It had been a bit of a gamble – after all, she'd had no idea what kind of jewellery Caroline wore – but something about the deep rich blue of the stone had caught her eye, and she'd felt instinctively that it was right.

Caroline must have read her thoughts, because she put the cup down, took the necklace between forefinger and thumb and stroked the topaz.

'I love it. It was such a thoughtful gift; I wear it all the time.'

Esme felt a warm glow of pleasure.

'Goodness!' Caroline straightened the shoulders of her top, pulled up the neckline and gave a little gurgle of laughter. 'There's so much to talk about. Where on earth shall we begin?'

Shall we go to the beach?'

Rosie was tired, her leg was aching and she had quite a lot of homework, but Rafael's big brown puppy-dog eyes and Brazilian accent proved irresistible.

'All right,' she said, 'but I can't be too long or my mum will get stressy.'

'I'll take your bag,' Rafael replied, gallantly removing the rucksack from her shoulder, which was laden with heavy books. Quite what he did with his own textbooks was a mystery as he never seemed to carry a bag himself, nor did he mention homework much or even lessons, come to that.

Having alighted from the bus some way up Humble Hill, they turned right down South Street towards the seafront. They had only been back at school for three days after the summer holidays, and already Rosie was feeling anxious about exams and worrying that she wouldn't be able to keep up.

She had been born with mild cerebral palsy, which made walking harder, and her left arm and hand didn't work as well as they should. She'd also suffered from a brain tumour some years ago, which had left her with impaired vision; despite thick glasses, which she disliked intensely, she still suffered from more than her fair share of headaches if she studied for too long. Comparing herself with others only made her miserable so she did her best not to, and there was no doubt that her life had improved since Rafael turned up in the village with his multicoloured Mohican, wooden crosses and flesh plugs in his ears.

Back in Rio, where he was born, his mother had washed her hands of him and his wild ways and packed him off to Tremarnock to live with his big brother Felipe and Felipe's partner, Tony.

Rosie had got to know Rafael the summer before he started at her school. It had helped to heal her hurt over a different boy called Tim, who'd been a close friend and ally until he'd dropped her for someone else. Being pals with Rafael had also raised her standing no end with the other girls, and anyway, she really liked him – it wasn't just show; he was kind, he didn't seem to mind her disabilities and he made her laugh.

Jenny Lambert's front door was open as they passed and there was a phone ringing somewhere inside. Seizing the moment while her mistress was distracted, her brown and white Jack Russell, Sally, made a bid for freedom and raced outside, yapping wildly at Rosie's and Rafael's heels, sniffing and wagging her stumpy tail.

Rosie, laughing, bent down to grab the dog's collar and give her a stroke at the same time.

'Hello Sally!' she said, scratching her behind the ears where she liked it most. 'You must wait for your mistress. You can't go out on your own.'

'She's always escaping. Jenny should give her more discipline,' Rafael said with a sniff, seemingly oblivious to the irony of his comment, for he had never been particularly keen on following rules himself.

'Rubbish!' Rosie replied, as the dog rolled over on her back and stuck her legs in the air to have her pink tummy tickled. 'She wouldn't be Sally if she wasn't always getting lost and making everyone run around after her.'

Her phone conversation done, Jenny came puffing out of the house and looked hugely relieved to discover that her beloved pet was in safe hands.

'Thank you.' She clipped the lead securely onto Sally's collar. 'I completely forgot to shut the door. She could have gone anywhere.'

The teenagers continued down the road past A Winkle in Time, which was on the ground floor of what was once a well-to-do sea captain's home. Painted white with smart bright blue wooden shutters, its name was emblazoned in swirly white letters on a matching blue board above the door; there was a two-storey flat above which Robert, Rosie's stepfather, rented out for the owner.

Nudging Rafael in the ribs, Rosie hurried by, looking the other way. She didn't want anyone to spot her. Robert would no doubt ask what she was up to, and Loveday and Jesse would tease her for being out with a boy. Sometimes she wished that she lived in a big anonymous city rather than a small village, where everyone knew everyone else's business.

It was reasonably warm, and she'd taken off her black blazer and stuffed it in her bag; Rafael's, meanwhile, was scrunched up and tied around his waist. But when they reached the seafront, a gust of cold air chased up the sleeves of her white shirt, giving her goose bumps and turning her thin bare legs reddish-blue. She didn't say anything, though; she hated the cold, but disliked drawing attention to herself even more.

The small beach, a mixture of shingle and sand, was horseshoe-shaped and flanked on either side by rocky promontories. Behind it was a row of gaily painted houses and shops in white, yellow and pink, as well as Barbara's pub, the Lobster Pot, festooned with hanging baskets. Although it was no longer the height of the tourist season, there were still a fair number of holidaymakers about. An older couple whom Rosie didn't recognise were huddling on fold-up chairs behind a wind break, determined to catch whatever rays of sun they could when it deigned to peep from behind the clouds.

Meanwhile, a dark-haired woman in shorts and a pink T-shirt was standing barefoot on the shoreline, throwing stones into the water and watching her golden retriever race in after them. It swam back empty-mouthed each time, but didn't seem to care.

'You want a cigarette?' Rafael asked, pulling a packet nonchalantly from the pocket of his black trousers and passing it to Rosie. He had an array of thick silver rings like knuckledusters on his fingers and thumbs, which he'd had to put on after school as he wasn't allowed to wear them on the premises.

Rosie's eyes widened. She'd tried a couple of puffs once and it had made her feel sick, but she didn't want to appear prudish.

'I, um—'

'Go on,' he pressed, pushing the packet towards her.

She glanced around furtively. 'Someone might see us!' She meant, of course, one of the locals, who would undoubtedly report back to her parents.

Rafael took the point and nodded. 'Come with me!'

Grabbing her gently by her good arm, he pulled her in the direction of the granite rocks on the right and they started to scramble up and over to the other side, where there was a small inlet that was invisible from the beach. It was tricky climbing with only one strong hand and leg, and Rosie scratched her knees and elbows as she followed him over the sharp stones. Bits of slimy seaweed squelched between her fingers and she yelped a bit, but didn't complain.

Finally Rafael took a big leap with Rosie's bag still slung over one shoulder, and sprang onto the shingle before turning around and offering her his outstretched arms.

Perching awkwardly, her bad leg sticking out at an odd angle, she was tempted to bend forward and allow him to lift her down. She was so light that he wouldn't have found it difficult. Instead, she half-slid, half-shuffled on her backside until she, too, could feel the ground beneath one foot. Only then did she accept a proffered hand.

'Here is good,' Rafael said, pointing to a dry patch a little way from the water's edge. He threw his poor, mistreated school blazer on the ground and signalled to her to sit on it.

The inlet was overlooked by some windows at the back of a row of terrace houses, but it was unlikely that anyone would be gazing down at that very moment; so Rosie decided to risk it, pulling up her knees and adjusting her skirt before hugging them tight to her body.

Once they were both settled, he fished the packet of cigarettes from his pocket again, took one out and tried to light it. A gust of wind blew out the flame so he had another go, this time hunching right over and cupping his hands around the treasured object. Several more attempts were required and he swore a few times, but eventually straightened up and took a deep, satisfied drag before blowing the smoke out ostentatiously through his nose.

'Ah, that is better,' he said, trying to disguise his cough by clearing his throat while his eyes filled with tears. Rosie pretended not to notice.

It took him a while to recover fully and then he announced, 'School was shit. Mrs Bailey is nincompoop.'

Mrs Bailey was his class tutor, and nincompoop was one of Tony's favourite words; Rosie had heard him use it often.

'She is,' she agreed, giggling. 'I had her in my first year. She can be a right cow.'

After taking another puff, Rafael passed her the cigarette and she tried to look relaxed, dangling it in the air between her index and middle fingers and nearly dropping it. 'Whoops!'

When she finally took a tentative drag, it made her retch. 'I like this brand,' she lied, eyeing the packet lying between them. 'It's my favourite.'

'You want a whole one?'

'Oh no,' she replied, a little too swiftly. 'It's not fair to smoke all yours.'

The sky had clouded over completely now and turned ominously grey, but they were well sheltered in their cove and completely cut off from the people on the neighbouring beach. Far out, a couple of fishing boats bobbed on the choppy ocean beneath the freewheeling seagulls, and Rosie watched a small reddish-brown crab scuttle towards a pool of sludgy water at the base of the rocks.

Although she felt guilty for smoking behind her mother's back, she was enjoying being beside Rafael, sensing the closeness of his body, aware of his strength and wiry athleticism. She thought that he was like a tiger, or a panther maybe, alert and springy, constantly shifting his body slightly, unable to stay completely still for long. She could have remained like that for ages.

He was still puffing away, trying to suck every last scrap of nicotine from the butt, when she noticed a clear bottle on the water's edge, floating this way and that as the tide pushed it towards the wet sand before dragging it out again. It wasn't unusual to find assorted objects washed up on the beach:

plastic bags, bits of crockery, dead jellyfish and sea urchins, the odd shoe. However, something about the bottle caught her attention and she got up to take a closer look.

'What are you doing?' Rafael wanted to know, but she didn't answer. The current was quite strong, and she was afraid that the bottle would soon be pulled beyond her reach.

Sure enough, a fierce wave stretched its foamy tentacles around the object and dragged it further out. Rosie hesitated. Was it worth the effort? But from where she stood now on the shoreline, she could see what appeared to be a cork in the top and inside, some rolled-up paper.

Quickly, she took off her socks and shoes, threw them on the beach behind her and waded in. The water was freezing and she had to go right up to her knees before she could reach out and grab the neck of the bottle, just before the tide sucked it even further.

'What is it?' Rafael's voice, whipped by the wind, sounded more like a seagull's cry.

Turning, she brandished her find in the air like a trophy. 'There's something inside – maybe it's a message!'

Now his interest was piqued. He jumped up while she half-ran, half-limped back to where they'd been sitting, her fingers grasping eagerly at the cork, trying to pull it out.

'It's stuck,' she said crossly after a few moments, and passed the bottle to Rafael. He tipped it one way and the other, making the paper slide up and down. 'Quick! Open it!'

He twisted the cork a few times until it broke off, leaving a section wedged in the neck.

Rosie frowned. 'What do we do now?' She was tempted to smash the bottle against the rocks in frustration.

'Maybe we can poke it down?' Rafael tried to push the cork with his thumb, but it wouldn't budge.

Rosie searched around for something long and sharp. Her eyes fell on a rusty metal stick with a round end that could have been washed up years ago; it looked as if it might have once been used to prop up a car bonnet. Rafael took it from her and used the rounded top to push the cork with some force. It broke up, some of the pieces slipping inside the bottle.

Unable to wait any longer, Rosie grabbed it back and tipped the contents, cork and all, onto Rafael's crumpled jacket.

The paper was yellowing and quite tightly rolled, fastened with a piece of rotting string. She carefully untied it, pleased to find that it fell apart quite easily. Rafael, caught up in her enthusiasm, tried to snatch the paper from her and open it himself, but she held it out of reach.

'No, I want to do it!'

He peered over her shoulder as she unfurled the scroll, and gave a little gasp. 'There's writing on it! Look!'

They both stared in amazement at the faded message on the page, still quite clearly visible, although the letters had turned brownish-grey. Miraculously, the paper itself was dry, but it was delicate as a fallen leaf.

'*My dear Little Bear,*' Rosie read out loud, before scanning to the top right-hand side of the page and gasping again. '*13th March 1946.*' She stopped reading for a moment to stare at her friend. 'That was just after the Second World War, wasn't it?'

Rafael shrugged. 'What else does it say?'

She resumed reading. '*I am writing this on the ferry and by the time you find it, if you ever do, I shall be far away, bound for my hometown of Munich, in my beloved Bavaria.*

There was so much that I wished to say to you, and to Winnie and Arthur, your dear Mutter und Vater, before I left, but there were tears in my eyes and the words would not come to my lips. Now that I have left, however, I can express my feelings at last and I want you to know that I will never forget the kindness you showed to a poor German boy who was alone, frightened and so far from home. You took me into your home and your hearts and turned what might have been the very worst time of my life into one of the happiest, despite the terrible things that were going on in the world.

Although I am pleased to return to my country, or what is left of it, and to see my family at long last, truly I shall miss the warmth of Cobbler's Rest and your charming little village, even the quarry, where I spent so many long hours. Most of all, however, I shall miss you, Little Bear, your funny smile and your silly English jokes. "Knock knock. Who's there? Egbert. Egbert who? Egbert no bacon!"

I have left a little part of me in Tremarnock and one day, when you are all grown up, I shall return for a visit and we shall have a cup of tea together and talk and laugh about old times and swap new jokes for the old ones that we once shared.

Until then, little one, God bless you and protect you, and thank you for all that you are and that you have meant to me. Your dear friend, Franz.'

When she'd finished reading, Rosie took a deep breath. Her imagination was running riot; she felt as if a voice from the past had risen up and was speaking directly to her.

'D'you think it's real?' she whispered, still holding the message reverently in both hands.

Rafael scratched his chin. 'I don't know. I don't think so. Maybe it's a joke.'

But Rosie was totally caught up in the romance of the moment.

'I have to go,' she said, carefully rolling the paper up again and popping it back in the bottle. Then she removed her blazer from her bag, wrapped it around the container, placed them both inside her bag and hoisted it onto her back before Rafael had a chance to stop her.

She seemed to have a new-found strength as she clambered over the rocks; this time, it seemed much easier. She didn't even notice when she scraped her hand on a patch of barnacles, drawing blood.

They could have spent only about half an hour in the cove but the beach was empty now, and there was no one on the seafront. As they approached the sea wall, they heard the iron hanging baskets outside Barbara's pub creaking in the wind, and wind chimes sang eerily.

Rafael was dragging his feet. Normally Rosie wouldn't have minded, but she had no time to waste. 'I'll see you tomorrow. I need to show the letter to my mum. It could be important.'

In truth, he wasn't much interested in History, but didn't want to miss out on any excitement.

'I will come with you,' he said, as she set off up South Street at an impressively speedy pace. 'I am hungry. I expect your mother will have something to eat?'

Chapter Three

MITZI THE TORTOISESHELL cat was on the windowsill licking her paws, but she jumped down when she saw Rosie and Rafael and waited by the door to be let in.

Most of the cottages on Humble Hill opened straight onto the street, but Bag End had a small front plot filled with cottage garden flowers: hollyhocks and catmint, phlox, delphiniums and geraniums, which had been glorious all summer but were faded and scrappy now.

Liz was the one who liked to garden; she picked up tips from Jean the childminder and her husband, Tom, whose house was just a few doors down. The couple spent hours tending to their plants, particularly Tom, who positively glowed with pleasure when passers-by stopped to compliment him.

'*Il faut cultiver notre jardin*,' he'd say knowingly over his white picket fence, in his broad Cornish accent. 'That's Voltaire, dontcha know. French. Means focus on your own little corner, make your own bit of happiness. No one else is going to do it for you.'

Then, if his admirers were still interested, he'd snip off a few blooms or fetch them a cutting a two. Liz had acquired many of her own plants this way and her skills were improving, though she'd be the first to admit that she still had a lot to learn.

Bag End, a former fisherman's cottage, was painted white, with sash windows, thick stone walls, oak beams, an impressive cast-iron fireplace in the sitting room and a flagstone floor in the kitchen. The family had moved in just before Robert and Liz married, and sometimes she and Rosie had to pinch themselves to believe that it was truly theirs. For many years they'd lived alone in the cramped rented apartment below Esme, and life had been tough. Rosie could still remember feeling guilty when she had to ask her mother for money, knowing that she had to work two jobs just to pay the bills, and often Robert had to remind them that they didn't need to worry about cash any more; he'd look after them.

Rosie let herself in with her own key and Rafael followed her down the hallway to the medium-sized square kitchen at the end. Lowenna was in her highchair at the table facing the door, with a beaker and a blue plastic bowl on the tray in front. Her eyes lit up when she saw her big sister.

'Wo-Wo!' she shouted in delight, waving her spoon in the air and scattering bits of food.

She could pronounce 'Rosie' perfectly well now, but the whole family had adopted 'Wo-Wo'; even some of Rosie's friends used it. She pretended to be annoyed, but secretly quite liked it.

'Ach! Careful!' Liz cried, jumping up from where she'd been sitting and grabbing the spoon off her daughter, while simultaneously mopping her face with a damp cloth. 'Hi, Rosie. Oh! Hi, Rafael,' she said, when she realised that he was there, too. 'Come in! Would you like a slice of banana cake? I made some this morning.'

Rafael looked keen but Rosie paid no attention, rootling in her bag for the bottle, which she unwrapped and placed triumphantly on the table.

'Look!' she said breathlessly. 'We found a message in a bottle. It's from someone called Franz, just after the Second World War. D'you think it's valuable?'

Lowenna, enraged by the twin insults of having her face wiped and being ignored by her sister, started to yell, and Liz quickly passed back the spoon, promising ice-cream for pudding, which seemed to do the trick.

Now that the room was quiet again, she took the piece of paper from Rosie and examined the contents.

'Wow!' she said, with a whistling sound when she got to the bottom. 'It looks genuine to me, but could it really have survived in the sea that long?'

Rosie explained where and how they'd found it, taking care to omit the reason why they'd been at the cove in the first place. 'I guess it could've been washing round the coast all this time. I wonder who Franz was.'

'Let's try to find out.' Liz placed the letter carefully on the table, out of Lowenna's sticky reach. 'Rick's pretty knowledgeable about local history – we can ask him. I can't wait to show Robert.'

Rafael, who was clearly more interested in the banana cake, which was cooling on the stove, cleared his throat. 'Mm! Something smells good!'

Taking the hint, Liz went to cut two large slices and soon the message in a bottle was quite forgotten while they chatted about school, the unpleasant lunches, Mrs Bailey's lengthy list of faults and homework – though Rafael was notably silent on this matter.

'I thought Mrs Bailey seemed quite nice when I met her,'

Liz said, remembering a particularly successful parents' evening at the school last year when all the teachers had sung Rosie's praises.

'Not at all,' replied Rafael gravely. 'She has bad breath – and ugly shoes.'

Liz laughed. 'What on earth's the matter with them? I didn't notice.'

'Crocs.' He looked at her meaningfully. 'Red plastic Crocs.'

Liz shook her head and laughed again. 'Poor Mrs Bailey. Condemned for her footwear.'

When they'd finished their cake, Rafael seemed quite keen to hang about, but Rosie told him that she had an essay to write for tomorrow.

'See you in the morning,' she said as she waved him off reluctantly at the door.

On reaching the gate, he turned around and blew her a kiss. 'Bye, Wo-Wo.'

He grinned, making red spots blossom on her cheeks, and she was still blushing as she walked upstairs to her bedroom, closing the door quickly because she didn't want her mother to see.

She needn't have worried. Liz was running a bath for Lowenna, who, having managed to get more food on her face and clothes than in her mouth, was roaring around the place, threatening to spread the mess on walls and furniture.

Robert popped back from the restaurant at around six. He usually came home between shifts to eat with the family, and Liz looked forward to it. Tonight, she'd bought fresh trout from the fishmonger, which she planned to bake in the oven with olive oil, parsley and lemon.

Following him into the bedroom while Lowenna played with her toys next door, she watched as he stripped off his crumpled white shirt and threw it in the linen basket in the corner before grabbing another, almost identical one from the wardrobe.

He was very tall, lean and muscular, with a sprinkling of dark hair on his chest that matched the wavy chestnut variety on his head. He'd been shy and awkward when they'd first met, and he still had no idea how attractive he was, which only made her love him more.

'Are you staying for supper?' she asked, secretly wishing that the children would dematerialise to allow time for something else.

'I can't.' He brushed her cheek with his lips. 'Sorry.'

Disappointment washed over her. 'Why not?'

'We're almost full tonight.'

'But you need to eat.'

'I'll grab something at the restaurant.'

He buttoned up his clean shirt before glancing in the mirror above the chest of drawers and smoothing down his hair, which had a habit of sticking out at odd angles, particularly when he was stressed.

'Rosie just found a message in a bottle. It was washed up on the beach.'

'Mmm?' He squirted on some eau de toilette. Really, he could have done with a shower and a shave to remove his six o'clock shadow.

'It seems to be from a German soldier, from the Second World War.'

'Interesting.' He didn't sound particularly curious.

'I've said we'll try to find out if it's genuine and trace who he was. I'm not sure how to go about it, though.'

'Good idea.' Robert wasn't listening, and checked his watch. 'Must dash. Don't wait up. Mark Tilley's coming by at eleven to discuss his quote for the café.'

That damned café. Couldn't he think of anything else? No doubt he and Mark, a local builder, would be up drinking and talking until the small hours.

'See you tomorrow, then,' Liz said stiffly, turning her back and picking up the dirty shirt from the linen basket.

'Don't be like that—'

She felt a pang of guilt. He wasn't doing this for himself, after all. The whole family would benefit if the Secret Shack got off the ground.

She turned to say goodbye, but it was too late. She could hear his footsteps rapidly descending the stairs before the front door slammed shut.

Lowenna, who'd heard the bang, toddled into the bedroom in her pink stripy pyjamas.

'Dada?' she enquired, clutching a battered teddy in one hand and a wooden brick in the other.

'Dada's gone,' Liz replied, picking up her daughter and burying her face in her soft hair. Then she muttered, 'What's the point in being married if you never get to see each other?' Fortunately, however, the little girl didn't understand.

When Esme woke the following morning, it took a moment or two to realise where she was. Everything felt different: the texture and weight of the hotel quilt, the smell of unfamiliar sheets and the light filtering through the cream curtains. Her own bedroom, with its thick shutters, was very dark.

But something else was unusual, too. Her eyes snapped open and she lay quite still, staring at the white sunflower ceiling rose, from which hung a brass chandelier, as she tried to work out what it was. Then it dawned on her: she felt lighter somehow, almost airy. The melancholia that normally sat so obstinately on her chest and shoulders until elevenish every day, sometimes longer, was no longer there. Instead, little bubbles fizzed and popped in her stomach. It was quite disorientating.

She turned on her side, closing her eyes once more. It was being on holiday, of course. This would explain her mood, although she seemed to remember that on other jaunts, the sense of bleakness seemed to cling stubbornly, no matter how interesting her surroundings or what plans lay ahead. She'd grown so accustomed to it that she barely even registered its presence. It had become a part of her, just like her hay fever in summer and the crunchy left shoulder that flared up painfully in damp weather. It was something to be borne, a burden made more endurable because she knew that it wouldn't last, but would eventually scuttle away, tail between legs, and the skies would brighten along with her spirits.

What sort of person would she have been, what might she have achieved, she wondered, had she not been dragged down by sadness in this way? Each morning she seemed to waste so much time floundering in greyness, gasping for air. She could have become a world-famous sculptress, perhaps, as celebrated as Barbara Hepworth, who'd lived not far from this hotel, or Henry Moore. She checked herself. Talk about illusions of grandeur!

For a moment she felt as if she were high above, looking down on herself, a middle-aged woman in a white cotton nightie, lying in bed lamenting her character flaws and missed opportunities. But then laughter gurgled in her throat, because this time she could spot where her negative thinking was trying to take her and she wasn't having it. Today was going to be *fun*.

She opened her eyes again, threw off the covers and walked to the window, drawing back the curtains and blinking as the morning sun flooded her senses. She'd asked for a sea view, and she wasn't disappointed. Beyond the hotel was a lawn, dark and moist with dew, and beyond that lay a crescent-shaped harbour sheltered by a pier on one side and a sea wall on the other. The tide was some way out and small boats, some protected by brightly coloured tarpaulins, lay stranded on the sand, trailing lengths of sinewy, seaweed-covered rope.

At one end of the pier was a white lighthouse, comically small from where she stood, and behind it rows of higgledy-piggledy cottages with lichen-stained roofs seemed to clamber up the hillside, eager to reach the top.

Tremarnock harbour was less than half the size and there were far fewer houses, whereas this was a proper, bustling town, you could tell – a place of business and enterprise, comings and goings, where plans were made and careers built and where celebrated artists chose to settle.

A niggle of doubt buzzed in her ear and she swatted it away. She could have lived here, or anywhere, come to that, if she'd really wanted; but she liked the smallness, the relative unimportance of her own village. Its isolation on a remote peninsula, flanked on three sides by water and battered by the elements, meant that in times of crisis, everyone had to pull together. It was reassuringly levelling.

She might feel claustrophobic occasionally, but she could always take off on her travels, safe in the knowledge that she had her haven to return to, her own personal cocoon. No, she thought, as the gloom receded again, she wouldn't want to have made her home in glitzy St Ives; Tremarnock suited her just fine.

Caroline had suggested meeting downstairs for breakfast at eight-thirty and it was already ten past. She'd better get a move on. As she showered and dressed, she found herself replaying parts of last night, which had been more enjoyable than she could possibly have hoped. There had been no awkward moments, not one; just plenty of conversation and laughter. They'd hurtled through the decades, touching on Caroline's later teens, after she'd left St Hilda's, her three years at university and her first research job for a homeless charity, where she'd met Philip, who had just left the army and taken his first civilian position. She also mentioned her two children, Helen and Andrew, both of whom were thriving, and her part-time job in Paris.

Her life was so full and colourful that Esme would have been content to listen all night, avoiding the subject of herself entirely, but Caroline had had other ideas. When she'd finally run out of steam, she'd turned the spotlight around and refused, despite Esme's best efforts, to be diverted.

'Tremarnock sounds heavenly,' Caroline had said at last, when Esme had finished. 'I'd love to come to one of your exhibitions.'

Esme had smiled, thinking that it would never happen, but told her friend that she'd be welcome any time.

When they'd retired at around half-eleven, after a large meal and several glasses of wine, both had agreed that they'd really only scratched the surface.

'There's so much more to discuss,' Caroline had said, hovering outside Esme's door before continuing down the corridor to her own. Then she'd wrinkled her nose and laughed in that slightly shy but infectious way she had. 'We need a month at least!'

As Esme had rootled for her key, she'd reflected happily on the fact that the years seemed to have melted away; within minutes, she'd almost forgotten that they were women of a certain age, 'on the downward slope', as Caroline had joked. In fact, she seemed like the least down person Esme had ever met. She had, as the saying went, grown into her own skin and gained in confidence, becoming at ease with herself and secure of her place in the world.

It was with this thought in mind that Esme descended the stairs this morning, so she was a little taken aback when she saw her friend sitting alone at the breakfast table, staring out of the window, her small hands resting very still on the white tablecloth, seemingly lost in reflection. She was wearing a pale beige top that was a little too big on the arms and shoulders and she looked thin and ever so slightly bent, almost vulnerable.

Esme hesitated a moment before approaching. Perhaps she had received bad news? One of the children? Philip? The dog? She was on the point of asking when Caroline turned. Her face lit up and she was the same as before – playful, curious and in control.

'How did you sleep?' she asked, rising to embrace her friend. 'I shouldn't have had that last glass of wine. I need gallons of coffee before we set off!'

They both decided against a cooked breakfast and helped themselves to cereal and yoghurt from the buffet. The array of fresh fruit reminded Caroline of the rather more meagre fare at St Hilda's, and soon they were laughing again, so that anyone watching would never guess that they hadn't met for decades.

'D'you remember Bossy Brokenshire?' Caroline put down her toast and marmalade and dabbed her mouth with a white napkin.

'With the frizzy hair? Always insisted on being captain?' Esme could still see the girl clear as day, with her buck teeth, freckles and smug little eyes.

Caroline nodded. 'She left her husband for a thirty-six-year-old ski instructor.'

Esme's mouth dropped open. 'Bossy? I don't believe it! How d'you know?'

'Facebook,' Caroline explained. 'We've been friends for a while. You should join. It's a good way of finding out what's going on.'

Esme stiffened. 'Not my thing' – before relaxing again. 'I say, though. I'd never have imagined Bossy behaving badly. She was always such a goody-two-shoes; she wouldn't even whisper after lights out.'

Caroline laughed. 'When Sister Bernadette made Susan Gilchrist form prefect, Bossy sulked for a week! She told me off once and made me cry for wearing my netball shirt for lacrosse by mistake. She thought she was head teacher.'

'Well, she's blotted her copybook now,' observed Esme, starting on her second piece of toast and honey. 'What would the nuns say? And does she still have that frizzy hair?'

'It's shorter now and sort of apricot-coloured. The ski instructor's *very* young.'

'My! I wonder if she still wears that awful flesh-coloured pointy bra and knicks.'

'I think she was rather proud of them.'

'I can't imagine why. They were like something my grandmother wore.'

'Perhaps they *were* her grandmother's.'

The conversation zipped along for a while more, then Caroline said that if they didn't leave now, they'd never manage to complete today's walk. They had decided to start their holiday with a section of the South West Coastal Path, from St Ives to the remote village of Zennor, and as they set off in comfy trousers and sturdy walking boots with backpacks, walking poles and bottles of water, as well as wet weather gear should the heavens open, Esme thought that she'd never felt happier.

The blue sky that she'd seen out of her window that morning was largely gone, though there were still a few patches in between the rapidly scudding clouds, and now that she and Caroline had broken the ice, the day ahead seemed set fair. They bought freshly made sandwiches and chocolate from a bakery and were soon leaving the town behind, following the acorn symbols on signposts and climbing the steep, winding path to the first headland. Tall hedgerows on either side were still a rich deep green, and they laughed at a pair of red setters bobbing in and out of the bracken while their owner traipsed behind.

Initially the women chatted non-stop – there was no shortage of material – but as the incline sharpened and their breathing became shallower, they fell silent, each lost in their own thoughts. The ground, which had started relatively even, became increasingly rough, until they had to scramble over crumbling stones and sharp rocks, hanging onto whatever they could to keep from falling. It was a good job they were both fit, or they'd never have managed it.

The wind was blowing fiercely at the top of the headland and when they gazed for the first time at the open sea, stretching to the horizon, it was a challenge to stand up straight on the very edge.

'It's spectacular!' Caroline shouted, turning to her friend with chin raised and arms spread wide, almost like an act of worship. She swayed slightly, her slim frame buffeted by the gale, and Esme noticed that her cornflower blue eyes were very bright, almost wild.

For some reason, she felt suddenly afraid. 'Let's go.'

She took Caroline firmly by the arm and led her away from the drop. It was only once they started to descend again that her heart stopped pitter-pattering and she wondered what that had been about. She must be getting nervous of heights in her advancing years.

Caroline, oblivious, fished a gooey chocolate bar out of her backpack and tore off a piece for her friend.

'I feel so far from everywhere here,' she said, sighing. 'I can't think why I haven't done this before.'

As they went lower, they used their hiking poles to take some of the pressure from their knees. Caroline was quicker than Esme, but they weren't in any hurry and she was happy to adjust her pace accordingly. There was something comforting about planting your pole in the soft earth, where you could find it, and focusing on the steady rhythm of your steps. Esme felt her brain emptying, aware only of the pumping of her arms and legs and the rise and fall of her breath. It was almost meditative.

Halfway across the next beach, they stopped to put on their waterproofs. The rain had started blowing hard into their faces and Esme's cheeks stung, though whether from a mix of hail or sand or both, she couldn't tell. After the second brief shower, the skies cleared and the sun came out again, watery but bright.

Another headland followed, and another, each crowned with weathered grey tors interspersed with coves, where cormorants fished from the barnacled rocks. They stopped and sat on a flat granite perch to watch seals swimming around their island colony, their soft, domed heads bobbing in and out of the water, their strong, lithe bodies riding the choppy waves effortlessly. When a motorboat buzzed lazily by, they vanished, only to pop up shortly afterwards somewhere else.

At one point a man with a bright red rucksack rain cover passed them, and they watched him gradually pulling away. Later, they stumbled on a chalk artist drawing the cliffscape and foaming water. He said a cheery hello, so they paused to talk and discovered that he and Esme had a few Cornish artist friends in common.

A youngish German couple with a dog joined them for a chat and explained that they were going the other way. Nearing the end of their walk from Penzance to St Ives, they said they loved the area and came back frequently, which made Esme swell with pride. She would have liked to ask which part of Germany they lived in, but they seemed weary and eager to reach their hotel.

'We might see you here another year!' the woman called cheerily as they headed off.

'*Auf wiedersehen!*' Esme cried back.

At the next cliff, they stopped again to look across the cove to Zennor Head, taking in the dark, volcanic stones and strange, otherworldly shapes, and the fulmars sailing the air currents on straight, graceful wings. Then finally they reached the head itself, covered in lichen-clad rocks and heather, gorse and wild thyme.

Here, they sat to eat their cheese and tomato sandwiches, basking in a profound sense of achievement as they savoured each bite, commenting on how delicious it all tasted because they were so hungry.

'I swear it's the best food I've ever had,' Caroline said, joking.

When they'd finished every last crumb, they lay back and closed their eyes, luxuriating in the warm sun on their faces, grateful for some rest at last.

'What's Philip up to while you're away?' Esme asked with a yawn. She wiggled her boots on the springy heather and settled into an even more comfortable groove in the earth. She could easily fall asleep.

'I'm not sure.' Caroline sounded half-drugged with sleep herself. 'I think he might be going to see a new house he's bought.'

'Oh! Where's that?' In truth, Esme was only mildly interested, assuming from her friend's tone that it was her husband's project; an investment property, perhaps, rather than somewhere they intended to live.

'In Burgundy, near a village called Vézelay. He's mad about the area, I can't think why. I much prefer the south.'

There was an edge to Caroline's voice that caught Esme by surprise; she'd imagined that they were the sort of couple who agreed about everything.

'Have you seen it?' she persisted, her curiosity raised, and Caroline said that she hadn't.

'What's it for? Are you going to rent it out?'

It seemed a harmless enough question, but Caroline rose suddenly and brushed the crumbs from her lap. 'Shall we get going? Otherwise my legs will seize up.'

It was clear that she didn't wish to pursue the subject, and Esme wondered why; but perhaps it was best not to speculate. She'd always found the workings of other people's relationships baffling, never having been married herself.

It was time to move inland and press on to the remote village of Zennor, where they were to call for a taxi back to St Ives. Away from the coast, the wind dropped and they stopped in a shaggy field to strip off a couple of layers and stuff them into their backpacks.

'That's the place with the mermaid!' said Esme, pointing to an ancient, lichen-covered church on the edge of the village, which seemed to be crumbling into the battered landscape stone by stone. 'Legend has it that a mermaid once lured a young villager to his death. He was the best singer in the parish and she fell in love with his voice and tempted him out to sea. There's a carving of her on a bench end, holding a mirror and comb. On warm summer's evenings it's said that their voices can be heard from beneath the waves.'

'Creepy!' said Caroline.

All the same, she wanted to go and see it. A hush seemed to descend as they approached the church wall, covered in ivy and sprouting wild flowers; the only sound was the distant lowing of cattle in a far-off meadow. They picked their way around tombstones, so old that you could no longer read the names, before pushing open a heavy oak door and entering the shadowy interior.

A man in overalls was kneeling on a platform above the organ, quietly doing some repairs, but other than that the place was empty. It felt much loved, though, with fresh flowers on the altar, and Esme noticed the beautiful hand-embroidered pew cushions, which looked brand new.

As they strolled around, admiring the mermaid chair, the stained-glass window above the altar and the Norman font, Caroline whispered that she rarely went to Mass these days.

'I used to when the children were little, but I haven't wanted to recently. I think I'm doing the Camino to try to reconnect with all that. It was such a major part of our lives, wasn't it?'

Esme nodded. 'I go to Mass most weeks, but only because

I love the peace and quiet. It must be comforting to have a strong faith.'

She watched as Caroline ran a hand along the smooth, polished surface of one of the pews, pausing at the end to wrap her fingers around the finial; she was frowning, as if deep in thought.

'I still feel angry with the nuns, don't you?' she said at last, and Esme hesitated, unsure what she meant.

'They were terrible teachers,' Caroline went on, warming to her theme. 'I can recite the catechism back to front but my general knowledge is appalling. I remember when I was revising for a history exam, Sister Michael walked into the library and told me to get on with my crochet. Imagine that! She wanted it for a display!'

Esme smiled. 'They were preparing us to be good wives and mothers, not career women. I'm afraid I didn't fit their mould at all.'

'Nor me.'

Esme was about to contradict this, but Caroline changed the subject. 'I say,' she said, as they left the church, blinking in the light, and started to stroll towards the village. 'What can you tell me about the Lost Lady of Tremarnock? Do you think she really exists?'

Esme had heard about the legend of the Lost Lady, an ancient shrine to the Celtic goddess Tremanthia, the goddess of love, healing, transformation and harmony. Old records suggested that there used to be a statue of her by a spring, and according to folklore, if you doused yourself in the water your troubles would be washed away and you'd be reborn.

'It's a good tale, but no one's ever found it. It's supposed to have been up in the hills above the village. I've walked there often enough, but I've never seen any evidence of a shrine.'

'Oh! What a shame! I'd really hoped there might be at least a kernel of truth in it.'

For some reason, Caroline seemed desperately disappointed, but it was only a silly story.

'There's the pub!' Esme cried, relieved to see a welcoming sign as they rounded the corner. Keep it light, she was saying to herself. Don't delve. The last thing she wanted was to scratch any wounds, old or new, and risk ruining their precious break.

Perhaps sensing that she'd made her friend uneasy, Caroline pulled back her shoulders and brightened her tone. 'I could do with a cup of tea and something to eat. And I think we've more than earned a G and T while we wait for the taxi, don't you?'

Chapter Four

THERE WAS NO point trying to talk to Robert about the message in the bottle; he was far too busy, so Liz went straight to Rick instead. She waited until Rosie returned from school, then together they wheeled Lowenna in her pushchair to Rick's gift shop, which was at the bottom of South Street, just past A Winkle in Time.

Stopping on the pavement outside for a moment, they gave Lowenna a moment to admire the enticing displays of postcards and brightly coloured spinning windmills, letting her reach with her chubby hands to whizz them around. Liz thought it rather optimistic to put them out today given that there were so few people about, but it certainly perked the place up.

Truth be told, without them Treasure Trove was rather a shabby affair, with peeling blue paint on the door and a cracked windowpane that had been like that for years. Liz never could fathom how Rick made a living from his cheap toys and models of lighthouses and dolphins, ice-creams and Cornish fudge and fairing biscuits, but he seemed to manage all right. He didn't complain, anyhow. A tall, big-framed man with a sizeable belly poking from the bottom of his grey polo shirt, he was behind the counter when they entered the shop, which was quite dark and smelled musty. He was flicking through a car magazine, but put it down as soon as he saw them and flashed a wide grin.

'Afternoon folks! How are we today? The usual, is it?'

They normally came in for lollies and an ice-pop for Lowenna. He started to move towards the giant fridge-freezer, but Liz stopped him.

'Actually, I've got a favour to ask…'

Rosie produced the bottle and after explaining their mission, his eyes lit up.

'Marvellous!' he exclaimed, nipping outside and glancing left and right to check if there were any potential customers, before shutting the door firmly and putting up the CLOSED sign. 'Let's take a look.'

Rick had a variety of interests, including sea swimming in all weathers, singing – he was extremely proud of his booming baritone – and local history. He was also very fond of the ladies, though it had taken him a while to get over the unfortunate débâcle with Esme, the reasons for which none but the two of them fully understood.

Happily, after a fallow period during which he'd moped around the village like a lovesick Romeo, he'd recently started dating Marie, an attractive mature blonde from Saltash who had given him a new-found spring in his step. Like him, she enjoyed all manner of activities, especially anything outdoorsy, and the romance seemed to be going marvellously, much to the relief of friends and well-wishers.

He hadn't received much formal education, having left school at sixteen to work in his father's hardware store; but history was an abiding passion, and his flat upstairs was packed with books and pamphlets, newspaper cuttings and historical memorabilia. The Tudors and Stuarts were an enduring interest and luckily for Liz and Rosie, he also happened to be particularly keen on the Second World War.

Lowenna was struggling with her restraints, trying to reach a plastic doll with purple hair and a fish's tail on the shelf beside it, so Liz pulled an apple from the bag dangling off the handle of the buggy and handed it over.

Rick, meanwhile, opened the message and spread it on his counter, propping the rectangular glasses around his neck on the end of his nose so that he could read properly.

'I say!' he said once or twice, and, 'Fascinating!'

Having reached the end, he held the paper up to the light and turned it over, as if searching for clues. Liz could tell that Rosie was getting impatient, shifting from one foot to another and fiddling with her ponytail, but was too polite to interrupt.

When at last he put the paper down again, he gazed first at Liz, then at her daughter.

'Well,' he said, scratching his not insubstantial nose in a ponderous sort of way. 'I think we've got quite a find here. It certainly looks genuine. Our Franz mentions the quarry; he might be referring to the old stone one in Mengleudh. They used prisoners of war to work it – Italians and Germans, mainly. The granite was loaded onto barges and taken downriver; most of it ended up at Plymouth dockyard. The PoWs slept in Nissen huts up on the cliffs. Some of the polite, anti-Nazi ones were allowed to find work in the village. Sounds like this one here struck up a friendship with the locals.' Rosie opened her mouth to speak but Rick held up a hand. 'Hang on a mo! I've got something you might find interesting.'

Without more ado, he disappeared to the back of the shop and they listened to his heavy footsteps on the stairs. He was gone for what felt like an age while they gazed idly at the dusty knick-knacks on the shelves. When he reappeared at last, he had a satisfied grin on his face and thrust a slim pamphlet into Rosie's hands.

'You can read about it here,' he explained, pointing to the words: *'GERMAN PRISONERS OF WAR IN SOUTH-EAST CORNWALL DURING WWII.'*

It wasn't a particularly inspiring title, but on the cover there was an interesting black-and-white photograph of some smiling men wearing an assortment of army uniforms and overalls, flat caps and berets, and clutching their tools outside the entrance to one of the quarries. They might have been prisoners but they looked pretty normal, despite their gear.

'Can I borrow it?' Rosie asked, and Rick nodded.

'It was written by an old chap from Polrethen way. Joss, he was called; published it himself. Nice fellow. He's dead now, but he was a boy during the war, grew up in Tremarnock, and he could remember the PoWs turning up. Said he and his sister used to hang around the camp and post their leftover sandwiches through the hedge to the men hanging about smoking. It's not particularly well written, to be honest with you, but there's a lot of information in it.'

'Thank you.' Rosie turned the pamphlet over and scrutinised the blurb on the back. 'But how can we find out who Franz was?' She looked hopefully at Rick, who scratched his nose again.

'Shame old Joss is gone.' He seemed quite crestfallen, until all of a sudden his eyes lit up. 'There's bound to be some records somewhere! There's the National Archives, of course, but local museums might be our best bet, or the Cornwall Record Office in Truro, come to that. I've got a good contact there – my old drinking pal, Des.'

Liz frowned. 'The problem is, we only know the man's first

name, and Franz is pretty common in Germany, isn't it? There might be dozens of them.'

'There weren't dozens at Mengleudh, I know that much. It says in there.' Rick pointed to the pamphlet again. 'I seem to remember there were only ten or eleven, though there were more in other parts of Cornwall. If I'm right,' he went on, smoothing his bushy grey beard, 'our chap worked round here, otherwise why would he be so fond of Tremarnock? Anyway, we've got to start somewhere.'

Liz agreed that it made sense, and Rosie piped up that she'd like to help with the research, too. She was keen on History and anxious not to be side-lined.

'By all means,' agreed Rick. 'Why don't you call the local museum, ask if they've anything we can look at? In the meantime I'll give Des a ring. Let's report back as soon as we've got some information.'

Rosie gave a little skip, clearly thrilled. 'I'll keep in touch,' she said, puffing out her chest importantly.

'Right you are, Sherlock,' Rick replied, grinning. 'I reckon you and me are going to be a dream team!'

They were about to leave when he mentioned the meeting of Tremarnock Resists at the Methodist church hall at 8 p.m. Liz had completely forgotten, despite the leaflet that had come through her letterbox at lunchtime.

'Damn,' she said, frowning again, because she'd been hoping to put the finishing touches to some homemade hairbands, which she'd promised to a woman in one of the nearby villages. She used to run her own small hair accessories business from home and although she'd wound it up, she still enjoyed making things for friends from time to time, using bits of fabric, sequins, rhinestones and whatnot that she picked up in local markets.

'The meeting is rather important,' Rick said sternly.

Liz sighed. 'You're right.' Then she glanced at Rosie. 'Can you look after Lowenna?'

She wasn't that keen on leaving her eldest in charge, not because she didn't trust her; quite the reverse, in fact – but if Lowenna got so much as an inkling that her big sister was babysitting, she'd be up all evening wanting to play.

This wasn't a problem for Rosie, however. 'Most of my homework's not due till Monday,' she insisted. 'You must go. We'll be fine.'

And so it was sorted.

On the way home, Liz popped into the restaurant to see Robert. The square low room was fairly dark inside, with pretty lead-paned windows that looked directly on to the street and old oak beams. Eight tables made of stripped bare wood were crammed together, creating a cosy, rough-and-ready feel, and there was a long bar near the kitchen on which stood two giant ceramic urns overflowing with sweet-scented flowers.

Robert was at one of the corner tables poring over his laptop; on the other side of the room, a couple of late lunchtime customers were nursing a pot of coffee. Other than that, the restaurant was empty.

'Any chance you could make the meeting – even just for an hour?' Liz asked hopefully, peering over her husband's shoulder at a headache-inducing spreadsheet, which she strongly suspected had something to do with the new business venture.

'Sorry, I have to go over to the Shack,' he replied, scarcely acknowledging either her, Rosie or Lowenna, still in her pushchair by the door. 'Ryan's cousin's coming over from

Looe to take a look. Says he'll do me a special deal on crab and lobster.'

Ryan the fishmonger's entire family were involved in the trade in one way or another.

'But you haven't even signed the contract yet,' Liz said crossly, 'let alone done the café up. Isn't it too early to start talking food?'

Robert flicked a hand in the air, as if swatting away an invisible fly, which irritated her intensely.

'The contract's just a formality. It's definitely going ahead.'

He looked at her properly for the first time and she noticed the dark circles under his eyes and the fret lines on his handsome forehead.

'This is going to be a GOOD THING, darling,' he insisted, adopting a new, soothing tone. 'Just you wait and see. I know you've had your doubts, but I've looked into everything carefully and there's very little risk involved. You're just going to have to trust me.'

Tears of anger and impotence sprang to her eyes, which she tried to disguise by clearing her throat. She didn't care that the couple at the other table had turned around, or that Rosie, standing by Lowenna, was fiddling with the cuff of her shirt and looking uncomfortable.

'It's not a question of trust,' she said hotly. 'I just hate it when you're so tired. I hardly see you these days and once the café's open, it'll be even worse. Why have all that stress? We were happy before, weren't we?'

Their eyes met and she pleaded with him to understand, to see her point of view, but his own eyes were blank and steely.

'You'll change your mind once it's up and running. You don't understand how the restaurant trade works. Why would you, when it's not your thing?'

Heat spread up to her neck and face and she felt her cheeks start to burn. 'I'm not stupid, you know. Have you forgotten I ran my own business – and made quite a success of it?'

'But you don't any more, Lizzie,' he said heavily. 'That's the point. We've only got one income now and it's important not to put all your eggs in one basket.'

She flinched, as if she'd been stung. He'd never seemed to mind that she no longer earned anything; in fact he'd positively encouraged her to give up work.

She started to say that she'd go back to cleaning and waitressing if he wanted her to, and that she'd only stopped because he'd insisted that they didn't need the money. Lowenna, though, was bored and had begun to whimper, and Rosie was having trouble undoing the buckles of the pushchair to lift her out.

'We can't talk now, in front of the girls, we'll have to discuss this later.'

Even as she spoke, however, Liz remembered that he would be back late and most probably up early, too. It was impossible to have a proper conversation with him any more. Tossing her hair and turning on her heel, she hoped to make a dramatic statement, but she'd hardly gone two paces towards the door when he went back to his laptop, and he didn't even notice.

Still smarting when she arrived at the meeting, Liz hadn't expected to see so many people, and certainly not Loveday. She'd spotted Robert's niece almost as soon as she'd arrived; it wasn't difficult. The extraordinary fat black buns perched on either side of her head, coupled with her glittery blue parting, made her stick out a mile.

'Come here!' the girl cried, patting the chair beside her as Liz moved along the row.

'Shouldn't you be at work?' Liz asked when she finally reached her seat, glancing around quickly at the sea of familiar faces: Rick and Felipe, Tabitha and Danny, Jenny and John and Barbara on the stage at the front, tapping the microphone importantly, making it hiss and squeak.

'I told Uncle Robert I had to run home and get a painkiller.'

'That doesn't take long. Won't he expect you back soon?' Liz waved at Jean in the row in front before settling down with her bag on her lap.

'Period pains,' said Loveday, tapping her nose and winking.

Liz frowned. She didn't approve of skiving, but couldn't help admiring the girl's cunning. Robert hated hearing about 'women's problems'. He found it embarrassing, and Liz herself liked teasing him and making him blush; she couldn't resist it.

The 1970s hall, with its tatty white walls and garish overhead lighting, had none of the charm of the nineteenth-century Methodist church alongside it. It was too hot in summer, too cold in winter and the roof leaked, so that big black wheelie bins had had to be strategically positioned around the edges to catch the drips. Locals had been fundraising for years for a new roof, but there was some way to go before they reached their target. Still, the hall was an integral part of the community, with numerous events taking place there from Mothers' Union lunches to toddler mornings, yoga sessions and meditation classes. The village would be lost without it.

'Hi!'

Liz swung around to find Bramble Challoner behind her, beside her partner, Matt. Bramble, who was twenty-seven, had inherited Polgarry Manor, the crumbling stately home on the cliff, from her grandfather, Lord Penrose. For a while it had seemed that she'd have to sell the house as she didn't have the cash to renovate or run it, but thanks to the discovery of a valuable painting that had fetched a very large sum at auction, she'd been able to start doing the place up.

Now, with the help of Matt, who managed a popular Plymouth fitness centre, she offered bed and breakfast accommodation and held numerous events at the manor, from weddings to open garden days and music festivals, all of which helped fund the upkeep. It was hard work but she seemed to enjoy it, and Polgarry had become quite a focal point for villagers, too.

'D'you think we can really stop the development?' she asked Liz now, leaning forward and lowering her voice. She was blonde, blue-eyed and very pretty, in a quirky kind of way.

Liz pulled a face. 'I'm doubtful, aren't you? I mean, it sounds like the council's made up its mind. They don't care about us – they just want their quota of new houses.'

'Oh ye of little faith!' Tony, who must have had very acute hearing, was several rows back wearing a distinctive blue and white floral shirt, open at the neck. He'd lost a bit of weight recently and bought himself a selection of dashing eye-catching tops, some in startlingly bright colours that meant you couldn't miss him.

'Quite right,' said Liz loudly, doing a thumbs-up. 'People power – it can move mountains.' She wasn't entirely sure that she believed it, though.

The microphone squeaked again and Barbara cleared her throat. She was quite short, but with a big presence that was further enhanced by her halo of heavily lacquered blonde hair, high red heels, tight white trousers and a plunging black top.

She held up a hand, adorned with chunky silver rings, and the chatter died down.

'Good evening, ladies and gentlemen,' she said. Behind her stood two youngish men, dressed casually in jeans and T-shirts, as well as Rick, Audrey from Seaspray Boutique and Reg Carter, the leader of the parish council, whom everyone tried to avoid because he was such a bore.

In a loud voice heaving with emotion, Barbara started to explain that as far as the proposed housing development went, the usual avenues of objection had been exhausted. Letters, petitions, even a large peaceful demonstration outside the council offices some weeks ago had failed; and yesterday, in the marketplace, the decision had been made to try something else.

'Quite what, though, is up for discussion,' she commented, before going on to introduce the two young men in jeans and T-shirts as members of the environmental group, Keep Cornwall Green, or KCG for short.

Some years before, the group had helped mount a successful campaign to prevent the site of an old tin mine in north Cornwall being turned into a theme park. They'd camped on the site for so long and caused so much aggravation that in the end, the developers had got fed up and decided to pull out.

Most of the younger residents, including Loveday, Rick and Nathan, were all for squatting in the play park for as long as it took, but Jenny, from Gull Cottage, was anxious.

'Isn't that trespassing? Couldn't we be prosecuted?' she said, in a quivering voice. 'I don't want a criminal record.'

Jean the childminder agreed. 'I've seen on the telly how the police come along and evict you. Some of them look quite rough. All my mums rely on me. I can't risk being beaten up.'

'Old Sergeant Kent won't beat anyone up, he's too soft!' her husband Tom cried, and everyone laughed. Sgt Kent ran the local police station and no one was particularly afraid of him, least of all the underage drinkers who could be a bother on a Friday or Saturday night after too many snakebites.

One of the young men from KCG stepped forward and asked if he could speak. 'I have to warn you that if you do decide to go down the route of direct action, things can get a bit unpleasant,' he said, tucking his grey T-shirt into the waistband of his jeans. 'What it boils down to is – how strongly do you feel about this, and how far are you prepared to go?'

'All the way! Viva the play park! Viva Tremarnock!' Everyone turned to stare at Loveday, who had risen up and was standing on her chair, her eyes blazing and right arm raised high. She looked courageous and magnificent, like the Statue of Liberty, sans torch or toga.

'Hear, hear!' came a shout from the front, and soon everyone was cheering and drumming their feet while Barbara stared open-mouthed – wondering, no doubt, what she'd unleashed.

Before long, Felipe the Brazilian had taken to the stage, too, brandishing a notebook and pen and promising in his broken English to take the names of all those who were willing to occupy the land. Jenny and John Lambert offered to donate tents from their shop for those who needed them, while Loveday, in her boyfriend Jesse's absence, volunteered his carpentry skills for treehouse building.

'I'll go to the timber yard and buy a load of planks,' Ryan shouted. 'There's plenty of room in the back of my fish van.'

Tony suggested that real eco-warriors probably used fallen branches and things that they'd picked up in skips, not brand-new wood, but he was shouted down by Tabitha's boyfriend Danny, who ran the Hole in the Wall pub.

'We haven't got time to go rummaging in skips, have we? Surely the whole point is to move really fast, before they get the diggers in.'

There was a general murmur of agreement.

Then Rick stepped forward. 'I say we start this very night. I'm going home to fetch my tent now. Anyone fancy joining me?'

'Me!' screamed Loveday, still on her plinth, and Liz pulled on the bottom of the girl's black waitressing skirt, which scarcely covered her purple fishnet tights.

'You're supposed to be working tonight, remember? You should go back now. Robert'll be missing you.'

Scowling, Loveday plonked down, muttering, 'Spoilsport' under her breath. It didn't take her long to perk up again, though. 'I know,' she said brightly. 'Me and Jesse will go there after work. We've got sleeping bags and we can kip on the ground. He can build the treehouse tomorrow.'

Liz swallowed. This was going to be chaos, she could tell. As soon as the other staff got wind of Loveday's plans, they'd be shinning up trees themselves and then where would A Winkle in Time be? Never mind the Secret Shack, it was going to be a devil of a job just keeping the main business running.

'I've got a load of old beds I don't need in one of the outhouses. I was planning to donate the frames to charity, but you're welcome to them if you want.' Bramble had risen, too, so that she could be heard above the hubbub. 'There's also various tables and chairs and things. They're not worth much. You could break them up and use the wood.'

'I love it! Filling the place with antique furniture will really piss 'em off!' Liz was delighted to see Osiris Turner, about halfway down with his back to the wall, grinning widely. A tall thin man with a straggly beard, he lived in one of the farm workers' cottages near Polgarry Manor and had been raising his three children alone since his wife died. He'd suffered from debilitating depression and hadn't been able to work; for a while, his teenage daughter Shannon had gone off the rails, but she'd calmed down a lot recently. Thankfully, her father seemed much better, too. He'd even found a part-time job as a farm labourer, which helped pay the bills, and Shannon, who loved gardening, often popped into Polgarry Manor to tend to Bramble's extensive grounds.

Barbara glanced at the two young men from KCG, who nodded in approval.

'Thank you,' she said. 'That could be very useful.'

Then Osiris offered to shift the furniture with Ryan and his van.

'I'll give you both a hand,' Rick chipped in.

'And me!' came various other voices including, rather surprisingly, that of Audrey, who wasn't known for her willingness to muck in. Today, however, she seemed so caught up in the general excitement that Liz thought she'd have volunteered for anything, even chaining herself to a fence, suffragette-style.

Before she knew it, Liz was filing forward to add her own name to Felipe's list of those prepared to take their turn at camping out. In fact hardly anyone held back, not even Jean, who seemed to be cheered by the prospect of sleeping in a proper bed, albeit out of doors, rather than on the ground or in a tree. About twenty villagers offered to set up camp with Rick that very night, so that by morning, when everyone awoke, it would be clear that the people of Tremarnock meant business.

Charlie, the *Tremarnock Bugle* reporter with the messy auburn hair, had been sitting at the back taking notes. She promised to be there at dawn with a photographer, and a group of locals who didn't work during the day agreed to take over from those who did.

Liz pointed out that it would be difficult for her to do much, as she had Lowenna to take care of, but she was soon shouted down.

'Bring her along with you, the more the merrier!' cried Tony, who hadn't actually committed to sleeping rough himself, though he'd insisted that Felipe and Rafael wouldn't mind the discomfort because they were 'used to that sort of thing'.

Only Reg Carter, leader of the parish council, who was still on the stage, wasn't joining in with the proceedings; instead he was rocking to and fro, his lips pursed and hands shoved into the pockets of his crumpled brown suit. All of a sudden he stepped forward, hustling Barbara aside so that he could reach the microphone, which made a piercing squeak that hurt everyone's ears.

'I've kept quiet up to now, because I wanted to hear what you all had to say,' he announced pompously, wiping a hand on the strands of sparse grey hair that partially covered his shiny bald spot. 'Before you leave this hall tonight, however, I feel duty bound to remind you that the actions you propose to take are highly illegal.' He coughed. 'I shall, of course, have to inform the relevant authorities.'

There were groans from the throng and cries of, 'Traitor!'

Tabitha, a former nightclub singer, who was in front of the stage, having just put her name to Felipe's list, raised her hands in a gesture of despair. 'How could you?' she called. 'Don't you want to preserve this village? Don't you care about its future?'

Reg's round, sweaty face turned red with anger, and he jabbed a pudgy finger in her direction. 'Don't tell me I don't care, young lady. I've devoted my entire life to helping this community—'

His voice was drowned out by the drumming of feet.

Ryan, the fishmonger, hollered, 'We don't want your help anyway, you old fool. We're better off without you.'

The gales of laughter were still ringing in Liz's ears as she left the hall and headed home down Humble Hill, past the rows of familiar cottages on either side: Dolly's Place, the Nook and Dove Cottage.

It was past ten o'clock when she arrived at Bag End but Rosie was still up watching television, having popped Lowenna into her cot after she'd dropped off in her sister's arms. Rosie was a little shifty about the exact time that she'd put her down, which was probably later than she claimed, but it didn't really matter; if the little girl was grumpy tomorrow, she could fall asleep in her pushchair at the play park.

The play park. The squatters' camp. Liz shuddered. Had she really just signed up to become a sort of eco-warrior? Didn't you have to sport dreadlocks and shun meat and leather and grow all your own vegetables?

Rosie, curled up on the sitting room sofa in her white onesie with little pink hearts on, wanted to hear all about the meeting, and brushed away her mother's concerns.

'I'll braid your hair and do cornrows for Lowenna. You'll look cool!'

Having finished doing the imaginary makeover, she mentioned that she'd put the message in a bottle in the cupboard in her bedroom, as she was scared that it might get broken. 'I hope Rick's friend can help us find out who Franz was.'

Quite how Rick was supposed to do the research as well as spearhead Tremarnock Resists was anybody's guess, but Liz supposed that he'd find a way somehow. He wasn't exactly busy in the shop, so perhaps he could take a little time out to make phone calls and surf the net. Anyhow, she was too tired to worry about that now.

'Come on,' she told her daughter, kissing the top of her soft, fair head. 'You might not be tired, but I've had quite enough excitement for one day. I'm off to my bed.'

'You'd better make the most of it,' Rosie said with a cheeky grin. 'You and Lowenna might be sharing a sleeping bag under the stars tomorrow!'

Chapter Five

AFTER RETURNING TO St Ives to bathe and change, Esme felt like a new woman. It was past eight o'clock by the time she and Caroline mustered once more in the lobby, and they decided to eat in the hotel rather than wander into town.

'We've got a big day tomorrow,' Caroline pointed out. 'We'd better conserve our energy.'

Having forgotten to pack evening shoes, Esme would have been stuck in her muddy walking boots, but Caroline kindly popped back to her room to fetch her a pair of silver flip-flops. They were far too small for Esme's size eight feet, but as you couldn't really see them under her long purple skirt, it didn't much matter.

She was glad that she'd remembered makeup and jewellery, as Caroline was wearing a pale blue shirt with a white Peter Pan collar that looked lovely with her newly washed fair hair and grey eyeshadow. An expensive-looking pair of diamond studs twinkled in her ears.

Esme felt like an elephant beside her small, neat friend, but hadn't that always been the case, even when they were girls? Some things didn't change.

'What a lovely top!' she said, when the younger woman settled on the sofa beside her. 'It looks freshly ironed. You always were immaculate, I remember. You never had a hair out of place. I didn't know how you did it then, and I still don't now.'

Caroline pulled a face. 'I can't help it. I wish I wasn't like this, to be honest; I'd love to be more free and easy like you.' She fiddled with the collar of her shirt, which was quite high-necked, and gave an apologetic sort of smile. 'Anyway, this is nice and modest so the nuns would approve. D'you remember how they made us do up the top buttons of our blouses even when it was sweltering? I think they must have loathed all things fleshly.'

Esme pretended to laugh, but a memory flashed through her mind that made anxiety nibble at her insides. Realising the significance of what she'd just said, Caroline's eyes flickered left and right, too.

'Let's find a table,' she suggested, rising quickly, and Esme, grateful for the distraction, followed her to the restaurant on the other side of the hotel.

It was a wide, square room with big windows that looked out onto the gardens; as it was dark, though, the heavy yellow curtains were drawn. They were greeted at the entrance by a waiter in a black suit and bow tie who showed them to a table for two, which was tucked away behind a pillar.

Hungry, they ordered quickly, and while they waited for the food to arrive Esme did her best to steer the conversation towards general chat about today's walk and Caroline's grown-up children. More nice safe topics followed, with no hidden booby traps, and the hour and a half whizzed by pleasantly.

Esme would have gone straight to bed after dinner, but Caroline suggested a nightcap; so they made their way to the small bar, where bright overhead lights destroyed any semblance of intimacy and a gaggle of foreign visitors were talking and laughing in raucous voices.

Choosing a spot by the window as far from the others as was possible in such a tight space, the women settled on some brown leather chairs arranged around a circular wooden table. Through gaps in the blinds they could just see the twinkling lights of the harbour in the distance, which provided a welcome diversion from their inauspicious surroundings.

They had already shared a bottle of wine at dinner and Caroline was in an expansive mood as she sipped on some whisky. Esme was quite happy to sit back and listen while her friend talked about her childhood in rural East Anglia, her father's hot temper and her brother, Peter, who was almost ten years older, who had left to go travelling at eighteen years of age and never come back.

'I missed him so much,' she mused, fiddling with the topaz necklace that Esme had given her. 'I think he couldn't wait to get away from home and once he'd made the break, nothing would make him change his mind, not even my father's threats to cut him off.

'He lives in Thailand now, has done for years,' she went on, swirling the ice in her glass before taking another sip. 'He married a Thai girl, Kulap, and they have two children. They run a language school together. He seems happy enough, but I think he misses England.' She smiled sadly. 'Especially the weather, oddly.'

Esme wanted to know if she'd visited, and Caroline said that she had.

'I went on my own as soon as I was old enough. My parents never did; they never forgave him for leaving. They were bitter to the very end, or my father was. My mother just did as she was told. Peter knows he can come to Paris any time but Kulap doesn't like flying. It's a shame, because they'd love it.

'Peter and I always got on well, despite the age gap. There was such a big hole when he went.' She glanced at Esme. 'You know, I can still recall the terror when my father told me I was going to boarding school. He never even gave me a choice. I think he'd decided I was spending too much time on my own, but I was so miserable at first. Do you remember?'

An image swam before Esme of a small, thin girl with a tight little mouth and big, frightened blue eyes, and she nodded.

'But it didn't last – thanks to you,' Caroline went on. 'It was such a shock when he pulled me out.'

Without warning, she reached across the table to touch Esme's hand, resting her fingers on the smooth, veined surface above her knuckles. The hairs on the back of her neck prickled and it was all she could do not to pull her own hand away.

'It took me years to get over it,' Caroline continued, oblivious. 'And you... I'm sorry—'

'Don't!'

The change of tone made Caroline start and she stared at her friend in surprise.

'It was all so long ago,' Esme said, more evenly. 'Let's not go over old ground.'

She swallowed, and to her dismay, tears welled in her eyes. She picked up a white paper napkin from the table and blew her nose. She couldn't remember when she'd last wept. Not for many years, for sure. Not since her previous, darling cat, Donatello, had been run over by a car and she'd thought that her heart would break.

She was aware of Caroline's gaze, confused and anxious at the same time, and felt guilty for causing her consternation.

'It's all right,' she whispered; but it wasn't, not really. She had been trying so hard to keep the atmosphere light and she'd been doing so well. Why rake things up? Things could so easily turn sour.

Telling herself to stay calm and not overreact, she took a few deep breaths and her pulse started to slow. She was hoping that her words would have drawn a line under that particular topic of conversation, but she was out of luck, because Caroline wanted to say more.

'I wasn't allowed to write for ages,' she said in a low, urgent voice, as if sensing that she didn't have much time and that at any moment, Esme might get up and leave. 'My father was watching my every move. I didn't have a choice.'

Esme was suddenly overcome with weariness. 'I know,' she said, sighing heavily. 'You don't need to tell me.'

'I always wondered how you were,' Caroline persisted. She was like a dog with a bone; she wouldn't let go. 'I thought about you often and I was so happy when you got back in touch.'

'Please!' Unable to stand it any longer, Esme raised a hand in warning. 'That's enough.'

Caroline opened her mouth to speak, but thought better of it and lowered her head while her eyes fell to her lap. 'Of course. I'm sorry.' She was backtracking furiously. 'I understand.'

At last, Esme managed to muster a smile. 'It's so lovely to see you.' She meant it, she really did. 'You know, we really must make the most of our precious few days.'

After that, the conversation petered out; they finished their drinks and made their way back to their rooms. They said goodbye at Caroline's door and she reached up to kiss her friend softly on the cheek.

'Thank you for organising the hotel. I hope you sleep well.'

The scent of her perfume hung in the air for some time after she'd gone.

It was only once Esme had put on her nightdress and cleaned her teeth that she remembered she'd forgotten to return Caroline's sandals. Having more or less decided to wait until morning, something made her change her mind. She tiptoed along the corridor and knocked lightly on her friend's door.

Oddly, there was no reply, and she waited for a moment with her ear pressed against the wood, thinking that perhaps Caroline was in the bathroom. Then all at once she heard her voice, loud and shrill.

'I can't believe you said that!'

Esme's heart fluttered and she hesitated, unsure what to do.

'I've already told you, Philip,' came the voice again, sharp enough to cut with. 'I want you to leave me alone.'

Esme was confused. Philip? Had she misheard?

'Don't you understand?' This time the voice cracked and there was a high-pitched wail, a childlike, primal sound that tore at the gut, followed by a bang, as if something had been thrown across the room. Esme felt an insane urge to smash down the door and rush to her friend's rescue, but managed to stop herself.

Should she knock again – or go? She hovered on the landing, paralysed with indecision, until she thought that she could hear Caroline moving about again, putting things back in order. There were no more shouts or sobs; there wasn't even any more talking. She must have hung up.

Somewhat reassured, Esme told herself that she'd been right not to get involved. It was none of her business, after all.

As she crept away, she was thinking that the situation would most likely resolve itself before too long. The majority of her married friends seemed to go through sticky patches and most came out, a bit battered and bruised but still together, on the other side.

Despite her exhaustion, however, she tossed and turned in bed that night, unable to sleep. She couldn't help remembering the molten anger in her friend's voice, the sheer, terrifying fury, followed by a howl of pain so raw and intense that anyone would think the spirit had been ripped from her body and hurled, torn and dying, at her size four feet.

The following morning, the sun rose slowly over Tremarnock, casting an orange glow across beach and harbour, cottages, pubs and shops. High above on the jagged cliffs Polgarry Manor, with its grand grey façade and fake turrets, seemed to peer down on the sleepy inhabitants like a stern parent and say, 'Wake up, wake up, you lazybones, the day has begun!'

Most folk weren't listening, but in one corner of the village, a little way away from the main streets as you headed out of town, there was an unusual amount of activity.

In the wide grassy play park dotted with sturdy oak trees, the children's swings, see-saw, climbing frame and slide stood silent and unused. Around them, however, was an assortment of tents of varying colours: red, yellow, brown, green and blue. Some were domed or mushroom-shaped; others had peaked tops like witches' hats and one was decorated with a very large picture of a black and white cow.

Many of the doors were zipped shut, but a few had been rolled open and bedraggled-looking folk were wandering about outside, tripping over guy ropes and rubbing their eyes, as if they couldn't remember for the life of them why on earth they were here.

Luckily it hadn't rained in the night, so Loveday and Jesse, who had declined Jenny Lambert's offer of sharing her and John's four-man tent and opted instead for a groundsheet under the stars, had remained reasonably dry. Even so, the outside of their double sleeping bag was moist with dew, and Loveday, sitting bolt upright inside it and wrapped in a bundle of old jumpers, was decidedly grumpy.

'I ache all over,' she moaned, poking Jesse in the ribs with a finger. Her hair, having largely escaped from her two fat buns, resembled beached seaweed after a storm, while tears of makeup dribbled down her cheeks like squid ink.

Jesse was lying on his stomach, eyes tightly shut, and didn't reply.

She tried again. 'I SAID, I ACHE ALL OVER!'

This time, the top of his blond curly head, only just visible above the bag, moved slightly and he groaned as if in pain.

'I know you're awake.' Loveday shook him hard with both hands.

'Go back to sleep, babes,' came a muffled voice. 'I'm having a nice dream.'

She bent over as if about to give him a kiss, then hollered, 'I CAN'T GO BACK TO SLEEP BECAUSE I NEVER SLEPT IN THE FIRST PLACE!'

It did the trick. He sat up, grimacing, with his hands glued to his ears.

'Morning!' said Loveday, smiling sweetly now she'd got his attention. 'Will you run back to the flat and make us some coffee?'

'Get it yourself.' He crossed his arms over his bare tanned chest. 'Now I'll never know the end of my dream. It's all your fault.'

She narrowed her eyes dangerously, but luckily Rick came to the rescue with a flask and two plastic cups. He was wearing a grey T-shirt and long johns, which were rather tight around the belly and groin area. Loveday looked the other way.

'Here you go,' he said, pouring out the drinks. 'I'm off with Ryan and Osiris in a minute to fetch the furniture from Bramble's place. We'll need your help with unloading when we get back.'

'Sure thing,' Jesse replied, taking a sip of coffee.

As soon as they were alone again, however, he and Loveday, who'd chosen a spot under some thick branches, flopped back, resting their heads on their hands and staring at the blue-grey sky peeping through the leaves, which were already starting to turn brown.

'I like sleeping outdoors,' Jesse said, his rude awakening already forgotten. Loveday was poised to disagree when a scream came from Audrey's tent. Jenny, in a long pink nightie and fluffy slippers, charged across the field after Sally, shouting, 'Stop! Bad dog!'

Too late. The Jack Russell had already begun digging a hole beneath Audrey's tarpaulin, spraying mud and grass everywhere and scratching and yipping wildly. Soon, Audrey unzipped her door and poked out her head. She looked different without her camouflage of red lipstick and blue eyeshadow, like a badly scrubbed potato, and bits of hair were sticking up in all the wrong places. She was incandescent with rage.

'I will NOT have that dog anywhere near my quarters,' she boomed. 'If it can't be controlled, you should have it put down.'

Loveday giggled; she couldn't help it. Audrey's face was such a picture, and to crown it all, Jenny uttered a very uncharacteristic swear word. The dog peed on one of the guy ropes before she could grab its collar and drag it off.

Loveday sighed happily; all her aches and pains had melted clean away. 'This is going to be fun. I can't wait for you to build our treehouse. Maybe we'll like it so much we'll want to live here for ever.'

Jesse put an arm around her and gave her a squeeze. 'Yeah, maybe. We could add a new room every time a baby comes along. Our kids'll be mini Tarzans, swinging round like monkeys – and you'll be Mamma Jane.'

The idea pleased Loveday so much that she couldn't help snaking a hand down inside the sleeping bag, prompting her lover to roll over for a passionate smooch. They would have carried on like that, oblivious, but someone shouted, 'Oi! You can't do that here!'

When they opened their eyes, Jean's husband Tom was towering above, hands on hips, in a navy top and bright red boxers with white go-faster stripes down the side. It was such a surprise to see him out of his usual gardening gear of baggy trousers, muddy shirt and battered green fisherman's hat that Loveday stopped what she was doing and pushed Jesse off.

'Sorry,' she muttered, but Tom had already turned his back and was stomping back to his tent, where Jean was attempting to boil a silver kettle on a gas ring. It looked as if she might have to wait a long time, as it was a very small flame.

The air was still cold and clung to the body like damp cloth, while the birds, Nature's own tubular bells, were chirping and chiming in different tones and frequencies, as if trying to summon the sun to be quick and warm up their feathers.

Jesse noticed a small white Fiat stop for a moment by the entrance to the field, before pulling into the car park opposite.

'Visitors,' he said, sensing that the brief, pleasurable hiatus after waking and before the day swings into motion was over.

Loveday opened her mouth wide and yawned noisily.

'I think it's that reporter,' Jesse went on, watching an auburn-haired woman in a pink and yellow stripy jumper and green Wellington boots leave her car and stroll across the road. 'And she's got a photographer with her.'

The effect on his girlfriend was instant. At the mere suggestion of a camera, she stopped stretching and started frantically smoothing her hair, redoing the buns as well as she could without a comb or mirror. All the while, she had her eyes fixed on the tall thin young man loping behind the redhead towards them, with a large camera hanging from a strap across his shoulders.

'Hurry, pass me my bag,' Loveday hissed, with one hair tie still in her mouth. 'I need my makeup.'

The visitors stopped in the middle of the field to talk to Jenny, who had put Sally firmly on a lead, and Rick, who thankfully had now changed into khaki shorts and a crumpled white polo neck.

'Bloody girls and their war paint,' Jesse grumbled, but he passed across the purple rucksack, then started pulling on the black T-shirt that he'd worn yesterday while Loveday rootled inside. As soon as he was fully dressed in jeans and trainers as well, he wandered over to the group.

'Ideally, we need a lot more people,' the reporter Charlie was saying, casting an eye over the thinly spread campers and their motley collection of tents. 'It'll make a better picture. Are there more expected?'

Rick nodded. 'Lots, I hope. Why don't you come back later?'

'I think I'll wait,' replied the girl, tucking her notebook and pen into the back pocket of her jeans. 'I'd like to have a wander round and chat to some people, if that's OK? It'd be good to get some colour.'

She turned to Jesse. 'I'm Charlie Pearce, by the way, from the *Tremarnock Bugle*. And this is Rory Clark.'

The tall thin young man beside her smiled shyly. He wasn't bad-looking, with short black hair, shaved at the sides and longer on top and a sprinkling of designer stubble, but his unusually large ears made him look rather as if he might take off in flight at any moment.

Jesse was about to offer to introduce them both to the campers when Liz arrived, stamping across the wet grass with Lowenna balanced on one hip and an extremely heavy-looking basket in the other hand.

'Breakfast,' she shouted, swinging the basket, while Jesse ran to help. 'I've got croissants and sticky buns and hot tea and coffee. I'm going to go back and fetch my sleeping bag and stuff later.'

The basket brought everyone over, including those still in their tents, who must have been able to sense food in the proximity. Jenny produced a couple of tartan blankets, which she laid on the rubbery playground surface beside the swings where it was dry, and Liz laid out paper plates, cups and two large flasks.

It was still only 6.45 a.m., so there was time before John Lambert and Ryan had to leave to open their shops; Audrey and Rick had already decided to take the morning off. Jean, though, said she'd have to be extra-quick as the first of her mums and children would arrive at eight-thirty and she'd need a shower first.

'I'll ask them if I can bring the littl'uns down here for a while. They'll enjoy seeing the tents and playing on the swings, and they'll swell the numbers, too.'

Audrey, in a white bathrobe and towelling turban, helped herself to a large Danish pastry and announced that she needed first dibs on the comfiest cast-off Polgarry Manor bed, as her back couldn't take another night on the ground.

'Make sure you remember the mattress,' she told Rick, who was munching on a croissant, dropping flaky bits into his bushy grey beard. 'I know what you're like.'

The pair had known each other since childhood and he was able to cope with her better than most.

'I'll do what I can, but I'm not promising anything. Mattresses are very heavy and there's only so much room in the van.'

'I'd like one too, if possible,' Jean squeaked, but Audrey shot her a look as if to say, *if there's only space in that van for one mattress, my name's on it.*

Poor Jean looked crestfallen until her husband Tom offered to take his old estate car up to the manor, too. 'I'll get you a mattress, love, don't you worry. I can squeeze a surprising amount in the boot with the back seat down.'

After the men set off, accompanied by Jesse, Loveday made a beeline for Rory the photographer who, to her delight, offered to take a few 'action' shots of her leaning against a tree and hovering over a camping stove – not that she intended to do any cooking. Meanwhile other villagers started arriving, carting with them bags of equipment, bedding and supplies. Barbara, who was going to share eco-warrior shifts with her son Aiden so that they could keep the Lobster Pot open, even had an inflatable three-piece suite – an orange sofa and two armchairs, along with a matching coffee table – which she'd bought for her grandchildren's den at the bottom of her garden. The only problem, she said, was that it had taken half a day to deflate them and she'd need at least as long to blow them up again.

'I'm hoping one of the lads'll give me a hand. It's blooming hard work, even with the foot pump.'

By the time the van reappeared, laden with furniture from Bramble's outhouse, followed by Tom and Jesse in the estate car and Bramble and Matt in her yellow VW, there were around forty villagers in the field, all talking and laughing as they put up their tents and compared groundsheets and sleeping bags. The sun had warmed up at last, banishing the early-morning chill, and before long, the air was alive with sawing and banging as Jesse set to work on some rickety tables and chests of drawers, cutting them up into varying sizes for his treehouse.

Meanwhile, the better-quality furniture was dumped in a pile in the middle of the field so that people could take what they wanted – including Audrey, of course, who plonked herself down on the best bed and refused to budge until some strong men agreed to move it to her corner of the field and put a temporary gazebo over it. This she draped with tarpaulin for added protection. She even had bits of rope to tie back the tarpaulin in the daytime, so that by the time she'd finished, she had a sort of makeshift boudoir, complete with four-poster, a bedside table with a cracked mirror on top and a couple of torn velvet chairs with tufts of wadding sticking out – 'For entertaining,' she explained.

Since time immemorial, humans have built themselves homes out of whatever happens to be available – be it ice, mud, brick, bark, cloth or straw – and today was no exception. By mid-afternoon, the play park had been transformed into an ingenious array of temporary residences, some with washing lines strung between them for hanging damp clothes on, others boasting bits of rug and carpet at the entrance, sofas, chairs and tables outside and broken lamps for decoration.

And in the centre of it all, just a little way from the swings and slide, were six or seven tables, some round, some square or rectangular, which had been put together and surrounded by high-backed wooden dining chairs, like an outdoor banqueting hall. Someone had even put a vase of wild flowers in the middle, and two large wooden candlesticks on either end. All they needed was food, crockery, cutlery and, ideally, some entertainment, and they were all set for an alfresco feast worthy of Titania, Bottom and the fairies.

Jesse was in the oak tree, bolting a rudimentary floor platform in place, while Liz stood at the bottom passing up the tools, when she spotted three suited figures and a uniformed police officer marching across the grass towards them.

'Uh-oh!' she hissed. 'Here comes trouble!'

'Reg jelly-belly Carter!' squealed Loveday, who, worn out after the photographic shoot, had already abandoned her post beside Liz and was sitting on the grass with Lowenna making a daisy chain. 'What does he want?'

'I don't know, but he doesn't looked happy,' Liz replied ominously, and Jesse poked his head out of the branches to take a look.

'He's got a clipboard with him, and that developer geezer who's been sniffing round the village. Quick! Warn the lads! Tell them to get their knuckles out.'

'There's not going to be a fight,' Liz said firmly, putting down her hammer. 'Whatever else happens, we must keep our fists to ourselves.'

Reg appeared to be in his element, ignoring the rude stares and heckles from campers gathering around. It looked as if Barbara might have got to him with her foot pump, for his short body seemed to be filled with air and his two chins waggled self-importantly. As soon as he was satisfied with the size of his audience, he cleared his throat and puffed his chest out even further.

'Ladies and gentlemen,' he said, straight-backed and officious. 'I am here this morning with my colleagues, Sergeant Roy Kent of the Devon and Cornwall Constabulary' – he gestured unnecessarily to the police officer beside him – 'Mr Rod Halliday from MegaCrest Homes and Mr Eric Bosomworth from Porthcaron District Council—'

The unlikely surname was too much for Ryan, who sniggered rudely, prompting a strict look from Sergeant Kent.

'We are here,' Reg Carter continued, unabashed, 'to warn you in no uncertain terms that you are trespassing on council property. This place is supposed to be used as a playground, not a campsite, and if you don't pack up and move the local authority, together with MegaCrest Homes, may have to take legal action to evict you.'

The MegaCrest Homes man, a tall fellow with an orange tie, flinched slightly at the word 'evict'.

'I'm sure it won't come to that,' he said, flashing a charming smile. 'These people seem eminently reasonable. I'm sure they won't want to cause any trouble. '

Reg coughed again. 'Obviously we'd rather find a peaceful solution, but if it comes to it—'

'This is a public space! You can't make us go anywhere!'

Liz, who was holding Lowenna tightly by the hand, glanced at Osiris Turner, now sporting a yellow bandana made from torn-up curtains. Coupled with his straggly beard and grubby clothes, he looked every inch the eco-warrior. He even had a smudge of green paint on his cheek that must have rubbed off some furniture.

'That's just where you're wrong!' spluttered Reg Carter, who had a very short fuse. He held up his clipboard and started waving it vigorously. 'It says here on this notice. It's about unauthorised encampments. There's rules against people like you, putting up your tents willy-nilly and your...'

There was a cheeky whistle and his gaze slid to Jesse, who was hanging out of his tree, grinning and waving.

'... you and your, your Wendy houses,' Reg stammered. He brandished his notice again. 'Look!'

Sgt Kent peered at the writing as if he didn't know where else to look, while the MegaCrest Homes man and the local authority representative stared hard at their feet.

'It's a treehouse, not a Wendy house!' Loveday cried.

Charlie-the-reporter, next to her, scribbled in her notebook and Rory, standing some distance off, snapped away furiously. Their presence only seemed to egg the villagers on, and now Rafael, whose Mohican was rather limp after his night in a tent with Felipe, piped up, 'The power in people is much stronger than the people in power!'

It seemed to catch on, and soon others were chanting, 'People power!' and singing, 'We shall not be moved!'

Then without even thinking about it, Liz pushed forward, hoisted Lowenna up high, and shouted, 'The future belongs to our children. Keep Tremarnock for the kids!'

There was a whoop of agreement and Lowenna clapped her hands obligingly and beamed from ear to ear. Her presence seemed to cause great consternation among Sergeant Kent and the suits, who huddled together, shaking their heads and conferring in low voices. Their anxiety increased still further when Audrey limped into the mêlée, rubbing her knee.

'You've got to be extra careful with minors and the elderly,' the local authority man muttered sagely. 'The law's very strict on it. It's about human rights, you see. You can't go shoving them around, causing distress. The old folks might have a heart attack.'

Audrey turned very red and was about to point out that she wasn't old – she'd only tripped over a tree root and banged her knee – but Jean poked her in the ribs and whispered something in her ear. After that, Audrey groaned a bit louder.

'It's my poor old bones.' She was laying it on a bit thick. 'I'm not the woman I once was.'

'You can say that again,' Tom joked, but she pretended not to hear.

Fortunately, her amateur dramatics seemed to do the trick and before long, Sergeant Kent and the suits turned tail, muttering about needing to take more advice. Only Reg hung back for a moment.

'Don't think you can get away with this.' He cast a steely eye over the assembled crew. 'You and all your rubbish. Ruining the place, that's what you're doing. Acting like common or garden tramps and vagabonds.' He growled menacingly. 'Make no mistake, we'll be back!'

Then, amid more whoops and jeers from the protesters, he practically ran on his fat little legs to join the others by the exit while Loveday stuck up two fingers and Jesse sang the Beatles' 'Revolution' at the top of his voice. Meanwhile Lowenna, now on her mother's shoulders, clapped her hands again and squealed with laughter as Liz jigged along to the music.

Chapter Six

CAROLINE MADE NO mention at breakfast of her argument with Philip the previous night, but she seemed subdued and spent ages getting her backpack ready. Then she forgot her sunglasses and had to go back to her room to fetch them.

She and Esme took a taxi from their hotel to the little church of St Uny, where they were to begin their walk, stopping at a bakery en route to pick up drinks and sandwiches. The air was close and still, almost suffocating, and ominous clouds obscured the sun, though the weather app on Esme's phone hadn't predicted rain.

Legend had it that the little church, overlooking medieval Lelant harbour, was originally dedicated to St Anta, a long-forgotten woman of the Celtic past, but it had become buried in sand. Later, in the sixth century, St Uny had arrived from Ireland and started to spread Christianity among the native Cornish folk.

Esme, who had a handy guidebook, was keen to honour the place by circling clockwise around the outside first, as the book suggested; but Caroline went straight inside. When Esme joined her, she was sitting in the shadows at the back, head bowed, seemingly lost in thought or prayer – Esme couldn't tell which. Caroline smiled on catching her eye, but there was no joy in it; she was putting on a brave show.

On leaving the church, they passed a wooden post decorated with the symbol of the scallop shell, which was used to direct pilgrims along the Camino towards St Michael's Mount and, eventually, St James's Cathedral in Santiago. Esme felt a tickle of excitement, for this was the beginning of their micro-pilgrimage. It was what they had come for, surely – to follow the path of the early missionaries, to tread the same steps that they had once trodden? But Caroline, whose idea it had been, scarcely seemed to notice, so lost was she in her own thoughts.

All the gaiety of yesterday had evaporated. As they headed across a golf course before joining the coastal path and following the dunes with the sea on their right, Esme was left wondering if they were destined to spend the rest of their short break in gloomy silence.

Today, her walking boots felt heavier than before and the toes pinched. Her neck ached, too, and suddenly the whole venture felt like a fiasco. Indeed, she half-wished that she were back in her cosy flat with Rasputin purring on her lap and a cup of coffee at her side, or in her studio, where she could lose herself in work and forget the outside world with all its harshness and disappointment.

As the route wound inland, the path narrowed to a thin track overhung with trees, and in places they had to bend to avoid them. It was lucky that they were both in long trousers, or their legs would have been stung by nettles and scratched by brambles. When they came to a railway crossing with no lights or barriers, Esme stopped and looked left and right, but Caroline walked straight over without checking.

Her insouciant, devil-may-care attitude made Esme jumpy and she almost ticked her off, but managed to bite her tongue;

she wasn't her friend's mother, for goodness' sake, and she could surely look after herself.

After about an hour and a half, they reached a giant granite obelisk, which had been built as a mausoleum by a wealthy customs collector in St Ives. The structure, some fifty feet high, dominated the landscape, presiding over St Ives Bay and Godrevy lighthouse, and for the first time that morning, Caroline stopped for a proper look.

'How vain he must have been!' she commented, after Esme had read out some information from her guidebook. 'Imagine building something like that for yourself. Typical man!'

Her sharp tone caught Esme by surprise. Caroline must have noticed, because her shoulders suddenly drooped, all her bluster gone.

'I'm afraid I'm very bad company today,' she said, shuffling uncomfortably from one foot to another. 'I had a filthy row with Philip last night.'

It was a relief, really, to have it out in the open, because Esme had felt squeezed so tightly by the atmosphere that she could hardly breathe.

'I'm sorry to hear that.' She paused, hoping that her words would be enough to prompt further explanation, but there was nothing. 'What was it about?'

Caroline sighed. 'I really don't want to involve you.' She nodded in the direction of the onward path. 'Shall we keep going?'

Esme concurred, sensing, however, that her friend hadn't finished. Sure enough, as they circled a hill, thought to have once been a Neolithic fort, Caroline started to explain that she and her husband weren't seeing eye to eye. It was a start, at least, but she was skirting around the issue, like a skater testing the depth of the ice around the edges before venturing into the middle. Her words hinted at something deep and complicated, but it was impossible to tell what it might be.

Esme felt frustrated because she wanted to assist, but without the full facts, she didn't know how. Down the years she'd learned to keep her feelings to herself; she wasn't one to wear her heart on her sleeve, and nor did she expect others to. Now, though, she mustered all her courage and plunged right in.

'Caroline, what is it? What's really going on? I'd like to help if I can. You can trust me, you know.'

They were passing some farm buildings, the first sign of habitation for a while; no one was around, but a silver car was parked just outside the entrance to one of the barns, which housed some heavy-duty farm equipment and a large pile of carefully chopped logs.

Caroline kept her head down, her eyes on the ground, but Esme's words had clearly touched her. Finally, something in her shifted, and she began to talk more honestly.

'I made a terrible discovery,' she said heavily. 'It's changed absolutely everything.'

She went on to explain that when Philip retired some six months ago, his secretary packed up the contents of his office for him and sent the boxes to their apartment in a special delivery van. 'I asked the men to put everything in our underground garage. Philip said he'd go through them but he never did. They just sat around unopened for months, taking up space and gathering dust.

'In the end I got fed up with waiting. So one day when he was away, I decided to start going through them. I wanted the space for my clothes, you see, things I never wore but couldn't bear to part with. I thought Helen might want them at some point, or even my grandchildren. They were nice, expensive pieces. I don't buy much designer stuff but I've collected a few bits down the years.'

She sounded almost apologetic, as if she were at fault in some way; but she didn't need to justify anything to Esme, who nodded, encouraging her to go on.

'I honestly thought I was doing him a favour.' Caroline gave a humourless laugh. 'If I'd known what was in the boxes, I'd probably have turned round, locked the garage door and never gone in there again.'

Esme made a sympathetic noise but didn't speak, not wishing to interrupt her friend's flow. It felt reassuring to continue the walk as the tale unfolded, as if whatever else happened, they were at least making progress, putting one foot in front of another towards their chosen destination. The fact that there was no eye contact also made it easier.

Hesitating for a moment at a large round granite rock at the side of the road, Esme started to read out loud what was written on the plaque at its base. '*According to local folklore, this rock was used by giants playing a game—*'

'Most of the boxes were full of rubbish,' Caroline interrupted, as if she hadn't heard a word. 'Old files, pictures he'd hung on his walls, stationery, that sort of thing. Most of it went straight in the bin.'

She cleared her throat, as if her voice had got stuck. Esme resumed walking once more, hoping that this might loosen the logjam.

'But in one I found a batch of letters. They were from his lover, a younger woman in the company. I knew her quite well. She was almost like a friend.' She made a strange noise, like a kitten's mew, and they paused again while she collected herself.

Esme reached out to touch her arm for reassurance, but she shook her head.

'It's OK,' she said, smiling bravely. 'It happened a few months ago. I'm sort of used to it now, if you can ever get used to something like this. It's become part of my narrative, if you know what I mean. I've had to absorb it. I'm at the stage now of trying to work out what to do with the next phase of my life. That's mainly why I'm walking the Camino. I need time away from Philip. I'm hoping I'll get some answers.'

Their breath quickened as they started to ascend a steep hill, and from the top they caught their first sight of St Michael's Mount, a rocky island assaulted by fierce waves, shrouded in mist and crowned by a medieval church and turreted castle.

'There it is!' Esme said unnecessarily, while Caroline merely nodded.

'It had been going on for years,' she continued, staring at the view without seeming to see anything at all. 'Fifteen years or more. All through Helen's and Andrew's childhood. I used to invite her to their birthday parties. Donna, she's called. I can hardly bear to use her name. We lived in the same compound in Islamabad. She stayed there for a bit after we moved to Paris, then she was transferred, too. I imagine she and Philip engineered it, though I didn't know at the time, of course. I honestly thought it was just a happy coincidence.

'She was single – no husband or children – and I actually felt quite sorry for her. She was always super-nice to me and so interested in the kids. They loved her because she gave them amazing presents. When Philip told me he was working late or away on business, he'd be with her. It's the lies I can't stand.' She choked.

Esme wrapped an arm around her shoulder and squeezed. 'I'm so sorry,' she repeated, wishing that she could think of something better. 'It must have been a terrible shock.'

'It was – it is!' Caroline broke away and looked at her friend squarely. 'There's something more,' she went on. 'The letters she sent him – they were very explicit, sexually explicit, I mean. They were into things, tying up, inflicting pain...' She winced. 'Things I had no idea he liked. Horrible.'

Esme's mind started racing, her brain filled with lurid images she'd rather not contemplate. She was trying to imagine how such a conversation would have unfolded. She was way out of her depth, she knew that much.

'What did he say when you confronted him?'

'He broke down. He didn't try to deny it; how could he? It was all there in black and white in the letters. He said it was just about sex. She'd do things he couldn't ask of me. He had these specific needs, these urges. He said he wasn't proud of himself, it's just the way he was made.

'He told me the affair finished some time ago, when she moved back to England to look after her mother. He was terrified of losing me – he still is – but I don't know if I can go on. I can hardly bear to look at him, let alone share a bed or even sit at a dinner table with him. The truth is, he revolts me. I can honestly say I hate him.' She was still fixing Esme with her big blue eyes.

Esme trembled slightly, shaken by what she'd just heard. 'I don't know what to say. I can't imagine what you must have been going through—'

'It's all right,' Caroline replied gently, assuming the role of comforter for a moment. Esme felt guilty, thinking it should be the other way around. 'I'm strong. I'll survive. I've discovered reserves of strength in these past months that I never knew I had.'

'Will you divorce him?' It seemed so obvious: Philip had been a bastard, Caroline loathed him and the marriage was over. End of.

But to Esme's surprise, her friend shrugged. 'I don't know. It's difficult.'

Esme frowned; she was already having great difficulty getting her head around the information and this latest response threw her even more.

'He's not well,' Caroline explained, as if reading her friend's thoughts. 'He's got Parkinson's disease. That's why he retired when he did; he'd just been diagnosed. The medication's working pretty well at the moment but he's shaky and slow and it's a progressive illness, of course. It'll only get worse. He's very scared for the future.'

Esme felt her face heat up. 'You can't feel sorry for him! Not after what he's done to you.'

'I don't, not really, but he's the father of my children and I do feel some responsibility towards him. The illness is an added complication; it makes it harder just to walk away.'

There was silence for a few moments while Esme tried to digest what she'd heard. There was so much to take on board, and her own emotions were in turmoil. The only certainty, right now, was that she knew she hated Philip, too.

The rocky ground beneath their feet gave way to soft tufty earth, prompting her to pause and check her watch. Amazed to discover that it was gone two o'clock, she suggested lunch. The very least she could do, she thought, was to make sure that her friend ate properly. 'You must be hungry. We can carry on talking while we have our sandwiches.'

Caroline seemed surprised, as if she'd forgotten all about food, but conceded that here was as good a place as any to take a break. They sat on a tussock, in full view of the castle, and chomped slowly through thick slices of bread filled with slabs of West Country cheddar.

'Have you told Helen and Andrew?' Esme asked, resuming the conversation between mouthfuls, but Caroline shook her head.

'They'd be devastated. I couldn't possibly do it to them.'

'What about close friends or relatives? I should think you could do with some support.'

'You're the only person who knows.' Caroline gave a meaningful look. 'I'd rather keep it that way.'

'I won't breathe a word,' Esme promised. She felt honoured to have been entrusted with her friend's secret but also somewhat daunted by the responsibility. 'When you first told me you were walking the whole Camino on your own, I thought it was a bit strange, but I completely understand now. No wonder you want to leave your burdens at the cathedral.' She smiled sadly. 'I hope it works for you.'

After lunch, the route continued across an ancient bridge; the trail led through the front garden of a former Wesleyan chapel, now a private house. Soon, they were passing Ludgvan Church, with its stone carving of a pilgrim with a staff above the porch, but they didn't go in, preferring to press ahead across flat, swampy timber plantations before reaching the reedy marshes of Marazion. Here, dragonflies buzzed in and out of the tall grasses while overhead, late-departing swallows and martins were hawking flies and feeding up in readiness for their flight south over the Channel.

'Are you all right?' Esme asked, sensing her friend's pace starting to slow.

'Just a bit tired. This feels a lot further than yesterday.'

They finally left the marsh and crossed a busy road before arriving at a stretch of sand dunes. From here, St Michael's Mount was well within reach. Before they could get there, however, they had to pass through an ugly car park full of tourist coaches, with a run-down café in the centre.

It was a bit of a let-down after the peace and tranquillity of the fields and marshland, but they were cheered by the sight of some brave souls on the beach wearing wetsuits and carrying surfboards, though no one was actually in the sea.

Settling for a moment on the sea wall, they gazed out at the island and its castle rising out of the water, grey, austere and formidable, while a flag on the very top flapped jauntily in the breeze. A few folk, little pinpricks in the distance, were tramping across the causeway, their heads bent against the wind.

'D'you think we'd better go across now?' Caroline said at last.

The island would become inaccessible at high tide. Esme was weary and had been there before, but knowing that this might be Caroline's only opportunity to make the trip, she didn't want to deprive her of the experience; not when she'd come this far.

After climbing carefully off the wall, Esme started to put on her backpack. Caroline hopped off, too, but as she reached the hard ground, she lost her footing and cried out.

Turning quickly, Esme saw her fall as if in slow motion. She rushed to assist but it was too late; before she knew it, Caroline had landed sideways on the tarmac, her arms splayed and one leg twisted beneath her at an odd angle.

'My ankle!' she yelled, her face contorted with shock and pain.

Esme tried to help her up, but she was too heavy. 'Oh God!' She dropped to her knees and tried to look at Caroline's right foot, which was bent awkwardly. 'Can you move it at all?' She started to unlace her friend's boot, taking care not to jerk anything.

'I don't know… It hurts… a little, I think.' Caroline wiggled the foot very gingerly to and fro before using her elbows to push herself up. 'Ow!'

As Esme pulled the boot off gently, then the sock, she could see that the ankle was already beginning to swell. It might be broken or sprained; it was impossible to know. She glanced around as if searching for inspiration and spotted several groups of people in the distance, but no one noticed the two women huddled on the ground.

'Shall I call an ambulance?' she asked desperately.

'I don't know… maybe it's not necessary.'

'D'you think you can hop to the car park, then, and I'll call a taxi?'

Caroline shuffled back a little, so that she was resting against the wall. Some of the colour had returned to her cheeks, but she was clearly still in pain.

'I can try…'

She attempted to rise on her own, but couldn't, so Esme crouched right down again and positioned herself alongside.

'Here, put an arm round my shoulder. Careful,' she commanded, and she slowly straightened with Caroline clinging onto her. 'Don't put any pressure on it.'

Once upright, Caroline took a deep breath. 'How stupid of me! I can't believe it.' She attempted to place her injured foot ever so lightly on the ground, but winced and pulled it back again quickly. 'It's impossible, it hurts too much. I've ruined our holiday... I'm so sorry.'

The consequences of what had happened were only just beginning to sink in.

'It wasn't your fault. It's just one of those things,' said Esme. signalling with her free arm to a middle-aged man in shorts and a bright blue cagoule some way off, who was staring at them. He must have clocked their predicament because he'd stopped talking to his companion and as soon as he saw her beckon, he strode towards them.

When he was close enough, Esme explained the situation and he gestured to his wife or friend, a plump woman with short grey hair, who hurried over to join them, too.

'She's hurt her ankle,' he told the woman, who clucked sympathetically.

'You'd best get to Casualty,' she advised, eyeing Caroline's poor puffy foot, which was already beginning to turn blue. 'You should get an X-ray to check if it's broken.'

Caroline couldn't stop apologising. 'It all happened so fast... just lost my footing... so careless of me...'

'It's easily done,' the man soothed, before offering to drive them to the local hospital. 'It's only ten minutes away. We don't live far from there. It's no trouble.'

Before they knew it, the women were tucked in the back of his blue Toyota while up front, his wife Ali chattered away nineteen to the dozen in her strong Cornish accent.

'My daughter, Hayley, she's twenty-one... her little boy, Noah... likes swimming pools but can't stand the sea...'

Though deeply grateful for their kindness, Esme couldn't take it all in; she was too anxious about her friend, sitting quietly beside her with her leg raised and her bad foot resting on Esme's knee.

As they drew up outside the entrance to the hospital, an ugly, sprawling affair, Caroline groaned for the umpteenth time, 'How could I have been such a fool?'

While the man and his wife helped her out of the car, Esme's mind started racing ahead. She was thinking, wondering – hoping a little, too, though she scarcely dared. She wouldn't have wished the accident on her worst enemy, but it might just open up some possibilities.

'Don't worry, we'll get you seen to,' she said, scanning the area for a porter with a wheelchair, or some other member of the hospital staff who could help. 'You'll be OK, just you wait and see. From now on *I'm* going to look after you.'

Chapter Seven

ALMOST A WEEK passed, and the villagers were well and truly ensconced in their new quarters. Jesse's treehouse, though not complete, was habitable, and he and Loveday had dragged up a mattress and even installed some makeshift curtains on the windows to keep out the morning light.

Loveday was delighted with her new abode and already had expansion plans; she'd asked Jesse for a room for her clothes, as well as a separate kitchen-cum-dining area so they wouldn't feel obliged to eat meals with the others if they wanted a cosy *à deux*. She had even threatened to have a housewarming party and invite along her friends from far and wide, but Rick had overheard and vetoed the idea.

'You can't go playing a lot of loud music and making a nuisance of yourselves. You'll turn the locals against us; at the moment they're all on our side.'

Audrey's boudoir was becoming more lavish by the minute; she'd hired a small white marquee with plastic windows to keep out the cold and rain. In addition, she'd requisitioned a dressing table, wardrobe and standard lamp with a jazzy purple shade from Polgarry Manor to add to her other furniture. Thanks to the loan of a rather noisy portable electric generator, she now had light, too, as well as a small fridge and portable TV, so that her tent was a bit of a magnet; though you could enter strictly by invitation only and she kept her hands tightly on the remote control.

The fact that they all lived close to the campsite meant they could pop home for showers whenever they wanted, or to use the loo. The rota system was functioning well, so that no one had to camp for more than two nights in a row, but some of the villagers found that they were liking the outdoor life so much they wanted to stay longer.

As each day went by, more and more stuff kept arriving in the field: Primus stoves, blow-up beds, duvets and pillows, cooking equipment, bicycles, rugs, you name it. Anyone would think that the protesters had been there for years, not just a matter of days.

Reg Carter had gone very quiet, but no one was under any illusions that he'd stay away. The good news, however, was that until contracts with the developer were exchanged, there seemed to be little that he or anyone else could do. Some days before, he'd discovered in some obscure old parish papers that there had once been a sign in the playground saying it was to be used only between 8 a.m. and 6 p.m. According to him, this meant that the villagers were in breach of the opening hours and the council would be well within its rights to take legal action. Charlie had duly quoted his words to that effect in her newspaper.

Since then, however, it had been established that as the sign had long since disappeared, and given the absence of photos or any other concrete evidence, it was difficult to prove its existence beyond all reasonable doubt. Furthermore, the fact that there was no fence around the field meant that any restrictions would be impossible to enforce; so for the time being, at least, the campers felt safe.

Living in such close proximity meant that there were plenty of clashes about noise, rubbish disposal, cooking smells and so on. Ryan had a habit of frying up mackerel for breakfast at the crack of dawn every morning before he went to work, which upset Jean, sleeping next door, who claimed the pungent smell got into everything, including her underwear.

There were frequent mutterings about Rick and his girlfriend Marie's noisy lovemaking, though no one dared complain to his face. Fortunately, she lived some way away and could only cope with one night at a time under canvas, so every other night, folk were able to sleep in peace.

Meanwhile Nathan the postman and his girlfriend Annie the fitness trainer had started running exercise classes on the grass behind the encampment at different times of the day and evening. Bramble and her boyfriend Matt often joined in and some of Matt's clientele came over from his Plymouth gym, too.

On a good day, there could be up to thirty people huffing and puffing around the site in trainers and trackie bottoms, doing press-ups and burpees, star jumps and planks, urged on in loud voices by Annie and Matt. Most of the campers found it highly entertaining and the more enthusiastic exercisers, including Tony and Felipe, were getting fitter and more toned by the minute. Audrey, however, moaned about the shouting and sweaty bodies, while Tom claimed that just watching the goings-on nearly gave him a heart attack.

Despite the inevitable grumbles, however, a lot of fun was being had. Alex, Robert's chef at A Winkle in Time, rustled up some amazing communal meals with little more than a couple of gas rings and a saucepan or two. When Jesse wasn't helping Alex, he entertained them all with his guitar while

Loveday and Rick sang, and Lowenna toddled around the place charming everyone. For her, it was like Christmas every day with so many people to play with and fuss over her.

Charlie-the-reporter was down frequently with her notebook, pen and photographer in tow. Although the *Tremarnock Bugle* came out just once a week, she had quickly established herself as the official stringer for a variety of other local newspapers, radio and TV stations; almost every day, it seemed she got something in the media about Tremarnock Resists, along with pictures of the ever-growing protest. She was clever, persistent and ambitious, and the fact that the villagers liked and trusted her also worked in her favour. They were beginning to feel like celebrities, especially when carloads of folk descended from other areas to show their support and see for themselves what was going on.

Only Robert, it seemed, couldn't enter the spirit of it at all. He refused to spend a single night with Liz, Rosie and Lowenna under the stars, insisting that someone in the family had to keep their head out of the clouds and the restaurant up and running.

When Nathan delivered the post a little late after a particularly strenuous early-morning outdoor boot camp session, Robert was the first to complain.

'How am I supposed to run a business if the letters don't arrive?' he said. And when Ryan turned up a few minutes past his usual time with the day's consignment of fresh fish, he moaned that the whole village was falling apart.

Sometimes, Alex, Jesse and Loveday would arrive for work with bags under their eyes and mud on their clothes, regaling anyone who would listen with stories of the previous night's activities. Robert would wring his hands and mutter under his breath about everything 'going to pot', but they still fulfilled their duties and never let him down. Liz couldn't understand what had got into her husband.

'You never used to be like this,' she said one afternoon, when she'd popped into the restaurant with Lowenna, who was asleep in her pushchair, to bring clean napkins and tea towels and rearrange the flowers. 'Don't you want to stop the development? Don't you care if they bulldoze the playground and build a bloody great estate in its place?'

Robert, who had been polishing glasses behind the bar, stood up straight and folded his long arms across his chest.

'Of course I care,' he said, frowning. 'But it's a done deal, isn't it? It's all very well trying to make a stand, but it won't do any good, and I can't afford to stop working.' He made a low growling sound. 'That said, the way things are going, soon I won't have any staff or customers any more, or a restaurant either.'

'Oh Robert, it's not that bad.' Liz reached over the counter and touched her husband on the shoulder. She felt sorry for him, she really did. He seemed so isolated in his truculence, stuck in the woods on his own. Yet no one was abandoning him. The restaurant was still full most nights and he was surrounded by willing hands. It was just that things *felt* different right now. Life would soon get back to normal.

'Let me help you,' she said suddenly. 'Lowenna's exhausted. She'll probably sleep in her pushchair for a couple of hours at least. What needs doing first? I can help the boys in the kitchen. Or shall I lay the tables?' She tried to grab the tea towel that he was using for the glasses. 'Here, I'll do that. Why don't you have a couple of hours on the computer? I'll take over – I know what to do.'

But Robert wasn't having any of it. Whisking the towel away, he picked up another glass and began polishing again furiously. 'I can manage.'

He sounded so stern that you couldn't argue with him. Liz sighed, wishing that she could make things easier for him, but it was difficult to reach out to someone who didn't want it.

As she replaced the clean napkins in the drawer of the wooden chest in the corner and threw out the dead flowers, she found herself wishing that she could spirit him away for a fortnight's holiday somewhere warm and sunny. Rest and relaxation was what he needed, she was sure; but there was no way he'd leave now, not while he was so busy trying to set up the new business. Besides, she couldn't abandon her neighbours in the middle of their dispute with the council either.

Needing a breath of fresh air after the grumpy exchange with her husband, she resolved to stroll home along the seafront. As she passed Treasure Trove, Rick came bustling out of his shop, waving a bit of paper.

'I've got some news about your German prisoner of war,' he declared. 'I spoke to my mate Des at the Cornwall Record Office. Tell Rosie to get down here as quickly as possible.'

As it was almost 4 p.m., Liz decided to meet her daughter off the school bus. She'd be keen to hear what Rick had to say, especially as her own research seemed to have stalled; as soon as Rosie had finished reading the pamphlet that Rick had lent her, she'd hot-footed it to the local museum and spoken to one of the members of staff. But to her great disappointment, she'd left empty-handed. Secretly, Liz suspected that she hadn't asked the right questions – or the right person, come to that. Since then, what with homework and all the excitement at the camp, she'd been too busy to pursue her investigations any further and the bottle and its message were gathering dust on a shelf.

As she watched her daughter scramble awkwardly down the stairs of the bus, Liz's heart hurt. Rosie hung on tight to the rail with her good hand, lurching on the steep bottom step as if she might fall. Liz's instinct was to reach out and grab her before lifting her down gently and placing her on the ground, safe from harm. It wouldn't be difficult; she was so small and light. With a supreme effort of will she managed to stop herself, knowing full well that Rosie hated feeling different and couldn't bear a fuss. If she found something difficult, she'd sooner fall flat on her face than ask for help. Her obstinacy could be infuriating, but Liz admired and loved her for it, too. She didn't have an ounce of self-pity.

There was a smudge of ink on Rosie's cheek, and one side of her thick fair hair had come out of its ponytail and was dangling messily around her face. Beneath the crumpled navy blazer, her white shirt was missing a button and her school bag was open and flapping. Liz smiled, thinking that she looked as if she'd walked straight out of the pages of a St Trinian's story.

'Good day?' she asked, kissing her daughter on the cheek before taking her heavy bag and slinging it over her own shoulder. It was something she'd done ever since Rosie was little, when she'd collected her from primary school in their old banger.

There was no time for the girl to respond, because Rafael came clattering down the steps behind her, his hands stuffed in his pockets. The large round holes in his earlobes were lined with silver flesh plugs, off which hung his favourite wooden crosses, and there was a silver stud in his nose; he must have popped them in after school, as usual. The Mohawk, with its brightly coloured strip down the centre, would most likely reappear tomorrow, too, as it was Saturday. Liz hoped so, anyway. She'd become surprisingly fond of it.

Lowenna was still asleep in her pushchair, worn out after another night in the tent. When Liz told Rosie about Rick, Rafael wanted to tag along as well.

'I am very hungry, I only had small lunch,' he said hopefully, as they trundled along the cobbles in the direction of Treasure Trove. Taking the hint, Liz suggested a detour to the bakery, where she bought iced buns and cartons of chocolate milk. She could remember feeling ravenous after school herself, and besides, she always leaped at an opportunity to try to fatten Rosie up.

The teenagers were still munching when they reached the shop, but they finished up quickly and shoved the empty milk cartons on the tray under the pushchair before going inside.

Rick was on his own, flicking through a magazine, but broke into a wide smile when they approached. 'You'll never guess what! I think I've found our man!' The others listened, rapt, as he explained that Des, his friend at the Cornwall Records Office, had pulled out some old files relating to the prisoners of war at Mengleudh Quarry. 'We're in luck. There was only one Franz. Maier, his surname was. M-A-I-E-R.' He spelled it out. 'Captured on D-Day in June 1944, sent home in 1946.

'Strangely, there's not much information about that time. Probably everyone was too busy with the war effort. But Des did find a couple of old newspaper cuttings, which were very useful.'

Rick peered at his visitors long and meaningfully over the top of his spectacles, and Rosie shuffled impatiently. He was clearly enjoying the moment, spinning it out for as long as possible.

'Look here.' At last he reached over to the corner of the counter and produced a couple of photocopies, but the words were too faded to read properly. 'The originals are clearer,' Rick went on, sensing everyone's frustration as they peered at the indecipherable script. 'They mention a German PoW from Bavaria, name of Franz, who went out in the boat sometimes with a Tremarnock fisherman named Arthur Kellow, of Cobbler's Rest—'

'Cobbler's Rest?' Rosie interrupted. 'That's the name he mentioned in the letter, isn't it? The house where Little Bear lived? It must be the same man!'

She glanced at her mother. Liz nodded, and a flicker of delight and anticipation licked through her.

'That's right,' Rick agreed. 'The very same. And what's more...' He leaned over the counter and lowered his voice conspiratorially, which only served to heighten the anticipation further. 'What's more, Arthur Kellow was married to a lady named Winnie Kellow and they had five children, including a daughter named Patricia – or Pat.'

Rosie's greeny-grey eyes opened so wide with wonder that Liz couldn't help laughing.

'P-Pat?' the girl stammered. 'You don't mean...?'

Rick grinned; he was enjoying himself immensely.

'The very same,' he said at last. 'Pat Kellow married another fisherman named Geoffrey Kersey. Lived most of her life at the Nook.'

He pulled himself up straight. 'It was our Pat who Franz called "Little Bear" and who he befriended when she was seven or eight years old. It was our Pat's parents, Arthur and Winnie, who took him under their wing and showed him so much kindness. He was only nineteen when he was captured, according to the records. Not much more than a boy. He must have been very homesick, and as he says in that note, Winnie and Arthur made his life that bit better. And Little Bear, of course.

'So you see,' he concluded triumphantly, 'our Pat had her very own prisoner of war friend and we never even knew. Now that's a piece of history worth having, isn't it? Who'd have thought it?'

There was silence for a moment as they all absorbed the information. Pat, who had been well into her eighties when she'd died the previous year, had been almost an institution in Tremarnock, having lived in and around the village all her life. She'd married a fisherman, Geoffrey, long since deceased, and they'd had no children – 'They never came along' – but she'd adored little ones, especially Rosie, who'd called her Nan.

Pat's house, the Nook, was just a few doors up from Bag End, and she had babysat Rosie when Liz had worked as a waitress at A Winkle in Time before her marriage. Money had been extremely tight back then and the old woman had refused payment, insisting that she liked the company. Liz was eternally grateful and had often done Pat's shopping for her, and stopped by for a cup of tea and one of the old woman's famous chocky bickies. Pat had been a mainstay in their lives for so long, always ready with a gentle word, some homespun wisdom or a piece of juicy gossip, and they still missed her like crazy.

'How amazing!' Liz said, before letting out a long sigh. 'If only she were alive now to tell us about it. Wouldn't she have loved to see the message? It's such a shame.'

'I don't understand – why didn't she tell us about him?' Rosie added, with a wail. 'We talked about everything, didn't we? I can't believe she never even mentioned his name.'

Rick knitted his bushy grey eyebrows and stroked his beard, twizzling the ends around between fingers and thumb.

'Aye, I wondered that myself. Pat was such a chatterbox, you'd think she'd have mentioned him to someone. Maybe she did, but they've forgotten; maybe her friends knew, but most of them have passed away, same as her.'

'Could be,' Liz agreed. 'And it was such a long time ago. I guess it's also possible that she was upset he never said goodbye. Maybe she just wanted to forget about him? I wish she'd known just how much she meant to him.'

'So what now?' piped up Rosie, who had been listening intently. 'I feel like we should do something with the information.'

Liz pulled thoughtfully on her bottom lip. 'I wonder if Franz is still alive. It would be fun to try to find him, wouldn't it? But how would we do that? I mean, Munich's a big place and he might not even live there any more. It would be like looking for a needle in a haystack.'

A squeak of excitement from Rafael, who'd been silent up to now, made everyone turn. His voice was breaking, and was a source of private entertainment in the village – you never quite knew what sort of sound would come out.

'What about that reporter, Charlie?' he said. 'Maybe she could write a piece in her paper asking for information? It happens in Rio all the time when someone goes missing. It's on the news with a photo of the lost person. Often the body is found after.'

Liz shuddered. She hadn't been to Brazil, but she'd heard some hair-raising tales from Felipe down the years; he loved to talk about the drugs murders, elaborating on the grisly details. As far as she knew, though, there were no favelas in

Munich and it was unlikely that Franz would have come to a gruesome end.

'That's a good idea,' she said, rallying. 'Maybe someone will recognise his name.'

'Even better, the story could get picked up in Germany,' added Rick, who was starting to run away with himself. 'It might go global!'

Liz giggled again. 'Unlikely, I think, but we can certainly ask Charlie if she has any German contacts. It would be fantastic to find out more.'

Bubbling over with enthusiasm, she and Rosie offered to speak to the reporter the next time they saw her.

As it happened, they didn't have long to wait. Rafael had arranged to camp in the play park with Felipe that night and after leaving Rick's shop, they all wandered over to drop him off. As they approached the site, whom should they see but Charlie herself, sitting on the grass outside Jean's tent, nursing a cuppa and chatting to Tom on a fold-up chair.

Liz waved and Charlie, who'd spotted them, too, waved cheerily back. Some way away, in front of Jesse's and Loveday's treehouse, Nathan hollered to a group of enthusiastic exercisers, which made Lowenna wake with a start. After her long nap, this was probably a good thing, Liz decided, as otherwise she might be up all night; there was no denying that the goings-on were wreaking havoc with both their routines.

There seemed to be plenty happening, but other than Charlie, Tom, the fitness class members and Rory the photographer, there weren't actually that many people about. Those who had jobs wouldn't be down until later and thanks to the absence of Audrey, the atmosphere was relatively calm and happy; she always managed to upset the applecart in one way or another.

Lowenna struggled to get out of her pushchair and made a run for the swings as soon as she was unbuckled, followed by Rosie and Rafael.

'Wait! Don't you want to speak to Charlie?' Liz called after her daughter, but Rosie turned and shook her head.

'You tell her. I'll mind Lowie.'

Liz was surprised, until she noticed two handsome young men, whom she recognised as Rafael's schoolmates, approaching the swings from the other direction. One raised an arm in greeting and Rosie gestured back. Clearly the message in the bottle was no longer top priority; she had better fish to fry. Liz smiled to herself. Fickle or what? But she supposed you were allowed to be at that age.

Having been abandoned, Liz strolled over on her own to Charlie, whose auburn hair was piled high on the top of her head and held up with what looked like two chopsticks.

'Can you spare a moment?'

'Of course! Come and join us,' Charlie said, smiling and patting the grass beside her while Tom got up to fetch more tea. Pale and lightly freckled, she had on rolled-up jeans, flip-flops and a red and white stripy T-shirt. Her hands, cupped around her blue and white mug, were caked in mud; Liz couldn't help noticing that her fingernails, short and bitten, were remarkably grubby, too.

'I helped Tom plant his bulbs,' Charlie said apologetically, registering Liz's look and pointing to a rectangle of neatly raked earth beside his tent.

'Goodness!' Liz's eyes widened. 'What does he want bulbs there for?'

Charlie flashed her wide, infectious grin, and the skin around her impish green eyes bunched into a mass of little wrinkles. 'He says he wants to be prepared in case he and Jean are still here in the spring. You know what he's like!'

Liz nodded. It was true that he couldn't do without a garden; he had to be surrounded by flowers. For all she knew, he was keeping the entire Cornish bee population alive single-handedly.

On returning with a mug of steaming tea for her, Tom settled down again and she started to explain her mission. She half-thought that Charlie would dismiss the story as not sufficiently newsworthy, but in fact she seemed extremely interested.

'Amazing!' the reporter muttered, scribbling some indecipherable shorthand in the ever-present notebook that she'd pulled from her back pocket. 'Incredible!'

When Liz had finished, she sat bolt upright, her eyes shining. 'We've got a front-page story here. I'm pretty sure I'll be able to flog it to local newspapers, radio and TV in Bavaria, too. Maybe even the nationals, you never know. It's got everything – war, suffering, friendship, a little girl from the past, a young lad far from home. It's a peach! Thank you! I promise I'll do everything I can to help you track Franz down.'

Liz hadn't even drunk her tea, but before she knew it, she was following Charlie over to Rosie and Rafael on the swings to get some quotes for the article. Charlie shouted to Liz over her shoulder that she needed to speak to Rick next, and after that she wanted a photo of all four of them together outside his shop, holding the bottle.

'My editor's going to love it!' she cried happily. She was clearly in her element, and as Rosie repeated the details of her discovery, Liz found her pulse quickening all over again and wished that Pat were here to enjoy the excitement. Even Rafael, who was normally so laid back, allowed himself to be whipped up with enthusiasm. He chipped in with the odd embellishment: 'It was a very old bottle, very dark and mysterious... I thought it was maybe from a pirate ship, or inside it was something magical, like Aladdin's lamp...' His voice cracked on the last two words and went surprisingly deep, like a cow's low.

By the time Liz returned to Bag End at around 7 p.m. she was quite worn out, but she still had supper to make and Lowenna to bathe. She was dismayed when she heard a rap on the door and might have ignored it, were it not for the fact that the radio was up full blast in the kitchen and she had been singing along to Mellow Magic while frying up a packet of mince and some chopped onions for a cottage pie.

It was quite a surprise to find Esme on the step, as Liz had only seen her once since she'd returned early from her walking trip; she'd understood that she was still nursing her injured friend, Caroline, who had a badly sprained ankle. The two women had spent last Sunday night in hospital, Liz knew, before returning to Tremarnock in a taxi at the crack of dawn on Monday morning. Of course she had offered to help in any way she could but Esme had refused, insisting that she could manage quite well on her own.

'How's the patient?' Liz asked now, standing aside to allow her friend to pass.

Esme shook her head. 'I won't stay. Caroline's in much better spirits, thank you, but the ankle's still painful and she's awfully immobile. She can't even get to the kitchen on her own to make herself a cup of tea. I don't like to leave her for too long.' She went on to explain that she'd run out of cat food and as the general store was now closed poor Rasputin would have to go hungry, unless Liz could help out. 'He won't touch human food, he's terribly fussy. He's been hanging round my ankles, purring like a steam train and making a general nuisance of himself, because it's past his suppertime. He might not be able to speak but he certainly knows how to get what he wants.'

Liz laughed. 'Mitzi's the same. She sits on my head when I'm having a lie-in, so I have to get up and give her breakfast.'

The two women chatted for a few more minutes, mainly about the encampment, but Liz couldn't help noticing that Esme seemed anxious to leave. It was most unlike her. Normally she'd have demanded an in-depth report of the day's activities, probably over a large gin and tonic. Come to think of it, she'd almost certainly have been camping herself, settled in a yurt, tepee or Bedouin tent festooned with multicoloured drapes and scarves. She'd hate to miss out on a creative opportunity and besides, the last thing she'd want was a big new housing development in the village.

'I really must go,' said Esme, checking her watch. Liz took the hint and hurried to the kitchen, returning shortly with two tins.

'You must be going a bit stir-crazy, cooped up inside for so long,' she commented, thinking how hard she herself would find it.

But Esme only laughed. 'Honestly, we've so much to talk about, we never seem to stop!'

The corners of her small grey eyes crinkled with amusement and Liz wasn't sure that she'd ever seen her friend so happy; she must be loving the company, which was surprising, really, as everyone had her down as a bit of a loner.

'Well, if there's anything you need, just shout. I must say, Caroline's lucky to have such a good friend.'

'I'm lucky to have *her*,' Esme added, before turning tail with a tin of cat food tucked under each arm.

As Liz set the kitchen table and gave the mince and onions a stir, it occurred to her that she'd have rather liked to fill Esme in on the letter in the bottle and tell her all about Charlie's interest and the potential newspaper article. She almost called Robert instead, but had second thoughts and replaced the phone before dialling. He'd be far too busy to listen to her; and in any case, he wouldn't be interested, would he?

Chapter Eight

PROPPED UP AGAINST a pile of cushions on Esme's sofa with her injured leg raised, Caroline laid the book that she'd been reading on her lap, closed her eyes for a moment and breathed in deeply. She could feel the air filling her lungs, expanding them so wide that her chest rose and her rib cage opened like a pair of wings. She imagined each curved, slender bone separating, giving its neighbour a little more air and space, allowing it room to move.

She held it there for as long as she could before exhaling, relishing the delicious sense of peace and calm flooding through her. It was a long time, she realised, since she'd been able to breathe like that. In fact she thought that she might have been holding her breath for her entire life.

She'd been in a great deal of pain when she'd arrived at the hospital last Sunday, and at first they'd suspected a broken bone. It had been a relief to discover that it was just a bad sprain, until doctors had explained that some ligaments were torn, the bone was bruised and it might take several months to recover fully.

Dosed up with painkillers and with her leg in a brace, Esme had had to wheel her to the taxi at around four in the morning; it had taken all that time for the X-rays and examination. On the ride home, her mind racing, she had babbled on about booking a flight back to Paris as soon as possible, not wishing to be a bother, until Esme had told her to shush.

'You can't travel for a few days at least – you need to keep the leg elevated. You heard what the doctor said. I think you should stay with me until you're fit enough. I'll look after you. We'll worry about flights when the swelling's started to go down.'

She had been so kind and pressing that it had been impossible to argue with her, and besides, Caroline didn't want to go back to Paris. The thought of being cooped up in the apartment with Philip for days on end made her feel sick. He'd see it as an opportunity to get back in her good books by fussing over her and playing nurse, pretending that he was doing it for her when in reality, it would be all about him as usual.

She hadn't yet phoned to tell him her news; there was no hurry. Best to wait till she was stronger and better able to fend off the inevitable demands for her to go home; in fact he'd probably suggest coming to collect her himself, such was his terror of being alone.

She picked up her book again and stared at the page, but the words failed to register. She was tired in a deep, relentless sort of way. Something about Esme's flat had made her relax so completely that most of the time she felt as if she were half-drugged, only just beginning to catch up on years of shallow, restless wakefulness.

Perhaps it was the seductive, jewel-like colours of the curtains, walls and rugs in the flat that made her so drowsy, or the scented candles dotted around the place that burned throughout the day and evening, filling the air with their sweet, heady perfume.

Or maybe it was Esme, who seemed to know exactly how Caroline felt and what she needed at any given moment, speaking gently to her in soft, hushed tones when she was weary, and regaling her with stories about life outside these four walls during livelier moments when she wanted to be entertained.

The days had passed so pleasantly that despite her injury, Caroline never wanted them to end. She adored the *objets d'art* scattered around Esme's flat, each one telling a story about her friend's interests and travels; her delightful little spare room, with the polished floorboards and Indian silk bedspread, and her shelves of books with glorious illustrations that had helped inspire her ceramic designs.

As for those, Caroline was full of admiration. Several times she'd asked Esme to fetch from a shelf an item that she'd made so that she could look at it properly, turning it around in her hands and feeling its smooth surface, the nooks and crannies in the glaze, marvelling at the sheer craftsmanship. She'd hadn't realised how very gifted her friend was, and she made it her business to tell her so often.

'I want everything in here,' she'd laugh. 'Every piece you've made, every item you've ever bought. You've got such a brilliant eye. I wish I had your talent.'

Esme, embarrassed, would try to shrug off the compliments, but she was pleased, Caroline could tell. She guessed that her friend wasn't much used to praise, which was a shame, as she deserved it.

She had only been gone ten minutes or so to get the cat food, but Caroline missed her already. They'd decided to call for a takeaway for supper from the Indian restaurant in the nearby village, and then rent a film on TV. It was such luxury to be able to choose whatever they fancied to eat, to watch whatever they desired. With Philip, everything always had to be geared towards him. If he were avoiding carbs for a period because he needed to lose weight, she'd cut them out, too. If he were restless and felt like a long walk rather than curling up with a movie, she'd put on her coat without a murmur and off they'd go.

He'd been so active before his illness, into running and cycling, skiing in winter and water sports in summer. Caroline had found it exhausting sometimes, especially on holidays, when all she'd wanted was to get stuck into her book. She'd put up with it when the children were little, believing that it was good for them to be busy and learning new skills. She did wonder now, though, why she'd continued to dance to her husband's tune when Helen and Andrew were all grown up and had flown the nest. She should have been more assertive.

That word – assertive, assertiveness. Like most young women, Helen had it in spades, but it had been leeched out of Caroline; that's if she'd ever had it in the first place. Looking back, she thought there might have been a window at St Hilda's when she could have grown in self-reliance, like a dragonfly that grows its wings, but the shock of being removed so suddenly from the school and plonked unceremoniously in another seemed to have arrested her development.

From then on, she'd got her head down, buried her own needs and wants, ignored her instincts and followed the path that was expected of her. She'd married well, had babies – and my, had she been a good mother and wife: poised, efficient, competent... and obedient. So different from Esme, who might seem a little sad and lonely from the outside; but in reality, which woman had remained truer to herself?

Philip, of course, was different now. He couldn't do half those active things that he'd once loved. On a bad day, even walking was difficult. Funny how her heart could still hurt when she saw him try to cover up his stumble on a bit of cracked pavement, or pretend that his drink hadn't spilled. She'd find herself starting to reach out to him, to try to comfort and reassure, then she'd remember and turn her head away as if she hadn't noticed.

Betrayal, cheating, selfishness and lies. They were loaded words but they applied to him, every one of them. It wasn't as if she hadn't voiced her doubts about their suitability for each other before they'd married, either; but he'd shot her qualms down, one by one. In the end she'd laid herself at his feet and he'd trampled all over her.

Forgive and forget, they said. Well, she might one day learn to forgive but she couldn't forget. This was her life now; she'd taken it back. The question was, what on earth was she to do with it?

She could hear Esme's steps on the metal staircase leading to the front door and her spirits lifted. The tread was quick and light, despite her friend's height and stature: you could tell that she was keen to arrive home, too.

'Success!' she exclaimed, bursting through the door, brandishing a tin of cat food in each hand.

She looked younger and more carefree, Caroline thought. Her cheeks were flushed; wisps of pepper-and-salt hair had escaped from her bun and draped girlishly around her face and neck, while the emeralds in her pendant earrings twinkled. A long, greenish scarf was draped around her neck and silver bangles dangled from her arms. Her style was arty and bohemian, adjectives that could never be applied to Caroline, but she loved just being in their presence and soaking them up. Who knew? Perhaps she'd even acquire a little bit of it herself, as if by osmosis. She smiled, sensing the dark thoughts of a moment ago melting away.

'Well done!' she told Esme. 'Rasputin joined me earlier but left in disgust when he realised I wasn't going to feed him. I bet he's back in a flash when he hears you're home.'

Right on cue, the marmalade tom slunk out of his mistress's bedroom and wound himself around her feet, purring loudly, while she bent down to give him a stroke.

'Liz was telling me about the protesters,' she said, tickling behind his ears. 'It sounds as if they're in it for the long haul. Apparently someone has even got electricity now, and a television. Perhaps we can wander down and have a look when you're up to it. I bet the developers are hopping mad.'

'They will be,' Caroline agreed. 'It's a shame we can't join the fun. I'd quite fancy myself as an eco-warrior, if only I hadn't got this stupid leg.'

A warm glow spread through Esme. She couldn't help feeling that the old Caroline, the one she'd met in St Ives, would have been too conservative to join a protest. In the short time that she'd been here, however, she seemed to have loosened up a little. She even looked different, wearing Esme's long loose orange crepe maxi dress because it was more comfortable than anything of her own. The dress swamped her, of course, but she loved it; she said it made her feel like a gypsy queen.

Esme went into the kitchen to feed the cat, returning with two glasses of gin and tonic on a tray and a bowl of crisps.

'What shall we watch?' She pulled up a little table for the drinks, fetched the remote control and started to scroll through the options. The women laughed at some of the corny-sounding plots and grimaced at the horrors.

'Andrew used to love those when he was a teenager – the more bloodthirsty the better,' said Caroline. 'He never seemed to get bad dreams, but I had to cover my eyes during the gory bits.'

They settled at last on an intriguing-looking psychological thriller, and Esme was just about to call for a takeaway when there was a loud clattering again on the metal stairs.

'Who on earth can it be?' She rose, frowning. 'I'll get shot of them as quick as I can.'

All of a sudden two, three, then four people barged into her smallish front room and Caroline found herself shrinking like a reclusive wood violet; it had been so quiet for the past few days with just the two of them, she'd quite forgotten about noise and crowds.

A smallish, stocky, middle-aged man in a distinctive floral shirt and rather tight jeans glanced over in her direction before flinging his arms around Esme, who responded with a stiff peck on the cheek.

'Darling, you've been hiding up here for so long we thought we'd better check if you were still alive! And this must be your school chum!' The stranger strolled over to Caroline and introduced himself as Tony, then took her hand with a flourish and bent down to give it a kiss. 'Welcome to Tremarnock! I do hope Esme's looking after you properly?'

He was so friendly and theatrical that Caroline couldn't help smiling. 'She's the perfect nurse. I've hardly had to move from the sofa since I arrived!'

'I'm very glad to hear it.' Tony's eyes slid down to the gin and tonic, as yet untouched, on the little table beside her. He clapped his hands. 'Cocktail hour? Marvellous! Yes please!'

Esme glanced at Caroline, who raised her eyebrows and gave an almost imperceptible nod. There was nothing for it but to offer drinks all round, and while Esme went to make them, Tony signalled the other visitors to come closer.

'This is my partner, Felipe,' he said, pointing to a handsome dark-haired man in his early to mid-thirties. 'And this is Rafael, Felipe's brother, who lives with us; and his friend, Rosie.'

There was no mistaking Rafael, who must have been about sixteen, Caroline decided; he looked exactly like Felipe, only smaller, with large, distinctive wooden crosses hanging from his ears.

Rosie, on the other hand, was pale and fair, very pretty but fragile-looking, with a heart-shaped face and large greenish-blue eyes behind light blue glasses. There was clearly something not quite right, as one of her arms was pulled up to her chest and held at an unnatural, flexed angle. She seemed to have a bit of a limp, too.

Caroline looked away quickly, not wishing to offend. 'Do you all live in the village? I've heard so much about it. I've been longing to meet you and see it properly for myself.'

Before she knew it, Tony, who obviously liked nothing better than the sound of his own voice, had pulled up a chair and was tucking into the crisps while feeding her dollops of juicy gossip. The others sat cross-legged on the floor, listening. They didn't seem to mind; they were probably used to it.

'Now Audrey – you can't miss her – nine feet tall and a voice like a foghorn – she's a nightmare...' He rolled his eyes. 'Dreadful busybody, always poking her nose in where it's not wanted... Liz, I expect you've heard about her?' He didn't wait for a response. 'That's Rosie's mum. She's an absolute sweetie, you'll adore her.' He winked at Rosie, who looked embarrassed and pleased at the same time. 'As soon as you're up and about, you must get Esme to take you to the local fish restaurant. Liz's husband Robert runs it. It's absolutely superb.'

He was so entertaining that Caroline's inhibitions quickly dissolved and she found herself prodding him for more information. 'What about Tabitha, the singer? I hear she has a wonderful voice. And the young woman who inherited the tumbledown manor on the cliff, completely out of the blue? Bramble? It's an incredible story.'

Esme, who had returned by now with more drinks and crisps, perched on the end of the sofa by Caroline's feet, taking care not to knock into her. She must have forgiven Tony for the intrusion because she was smiling, too, no doubt buoyed by his enthusiasm, Caroline's evident enjoyment and the general laughter.

'Come on then darling, tell us about you,' Tony said at last, leaning across and patting Caroline's good knee. 'I mean, I know you've hurt yourself, you poor dear, but why are you really here in windswept Cornwall? Give me your life story. Immediately.'

Being the nosy sort, he was only half-joking, but she couldn't feel offended; so while Esme handed around the nibbles, she tried to satisfy his curiosity by explaining her new-found enthusiasm for walking and her desire to complete the famous Camino de Santiago.

'I was asking Esme about the Lost Lady of Tremarnock, but she says the shrine probably doesn't exist any more, if it ever did. I know it's got nothing to do with the Camino but it's an interesting legend. I'd love to have gone there.'

Tony took a swig of his drink and scratched his neatly cut silver-grey hair. 'Really? What on earth for?'

'That's a silly question,' Rosie piped up. 'Everyone knows that if you wash yourself in the water, all your troubles will disappear.'

'Surely you don't really believe it, do you?' Tony scoffed. 'What a load of nonsense!'

But Felipe cleared his throat and assumed a sage expression. 'The old saints and goddesses, they have many powers, you know. My mother, she prayed every day at the shrine of Saint Escrava Anastacia in Rio, and her – what do you call them?' He glanced at Tony. 'Her knobbly feet—'

'Bunions?' Tony said helpfully.

Felipe's eyes lit up. 'Yes! Her bunions – they completely disappeared!'

Rosie giggled. 'Maybe she could take away Tony's sweet tooth, too?' She glanced at Caroline. 'He's mad for chocolate and puddings.'

His mouth dropped open in mock disbelief. 'Excuse me! I'm fitter than a butcher's dog these days! No puddings at all! Haven't you seen me doing those ghastly planks and press-ups? You must have heard Nathan and Annie shouting at me. Look!'

He pinched his stomach, which was impressively flat. 'There's hardly an ounce of fat on me! Speaking of which...' he looked slyly at Esme and reached for the crisp bowl on the little table, tipping the very last crumbs into the palm of his hand and sucking them up like a vacuum cleaner. 'I only had a small salad for lunch and that was hours ago...'

There was no mistaking his meaning and Caroline didn't stop to think. 'Why don't you join us for a takeaway?' She paused and checked herself. 'That is, if it's all right with Esme?'

'Of course!' Esme didn't sound put out. 'I was about to order an Indian,' she went on, rising and fetching a menu from the shelf above the television. 'What would you all like?'

A quick phone call to Liz soon established that Rosie was allowed to stay, as it was Friday night and there was no school tomorrow.

'Mum's made cottage pie for supper.' She pulled a face. 'And cabbage.'

'Good job you've got out of it, then,' Esme said dryly.

Rosie shook her head. 'There's bound to be leftovers for tomorrow.'

Before long, Tony, Felipe, Rafael, Rosie and Esme were settled on an assortment of odd chairs around the oval gate-legged table that was normally pushed up against a wall. They helped themselves to spicy curry, rice, nan bread and crispy poppadoms, and Tony kept the adults' glasses topped up with red or white wine. The teenagers were allowed a thimbleful, too.

Just a little way away, Caroline, still on the sofa, sat as upright as she could with one leg stretched out in front of her, a plate of food on her lap and a fork in her hand. For a few moments, she allowed herself to zone out, focusing on the flickering candles that were dotted around, the delicious scents of cumin, garlic, turmeric and fenugreek and the steady hum of chatter, punctuated by bursts of laughter.

Right now she felt so far from her old life in Paris that she wondered if it had all been a dream: Philip, the apartment, the dog, even Helen and Andrew. She stopped herself. Not the children; she must leave them out of it. None of this mess had been caused by them, yet when she'd looked into their eyes recently, she'd hardly recognised them. They were both so like their father that it was almost as if he had created them singlehandedly, and she'd had nothing to do with it.

She felt a stab of sorrow and regret so sharp that it almost winded her. The ramifications of Philip's affair seemed to have spread so far and wide, further than she could ever have imagined. Indeed, it was as if her very sense of self had started to crumble, the self that she'd spent her whole adult life carefully constructing. She no longer knew who she was or what she wanted. The only reality was here, now, within these walls.

'Caroline, are you all right?' Esme's voice brought her back to the present. 'You've gone very pale. Can I get you anything? A drink of water? Do you want to lie down?'

'I'm fine, honestly.' Caroline smiled but Esme was no fool; she'd probably ask questions when they were alone again.

With their tongues loosened, perhaps, by the wine, Rosie and Rafael started telling the adults about school, the teachers, the other pupils and some of the daft, naughty things they got up to. Before long, they'd moved on to the encampment, Audrey, silly old Reg Carter, huffing and puffing his way around the site, Loveday's and Jesse's treehouse, Ryan the fishmonger's smelly mackerel breakfasts, whiskery Rick's noisy lovemaking, Bramble's antique furniture and Nathan the postman's bulging biceps, which were only marginally larger than those of his super-fit girlfriend, Annie.

Caroline was grateful for the distraction. By now she felt that she'd built up a fairly accurate picture of Tremarnock, although she'd scarcely set foot outside Esme's front door; and the small, close-knit community intrigued her.

'Do you think you'll stay in the village when you're older?' she asked Rosie.

The girl's eyes opened wide. 'Oh yes. I mean, it's my home. I love it here. I couldn't really imagine wanting to be anywhere else.'

Her affection for the place was touching and Caroline smiled, wishing that she felt the same way about her own home. In fact, she wasn't sure that she'd ever felt comfortable anywhere except, perhaps, briefly at St Hilda's...

'I prefer Rio, it is much more exciting.' Rafael's dark brown eyes flashed and he gave a cheeky grin. 'More dangerous.'

'Yes, well, you can stay here until you've done your A-levels,' Tony said quickly. 'We'll talk about the next step after that.'

'What do your children do, Caroline?' Felipe wanted to know.

She explained that Andrew, twenty-eight, lived in Washington DC and worked for the World Bank, while twenty-six-year-old Helen was a graphic designer in Paris. 'They both went to international schools, as I didn't want to send them away. So they followed the UK curriculum. Andrew says he feels English but I think Helen's more French. She has a steady boyfriend, Thierry, and they've bought a flat together in Paris. I can't imagine they'll ever want to leave.'

'Don't *you* miss England?' Rosie, who was clearly not given to wandering or travel, looked quite upset.

'Not really. Well, a little perhaps, but I left so long ago. I did love my school in Canterbury, but that was mainly because of the other girls...' Her eyes slid across the room and fixed on Esme, who returned her gaze, lingering there for several moments. She might have stayed longer, but Tony was watching and it was quite a struggle to pull away.

If the incident had made Esme feel uncomfortable, she did a good job of hiding it.

'It's taken over forty years for you to come to Cornwall,' she told Caroline, straightening up and adjusting the clip that held her bun in place. 'Lord knows when you'll be back, so we'd better make the most of the here and now.' She started to rise. 'Would anyone like any more, or shall I clear the plates?'

There wasn't any pudding but several people wanted tea or coffee. Then Rafael agreed to walk Rosie home while the adults talked for a little longer.

'What lovely young people!' Caroline commented, once they'd left. 'So articulate and interesting.'

Clearly taking it as a compliment to himself, Tony smiled graciously.

Esme mentioned that she'd known Rosie since she was three years old. 'She and her mother were such a sad pair when they first arrived from London. It's a miracle how much they've changed.'

'Tremarnock can do that to you,' Tony agreed, before taking a sip of coffee. 'It's more than just a place, it's a state of being.'

Caroline pondered this for a moment. 'It must be something to do with the sea air. I feel so lovely and relaxed here, as if I've been to a spa. I hadn't realised how stressed I was before I came. You're very lucky to call it home.'

Tony, who had clever dark eyes, looked first at her, then at Esme. 'Were you two always good friends at school? Did you hit it off straight away?'

'Oh yes,' said Caroline, quick as a flash. 'I thought the world of Esme. She was two years older than me and I'd never met anyone like her. I really looked up to her. She was so funny, talented and kind. She was just beautiful.' She stopped, realising what she'd just said. 'I mean she had a beautiful character. She looked after me and brought me out of myself. I was so shy...'

'I only did what anyone would do,' Esme said softly. Her voice sounded strangely hoarse and she was examining her hands, picking at the edge of a fingernail.

'No!'

Everyone turned, surprised by Caroline's vehemence. She wanted to stop but at the same time she was determined to get her point across. She'd been meaning to say this for years, after all.

'I wouldn't have survived without you,' she went on, mustering all her courage. 'I mean it. I'm so glad I've found you again. This time, I'm not going to let you go.'

There was silence for a moment as her words sank in and she wondered if she'd overstepped the mark.

To her relief, Esme smiled. 'Well, that's good news!' She was trying to make light of it, but her eyes were moist and glittered strangely.

Tony must have noticed, too. 'It seems you two have a lot to catch up on,' he said softly, before squeezing Felipe's shoulder. 'C'mon then, it's time for my bed. Let's leave these two ladies in peace.'

When they'd gone, Esme moved quietly around the flat, putting back the chairs in their original positions and folding the leaves on the table. Caroline watched, too nervous to speak, wondering what, if anything, she might have unleashed.

When at last Esme had finished, she sat by the sofa on the chair that Tony had previously occupied, leaning forward and staring at her feet. It was clear that she wanted to say something and Caroline waited with bated breath.

'That thing that happened at school...' Esme started, and Caroline's stomach keeled.

'Yes?'

'I, I meant what I said...'

Caroline swallowed. 'So did I…'

There was a moment when they both remained stock still, listening, as it were, to the silence and to the sound of their own beating hearts.

Steeling herself, Caroline opened her mouth to speak again but just then, the phone rang in the bag that was gaping open beside her and split the air in two with its loud, insistent buzz.

She started, gasping, before reaching down to retrieve it.

'Mum,' came a familiar voice on the end of the line. 'It's Helen. I've got some big news. I wanted to wait till you're back but I can't keep it to myself any longer. Guess what? I'm pregnant!'

Chapter Nine

THE TWO WOMEN stared at one another for what seemed like an age after the call ended. When at last Caroline opened her mouth, all that came out was, 'Well, I wasn't expecting *that*.'

'No.' Esme's body suddenly felt terribly heavy, as if gravity had somehow strengthened its pull and was dragging her down, down to the earth's core. 'What will you do?' Her voice sounded odd and far away.

'She wants me to go back as soon as possible.' Caroline hesitated, as if searching for the right words. 'It's natural, I think, to want your mother at a time like this. It's good news, of course…'

'Oh yes.'

'I'll be a grandmother! How extraordinary!'

'You'll be wonderful at it.' Esme meant it.

Caroline's gaze fell to her lap and Esme leaned forward to touch her friend's arm.

'You will, truly – you'll be wonderful, I mean. Don't worry.' Then she straightened up and made to rise. 'We should celebrate. I've got a bottle of champagne somewhere. Shall I open it?'

She was halfway up, but Caroline shook her head. 'It's too

late. Thank you, though. Tomorrow, perhaps. I need time to process.'

'Of course.'

'It's come as a bit of a shock, after all this...' Her voice trailed off and the air between them seemed to fizz and crackle with unspoken meaning. 'I w-wish—' she stammered, still staring at her lap.

But Esme raised a hand. 'You're tired and emotional, which isn't surprising. We should both go to bed. Everything will seem different in the morning – it always does.'

All of a sudden, it was as if an invisible barrier had sprung up between them. Caroline nodded and Esme bent down, wrapped an arm around her waist and helped her to stand, then together they shuffled towards the spare room.

'Can you manage now?' Esme stood at the door as Caroline hobbled in. The little light on the bedside table sent out a warm glow and the pinkish-red Indian silk bedcover glittered like garnets and rubies.

'Yes, thank you.'

'Sleep well, then.' Esme started to pull the door closed.

'You, too. Goodnight.'

Rasputin appeared from nowhere to slink after Esme as she padded across the corridor to her own room, where he jumped on the end of the bed. She undressed and climbed under the duvet but she wasn't ready to sleep, so she opened a book on contemporary ceramic design and browsed the beautiful illustrations that she'd pored over countless times before, looking for inspiration.

Tonight, though, she found the photos flat and meaningless. Nothing in them made her itch to get back to her clay, wheel or kiln or the blissful solitude of her quiet studio. Indeed, in the past five days, since she'd stayed at home to nurse

Caroline, she realised that she hadn't missed her work at all; she'd felt perfectly content.

But Caroline would soon be gone, and then what? Quickly she flicked over the page and an image of a mother and child in pale, painted clay caught her eye. All soft, sensuous curves, the mother was cradling her baby, a small round ball, in the gentle slope of her lap and gazing down at it adoringly.

Esme's insides seemed to shrivel, leaving an empty hollow within. She'd have adored a child of her own, and grandchildren, too, though she'd never told anyone. Even more, she'd have loved a life partner, someone to share things with. The long-buried knowledge of all that sacrifice seemed to rise up now and batter her with its full force, almost taking her breath away, and she wasn't sure that she was strong enough to withstand it.

She shut the book quickly. Of course she was. After all, she was the one who'd made the decision all those years ago at her aunt's house in Truro that she'd remain alone, and since then, she'd never really doubted her resolution, had she? Her life had been cleaner and simpler with only herself to worry about, and most importantly of all, she'd never been hurt or hurt anyone.

Once Caroline had gone, she thought, giving herself a mental shake, the regrets would surely fade and things would return to how they were before. Better that way. Better to be safe than sorry...

A seagull landed on her windowsill a few feet away and uttered a salty, heartless cry, which was soon answered by countless others. Esme leaned over to switch off the light and closed her eyes, surrendering herself to their wonderful, terrible music.

A Winkle in Time was closed on Mondays, and it had once been Liz's and Robert's special day when they'd do something together, just the two of them. Quite often, they'd leave Lowenna with Jean or Tabitha for a few hours and go for a long walk along the cliffs, usually ending up in a cosy pub for a ploughman's lunch and a pint or two, in Robert's case, and a half of lager and lime for Liz.

She missed those occasions and, as she opened her eyes and blinked at the morning light peeping through a gap in the bedroom curtains, a deep sense of longing flooded through her.

Reaching out a hand, she touched her husband's warm, inert body beside her. He was dead to the world after another busy weekend of work, work, work.

'Robert?' She gave him a poke and he muttered something in his sleep.

She tried again, louder this time. 'Robert? Are you awake?'

This time he groaned and pulled the pillow over his head.

Liz could hear Rosie in the bathroom across the landing, getting ready for school. Lowenna, too, would be up and about soon; it was unusual for her to sleep beyond 7 a.m.; the camping nights must have worn her out. She knew she didn't have long, so this time she sat up, grabbed the pillow from Robert's head and whispered loudly in his ear.

'Let's do something nice together today. I haven't seen you for ages.'

His body twitched and she could tell that he was properly awake now.

'Please?' she wheedled. 'Forget about work, just for once. Let's have some fun.'

'I can't. I have to go to the Secret Shack. Someone's coming to give me a quote for catering equipment.'

Liz grimaced. 'Another one? You've already had three! I thought you'd settled on the St Columb man?'

At last he rolled over to face her and half-opened his hazel eyes, which were flecked with amber. She'd always loved his eyes.

'I wasn't happy with him. It just didn't feel right somehow. A bloke from the waterfront coffee house in Newquay gave me the name of the company he'd used; I thought I'd better check them out.'

Liz noticed her husband's thick black lashes that curled gently at the ends, his chestnut brown hair, boyishly messed, and the soft fullness of his lower lip. She thought that he was beautiful, as always, but today there was something strange behind the irises, a disconcerting distance.

'Newquay? When did you go there?' A jumpy tone had crept into her voice, which she didn't like.

'Last week. I told you. Alex was raving about the coffee house, remember? So I went to see it. It's really well done.'

Now that he mentioned it, Liz did vaguely recall the conversation, but it had been very much in passing when he'd popped back from the restaurant in the evening to collect something and she'd been on her way to the campsite with Lowenna and Rosie. They'd spent the night there and she hadn't seen him all the following day, so it was no wonder that it had slipped her mind.

She realised how out of touch she was. Before, they used not only to spend far more time in each other's company, they'd also speak frequently on the phone so that even when they were apart, it didn't really feel like it. But the calls had tapered off and now they seemed to go for ages without communicating. A shiver of anxiety crept up her spine.

'I'll come with you to the Shack. Jean will have Lowenna for a couple of hours. I'd like to see it again.'

She'd rarely been, which wasn't exactly unintentional, given that she'd never approved of the project. When reasoning with Robert had failed, refusing to visit had felt like the only form of protest at her disposal. But now that a price had been agreed, contracts had been exchanged and it was just a question of waiting for the lawyers to complete, staying away seemed pointless, and it was only creating a distance between them.

Robert frowned. 'We'll be discussing electric top hot cupboards, chargrills and glass washers. You'll find it very boring.'

'I don't mind. I might have a walk along the beach.' She glanced at the patchy blue sky out of the bedroom window. 'It looks like a nice day.'

Once Rosie left for school, she wheeled Lowenna in her pushchair down to Jean's house before jumping in the car beside her husband. It was just a short drive to Polrethen beach but it took over half an hour as they got stuck behind a tractor and then had to wait while a farmer herded his cows across the road.

Robert was quiet behind the wheel and seemed distracted, so Liz resisted the urge to chat about her own life and tried, instead, to draw him out.

'When do you think you'll complete?'

'Friday, I hope.'

'Wow! So soon!' He glanced at her, no doubt expecting signs of disapproval, but she forced a smile. 'Exciting!'

'It's definitely going ahead, Lizzie.' That stern voice she'd come to dread.

'I know.'

'It'll be a lot of work, but it's going to be worth it.'

'Of course.' She paused, searching for something uncontroversial. 'How soon do you want the builders to begin?'

'Next week, with luck.'

'D'you think it'll be ready by the spring?'

He looked serious. 'It'll have to be.'

Her stomach knotted and she wanted to ask why he had that grim expression, though she knew, really. He'd obviously committed a great deal of money to the project and would need to recoup the costs as quickly as possible, though he wouldn't tell her that.

Of course in business you had to take calculated risks, but the tired worry lines on his face only brought her back to her original conclusion, which was that they didn't need more money and had been perfectly happy as they were. On this subject, she believed that they could never be a partnership; they'd never see eye to eye.

Finally the last brown cow lumbered through the gate into the right-hand field and they could pick up speed again. Soon, they were taking a sharp left down a steep winding tree-lined lane, and as they reached the bottom of the hill, a smallish crescent-shaped sandy beach came into view.

The sky was pale and watery with wisps of grey cloud, while the sea, though calm, looked chilly and uninviting. There was hardly a soul about as Robert pulled into the gravel car park, which got so packed in summer that folk had to risk the wrath of traffic wardens by pulling up on the grass verges, or wedge each other in so tightly that you could barely open your door.

He got out to put money in the pay machine while Liz fetched her coat from the back seat. She was dressed in jeans, an olive green round-necked sweater and sturdy walking boots, but when she left the car, an unmistakable autumn chill in the air made her wish that she'd brought a scarf. Robert, though, in dark brown chinos and nothing but a blue and red checked shirt with the sleeves rolled up, didn't seem bothered.

'C'mon then.'

A warm glow spread through her body as he took her hand and together they tramped along a stony walkway to the beach. Their boots sank into the damp sand that had been transformed into myriad patterns by the wind: ripples and crests like giant fingerprints, root-like channels and strange, branching shapes that reminded Liz of the tops of swaying trees.

Turning right, they picked their way over leathery fronds of greenish-brown seaweed, tipped with rounded nodules like bunches of grapes, and sploshed through shallow pools of water that glittered glassily in the sunlight. At one point she stooped to pick up a rather handsome pale whelk shell heavily encrusted with barnacles, and tucked it in her pocket; Lowenna would enjoy investigating the bumps and ridges later, turning it over and over in her small hands and holding it to her ear to try to hear the ocean.

A little way back from the beach, they passed a surfing school, its metal doors shut tight and padlocked. Just after that was a breeze block beach shop selling body boards, towels, buckets and spades and the like, but that, too, was closed today. There was a gap, filled with broken boats, bits of rope and cracked lobster pots and then they came to a long low wooden hut atop a gentle mound, surrounded by sand and sea grass and with a rickety bench in front.

Several of the shack's wooden slats had been pulled off, leaving holes in the side that let in the wind and rain. The asphalt roof gaped in places and was covered in bird droppings, while a section of the front window frame dangled sadly from a bent, rusty nail.

It must once have been painted white, but the colour had long since faded and chipped and weeds sprouted everywhere. All in all it was a sorry-looking affair and Liz, who was usually bursting with creative ideas, simply couldn't envisage how it could ever be made appealing. She thought that Robert must have gone mad, but she didn't say so.

'You'll have to have a sign. Where will you put it?' She was trying to sound cheery.

He scratched his head. 'I haven't thought about it.'

'I could ask Felipe to design one? He's so good.' The Brazilian was an enthusiastic member of the Tremarnock Art Club, which met every Friday in the leaky church hall, and he often made the posters and leaflets for village events.

Robert looked pleased. 'That's not a bad idea. Or do you think we need a professional sign maker?'

Before Liz could respond, a balding, stocky chap in jeans and a white polo shirt appeared from behind the shack and introduced himself as Gavin, from a catering company in Newquay.

'Needs a bit of work,' he said in his rolling Cornish accent as he nodded at the wreck behind him.

'You can say that again.' Liz couldn't stop herself.

The door wasn't locked but the wood was badly swollen and Robert had to give it a hard shove. When it finally opened, a cloud of dust, paint and splinters fell from the lintel above, covering his head in a shower of debris, which he brushed away carelessly. Strictly speaking he was trespassing, as the shack wasn't yet his, but there wasn't a soul around to complain. Gavin went next, followed by a tentative Liz. The inside was dark and musty and there was no electricity, so Robert pushed up the corrugated-iron shutter to let in some light.

There was a surprising amount of space, at least, but with no proper insulation, the cold seeped into your bones. The concrete floor felt damp to the touch and there was evidence of mouse or, even worse, rat droppings, along with the tell-tale, pungent stench of ammonia.

While Robert started to describe to Gavin what he wanted in the way of kitchen equipment and where it would go, Liz wandered into the little room at the back. It had obviously been used once by fishermen as a storeroom, as a broken rod still stood in the corner and the ground was littered with hooks and bits of twine and netting. Installing a lavatory and washing facilities here was going to be a problem as there was no running water, but she supposed that the builders would come up with a solution – at a cost.

Back in the main room where the men were still talking, she had to concede that while the shell was a mess, the location was second to none. As you looked out of the wide rectangular window-cum-serving hatch, all you could see ahead was sand and miles and miles of ocean. What's more, this would be the only café for quite some distance; you'd have to wander into the village to find anywhere else for a cup of coffee, piece of cake, a crab sandwich or a lobster roll.

'What do you think?' Gavin asked as Liz approached. He had his tape measure out and was jotting things down in a notebook with his thick, sausage-shaped fingers.

'It has, um, potential.'

He laughed. 'Your husband's got vision, I'll give you that. Can't be many folk would be willing to take it on in this state. Personally I think I'd be tempted to knock it down and start all over again.'

Robert took a deep breath. 'Well, I could do that, but planning permission would probably take ages and besides, I like the idea of using what's already here. The place has an authenticity about it – it's not trying to pretend to be what it's not. I don't want to create some fancy eyesore. I want the café to blend into its surroundings, so you hardly even notice it's here.'

'Whatever you say, guv.' Gavin grinned. 'Anyhow, I guarantee I can do you a better price than those other chancers. You saw what I did at the coffee shop?'

Robert nodded.

'You've got pretty much the same dimensions here.'

Liz could see that Robert wanted to talk money. She was about to take a walk, thinking that he might find it easier to haggle on a one-to-one basis, when Gavin suggested popping over to his Newquay showroom straight away.

'Now I've got the measurements we can do a rough design and costings. I've got a tip-top computer program that shows you what it'll look like. It'll speed things up if you come. I know you're keen to get going as soon as possible.'

'Great idea!' said Robert, before turning to Liz. 'Is that all right with you?'

She nodded, but disappointment had washed over her. She'd been hoping they'd have lunch together, but she couldn't even go with him on the drive. It would take over two hours to travel there and back, and he'd need at least an hour in the showroom with Gavin, probably more. She couldn't leave Lowenna with Jean for all that time; it would be taking advantage, and besides, she wanted to be home when Rosie returned from school.

She was hoping that Robert would notice her expression and have a change of heart, but he didn't even look at her properly.

'Darling, do you mind getting the bus back? I'm sorry, but it makes sense to sort this now—'

'Of course. It would be silly to drive me all the way. It'd add ages to the journey.'

But still she couldn't quite believe it when he dropped her at the bus stop, pecked her on the cheek through the open window and sped off without so much as a backwards glance or wave. It seemed to her that she'd fallen way down his list of priorities. Whoever would have guessed that his heart would be stolen by a stupid, derelict beach shack?

The bus was late and by the time she reached Bag End, her mood had turned really black. To add insult to injury, Nathan the postman had delivered two nasty bills and Jean had left a message on the answerphone to say that Lowenna had diarrhoea. It seemed that it couldn't get much worse.

Liz put on the kettle and was about to grab a quick cup of tea before picking up her daughter when Charlie-the-reporter appeared on the doorstep, waving a rolled-up newspaper. Her cheeks were flushed, her eyes shining and her messy mop of curly auburn hair seemed to have a life of its own. She was in jeans, trainers and an oversized pink sweater that could have been knitted by her grandma, and she clearly had something very urgent to impart.

'It's in the paper, have you seen it?' She didn't stop for a reply. 'There's been a response already! They want to interview Rosie!'

She was talking so fast that Liz had trouble making out the words.

'Look!' Charlie thrust the newspaper into Liz's hands but didn't wait for her to open it. 'They're sending a German reporter and camera crew. They think it's a GREAT story!'

Liz was conscious of the time but nevertheless ushered Charlie in, fearing that the poor girl might explode.

'Hang on! Can you start again?' They were standing in the hallway. 'No, wait. I've got a better idea. You make the tea, I'll get Lowenna from Jean's – it won't take long – and then I'm all yours.'

The childminder looked distinctly harassed. Even her house, Dynnargh, seemed to give off agitated vibes. The downstairs front window was partially open and a child was screeching inside, while the normally tidy hallway was littered with toys. As soon as Liz was close enough, Jean thrust a rather pale Lowenna into her arms; it had clearly been a difficult morning.

'She's not well, I'm afraid she's going down with something.' A sullen, red-faced toddler appeared from the playroom to the right and Jean shooed him away. 'Her tummy's bad and she's been that clingy, she wouldn't let me put her down for a second. I hope we don't all catch it.'

Jean was normally the mildest, gentlest person, and her sharp tone took Liz aback.

'I'm awfully sorry. She seemed fine earlier on.' She hurriedly popped her daughter in the pushchair and fastened the straps, making a mental note to drop off some flowers later as a peace offering. 'I wouldn't have brought her otherwise.'

'I know, love.' Jean couldn't be cross for long. 'Keep her warm for the rest of the day and make sure she drinks plenty of water. I expect she'll be right as rain in the morning.'

She ruffled Lowenna's hair, but didn't bend down to kiss her. If the child had a bug, the last thing she'd want would be to pass it around. She was probably thinking that one sick child was bad enough; a whole houseful would be a nightmare.

Charlie was at the kitchen table nursing a mug of tea but she jumped up when Liz walked back in, balancing Lowenna on her hip.

Spread out in front of the reporter was a copy of today's *Tremarnock Bugle*. Liz started, because gazing out at her was a large photo of none other than herself alongside Rosie and Rafael, smiling in front of Rick's shop, while Rosie held out her precious bottle, complete with the message inside.

'Goodness!' Liz exclaimed. 'The picture's awfully big!'

'You're front-page news!' said Charlie, grinning. She was still twitching with excitement. 'You're famous!'

Lowenna sat quiet and forlorn on Liz's lap, sucking her thumb while Liz read the headline: '*TREMARNOCK GIRL FINDS WWII MESSAGE IN BOTTLE.*' Underneath was Charlie's byline, and beneath that, the whole saga up to now, including quotes from Rosie, Rafael and Liz. At the very bottom were the words:

Do you know Franz Maier? If you have any information regarding his whereabouts or that of his family, please contact Charlie Pearce.

Charlie's number was given next to it.

'I wonder if anyone will respond?' Liz mused.

Charlie clapped her hands, making Lowenna jump. 'That's just it! I've been trying to tell you! I had a call from a German TV station. They're going to do a follow-up. It'll be on the national news! Someone's bound to know something about him over there.'

Liz's eyes opened wide. 'D'you think so? Really?'

Soon, Charlie was on the phone to a man in Hamburg, confirming that a camera crew would be arriving at Bag End at 4.30 p.m., by which time Rosie would be home from school.

'You'd like the shopkeeper and the boy, too?' Charlie nodded, her mobile wedged between shoulder and ear while she scribbled in her notebook. 'The light's OK here, yes...' She glanced at Liz. 'They're all very photogenic.'

'Don't say that!' Liz felt panic rising, and her mouth went dry. Being shy, the thought of appearing in front of a camera filled her with horror; in fact she wasn't at all sure that she could do it, and Rosie wasn't a natural performer either. It was hardly surprising, given what the poor girl had been through. Liz's fiercely protective instincts kicked in. Because her daughter was doing so well, it was all too easy to forget that her short-term memory wasn't what it had been before her brain surgery, and that she'd lost a lot of her peripheral vision. In fact it was amazing that, aside from regular three-month scans and physiotherapy, she managed to lead such a normal life.

As soon as Charlie put down the phone, Liz reached across the table and shook her arm. 'This is too sudden! Rosie and I can't manage it. We'll freeze up! You'll have to do it. You know the story just as well; you'll be far better at it.'

But Charlie only laughed. 'It'll be just like having a chat, honest. All you need to do is tell them what you've told me. Rosie will be great. They'll love her.' Liz opened her mouth to protest again but the reporter wasn't paying attention. 'You'll never forgive yourself if you turn them down.' She gave a sly glance. 'And anyway, think of Pat. Wouldn't she have loved all this? She's probably looking down on you now, willing you on.'

She knew exactly what she was doing. The mere mention of Pat's name sent ripples of remorse cascading through Liz, who was well aware that the old woman would, indeed, have enjoyed the drama and would have wanted very much to locate her German friend. Moreover, in the unlikely event that he did turn up, hearing his version of events would be a wonderful way of remembering her and paying tribute to her kindness, far better than any dusty tombstone epitaph.

'All right, we'll try,' Liz said, swallowing. 'But you'll have to give us a lesson on how to behave in front of the camera.'

'Oh, it's easy,' Charlie replied breezily. 'You just have to be yourselves.'

To her mother's surprise, Rosie was remarkably composed when she heard about the camera crew and popped straight upstairs to shower, change and put on makeup. Meanwhile, Liz got in touch with Rick and then Rafael, who hurried to the house accompanied by Felipe; Tony was back in London for a few days, working on one of his many projects.

Rick had put on his best blue and white checked shirt and tie and oiled his greying beard and moustache, which gleamed lustrously. Rafael, too, must have done some hurried grooming, as his Mohican, though not coloured, was standing proudly to attention, having been waxed upright to within an inch of its life. The wooden crosses were firmly in his ears and his fingers were weighed down with chunky silver rings.

Liz decided that under the circumstances, she'd better make an effort, too, so she left Lowenna with the others while she dashed to her room to put on her favourite pale pink sweater and gold earrings. Then she brushed her dark hair, applied a slick of black mascara, a dab of brown eyeshadow and blusher and she was ready.

She didn't know what she was supposed to do with Lowenna while they were filming; the little girl was bound to make a fuss, especially as she wasn't feeling well. Luckily, though, Felipe, who had countless younger brothers and sisters back in Rio and was very good with small children, offered to take her for a walk in her pushchair.

When Liz pointed out that she had an upset tummy, he waved his hand in the air dismissively.

'My baby brother, he had terrible diarrhoea until we found he was allergic to dairy. Sometimes he would poo fifteen times a day. It was like a dam bursting, it would go everywhere.' He made a noise like an explosion, complete with gestures. 'My mother always said she was too busy to clean him up so she made me do it.'

Liz rather wished that he wouldn't be quite so graphic.

'Lowenna's not as bad as that,' she said, feeling slightly nauseous. 'But I'll give you some spare nappies just in case.'

Before long, Charlie was springing up and answering the door to two attractive young foreigners: a tall slim woman reporter with a long blonde plait hanging down her back, and a short camerawoman in a back-to-front blue baseball cap, white T-shirt, green cargo pants and a brown gilet with bulging pockets. The heavy black bag on her shoulder looked almost as big as she was. It quickly became apparent that they both spoke perfect English; in fact Liz thought that it was probably better than her own.

They were so smiley and friendly that it was difficult to feel too tense. Liz made mugs of tea and coffee that Rafael passed around while the camerawoman strolled about downstairs, deciding on the best place to do the filming. Meanwhile the reporter, who was called Lena, talked to Rosie in particular about the types of questions that she wanted to ask.

'Don't worry, I'm not trying to catch you out or anything. I just want you to tell your story.' She grinned. 'You'll be a celebrity in Germany. How do you feel about that?'

Rosie blushed.

Lena laughed and cuffed her arm. 'I'm only kidding, but wouldn't it be fun if we can find out who Franz Maier is – or was? Maybe you'll want to write a book about it one day.'

The landline rang several times, but it was on answerphone and Liz ignored it. It was no doubt one of the villagers; someone would have spotted the camera crew arriving and the tom-toms would be beating. Nothing stayed secret in Tremarnock for long. Soon after, her mobile pinged. A text message from Audrey. She turned the phone to silent. Audrey would only make her agitated again; she'd just have to wait.

In the end they settled on doing the interview in the cosy sitting room at the front of the cottage, where there was plenty of light from the bay window. It was Liz's favourite place. On winter evenings, she loved to draw the thick taupe curtains, light candles and huddle on the dove grey sofa around the open fire, sometimes with a tartan blanket on her knees and Mitzi the cat on top.

There was a striped hessian rug on the bare floorboards to keep out the chill, and the stone-coloured walls were lined with wooden shelves for Liz's and Robert's favourite books and artefacts: photographs, interesting little boxes, bits of driftwood and handmade pottery. On one side of the fireplace was a giant basket filled with chopped logs; on the other, a deep, mulberry-coloured armchair that you could sink into. Liz always kept a vase of fresh flowers on the mantelpiece along with the antique clock given to her by her father.

Lena was charmed. 'It's so pretty, so cute!' she kept repeating. 'I think it sums up that Danish word, *hygge*.'

'What's that?' Rosie raised her eyebrows.

'It means comfort and cosiness. It's all about snuggling up with your loved ones and keeping warm and comfy.'

Liz was pleased until the camerawoman started moving the furniture around to find the perfect angle. Suddenly the place felt terribly hot and cramped, but there was no time to fret; soon she was being ushered with Rafael and Rick onto the sofa with Rosie between them, and microphones were fastened onto their tops. Lena, meanwhile, sat facing them in the armchair, scanning a page of questions.

'Forget about her,' she said comfortably, as the camerawoman finally took up her position. Then she crossed one black-trousered leg over another and licked her lips. 'Just pretend we're old friends.'

It was easier said than done. Lena might be cool, calm and collected but Liz wondered how on earth she was supposed to act normal with a camera practically stuck in her face.

'What if I fluff my words?' she squeaked, feeling the blood rush to her neck and cheeks.

'It won't matter, we can edit it out.'

'I might need the loo!'

'Do you want to pop out now?' Lena said patiently, but Rosie tutted.

'Mu-um, you only went a moment ago. Stop flapping, will you? It's just a TV interview, for God's sake!' She smoothed down her top and tucked her hair behind her ears. 'C'mon. Let's get on with the show.'

Liz felt rather ashamed. If her daughter could cope, then so could she.

'All right.' She gave a brave thumbs-up. 'Action!'

In the end it only took about half an hour. Rick, who was usually talkative, particularly when it came to local history, seemed to have been struck dumb. Rafael, too, had apparently lost his tongue and forgotten most of his English. Only Rosie seemed at ease, chatting and laughing with Lena about her discovery and Rick's subsequent research, and explaining a bit about Pat.

'I used to call her Nan – she was like my grandmother.' She turned to Liz, who managed a nervous smile back. 'She looked after me when my mum went to work and she was really kind and made me laugh. It would mean so much to me to find Franz because it would be a link to Pat.' Lena, opposite, nodded with encouragement, urging her to go on. 'If you know anything about him or his family, please get in touch.'

'Yes, do.' Liz's voice sounded sort of strangled and high-pitched, like a child's, and she kicked herself for speaking out. What if the camera zoomed in on her? She'd go bright red and might start gibbering.

Fortunately Rosie, sensing her panic, came to the rescue. 'Mum misses Pat terribly. We all do. We'd love to meet Franz and hear about their time together.'

'What would you say to him?' Lena asked gently.

Rosie paused for a moment and bit her lip. 'I'd say...' she hesitated again and Liz felt herself tense, wondering if her daughter had lost her nerve. 'I'd say come to Tremarnock – we'd love to meet you, and you're welcome any time. Any friend of Pat's is a friend of ours!'

'Wonderful!' Lena sat back with a triumphant smile, signalling that the interview was over, and the atmosphere instantly relaxed. 'You smashed it, Rosie!' she went on. 'You were absolutely brilliant.'

Liz couldn't help but agree. She put an arm around her daughter's slim shoulders and gave her a squeeze. Of course she'd always thought Rosie a star – she was her mother, after all; but never in a million years would she have imagined her holding forth in front of the camera. It was amazing!

Lena seemed to read her thoughts. 'She's a natural. I'd better watch out or she'll be after my job.' She winked at Rosie. 'Seriously, you should consider a career in TV. You'd make a great presenter.'

Rosie coughed with embarrassment, but Liz could tell that she was secretly thrilled. Up to now, her daughter's main aim in life seemed to have been to blend into the background so that no one would notice her disabilities. Who knew? Perhaps this experience would give her some much-needed confidence.

They were interrupted by Rick, who seemed to have found his voice again now that the camera had stopped filming.

'I could do with a drink of water. I'm parched after that.'

Liz offered wine or a soft drink all around instead, but he shook his head. 'I need to get back. Marie's coming over this evening. In fact she might be waiting outside my flat now.'

Lena, too, declined the offer as she had to get back to work, and she informed everyone that the report would most likely be broadcast the following morning unless something big happened to bump it off the schedule. She handed Liz her business card and promised to be in touch the moment she had any information.

'This'll probably get picked up by local news channels, so don't be surprised if you get some calls. Everyone loves a good human interest story.' She crossed her fingers. 'Especially if there's a happy ending.'

They were saying goodbye in the street when an ear-splitting screech made them spin around sharply and they spotted Felipe rounding the corner, pushing Lowenna as fast as he could down the hill in her red and white striped stroller. The little girl was in a terrible state, beating her feet against the footrest and lunging backwards and forward in either distress or fury; it was impossible to tell. Meanwhile Felipe, who was normally a picture of understated elegance, looked as if he'd been trapped in a wind tunnel, with his blue jacket flapping, black hair flying and eyes wide with panic.

'What is it? What's happened?' Liz raced up the hill as fast she could, her mind filled with lurid images of rabid dogs and axe-wielding murderers.

When she finally reached Felipe, he stopped abruptly in the middle of the road and bent double, panting hard and trying to catch his breath.

'She wanted them... I put them back... Would not take no for an answer...'

Liz, none the wiser, quickly unfastened her daughter's straps and picked her up, smothering her damp face with kisses and jiggling her around to soothe her. Within a few moments the shrieking stopped, although the child's body still shook and shuddered with what felt like the aftershocks of an earthquake.

'Poor baby, poor darling,' Liz was saying, while Felipe, still out of puff, continued to make unintelligible sounds.

When at last the aftershocks lessened, Liz became aware that her daughter was staring hard at the still-stooping Felipe and pointing an accusing finger.

'Feepay not nice. Bad boy.' She sounded like someone scolding a naughty puppy.

Liz, bewildered, stared from her daughter to Felipe and back again. By now the others were alongside, too, and when the Brazilian rose at last, he fixed on his audience with his large, dark brown eyes and spread his palms beseechingly.

'I took her to the general store to buy her a little book. You know they have some on the shelf?'

Liz nodded. She'd bought a few down the years for Lowenna and Rosie.

'I thought I could take her back to my house and read it to her, until you had finished filming,' Felipe went on. 'But then she noticed the sweeties.' Now it was his turn to shudder. 'She wanted chocolate but I said no, you have a bad tummy and your mother won't like it.

'The next thing I knew, she was crying and screaming, screaming and crying.' He put his hands over his ears and pulled a face. 'I tried to buy her another book instead but she threw it on the floor and screamed louder. Then one of the customers shouted at me, saying I should control my child, so I ran out of the shop and down the street to find you.' He looked close to tears. 'I'm so sorry. I didn't know what to do. My brothers and sisters, they never screamed like that—'

'Please, you didn't do anything wrong.' Now that Liz understood what had happened, she felt nothing but sympathy for the poor man. 'She's terrible with sweets, really shocking. It was so kind of you to look after her.' Then she gave her daughter a stern look. 'Naughty girl for giving Felipe such a hard time.'

The child's eyes opened wide in surprise and indignation. 'Not naughty, nyshe.' She was the picture of innocence.

'Ooh, she's going to be a right madam when she's older,' said Lena, laughing.

Liz couldn't help giggling too. 'I know what you mean. She's dreadfully strong-willed!' Then she took Felipe by the arm. 'I'm sorry she was such a monster. Thank you for helping, though. I think I'd be wise to avoid the general store for a while. She's probably been banned!'

Chapter Ten

ESME WAS CROUCHED in her small kitchen opening the oven door when the landline rang, making her jump. She checked the clock on the wall above the radiator. It was still only 8 a.m. Who would call at this time?

Turning down the oven quickly, she hurried into the sitting room to pick up the phone, which was on a shelf near the TV.

'It's Philip Goulbourne, Caroline's husband,' came an abrupt voice, laced with uncertainty. 'Is she there? I need a word with her. I can't get through on her mobile; I think it's switched off.'

Esme's insides clenched. She wondered what to do. She was almost certain that Caroline wasn't expecting the call and wouldn't wish to speak to him, either. There again, if he had news of their daughter, Helen, it would be a different matter.

'I think she's still asleep.' She was playing for time, though she wasn't sure why until it dawned on her that every phone call from Paris seemed to drag Caroline mentally just a little further away. They had precious few hours left together; why did he have to phone now? Couldn't he at least let them have breakfast in peace?

It was Tuesday morning and she was surprised, really, that her friend was still here at all. She'd seemed frequently on the point of departing ever since Helen had announced her pregnancy. It was only when Esme had reminded Caroline that she still couldn't walk far unaided and would need assistance to get home that she'd backed down and conceded that it would, in fact, be better to wait another few days.

Still she'd repeatedly asked, 'Helen will understand, won't she?' only to be reassured that her daughter was an adult now and that her partner would be perfectly capable of looking after her until Caroline was well enough to return.

'She's pregnant – not ill,' Esme would say patiently. 'Nothing's going to happen for a while. She's seen her doctor and everything's fine. She's in very good hands.'

But Caroline had frowned, biting her lip, despite the fact that Helen herself had insisted that she stay in Cornwall a little longer to recuperate now that she understood the full extent of her mother's injury. It had made little difference. Caroline was a mum through and through, and Esme supposed that the maternal feelings never disappeared. You always wanted to be there for your children, no matter what.

'Can you still hear me?' Philip's voice dragged her back to the present.

She'd have liked to tell him to push off, but didn't, of course. It was up to her friend to do that. 'I'll go and get her.'

Caroline wasn't asleep but was sitting on the end of her bed reaching for her crutches when Esme knocked and entered. She vanished discreetly into the kitchen again while Caroline hobbled to the phone, but there was a gap between door and floor that made it almost impossible not to catch her words.

'Yes, I know,' she heard Caroline say, and, 'I'm perfectly well aware of that, Philip. I'm still in some pain, as I've told Helen.'

Silence reigned for a few moments while Philip was speaking, then she piped up again, louder this time. 'This isn't really about her, is it? It's about you!'

Esme gritted her teeth; she could well imagine the games of emotional blackmail that he was playing, and she hated him for it.

'She's told me she's fine... I know she'd like me there... I'll come as soon I can.' Caroline again, followed by another pause.

'No! Absolutely not!' Her panicky tone made Esme start. 'I'm not a child, Philip. I don't need your help.'

Another gap, during which he was no doubt testing a range of different tactics, bringing out every weapon of persuasion in his arsenal.

To distract herself, Esme took two now rather dry and overheated croissants out of the oven and put them on a tray, along with some butter in a white ceramic dish, jam, knives, napkins and a spoon. Then she made a big pot of coffee and heated some milk, which she poured into a small jug.

She came out only when she was sure that the conversation was over.

'Breakfast!' she smiled, fake-brightly. 'Come and sit on the sofa. We'll have it on our knees.'

Sunshine flooded through the bay window, but it looked different from the light of spring and summer. Long, slanted beams seemed to lend walls, floor and furniture a rich golden glow, while the leaves on the trees across the way were starting to turn yellowy brown.

Caroline's normally neat blonde hair was knotty and tousled. She was in one of Esme's wrinkled nightdresses – a baggy purple robe made of Indian cotton – and her face, too, was creased with sleep, but she looked beautiful even so: pale and slightly fragile, but with a brave and rather magnificent inner strength that flickered like a candle without blowing out.

The pity of it, Esme thought, was that she didn't know she had this inner resilience; she thought that she was weak. If she could only learn to trust herself more.

'He seems to think I'm a monster for not rushing home this second to see Helen,' said Caroline, picking at a corner of croissant. 'Really, it's just an excuse to get me back. He knows Helen's fine. In any case, if he's that worried he can go and look after her himself.'

It was just bravado. Esme could tell that the conversation had troubled her; Philip knew how to push her buttons, she'd give him that.

'He threatened to come here and "help me" get home.' Caroline gave a wry look. 'Help? You've got to be joking. I'd be helping *him*.'

'Did you manage to put him off?' The thought of Philip turning up at Dove Cottage made Esme shiver. She wasn't at all sure that she'd be able to look him in the face, let alone speak to him.

'Oh yes, but he'll ring again soon. He won't give in.'

'Why don't you just hang up?'

Caroline frowned. 'I can't do that. It would be so petty and childish after all we've been through together, don't you think? If we separate I want to do it properly, in a dignified way, for the children's sakes if nothing else.' She hesitated. 'And for our grandchild. I have to think of him or her now, too.'

Esme took a sip of coffee from her porcelain mug. It smelled fruity and delicious. The warm liquid flowed down her throat and into her stomach: the first thing she'd consumed this morning. She couldn't understand her friend's viewpoint, not properly. It was so obvious that Philip made her unhappy. She wanted to shake her, to make her see sense.

Instead, she took a croissant herself and smothered it in homemade strawberry jam that Jean had given her. She could sense time ticking by; she could almost feel it trickling through her fingers.

'Would you like some fresh air?' she said suddenly. 'You haven't been out for ages. How about I take you down to the harbour? I'd love you to see it.'

Caroline's eyes lit up momentarily, then a shadow passed across her face. 'But how would I get there?'

It was true that Esme still had no car, and in any case, the streets around the harbour were pedestrianised. 'I'm not sure, but I'll think of something. Leave it with me.'

After they'd eaten, Caroline washed and dressed while Esme fetched the laptop that she kept in her room and made some phone calls. She knew that what she wanted was possible, but wasn't sure how to go about getting it. The first people that she spoke to couldn't help, but on the third call, she struck gold.

'Eureka!' she cried, prompting Caroline to poke her head around the bathroom door, letting out a cloud of hot steam.

'Everything all right?'

Esme gave a thumbs-up. 'I'll explain later.'

Soon Caroline reappeared in a red sweater and a pair of Esme's baggy black and white harem pants, fastened with a belt and with one leg rolled up to accommodate the boot. Before long, Esme was bundling her into a taxi and they were heading away from Tremarnock, on the road to goodness knew where.

'I thought you were going to show me the harbour?'

'I am.' Esme smiled enigmatically.

'So why are we going out of town?'

'Wait and see.' Rather enjoying the mystery, Esme deliberately shut her mouth like a clam.

Realising that there was no point trying to press any further, Caroline sat back and savoured the journey, basking in the natural light and taking in the trees, fields and cottages as they zoomed past. When they slowed down, she admired the abundant hedgerows, bristling with glossy green ivy, plump blackberries, bright red hawthorn berries and orange rosehips. The world seemed quite magnificent to her after so long indoors.

'The colours! They look so bright! It's like watching high-definition TV!' She opened the window a little and closed her eyes, enjoying the wind in her hair, sniffing the unmistakable scent of damp earth and decaying leaves. Autumn.

At last the car rounded a bend and drove into an ugly out-of-town industrial estate, coming to a halt in front of a giant warehouse. On the side, in enormous yellow letters, were the words 'THE CORNISH MOBILITY CENTRE'.

Esme got out without a word and went inside, emerging soon after with a smiley woman in an ill-fitting navy suit, who was pushing a wheelchair that she proceeded to fold up and place in the boot.

Caroline was silent until her friend climbed once more into the back seat beside her. Then the words spurted like water from a hosepipe. 'Whatever are you thinking? What have you got that for? I can't go round in that thing – I'm not an old woman, for goodness' sake! I hope you haven't paid for it! What a waste of money!'

Esme put a finger to her lips. 'Shh. It was just a few pounds. I've only rented it. They could have delivered it tomorrow but we need it now. You do want to see the village, don't you?'

She eyed her friend, who nodded.

'Well, then, you'll just have to put up with it. You can wear a disguise if you want. I'll lend you a scarf and sunglasses!'

In the end, Caroline managed to lay her embarrassment to one side, so eager was she to have a look around Tremarnock. It wasn't cold, but Esme made sure that she had plenty of warm clothes on; then, once the taxi driver had been paid, they set off up Humble Hill in the direction of South Street, giggling like a couple of schoolgirls.

The wheelchair was much heavier and more cumbersome than Esme had imagined and although she felt light in spirits, she warned Caroline that she might have to jump on the back during the downhill bits to give herself a rest.

'Do you think you can steer with your crutch?' she joked. 'You can use it like a gear stick.'

Caroline didn't reply; she was too busy looking this way and that.

As they passed certain landmarks, Esme told her what they were. 'That's where Pat used to live... That's the way to the cliffs. The views are magnificent.'

'Isn't the shrine to the Lost Lady of Tremarnock supposed to be up there somewhere?'

Esme said that it was. 'I'd take you but I'm afraid it's too steep for a wheelchair. We might roll back down and end up in a messy heap at the bottom.'

They stopped for a moment or two outside Seaspray Boutique to admire the fashions in the window. Unfortunately, Audrey spotted them and came dashing out – eager, no doubt, to meet the visitor whom she'd have heard about on the grapevine.

'You must be Caroline. I'm SO pleased to meet you,' she gushed, as Caroline sank a little further into her chair. 'I hear you live in gay Paris?' Audrey pronounced it 'Paree'. 'How wonderful! I love the city so much. In fact, this is by a Parisian designer.' She took a step back and pulled at the hem of her rather striking black and white polka-dot blouse to show it off.

'I stock it in my shop,' she said hopefully. 'I still have a few left.'

'Do you?' Caroline was non-committal. 'It suits you.'

When they finally managed to extricate themselves, Esme pushed on towards the beach. It was hard work, as the wheels kept getting stuck in the cobbles and she needed to shove hard to get them out. She indicated the turning to Market Square, then A Winkle in Time.

'It's quite small, a bit like eating in someone's front room, only the food's a lot better.'

Caroline, turning, peered at Esme over her shoulder. 'I know! Let's eat there tonight. My treat. It's the least I can do after all you've done for me.'

'There's no need, really...' It sounded to Esme too much like a mournful Last Supper, but her discomfort went unnoticed.

'Come on,' Caroline insisted. 'Let's see if we can reserve a table.'

The doorway was only narrow, so in the end she had to remain outside while Esme popped in to book.

'Success!' she said, on her return. 'We're eating at seven-thirty. You'd better be in the mood for fish.'

On they went, but the pavement on the corner by Rick's shop was blocked by his displays of postcards and brightly coloured spinning windmills, so they were forced to use the road. Esme would have passed by without stopping, but Caroline wanted to admire the cards.

'I wouldn't mind getting a couple.' She reached out to spin the rotating stand while her friend, spotting Rick's bulky outline through the window, looked quickly in the other direction.

Esme knew perfectly well what the locals had been saying about her since she'd ended their brief liaison: it was no wonder that she'd never married, as she liked her own company and space too much to want to share it with anybody. Let them talk, she thought; only she knew the truth. Still, bumping into Rick was awkward and she made a point of avoiding him when possible.

To her relief, Caroline changed her mind about the postcards and suggested they move on. 'They look a bit moth-eaten, to be honest,' she whispered, 'and I can't be bothered to get out my purse.'

'He sells good fudge,' Esme replied, giving the wheelchair a firm push. When they were well and truly out of earshot, she added, 'But that's about all that's worth buying in there – unless you're into lighthouse souvenirs, that is.'

The hanging baskets outside Barbara's pub, the Lobster Pot, were tired and bedraggled. It was almost time to empty the summer flowers and plant something new; but the place still looked cosy and inviting. The door was open and a soft light shone through the leaded windowpanes in the front window. Before long, there would be an open fire crackling away, too.

On a blackboard on the pavement someone had chalked the words, 'Moules Frites – Hand-baked Cornish Pasty and a Pint – Potted Shrimps – Village Scrumpy. Come on in!' Alongside was a rough drawing of a jolly farmer on a haystack, waving a dumpy cider bottle. It wasn't long since breakfast, but Esme's taste buds tingled all the same in a Pavlovian-style response.

Several yards on, they came to the window of Oliver's, the fishing tackle shop, which belonged to Jenny and John Lambert. After casting a glance over the rods, waterproof jackets and waders, Caroline decided that she rather fancied an olive green waxed cotton hat with a wide brim, until Esme spotted the price tag and suggested that it might look a little out of place in Paris.

'You'd be better off with that,' she said, pointing to a black beanie with a red stripe. 'D'you think it might pass as chic in France?'

Caroline laughed. 'Hmm. Not sure. I've always felt a bit silly in hats. They don't suit me. You'd look great in it, though. You've got the right shaped face.'

At the harbour wall, Esme parked the wheelchair and sat on the bench alongside Caroline while she gazed at the view. Several fishing boats had been dragged up and lay on their sides, their hulls covered in barnacles and slimy seaweed that gave off a tangy odour. The sand was a damp brown colour, while the greyish sea turned white at the edges, nipping at the shore like sharp teeth before receding.

'It's so quiet,' Caroline said, before inhaling deeply. There was no one else in sight. 'I love the salty air. I'm sure if I lived here I'd never feel down or unwell. I think I'd take up writing or painting, maybe. Landscapes. I used to love art at school, do you remember?'

Esme nodded. 'You were very good, as I recall.'

'Oh no, I was pretty rubbish, but I enjoyed it. I'm not sure why I stopped. I did think of signing up for some art classes once but I never got round to it. I guess things just got in the way.'

She looked troubled and, without thinking, Esme reached out and took the hand that had been sitting in her friend's lap, folding it in her own.

'You don't have to go back, you know.'

Her softly spoken words seemed to dangle in the space between them, like scraps of washing on a line, and her heart started to thump while the blood rushed to her ears. She couldn't quite believe what she'd just said; her instinct was to backpedal, but something forced her to hold her nerve. She'd been running in the other direction for forty-odd years, hadn't she? Maybe it was time to stop.

Caroline's hand, which was small and cold, remained where it was, but you could sense a fluttering unease.

'I... I mean, of course you'll want to go back and see Helen,' Esme stammered. Her cheeks burned, but she had begun now and might as well finish. 'But you don't have to live with Philip in Paris any more. You can live here, if you want – with me.'

Caroline flinched, and Esme thought that any second she might pull away, but she didn't. Instead she turned and rested her other hand on Esme's own, wrapping around it like a glove.

'You're amazing, you know.'

'What do you mean?' Esme asked hoarsely.

'I mean – if only things were different.'

'Different? How?' She felt giddy, as if she were standing on the edge of a skyscraper, looking down.

'I wish—' Caroline stopped again, and Esme held her breath. 'I wish the nuns hadn't burst in,' she said at last. 'I wish they'd never told my parents. I wish we'd run away to some place where it doesn't matter who you love; where no one cares.' She sounded savage, as if she wanted to lash out with her bare hands.

'I wish we'd had the courage to ignore everyone else,' she continued. Her shoulders slumped, all her anger gone. 'But then I wouldn't have Helen and Andrew, would I?' She looked at Esme with damp, imploring eyes. 'How could I wish them away? I couldn't, could I? They're my life.'

'Oh, Caroline!' Esme's voice cracked. Suddenly it was as if the earth had ripped in two; decades of pent-up suffering shot high into the air, like molten rocks lighting up the sky. 'I didn't know. I thought you'd forgotten me.'

Her whole body shook. She thought she'd never been so cold – or was it hot? She couldn't tell. It was like reaching the summit of life, the point beyond which life cannot rise; it was like a pain that seemed to know no bottom, no limit. How could these two reside in one body at the same time – and could she stand it?

Caroline, too, was shaking as she continued to wrap Esme's hand in hers. 'I tried so hard to forget,' she went on, falteringly. 'My father told me I was wicked and disgusting. He said if I carried on like that I could never be happy or lead a normal life or have friends, a home, children. He said I'd be ostracised by society and that our relationship wouldn't last.' She swallowed. 'I was only fifteen. I didn't know anything. Part of me believed him; I was terrified and it seemed easier to do as he said. I didn't feel I had any choice. I forced myself to push you out of my mind. I made myself date boys, even though it didn't feel right. I did like Philip, though.' She frowned, as if searching for the right words. 'He was interesting and well travelled. I loved the fact that he was into human rights and wanted to make a difference to the world.

'I never thought he'd look twice at me so I was flattered and amazed when he started paying me attention. It wasn't an all-consuming passion, not like a romantic film.' She smiled wryly. 'But when I agreed to marry him I did really think we could be happy; I was determined to make it work.

'Maybe it's my fault he had the affair,' she added, wiping an invisible speck of dust from the corner of her eye. 'Perhaps deep down he always knew something was wrong.'

A man in a navy jumper strolled by with a golden Labrador on a lead and smiled pleasantly at the women. 'Morning.'

Esme nodded back. If he thought they looked peculiar, huddled together as if their lives depended on it, he didn't show it, and she was grateful to him. He provided a welcome flash of normality in a world that had turned upside down.

'Why didn't you tell me all this?' she whispered, when he'd gone. She was thinking of herself now, not Caroline: all those wasted years when she had bottled up her feelings and struggled to convince herself that she wasn't lonely, and that she was meant to live this way. 'If only I'd known...' A hard lump formed in her throat. 'I would have waited. I would have come to get you. We'd have found a way.'

But Caroline shook her head. 'It wouldn't have made any difference.'

'Why not?'

'Because I'd never have left Philip, not when the children were still at home.'

'But you can leave him now?' Esme gazed deep into her friend's blue eyes. Everything seemed so simple suddenly: she loved Caroline, Caroline loved her and nothing else mattered.

'I... I'm not sure...' Caroline looked confused. 'Helen and Andrew, my friends – your friends, too. What will people—?'

'It doesn't matter,' Esme said passionately. 'I'm sick of shame, aren't you? Helen and Andrew will cope. They'll still love you. Surely they want you to be happy?'

Caroline fell silent as she absorbed the comment, while an unwelcome vision of Audrey floated through Esme's mind. She heard her speak as clearly as if she were standing there in front of them: '*So! Esme and Caroline! Fancy that! I never realised, did you? Though now I come to think of it...*'

Familiar old emotions licked through Esme's body and she felt herself heat up like a cauldron. It would be a lie to pretend that she hadn't carried more than her fair share of guilt, fear and self-loathing for most of her life: ever since she was ten or eleven, probably, when she first found herself looking at the other girls in the school changing room.

Back then she couldn't quite place the feeling; she just knew that she wanted very much to carry on looking. Then later, when schoolmates talked about their crush on some male pop star or other, or an actor in a TV series that they were glued to at the time, Esme would pretend to agree, when really it was the female lead that she wanted to be close to, though she didn't understand why.

She swallowed, wishing that she could block out her thoughts, but they kept on coming, one after the other, relentlessly. It was around that time, she remembered, that she first heard the words 'lezzy' and 'dyke' and she never forgot them. She could still picture the two girls sitting on a bench in the playground holding hands, and the other girls teasing them, making them cry.

That very night, Esme had looked up the word 'lesbian' in the dictionary. It was a massive shock to discover that it meant a woman who was attracted to someone of the same sex, because she realised that this might be her.

All at once the difference that she'd always felt, that sense of not quite fitting in, had a name, a label, like an illness; and she concluded that there must be something terribly wrong with her. It was almost as if she could see herself now, a poor lonely confused little girl, and wished that she could go back, take her own hand and tell her that everything would be all right.

A sudden gust of wind blew an empty paper bag out of the nearby rubbish bin and sent it dancing across the path in front of them. Caroline, not noticing, continued to stare at the sea, and it was Esme who bent down to pick it up.

The bag, so clean and white, reminded her then of Becky, her first proper infatuation, who had arrived at St Hilda's when Esme was thirteen. Tall, blonde, American and sporty, Becky had the whitest teeth and longest legs that Esme had ever seen, browned to the colour of warm toast after a sunny Californian summer. All the girls wanted to be her friend and Esme, too, was drawn to her like a moth to a flame, though she did her best to hide it.

By day, she was careful in the new girl's company, watching how her classmates interacted, keen to please but not toadying. But at night, Becky came to her in her dreams and led her away to a private place where they were completely alone. Quite what they did there, Esme could never visualise. She just knew that she wanted very much to be near her and to have her all to herself.

Becky didn't stay long at St Hilda's but by the time she left, Esme felt certain that she could never give herself to a man. In some ways it was a relief finally to bring to an end the plague of doubts in her mind, but the pain of having to keep this fundamental part of herself hidden away almost drove her mad.

As a form of self-protection, she developed her own safe world, like a parallel universe, becoming increasingly solitary and losing herself in art, music and novels. Amid the bleakness, she found that writers like Radclyffe Hall and Virginia Woolf offered some hope and comfort, because while they'd seemed to exist on the margins, they'd still had a life.

Throughout all this lonely period, Esme confided in no one. Homosexuality had never been discussed in her house and she wasn't sure how her parents would react, but she knew full well that in the eyes of the Catholic Church it was a wicked sin for which she could be severely punished.

She became so adept at repressing her innermost feelings that when Caroline arrived, it was a term at least before Esme realised that she had fallen in love. For Becky she had felt a sickly, destabilising, hopeless sort of longing. Now, it was like finally finding the piece that fitted into the puzzle of her life.

The memory of that sudden, glorious realisation made her want to cry all over again, and she took a tissue from her coat pocket and wiped her nose.

For one whole year, she recollected, she had felt complete. Having decided that her sole purpose was to be with Caroline, to wrap her in love and protect her from the harsh external world, she became a willing slave. She knew that she was the stronger personality and made it her role to shore Caroline up.

They didn't declare their feelings for one another, but it wasn't necessary; through stolen looks, touches and whispered moments together, they both simply knew. Then just once, when the whole school had assembled on the playing fields to watch a sixth form open-air production of *Twelfth Night*, they found themselves alone together in the dormitory, looking for Esme's misplaced glasses.

It was a beautiful June day, warm and sunny, and there was a low, happy rumbling coming from the crowd that had assembled outside the open first-floor window. Both girls were in their blue and white checked summer frocks, sandals and white socks, having run upstairs when they'd realised that the glasses were missing. Caroline was panting slightly and her blonde fringe stuck to her forehead, which was damp with sweat.

Bending down to look under Esme's bed, she shouted triumphantly, 'Ta da!'

Then, when she stood up with the glasses and turned around, their eyes met; and something took over, some force that neither could control.

Instinctively, Esme leaned down and kissed Caroline softly on the mouth. She responded by twining her hands around the back of the older girl's shoulders, pulling her close.

Esme's soul stirred and her body seemed to be on fire. Tiptoeing over to the door, she closed it softly; then they undressed quickly and wordlessly and climbed beneath the cool sheets.

They were both aware that they didn't have long, but it was long enough for Esme to know that if she had been in any doubt at all about her feelings before, she had none now. That sensation of skin on skin and the magical softness of her lover's body, combined with the hard edge of their mutual desire! Never had she known such utter bliss. But it was the spiritual connection that mattered most. It was as if she had come home.

Then: catastrophe. Sister Maura had also mislaid something – her camera. When she couldn't find it in the refectory, she decided that she must have left it in her bedroom, adjoining the dormitory; she'd always been a little absent-minded. She was one of the youngest nuns, probably not more than thirty, quite pretty and funny with a soft Irish accent, and the pupils liked her. Esme heard her open the dormitory door and saw her staring wide-eyed at the two naked girls.

For one wild moment, she imagined that Sister Maura might tiptoe out again and pretend it hadn't happened; but within seconds, her fluid features seemed to stiffen and set. She let out a cry and ran towards the bed like a woman possessed, throwing off the covers, slapping their heads and arms and shouting at them to get dressed.

'What will Sister Mary say?' Sister Mary was the head teacher. 'It's disgusting, that's what it is! Hurry up and put on your things.' And when they were clothed and shivering with fear, she ordered, 'You come with me now. Oh my!' Sister Maura crossed herself and reached for her rosary, dangling on a chain from her waist. 'You'll never, ever hear the end of this, to be sure.'

'Esme?'

Caroline's voice brought her out of her daydream. She was still sitting beside her on the bench, clutching the scrunched-up paper bag in her hand.

'You were miles away,' Caroline said gently. 'What were you thinking?'

Esme sighed. Time seemed to have done nothing to dull the pain of all that remorse, anger, longing and humiliation. The look on Sister Mary's face the following morning, when she'd told the girls that she'd called their parents, was just as vivid now as it had been then.

'Pack your things, Caroline,' she'd said, curling her thin lips with a flash of triumph in her eyes. 'You're going home.'

She'd turned to Esme, who was trembling so much that she feared she might collapse. 'You're to stay here. Your mother and father will be writing to you.'

It seemed strange to feel grateful to her parents for their reaction, but she was. They could never bring themselves to discuss what had happened or talk about what it meant, but unlike Caroline's mother and father, they didn't get angry or seek to change their daughter's nature. They must have accepted on some level that she was different, and no doubt sent her to her aunt in Truro in the hope that she, most probably a lesbian herself, would be able to teach Esme a good way of living. And it had worked, hadn't it? Esme had made the best of it. Only she had been so very, very alone.

'I love you, Caroline,' she said heavily now. 'I always have, but it hasn't been easy. For my sake, please make up your mind. I want you to stay but if you can't, then go quickly. Don't torture me. I'm sure you understand.'

Caroline let out a cry, like an injured animal. 'But I don't know what to do. I want to be with you but I have a family. It's not straightforward.'

'Think about it,' Esme replied steadily. 'I can't make up your mind for you. Let me know tomorrow or the next day. By Friday at the latest. That's long enough, surely? I'm not being unfair?'

Caroline paused before nodding. 'OK, by Friday. I promise.'

She gave a small smile and Esme felt a faint quiver of hope in her breast, like the flutterings of a baby bird. There was very little that she wouldn't do for Caroline. She would lay down her life for her, but she wouldn't beg or grovel. If Caroline were to choose her, she must do so freely and gladly.

Having finally spoken, she felt lighter, almost insubstantial, as if the wind might blow her down the street just like that

paper bag. Could she suppress the dread of possible rejec
for a day or two? She must, or it could spoil everything.

'Is the village how you imagined?' she asked, attemptin
row back to shore.

'Oh yes,' Caroline replied. 'But even lovelier.'

They decided to have a drink at the Lobster Pot; it was
early for lunch. They chatted for a while with the landla
Barbara. There was only one other customer – an elder
man in the corner, sipping a pint of beer and reading
newspaper – so she had plenty of time. She was in red lipstic
gold earrings and a sparkly low-cut black top that showed o
her impressive bosom, while her chin-length blonde hair w
so heavily lacquered it didn't move.

'It's so cosy in here!' Caroline commented, admirin
the low oak-beamed ceilings, the large fireplace and
uneven floorboards half-worn with use. The walls, simply
whitewashed, were adorned with old photographs of former
village residents and classic fishing scenes – a reminder of
how Tremarnock must once have been.

Barbara explained that the pub was a Grade II listed building
that had changed little since it was built in the seventeenth
century, when it was a favourite haunt of smugglers.

'The kitchen's been renovated since, mind,' she added wi
a grin, 'but that's about it.'

She was keen to offer them something to nibble on – so
potted shrimps, perhaps, or her famous thick-cut chips
some garlic mayonnaise – but Caroline refused.

'We just had breakfast, and we've a table booked
restaurant tonight, haven't we?' She glanced at Esme
nodded. 'We'd better not eat too much now.'

The 'we' seemed to reverberate around the room. Th
a pause while Barbara looked from one woman to th

Something crossed her features – a flash of clarity, perhaps, as if she were observing the same view from a slightly different angle and all at once the picture made sense. She inhaled sharply before breaking into a wide open smile, and Esme felt a new and unfamiliar kind of warmth spread through her. So this, she thought wonderingly, was how it felt to be accepted.

'Lucky you! I'm working again tonight,' Barbara said, unaware of the significance of what had just passed. 'No rest for the wicked!'

'Bad luck.' Esme fiddled with a beer mat on the table, anxious not to give herself away.

It was chilly when they left the pub and she pushed the wheelchair as swiftly as she could along cobbled Fore Street. The Hole in the Wall pub was open and she said hello to Danny, the landlord, through the open door.

Caroline was keen to see the encampment, so they went on up the hill. All the while, Esme found herself going over and over their conversation on the seafront, wondering where she'd found the courage to speak up and what the outcome would be. Had she done the right thing? There had been a certain sense of security in the old, familiar way of life and now she felt afraid, as if she were standing on the prow of a ship facing a gigantic wave. Would the vessel make it safely over the top, or be engulfed?

At last they reached the entrance to the campsite and paused for a moment, taking in the large number of tents and noticing how settled everyone seemed, as if they'd been there years. Children's toys were strewn about the place, washing was drying on makeshift lines and someone had put fresh flowers in a vase on the long refectory-style table in the middle of the field.

The largest dwelling was a white marquee with plastic windows, but the door was zipped firmly shut and there was no evidence of an inhabitant. A little further off, peeping out of a bushy round oak tree, was Loveday's and Jesse's rather magnificent treehouse.

'Where's everyone gone?' Caroline asked, for despite all the equipment, the place seemed deserted.

'Mostly at work, I suppose,' replied Esme. 'You'd think there'd be someone here just to keep an eye on the stuff.'

At that moment, a blonde head popped out of a small green tent to the right of the children's slide and waved at the two women. It was Bramble. Soon the rest of her emerged, and she padded in bare feet across the grass towards them. She looked a little odd in a voluminous white garment with big sleeves and a frilly collar.

'You've caught me in my nightie!' she explained sheepishly, as soon as she was close enough. 'I've only just woken up. I had a dreadful night because my blow-up bed had a puncture. As soon as Matt left for work I rolled over onto his and went back to sleep.'

'Oh, you poor thing!' said Caroline, with a laugh, before complimenting her on the nightdress. 'What an amazing garment!'

On closer inspection, she could see that it was made of fine cotton with subtle embroidery on the bodice and tiny shell buttons.

'I found it in a chest of drawers in one of the guest bedrooms at the manor,' Bramble told them. 'The whole place is stuffed with treasures. If I'd known you were coming, I'd have put on my grandfather's plus fours.'

Caroline laughed again and soon Esme was half-pushing, half-dragging her in her wheelchair across the muddy field towards Bramble's tent, where she quickly produced two fold-up chairs before proceeding to boil the kettle on a small Primus stove.

The sound of voices soon brought out some other villagers, too, including Jean's husband Tom, who claimed that he'd been in his tent all this time learning Russian vocabulary for his night class. It seemed pretty unlikely, though. His face was crumpled and his eyes were suspiciously bleary; he looked for all the world as if he'd been enjoying an unscheduled nap.

Annie's story was more plausible. She said that she had been meditating in preparation for her yoga class this afternoon, and her purple Lycra leggings and black sweatshirt seemed to bear this out. Two tight blonde plaits stuck out on either side of her head and under one arm was a pale blue yoga mat, which she spread on the grass, motioning to Tom to come and sit beside her.

Soon the five were drinking tea, chatting and laughing like old friends, and Esme could tell that Caroline was enchanted.

'You've managed to get yourselves so organised in such a short space of time,' she said, glancing around at all the evidence of a community, albeit an unconventional one. 'I hope you succeed in your mission.'

Annie, in the lotus position and with her hands clasped behind her back, proceeded to bend forward, stretching her arms over her head.

'We're a pretty good team,' she agreed, before exhaling loudly. As she did so, her body and limbs visibly lengthened by at least a couple of inches; soon, her nose was practically scraping the ground. 'Not everyone gels, but on the whole, we work great together.'

Caroline, who had been watching the young woman's contortions with fascination, exclaimed, 'I wish I was bendy like that!'

'It just takes practice,' Annie insisted, taking two more deep breaths before rising up and shaking out her arms. 'Anyone can do it. I can teach you, if you want.' She glanced at Caroline's boot. 'When your leg's better, of course.'

'I'd really like that.'

'How long are you going to be here?'

It seemed like an obvious question after what had gone before, but Caroline appeared confused, glancing from one face to another and then back again, as if searching for the right answer.

'Caroline?' Esme said softly, because everyone was waiting and her friend's eyes had started to glaze over.

'Sorry,' she said, jolting herself awake, 'I was a million miles away. The truth is...' She hesitated once more, frowning, and Tom coughed to fill the awkward silence while Esme's senses crackled. 'The truth is... I really don't know...'

Chapter Eleven

ALMOST AS SOON as they arrived back at Esme's flat, the phone rang. It was Philip again. This time, she passed the receiver across without speaking and went to hang her coat on the wooden stand near the door. She was so angry with him for hassling Caroline that she feared what might come out of her mouth.

'I'm sorry about that,' she heard Caroline say, and, 'So, are they going to change your meds?'

Esme didn't catch his response but was buoyed by the fact that she could, perhaps, detect something a little different in Caroline's tone this time – a firmer, calmer quality; but she might have been imagining it.

To distract herself, she made sandwiches for lunch. Before long, Caroline finished the call and disappeared into her bedroom, re-emerging shortly after with a well-thumbed paperback.

'It's for you,' she said, passing it to Esme. She settled on the sofa and took a sandwich from the plate that Esme had set on the little table in front of her. 'I've finished it now. I'd like you to have it. It's about the legend of the Lost Lady of Tremarnock. I think you'll find it interesting.'

Esme glanced at the illustration on the cover of a beautiful young woman in a forest with a tumbling waterfall behind. She was wearing a flowing green dress and had long red hair; her pale, slender arms were outspread, and in one hand she was holding a leafy green branch while from the other, she appeared to be releasing a brilliantly coloured butterfly.

'It's Tremanthia,' Caroline explained. 'The branch, part of an evergreen tree, represents strength, healing and harmony, and the butterfly is a Celtic symbol of rebirth. That's the purifying water behind, look.' She pointed to the cascade. 'The writer describes the spot in Tremarnock where the shrine is supposed to have been.'

Esme smiled. It was a lovely image, for sure. 'I have a feeling if anything was still there it would have been discovered by now.' She glanced at the blurb on the back. 'But I'll certainly read it. Thank you.'

Taking a sandwich herself, she nibbled on the corner before broaching the subject of Philip. 'What did he say?'

'He had a nasty turn a couple of hours ago. He said he couldn't move – it was as if his feet were stuck to the floor. Apparently they're called "freezing episodes" and he's afraid it's a sign his Parkinson's is getting worse. Luckily it was over quite quickly, but he had a terrible fright. He went to the doctor straight away.'

'So what did *you* say?' Esme asked, eyeing her friend.

'Nothing much. I just asked about the consultation.'

'Good.' Esme nodded, relieved. 'Leave it to the experts. You mustn't worry. It's not your responsibility, you know.'

'You're right,' said Caroline, sighing. But after they'd eaten, she decided to go to her room for a lie-down, and Esme was sure that behind closed doors she would be trawling the internet for information, trying to gain a better understanding of what the episode meant and what could be done.

Feeling restless and uneasy, Esme kicked off her shoes, settled into her favourite armchair by the fireplace and opened the book that Caroline had given her. She'd never been much interested in the Celts and didn't think the writing would hold her attention, but it was fresh and accessible; to her surprise, she was soon drawn in.

There was more, it seemed, to Tremanthia than Esme had realised. According to legend, which had been passed down the generations by word of mouth, she was the daughter of a beautiful peasant girl who had fallen in love with the local cowherd. They wanted to marry but the girl's father forbade it, thinking that he could barter her for a tidy sum to some wealthy landowner instead.

When the girl became pregnant, he was so enraged that he resolved to dash her brains against the rocks and throw her into the Cornish sea. In desperation she prayed to Kerensa, the goddess of love, who took pity on her and promised to help. But the father was too quick; when Kerensa arrived at the cliffs, the girl was already dead. Before he could throw her body into the ocean, however, the goddess killed him, too. She then cut the child, still living, from her mother's womb and took her away to raise as her own.

Thanks to her proximity to the great gods and goddesses, Tremanthia, though human, developed special powers. Aware of the terrible tragedy that had befallen her mother, when she grew up she dedicated her life to healing rifts, spreading harmony and in particular to helping all the women and girls of Cornwall. She also created a magical waterfall especially for the Cornish people that would wash away all their troubles and give them new life. She deliberately placed it in a very secret place, however, so that only a select, handpicked few would be able to find it. According to folklore, thousands of despairing souls tramped the fields and moors in search of the precious water, to no avail; some even died in the attempt. But a small number, whom Tremanthia favoured, found the sacred cascade, plunged in the water and returned to their homes happy, healthy and transformed. Esme read on:

One such was an old woman named Jowanet who had lost three husbands. All six of her offspring had died at birth. Full of despair when the final child passed away, she set off to find the waterfall, mocked and sneered at by the villagers who said she wouldn't survive so much as one night on her own. But the goddess Tremanthia looked kindly on Jowanet, who had led a blameless life and whose husbands and children had died through no fault of her own. She led the woman to the waterfall, where she bathed in the water and was transformed.

Some time later, she returned to the village and no one recognised her, because she was now a beautiful young woman with long golden hair, strong limbs and the voice of an angel. When they heard her singing, all the young men of the village wanted to marry her, including an arrogant shepherd named Hedrok, who had slain his own sister and mother, also a widow, because they were starving and had stolen his bread.

He begged for Jowanet's hand but she refused, knowing what he had done. Finally, when he would not give up, she grew angry and summoned the villagers to the marketplace. There, she stood on the trunk of an evergreen tree and shouted so that all could hear, 'Do you not recognise me, Hedrok?' And the shepherd said, 'No.' Then she told the crowd that she was the old woman, Jowanet, who had buried three husbands and six children and that she had been reborn, thanks to the goddess Tremanthia.

The crowd were amazed. Hedrok got down on his knees and swore that he would be a faithful husband and would never beat her if she would grant him his dearest wish and become his wife, but Jowanet was unmoved.

'Tremanthia has spoken to me,' she said. 'She has decreed that I shall be her handmaiden and dedicate the rest of my days to helping womankind. Never again shall I take a husband or give birth to a child of my own, but my joy will be to assist young women who have fallen in love, to watch the offspring of their unions enter this world and see to it that the mothers do not suffer, as Tremanthia's did. All these children will be my sons and daughters. I shall be known as the mother of the village, and Tremanthia will be my guide.'

Then she pointed a slender white finger at the shepherd Hedrok, who trembled in fear. 'You, who dealt so cruelly with your sister and mother – you, too, shall not marry. Instead, you shall go from this village and travel far and wide, using your skills as a shepherd to bring enemies together and guide them in the ways of understanding and peace. You are to tell them also of the power of Tremanthia, protector of women. Tell them that she is watching and that if they beat their wives or kill their mothers or tear their sisters from the arms of their lovers and force them to marry against their wishes, then Tremanthia will wreak a terrible vengeance. They will never find contentment in this life, nor the next.'

After that, the book said, it became customary for Cornishwomen to give each other twigs from evergreen trees as good luck gifts. Young girls thwarted in love would also douse themselves in running water in the hope that it might come from Tremanthia's magic cascade, and that she would look kindly on their passion and remove the obstacles standing in their way.

The tradition has long since died out, but in some parts of Cornwall today, women still mix evergreen leaves in with their bouquets of fresh flowers – unaware that the tradition started well before the birth of Christ, when folk worshipped the old Celtic gods and goddesses, including Tremanthia.

When she had finished the story, Esme took a deep breath and stared out of her first-floor window at the whitewashed stone cottages opposite. It must have rained while she'd been reading, though she hadn't noticed, because the uneven slate rooftops were always a damp dark grey.

She was touched by the stories of the poor peasant girl, her daughter Tremanthia and then Jowanet, and found herself wishing for the first time that some sort of shrine or waterfall did still exist where troubled women could go to find peace and solitude. When she returned to her pottery studio, she might weave the tale into her designs or make a sculpture of Tremanthia herself.

It was dark by the time she and Caroline set off for A Winkle in Time. Caroline, in the wheelchair, was wrapped in a bright red tasselled woollen shawl that Esme had picked up on her travels in Peru, while she herself wore her long multicoloured coat. Lights were on in quite a few of the cottage windows but the street itself was empty, and Rasputin the cat followed the women a little way before slinking into a doorway. As a kitten, he'd frequently wandered off and got lost, but these days, having settled on his home range, he rarely ventured far.

As they rounded the corner into South Street, they saw Jenny Lambert outside her cottage, about halfway down. Sally, her Jack Russell, was scrabbling at the door and raced inside as soon as Jenny opened it. She didn't notice the two women, and looked eager to get inside. Perhaps she and Sally had camped out last night and were both looking forward to a good meal and an early night in a comfy bed – and who could blame them?

The restaurant looked very welcoming. Candlelight flickered through the leaded front windows; the glass bottles on the shelves behind the bar, entwined with glossy decorative vine leaves, twinkled enticingly. Esme parked the wheelchair by the entrance and Robert himself came to help Caroline. While she hobbled on his arm to the table, Esme folded the wheelchair up and put it in the corner.

Delicious cooking smells wafted from the kitchen at the back, and the occasional raised voice and clattering of plates suggested a mass of activity. In the eating area, however, the atmosphere was calm and relaxing. There were only two other couples in the room, talking quietly, and someone had placed a little vase of fresh freesias on Esme's and Caroline's scrubbed wooden table, along with a white candle in a green bottle whose sides were coated in a waterfall of dribbled wax.

Robert, in a blue and white striped shirt that was open at the collar, handed them each a menu. He was smiling but seemed harassed, running a hand through his messy brown hair; he glanced over his shoulder more than once.

'Where's she gone?' he said, more to himself than anything, before pointing to a blackboard near the bar on which someone had chalked the day's specials – a hot shellfish starter with garlic, olive oil and lemon juice; turbot with artichokes; and John Dory with clams and Mangalitza, which he explained was a type of Hungarian pork. All the fish was locally sourced – what they couldn't obtain from the one bona fide fisherman left in the village they'd buy from the markets of Looe or Plymouth.

'I also recommend the fish stew,' he added. 'Our chef, Alex, makes it with sea bass, coconut, tamarind and chilli. It's quite spicy but delicious. The waitress will take your order.' He glanced over his shoulder again and muttered, 'When she bothers to turn up, that is.'

Esme wasn't in any hurry and, wanting to put him at his ease, she asked about Liz, Rosie and the message in the bottle. She'd seen the article in the *Tremarnock Bugle*, of course, and heard about the piece for German TV. 'Has there been any response yet? It would be fantastic if they could find whoever wrote it.'

At that moment there was a crash in the kitchen and Robert spun around sharply, cursing under his breath. He looked about to leave, but when no one scurried out to find him, he changed his mind.

'I don't know what the hell's going on in there,' he said, returning to the women. 'They've got butter fingers. Must be lack of sleep.' He shifted from one foot to another and scratched his head. 'Sorry, what did you just say?'

'The message in the bottle,' Esme repeated patiently. 'Has anyone got in contact about the German prisoner of war?'

Robert shrugged. 'I don't think so... I don't know.' He fixed on Esme with his hazel eyes. 'This protest, the campsite – it's a bloody nightmare, don't you think?'

She raised her brows. 'I'm in favour, to be honest. I admire everyone for taking a stand. If it weren't for Caroline's injury, I'd be camping out myself.'

It wasn't what he wanted to hear. 'They're all obsessed. Can't seem to think about anything else. The whole village is falling apart.'

Esme peered at him over the top of her glasses. She'd never seen him so out of sorts, and it reminded her of the conversation that she'd had with Liz on the morning she'd left for St Ives. She'd been distracted and hadn't been listening properly, but she did recall that Liz had seemed quite concerned that her husband was working too hard and not seeing enough of his family.

'How's the new project coming along?' she asked, fake-innocently. 'Are you going ahead with the beach café?'

'No thanks to that lot, though,' he replied, nodding. Then, tipping his head in the direction of the kitchen to indicate his staff, he added, 'They're far too busy sitting round campfires and climbing trees.'

Esme was about to say something to cheer him up when a young woman flew into the restaurant, wobbling precariously on high heels with her black hair tied in two strange upside-down braid pigtails, fastened with pink ribbons: Loveday. The white foundation on her face contrasted sharply with her dark eyes, which were rimmed with thick black kohl, and she was wearing a very tight black top with a gold zip down the front that was open to the cleavage, along with big gold hoop earrings.

'Sorry I'm late!' she cried, flinging her arms around Robert, who staggered slightly before righting himself. 'I couldn't find my shoes.' She raised a foot to show off a pair of purple platforms. 'It's hard to see in the treehouse when it's dark. I've told Jesse we need electricity. Bramble said I could have some of her old chandeliers if we get a generator. I might move in permanently.'

'Not if you want to keep your job,' Robert snapped. 'Waitressing and living in treehouses don't mix.' He tapped his watch. 'You're an hour and a half late!'

She stuck out her bottom lip. 'Aww, sorry, Uncle Robert. Don't be cross.' Then, straightening her mini skirt, she smiled sweetly at Esme and Caroline. 'I'll just pop my bag in the cloakroom then I'll come and take your order.'

While she disappeared, Robert went to get the drinks, leaving Esme and Caroline alone. They were sitting directly opposite one another with the candle to one side, and suddenly the room seemed to go very quiet. Esme felt shy, and a little afraid. It wasn't as if they hadn't eaten in restaurants together before, but this felt different. Words had been spoken that couldn't be unsaid and there was a new layer of meaning between them, coupled with a sense of rawness and urgency.

'Are you all right?' Caroline whispered, leaning forward; clearly she could feel it, too.

Esme attempted a smile, but the corners of her mouth wouldn't go up. She felt foolish and gauche, like a teenager. Perhaps they shouldn't have come.

It was a relief when the bottle of wine arrived with a small bowl of olives, and then again when Loveday bustled back with a notepad and pen. Neither woman seemed to know what to talk about so they discussed the menu, the weather, Tremarnock Resists and the message in a bottle – anything except the subject of themselves.

Caroline, though pretty in a pale blue top and the topaz necklace, looked pale and fragile, Esme thought; the skin around her eyes was paper-thin, almost translucent. Was she worrying about Philip and Helen, or trying to analyse her feelings for Esme? Who knew?

In any case, neither of them seemed hungry. When the first course arrived, Caroline picked at her salad while Esme pushed her scallops around the plate. So busy was she trying to disguise her awkwardness that she barely noticed Liz turn up with a pile of freshly laundered tea towels and black and white checked overalls for the staff, which she proceeded to place in a drawer in the large mahogany sideboard near the door.

She noticed Esme and Caroline, however, and strolled over when she'd finished to say hello. She was wearing jeans, black plimsolls and a green parka coat with a fur hood that almost swamped her small frame, and her dark hair was tied back in a ponytail.

'I hope they're looking after you,' she said, smiling.

Esme nodded. 'I hear the Secret Shack is going ahead?'

She glanced furtively at Liz, who pulled a face. 'Worst luck.'

'I don't suppose it'll take up so much of Robert's time once it's up and running.'

Liz snorted. 'Don't you believe it.'

'Oh dear.' Esme felt troubled. She'd watched Liz's and Robert's slow, tentative courtship – it had taken him ages to pluck up the courage to ask her out, and then everything had stalled when Rosie had fallen so ill. The whole village had breathed a sigh of relief when they'd finally got together again, and Esme had been particularly thrilled. She of all people knew how unhappy Liz had been, given that she'd been living in the flat below. Her marriage to Robert had seemed like the perfect fairytale ending, and Esme couldn't bear to think that they might be having problems.

'Couldn't you persuade him to have a weekend away with you somewhere nice?' she suggested. 'Or just go out for dinner? I'll happily have Lowenna.'

Liz frowned. 'That's really kind, thank you, but I know for a fact he'd say no.'

'Well, if you want my help, you only have to ask...'

They changed the subject and after enquiring about Caroline's ankle, Liz perked up and told them that she had some amazing news. 'You'll never guess what!'

Esme dabbed her mouth with her napkin. 'Go on then, spill the beans.'

Liz explained that she had just received a call from her German reporter friend to say that someone had been in touch with the TV station about Franz Maier. 'He says he's the grandson. He's going to email me and Rosie.'

'How wonderful!'

Caroline had heard the whole story and was agog, too. 'You must tell us what he says.' Then she frowned. 'You should be a bit careful. How will you know he's telling the truth?'

Liz assured her that the TV station had carried out some checks and it was all quite legitimate. 'Anyway, we'll wait and see what he says.' She hugged herself tightly. 'I can't quite believe it! Rosie's excited, too.' Noticing the women's unfinished food all of a sudden, she apologised for keeping them. 'I just had to tell someone, and you're the first people I've seen – after Rosie, of course. I can't find Rick and he's not answering his phone.'

'You must tell Robert,' Esme said quickly. 'He's around somewhere.'

But Liz shook her head. 'He's busy and anyway, I need to get back to the girls.'

Esme watched Liz leave the restaurant and hurry past the window, glancing around just once to give a small wave. In the past, Robert would have been the first person she'd have wanted to tell; but with luck, this new distance between them would only be temporary.

The women had to wait ages for their second course, and before Loveday could even put the plates on the table, Robert emerged from the kitchen with a face like thunder and wrestled them off her.

'I told Jesse not to bring them out before I'd checked the sauce,' he barked, before turning to the women with the plates still in his hands. 'Sorry, I'll just be a moment…' Then he vanished back into the kitchen while Loveday, open-mouthed, stared after him.

'Honestly, I don't know what's got into him. He's in a foul mood all the time. D'you think it's the male menopause?'

Esme laughed; she couldn't help it. 'Is there such a thing?'

'Women get it, so I don't see why men shouldn't too,' the girl replied, huffily. 'Anyway, he's a pain in the arse. I don't know how Liz can stand him.'

She went off to collect their dishes, but Robert didn't appear again until a youngish couple arrived and settled at a nearby table. They seemed enchanted by the restaurant, pointing things out to each other and making appreciative comments in accents that Esme couldn't place.

They ate, but picked at their food; and when Loveday came to collect their plates, she was dismayed to find that they'd left so much.

'What was the matter with it?' She looked quite cross.

Esme explained that they just weren't very hungry. 'It was all delicious, though,' she added quickly, hoping to smooth the girl's ruffled feathers. She was quite capable of holding a grudge for weeks.

The women didn't want pudding, but stayed a little longer to finish their wine. While Caroline settled the bill, Esme's mind wandered off again and her thoughts turned dark and bleak. It occurred to her that her friend might already have resolved to go back to Paris, having realised in just this short space of time that her feelings for Esme weren't as strong as she'd imagined, and that Philip exerted a stronger pull.

She was still reflecting on this as she pushed the wheelchair back to the flat; when Caroline mentioned that she didn't like Robert, she let the criticism pass rather than defend him.

On arriving home, she fully expected Caroline to go to bed, but she said she wasn't tired. 'Can we talk for a bit?'

While Esme fetched another bottle of wine and two glasses, Caroline dimmed the lights and managed to hobble around the room lighting scented candles, which illuminated the rich, iridescent colours of the soft cushions and thickly patterned throws and rugs.

'I feel sad tonight,' she said, taking her glass.

Esme sat beside her on the sofa. 'Why's that?'

'Oh, I don't know.' Caroline took a sip of wine and winced as if it hurt to swallow.

Esme understood for she, too, felt a pain somewhere, most probably in her heart. 'Try to explain – please.'

Setting her glass on the table beside her, Caroline pulled up her good leg, resting her chin on her knee.

'I just feel...' She paused.

'Yes?'

'I feel sorry for the person I could have been. All these lost years, all that pretending to be someone I wasn't. And for what?' A tear trickled down her cheek that she brushed away with the back of her hand. 'For a sham marriage based on nothing but deceit. It turns out we're both liars.' She laughed humourlessly. 'What a mess! I feel like my whole life has been one big failure.'

'That's not true! You mustn't say it!' Esme couldn't bear to see her friend like this. 'Think of Helen and Andrew and the good years you had with Philip. Think of the travelling you've done, and your work – and his. You rarely talk about your job, as if it doesn't matter because it's only part-time. But it's quite something to be an English language lecturer; I bet your students love you. You've achieved so much. You can't ignore the positives. It hasn't all been bad.'

'You're missing the point,' said Caroline, smiling sadly. 'You asked me earlier today not to torture you, remember? Well, I've been tortured, too. I play-acted all through my marriage and I'm not even sure I realised it, half the time. I was genuinely fond of Philip once, and I thought that would make everything all right; but it never really did. Deep down, I was terrified of being found out and I didn't even know why, because I didn't understand it properly myself.

'You see, I wouldn't allow myself to think of you, or any woman, for that matter – not in that way. I worked so hard to blot the feelings out. I'd swim a hundred lengths then go home to cook dinner for ten. That's the sort of person I was. Everyone told me I was incredible and all the time I felt like such a fraud.'

She shook her head, indicating that she couldn't continue, and Esme rose to fetch a box of tissues. When she returned, she sat close to her friend and put an arm around her shoulders, hugging her close to absorb the shudders and whispering comforting words: 'There, there… you just let it all out… that's right… it's going to be OK.'

The weeping seemed to come from deep within and went on and on, a build-up of suffering that exploded like boiling water from a geyser. No human power could halt its flow.

When at last it started to lessen and Caroline stopped shaking, she took Esme's hand and placed it on her lap.

'Thank you for listening. I didn't know I had so many tears in me.'

'You needed to cry,' Esme said simply.

There was silence for a few moments, the only sound the ticking of the carriage clock on a shelf near the TV mingled with Caroline's juddering breaths. After a time she leaned over for her glass of wine, but she couldn't quite reach.

She thought better of it, turning instead to look her friend in the eye. 'Do you think...?'

She didn't finish what she was saying because something passed between them, like an electrical charge. Esme felt sick. Caroline must have experienced it, too, because her eyes widened and her mouth uttered a wordless, 'Oh!'

Moving closer and leaning in so that their foreheads were resting against each other, Esme blinked slowly several times. Now her breathing was shaky and shallow too.

Scarcely daring to think, she inched even nearer, brushing her lips lightly against Caroline's, which felt soft and warm. Her friend might pull back at any moment... but she didn't. She just remained there, frozen.

'If you want me to stop, tell me now,' Esme whispered huskily.

Ever so slightly, Caroline's chin tilted up. 'Don't stop.'

It was the sweetest thing that Esme had ever heard. Her world fell away as her hands reached for Caroline's dear, precious, beautiful face. Her thumb caressed her warm cheek and then she kissed her properly, deeply and carefully, and it was slow and comforting, in ways that words could never be. It was solid and grounding: a secret told, a promise kept. It was silver rain falling all around them and a kind of whoosh that meant nothing would ever be the same again.

Chapter Twelve

Dear Mrs Hart,

I would like to introduce myself. My name is Max Maier and I
live in Munich, Bavaria, where I own a publishing company.

LIZ'S HEART PITTER-PATTERED as she scanned the email on
the laptop on the kitchen table in front of her. It was early on
Wednesday morning; Rosie had just left for school and peace
reigned as Lowenna sat happily on the floor, playing with her
toy ponies.

Eagerly, she read on:

I saw the report on television about the bottle your daughter
found on the beach with a message inside, and I believe I can
help.

My grandfather was Franz Maier, who lived in a little village just
outside Munich up until his death in 2007 at the age of eighty-
two. In 1942, aged seventeen, he was conscripted into the German
army as a regular foot soldier. He fought on the Normandy
beaches on D-Day, 6th June 1944, where he was captured by the

Allied forces. Soon after, he was taken to a prisoner-of-war camp near the village of Tremarnock in Cornwall, where he remained until his release in 1946.

He sometimes spoke to me and my siblings of his wartime experiences. You might think his capture would have been the worst time of his life, but in fact it seemed to have been one of the happiest. He was a gentle man who'd never wanted to fight; in fact he hated violence and all that Hitler stood for. He was deeply ashamed of his Nazi associations and wished that he could erase them from his past. When he was seized, far from being angry, he regarded himself as lucky to be alive and safe, unlike so many of his unfortunate peers.

He was put to work in a stone quarry, which he enjoyed because of the camaraderie. He said he was also amazed by the beautiful countryside of Cornwall and the kindness of the local people. He mentioned in particular a little girl with red hair called Pat, short for Patricia, whose family invited him to spend Christmas Day with them. He said Pat was very sweet and funny and he called her 'Little Bear', which is a German form of endearment.

Surprisingly, I think he was actually quite sad to leave Cornwall and return to Bavaria. He said he'd always intended to go back to Tremarnock but was too busy.

Germany was in a terrible state after the war, but he worked hard and became quite successful. He was good with cars and eventually, after some years as a mechanic, he bought his own garage, which still exists today. He married my grandmother, Onika, now also deceased, and they had four children, including my late father, and eight grandchildren. Franz was very much a family man who also loved nature and walking. I think it's fair to say he lived a decent, honest life.

He would have been astonished to know that his message had washed up on the beach all these years later and I, too, am amazed. I wish I knew more of his time in Cornwall and I'm sorry I can't ask him now.

I hope this doesn't sound too presumptuous, but I'd very much like to visit Tremarnock and meet you and your daughter and find out more about Pat. I'm lucky that my time is quite flexible, so I can come whenever suits you.

I've attached a few photos that you might be interested in, including one of my grandfather and grandmother, and of me and my daughter, Mila, who lives with her mother but I see her often.

I look forward to receiving your reply.

Yours very sincerely…

After reading the final line, Liz pushed back her chair and stared out of the window at her smallish back garden. The wind had blown quite a few leaves off the trees and she watched a squirrel bound across the damp grass and bury a nut in one of her plant pots.

She felt excited and rather pleased with herself, although in truth it was thanks to the power of television that Franz, or rather his grandson, had been traced; her own part in it was considerably smaller. Rosie would be thrilled, as would Rick, and she couldn't wait to tell them.

Glancing back at the email, she realised that she hadn't yet scrolled down to the photographs; as she did so, she felt rather as if history were coming alive in front of her. First there was an old black-and-white photo of an attractive young man in a uniform and beret with the Nazi eagle insignia pinned on the front. He had large pale eyes, a full bottom lip and baby-soft cheeks, and wore a troubled, slightly uncertain expression: Franz.

The next picture, in colour, was clearly of the same man but now elderly and stout. This time, he was standing by a house in a checked shirt and brown cardigan, smiling at the camera with his arm around a plump woman with short grey hair. They appeared similar, in the way that long-married couples often do, and as solid and content as the handsome white house behind them with its neat wooden shutters, bulging window boxes and pink roses around the front door.

How Pat would have loved all this! Liz could imagine her now, peering at the photos through her tortoiseshell-rimmed spectacles, commenting on the young Franz's eyes, mouth and nose – 'He was proper nice-looking, he was' – and the older Franz's girth – 'Look at the belly on him! If you ask me, he's been eating too many of them German sausages!'

She would have wanted to write a letter to Max herself in her spidery, old-fashioned handwriting – none of this new-fangled email business for her. And the prospect of actually meeting him – well! She'd have needed a month to get herself ready, never mind preparing her home for the very special visitor.

Remembering what Caroline had said in the restaurant about being careful, Liz scrolled down a little further to the final picture, which was of Max himself with his daughter Mila. It might have been a holiday snap, because the sun was shining and they both looked casual in shorts and colourful tops, sitting side by side on a wall with a pine tree in the foreground and a mountain behind. Their bodies were touching and Mila, with long straight brown hair, was resting her head against her father's shoulder while he held her hand. They looked confident in themselves as well as relaxed and happy in their surroundings.

Max was rather striking, with a close-cropped beard, short dark hair with a few silvery streaks and intense blue eyes. His broad shoulders and wide neck suggested that he was athletic, perhaps a rugby player, while the eyes and mouth reminded Liz of his grandfather's. He was quite tanned, with dark sunglasses on his head, and there was an air of affluence about him despite the informal dress. His pale blue shirt, though creased, was open at the neck and rolled up at the sleeves; it had a discreet little logo on the top right-hand pocket that hinted at exclusivity. With it, he wore sand-coloured chino shorts and brown leather boat shoes, while his daughter was in a pretty red sundress and white sandals. All in all, they were an appealing pair – especially Max, who was probably in his late thirties or early forties.

Liz wondered whether to wait until Rosie was home before replying; they could compose a response together. But the email wasn't addressed to her, only to Liz, and it was so warm and friendly that she couldn't resist writing back immediately. She didn't think Rosie would mind too much; her interest in the message in the bottle seemed to wax and wane depending on what was happening at school and in her social life. Besides, she could always write her own note to Max later if she wanted to.

Liz began by telling him a bit about herself and Rosie: how they'd moved to Tremarnock from London when Rosie was three years old, and how they'd grown to love the village and its people. She also said that Pat was one of the first locals they'd met, and that she'd looked after Rosie in the evenings while Liz worked:

She was like a grandmother to her; she was incredibly kind. She might have been old, but she was full of fun and laughter and Rosie loved her company. Although Pat didn't have any children herself, she had a wonderful rapport with them. She also loved to gossip, but it was harmless.

She was the sort of woman who saw the good in everyone and would do anything for you. She had loads of friends. She was in charge of the flowers at our local church for years and I always went to her for advice or a shoulder to cry on.

I think she'd be thrilled to know Franz had lived a happy life and I wish you could have met her to tell her all about him. In any case, if you come to Tremarnock we can point out where she lived and show you lots of photographs.

She went on to explain a bit about the location of Tremarnock and how to get there by plane or train. Then she mentioned some possible places to stay, ranging from hotels to bed and breakfast establishments, though she imagined that the former might be more his style. She was half-inclined to offer to put him up at Bag End but stopped herself, thinking how little she knew about him. Then she added:

I'd be delighted to show you around the village and introduce you to some of the locals. I can also take you to the site of the old stone quarry where your grandfather worked.

Finally, she attached a few photographs of herself and Rosie, a couple of Pat and one view of the seafront including the harbour.

It was only when she was debating how best to sign off that she realised she hadn't referred to Robert once. It wasn't all that surprising, given that he'd had nothing to do with the search for Franz, but it might seem strange if she didn't even mention him; so she found a nice photo of them together with the girls and added that, too, along with an explanatory line:

My husband Robert, me, Rosie and Lowenna, aged two.

After that, she quickly pressed 'send', because her youngest had disappeared into the next room and gone quiet, which was always a worrying sign.

A sudden gust rattled the windowpanes. When Liz glanced out at the garden once more, her heart sank as she remembered that it was her turn to camp out again. It would be her fourth night under the stars since the protest had begun and although Lowenna, who always came too, had adapted reasonably well, it took her much longer than usual to get to sleep and she'd normally wake at the first sounds of activity. Liz had put her foot down and insisted that Rosie could join them only on weekends.

Like the other villagers, they were gradually accumulating more and more stuff in and around their tent, while Bag End was looking increasingly neglected as the ironing piled up and the pot plants wilted. There was no doubt that the whole place could do with a jolly good clean but Liz tried not to fret, telling herself that the protest would surely be over soon and everything would return to normal.

It was somehow symptomatic of the general state of affairs, however, that when she went to find Lowenna, she was picking the petals off a bunch of dead flowers in the sitting room while bits of broken vase lay scattered around her.

'Oh dear,' said Liz, checking that the little girl wasn't hurt before scooping her up and closing the door swiftly behind them. The culprit was most likely the cat, Mitzi; and the clean-up, like most of the household chores, would have to wait till later.

Back in the kitchen, Lowenna pointed a demanding finger at the cereal cupboard and Liz realised that she hadn't yet had breakfast.

'Poor baby,' she said.

She pulled out a box of rice pops and set them on the table, along with some milk and a bowl and spoon, only to discover that there was hardly any cereal left. What's more, the orange juice had run out, there was just a small knob of butter left in the dish and as for honey to go on the toast – no chance.

Liz sighed. A big shop was well overdue, but she'd been planning to find Rick to tell him about Max's email and call Charlie-the-reporter, who'd asked to be kept fully informed. The children couldn't live on thin air, however, and Rosie especially would need a good meal this evening when she came in from school.

Resolving to find Rick later, Liz spoon-fed Lowenna the remains of the cereal before strapping her in the car and setting off for the supermarket about twenty minutes away, armed with a long list of groceries and a thermos of coffee for herself for the journey.

'We'll buy oranges, apples and kiwis,' she said to her daughter in the back seat, hoping that the promise of fresh fruit salad for lunch would keep her sweet. Lowenna loathed supermarkets and was perfectly capable of making the trip an absolute misery if she so desired.

Fortunately, the shop wasn't crowded and they managed to zoom up and down the aisles at record speed. It was only when they reached the checkout that Liz discovered several items in the trolley that had been sneaked in when she wasn't looking. It was too late to put them back now, though, so the chocolate biscuits, sugar-laden cereal and tooth-rotting juice drinks went in the boot of the car along with the other groceries.

By the time she'd unloaded and put everything away, several hours had passed and Lowenna was getting scratchy. After a lunch of scrambled eggs, the little girl settled down for an afternoon nap and Liz breathed a sigh of relief; she was itching to get back to her laptop.

On opening it up, she was surprised and delighted to find another email from Max. So soon! She'd imagined that she might have to wait another day, at least. Quickly, she scanned the contents and her eyes widened as the information sank in.

Dear Liz,

He used her first name this time, which pleased her.

My daughter often tells me off for being an impulsive person, and guess what? I've taken the liberty of booking my flight to Cornwall. I'll arrive at Newquay airport via London Gatwick at 14.05 on Friday, returning at the same time on Sunday afternoon.

I'll be staying at a cottage in the village owned by a lady named
Audrey Chatterton...

Liz grimaced. Bloody woman! She'd forgotten that Audrey
offered bed and breakfast and could imagine her sniffing
around already, trying to find out as much as she could about
the German stranger. For some reason, Liz felt strangely
proprietorial; he was hers and Rosie's contact, this was their
story, and Audrey had better back off.

But still – this weekend! He'd be here in just two days! Her
stomach fluttered as she read on.

I hope this is convenient for you and your husband, but if you
have prior arrangements, I'm perfectly happy to look after
myself. I've been working very hard recently and I fancy a
weekend away. Mila will be with her mother so I'm free as air. I
shall bring a map, a guidebook and my walking boots and I look
forward to exploring the area...

Liz's mind started racing. Robert would probably be working,
but she herself had nothing planned; nor, as far as she knew,
had Rosie. There was no way they'd be leaving Max to
explore on his own – they'd be his very willing guides. She
could hardly wait to start planning the schedule.

She wrote back, offering to pick him up at the airport, and
told him to bring warm clothes and wet weather gear, just in
case. Then she finished with:

I'm sure Charlie, our local newspaper reporter, will want
to interview you – I hope that's all right. You'll be quite a
celebrity round here. I hope you don't get fed up with all the
attention!'

As she prepared chicken casserole for supper, she made a mental itinerary. She wanted to give Max the full-on Cornish experience, including a coastal walk, at least one pub lunch, a cream tea and, of course, a pasty or two.

He'd want to meet Rick, and if possible Pat's oldest friend, Elaine, who had known Pat since she was a girl and had spoken at her funeral. Elaine was very elderly but had all her marbles, and it was quite likely that Pat would have told her about Franz. Who knew? She might even have met him.

Another must was a visit to the old stone quarry in Mengleudh, which was now a boatyard; and the site of the Nissen huts on the cliff, one of which still survived today and had been turned into a café with a difference. The truth was with only two days, there simply wouldn't be enough time to do everything. It was a good job, really, that Robert would be busy, as it meant that there would be one less person to consider when it came to the preparations.

Rosie was surprised and a little irritated when she returned from school and read the email correspondence; she said that Liz should have waited before replying. But then she conceded that it was best for her to make the arrangements. Rosie wouldn't have had time to do it and besides, Max was an adult and she might have felt shy writing to him herself.

Excitement took over and she had to call Rafael, even though she'd been with him on the bus only moments before. Then she, Liz and Lowenna walked to Rick's shop, from where they telephoned Charlie-the-reporter.

'I'll ask the news desk if I can accompany you on the visits,' said Charlie, on the other end of the line. 'It'll make a fantastic colour piece.'

Now, it was Liz's turn to feel a twinge of annoyance. Charlie's presence would undoubtedly change the dynamic, but she was a nice girl, if a little pushy, and it was thanks to her that they'd found Max in the first place.

'Of course,' she replied, but she was a little relieved when Charlie said that she wouldn't be able to make it to the airport to collect him as she had an important interview lined up. 'I'll join you with the photographer once I'm done,' she went on, adding, 'don't mention this to the German TV people yet, OK? I want the exclusive. They won't mind, they can do the follow-up. They'll be none the wiser.'

As soon as she'd finished supper, Rosie vanished upstairs to do her homework while Lowenna had her bath. Liz put her in her warmest pyjamas; it was dark outside now, and the prospect of camping was even less appealing. But they'd made a promise and they'd stick to it. At least it wasn't raining, and they could hurry home in the morning for breakfast and a hot shower.

As Liz popped Lowenna into her stroller and pushed her out of the front door, the little girl squealed with delight. It seemed she couldn't believe her luck – instead of heading for her cot, they were off on another adventure. The lights were on in most of the cottages, and plumes of smoked billowed temptingly from the chimneypots. Liz would have loved to light her own fire in the front room and settle down in front of the TV, but tried to wipe the thought from her mind.

Although it wasn't cold, she was wearing several layers beneath her thick fleece and tracksuit bottoms, and had brought filled hot-water bottles for herself and Lowenna to warm their sleeping bags.

'Moon!' said Lowenna, pointing in awe at the perfect silver crescent smiling down at them from the velvety black sky.

A dog barked in the distance and the sound bounced eerily off the cobbles, then echoed around the old stone walls.

'Can you see the man in the moon?' asked Liz, trying to be cheery.

Fortunately, there was plenty of activity at the campsite, with some folk huddling around a burning brazier in the centre of the field while others bent over gas stoves and portable barbecues. The smell of cooking sausages hung in the air. Loveday and Jesse had strung dozens of multicoloured fairy lights around their oak tree, which dazzled like Blackpool Tower, and Audrey's marquee was so bright that you could probably spot it from space.

As they came closer, Liz could hear guitar music and recognised the sweet, husky voice of her friend Tabitha, a former nightclub singer; but it wasn't until a few people moved away from the brazier that she could see her perched on a stool, her guitar resting on one knee and her jet-black hair fanning out around her face, which glowed mysteriously in the firelight.

The ground was slightly damp and the grass quite high, so to Liz's annoyance, the wheels of the pushchair got stuck in the mud. Thankfully, two strong young men quickly raced over to help, lifting Lowenna and stroller aloft as if they weighed absolutely nothing and depositing them in front of Liz's tent, where they unzipped the door and helped light her electric lanterns.

After her first terrible night, she had splashed out on high-rise airbeds which were superbly comfortable, and she was relieved that it looked quite cosy in there, with pillows, tartan blankets and sleeping bags, into which she popped the filled hot-water bottles.

There was no way that Lowenna would sleep for a while, so Liz grabbed a portable chair and took her over to the brazier, where her brown eyes grew to the size of dinner plates as she gazed around the assembled crowd. Some, in woolly hats and scarves, were just warming their hands, while others sang along heartily to a variety of well-known folk songs: 'All Around My Hat', 'Early One Morning' and 'Greensleeves'.

During a lull, when Tabitha needed a break and a mug of tea, Bramble and Matt updated Liz on where they were at with the local council and the developers. Just a few hours previously Reg Carter and Sgt Kent had been down to the campsite to deliver a threatening letter. The council would, it said, go to court and get an injunction unless the squatters were out first thing Monday morning.

However Barbara, who was pretty savvy, insisted that having spoken to a lawyer friend, she was pretty certain that it was just scare tactics. The fact was that legal action would cost a good deal of money and take ages so the council was probably hoping to frighten them off instead.

'In any case, my friend insists we've got time on our side. They'll try every other method they can before they get the law involved. I reckon we should hold onto our hats and sit tight.'

'I hope they don't come in the dead of night and squish us with their bulldozers,' commented Loveday, who had been listening in. She and her friend, Annie-the-fitness-trainer, were wrapped in a pink fluffy blanket so that they looked rather like a double-headed monster with four bright red cheeks heated up by the flames.

Barbara assured her that this wouldn't happen; and when Tabitha took up her guitar again and sang 'Green Grow the Rushes, O', Loveday celebrated by throwing off her blanket, grabbing Lowenna by the hands and dancing around in a circle until the little girl was quite giddy and had to sit down.

Shortly after, a well-wisher from one of the surrounding villages arrived with plastic cups and two giant flasks full of hot chocolate – enough for everyone. Of course Lowenna poured hers down her front immediately, but luckily Liz had brought a spare set of pyjamas in a backpack, just in case.

It was well after 11 p.m. when she finally carried her daughter, now drugged with sleep, back to their tent and slipped her into her sleeping bag before climbing into her own. She was about to close her eyes when the mobile buzzed in her pocket. She got up again and tiptoed outside to answer, not wanting to waken Lowenna.

'Where are you?' Robert sounded quite cross; he'd clearly forgotten that she wouldn't be home tonight. 'I suppose Loveday's there again, too? Tell her she's on duty at midday tomorrow. She'd better have a proper wash this time or I'll send her home without her wages.'

It was nonsense, of course. He was a soft touch where Loveday was concerned and would never dock her pay. Liz promised to remind her all the same, but Robert was off on a rant again and didn't hear.

'Ryan didn't gut the fish properly before he delivered it this morning, so Jesse had to do it again. It made everything late and he was so tired this evening I thought he was going to fall asleep in the kitchen. I told him to get some proper rest, but he said he'd promised to stay with Loveday again in that bloody stupid treehouse. Sometimes I feel like shutting the restaurant for good and throwing away the key.'

Liz listened patiently until he'd finished. There was no point trying to argue with him in this frame of mind; he just needed to get it off his chest. When he'd run out of steam at last, she whispered that she'd be in tomorrow night and suggested an early family meal before he set off again for A Winkle in Time at around six.

'No chance,' he snapped, sounding for all the world as if she'd asked him to unblock the drains or fix the loo. 'I'm getting the keys to the Secret Shack after lunch, then I'm meeting Gavin over there with his team.'

Liz started. 'I thought you weren't completing till Friday!'

'They brought the day forward.'

'And you've definitely decided to ask Gavin to do the job?'

'He seems efficient and the price is right, so yes. All being well, he'll start on Monday.'

Liz swallowed. She'd already resigned herself to the fact that this was going to happen, but it hadn't felt properly real until now. She knew that it was the wrong time to mention Max, but for some reason the words slipped from her mouth before she could stop them.

'We've found Rosie's German PoW. Well, he's dead now, but his grandson's coming to Tremarnock at the weekend.'

There was a pause before Robert said more softly, 'That's great! I bet Rosie's excited. It's a shame I'll be busy most of Saturday and Sunday. I've got a ton of stuff to catch up on.'

This wasn't exactly a surprise, but there was genuine regret in his voice, as if he'd suddenly remembered that there was life outside work and he missed being part of it. Still, Liz felt anger and disappointment bubble up inside.

'Why don't you bring him to the restaurant to eat? I can meet him then,' Robert suggested.

Liz shook her head. 'That won't be possible. We'll be very busy, too.'

After a curt goodbye, she crept back into the tent but found she couldn't sleep; she lay there instead with her eyes closed, listening to Lowenna's slow, steady breathing and the occasional hoot of an owl in the distance as it went about its night-time excursions. She thought about her first impressions of Robert when she'd gone to waitress for him at the restaurant. He'd seemed so awkward and harassed, one of life's loners, with a way of avoiding eye contact that had made her think he didn't like her much – or anyone else, come to that.

Then Loveday had revealed that his fiancée had called off their wedding days before it had been due to take place, which had given Liz a different perspective. Little by little, as she'd started to be kinder to him, his barriers had come down, and eventually she'd learned to love him for the generous, loyal, sexy and big-hearted man that he was.

The relationship hadn't progressed smoothly, however. When Rosie's brain tumour had been diagnosed, Liz had been so distraught that she'd been unable to focus on anything else, and had turned her back on him. A lesser man might have been put off, but not Robert. He'd never given up hope, sticking by her through thick and thin, quietly supporting her without expecting anything in return and giving her the strength that she needed to keep going.

Where had all his strength and support gone now? And what about her capacity to sustain and comfort him back? It seemed as if they were operating in a parallel universe, each attending to their own needs and worries with little or no thought for the other. She wanted to shake him; she wanted to wake him up and make him see sense. Couldn't he see that they were in trouble? Didn't he understand that marriages, like flowers, needed sunlight and water to survive?

Lowenna stirred slightly and turned over and Liz held her breath, praying that she wouldn't wake. On the bright side, she thought, there was the weekend to look forward to; with luck, Max would take her mind off her worries and the children would enjoy showing him around, too. It was great that he was fluent in English, and the fact that he was so nice-looking was an added bonus. She wouldn't say that to Robert, though. Best keep it to herself.

Chapter Thirteen

SIPPING ON A large latte in the coffee shop at Newquay airport, Liz watched as a dishy workman strolled in, wearing white overalls and with a newspaper tucked under his arm. The young woman behind the sandwich counter nudged her friend, the barista. The barista, in a black T-shirt with her dark hair tied back in a ponytail, giggled nervously before composing herself. Then, as the man approached, she flashed a simpering smile.

He fiddled with the change in his pocket as he placed his order, seemingly oblivious to the excitement he was causing. Liz smiled. The place was so quiet, she could well imagine that the girls would welcome distractions, especially in the form of a hunky young male.

His coffee ready, the man strolled over to a table, sat down and opened his paper. Liz glanced at the arrivals board for the umpteenth time. Max's flight was due any minute and she was sure that it wouldn't take long to get his bags and pass through security. Fumbling inside her handbag, she took out her peachy-brown lipstick and little mirror, then thought better of it and put them away again. Lipstick wasn't really her thing; she only kept it in there because it had been a birthday present from Rosie. It had hardly been touched.

Still, she hoped that she looked presentable enough. She'd washed and blow-dried her hair this morning and put on a little eye makeup and her favourite gold earrings, which resembled miniature flying swallows. She was wearing jeans and a softly ribbed navy polo neck that seemed to cling in all the right places. Quickly, she ran a comb through her hair and tucked one side behind an ear before glancing at the board again. Her stomach turned over: LANDED.

There was still an inch of coffee in her cup, which she swiftly drained before rising. She called out her thanks to the girls behind the counter, but they were too busy gossiping to notice; grabbing her bag, she wandered over to arrivals.

The airport was so small that it would be hard to miss anyone. Even so, she stayed close to the metal barriers, idly scrolling through Facebook on her phone without taking it in, trying to appear nonchalant.

A message flashed up from her friend, Tabitha:

Is he here yet?

Liz didn't reply. Tabitha was dying to meet Max, like everyone else who knew of his impending visit, but Liz wanted to get to know him a little bit herself first. To that end, she had left Lowenna with Jean for the afternoon, so that she could have a couple of hours with him alone. There would be plenty of time for introductions this evening and tomorrow; in fact it was quite likely that someone would be knocking impatiently on the door the moment she arrived home.

Noticing a smudge on the toe of one of her brown suede Chelsea boots, she bent down to wipe it off. When she stood up again, a small flurry of travellers had started to trickle through the exit. They were mostly men carrying briefcases and overnight bags – returning home from business trips, she guessed. A few wives had joined her by the barriers and one by one, they and their spouses paired off and headed in the direction of the car park.

At other times of year the airport would be humming with holidaymakers, but it was the start of the quiet season now, when Cornwall became a different place. No longer heaving with tourists, the streets were quiet, the beaches almost deserted and locals had the pubs and shops to themselves. Liz loved these months the best, when Tremarnock seemed to come out of its shell and villagers had the chance to linger a little and ask each other how they really *were*.

Three middle-aged women appeared now, pulling neat, brightly coloured wheelie bags. And behind them came a handsome man in a checked shirt and well-worn brown leather jacket with a sheepskin collar, a laptop case slung casually over his shoulder. He was shorter than Liz had imagined, broad and athletic-looking. He glanced left and right before his eyes alighted on her and instantly, her cheeks burst into flame.

Cursing herself, she bent down again to pick something invisible off the floor and give herself a quick talking to. *For goodness' sake, pull yourself together.* Anyone would think she'd never met an attractive man before!

To her relief, by the time she'd straightened up the blush had subsided, and she raised a tentative hand in greeting. Instantly, the man smiled widely back and waved in return.

It was definitely Max, then; not that she'd really been in any doubt. There was no mistaking him from his photograph, and besides, you could tell that he was foreign. His clothes, his bag, even his haircut and neat beard marked him out as slightly different. He didn't look like any of the men from around here and certainly not Robert, who was considerably taller, thinner and frankly more dishevelled.

'Liz!' Max leaned over the barrier and shook her hand. 'Have you come alone?' He glanced around as if expecting her to be in company. 'I thought Rosie might be here and your husband and, um…' He frowned, as if trying to remember something.

Liz stepped in to help. 'Lowenna. It means joy in Cornish.'

'Lowenna,' he repeated, as if testing the word on his lips. 'Of course. It's a lovely name.'

As they strolled to the car, Liz explained that Rosie was in school, Robert was working and Lowenna was with the childminder, but that he'd have the opportunity to meet everyone later. 'At least, I'm not sure about Robert. He's so busy with his restaurant and the new business. Hopefully we'll be able to catch him at some point, though.'

She asked Max about his journey, and he told her that he'd left home early this morning and flown via Gatwick. 'Mila was very upset she couldn't come with me. We've been to London many times, as we have friends there, but I've never taken her to Scotland, Ireland or Wales – or Cornwall, come to that,' he added.

He had a pleasant voice, deep and low, and his English was faultless, although his accent was quite strong. Liz felt rather embarrassed about her own lack of language skills and resolved to learn a few words of German before he left, so that she could at least say goodbye to him in his own tongue.

Once he'd loaded his small suitcase in the boot and climbed in beside her, she talked him through her plans for the weekend, including a visit to the site of the old stone quarry on the way home. 'There's not a lot to see, to be honest, but we can have a walk along the river and you can get a feel for the place. It's only a suggestion,' she added hesitantly. 'I can drop you at your bed and breakfast now, if you prefer?'

'Oh no.' Max was adamant. 'I'd love to see the quarry, or what's left of it. I'm totally in your hands.' He paused. 'It's very kind of you to give up your time like this. I hope I'm not getting in the way?'

Liz assured him that he wasn't, and they chatted a little about Pat and Franz, Max's work, Robert's restaurant and her former venture into business with her hair accessories website. Max was most polite, and seemed to want to know everything about her as well as his surroundings.

All the while they talked, he gazed out of the window, asking about the landmarks they passed and picking her brains about the history, climate, religion and culture of the county: 'Does anyone still speak the Cornish dialect?', 'Who was St Piran?', 'Is the weather really better here than in other parts of the UK?', 'Are there any tin mines left?' and 'What about pirates and smugglers – and what can you tell me about *Poldark*?'

His open, relaxed manner soon put Liz at her ease; it was easy to forget they'd only just met. She even found herself singing, at his request, 'The Song of the Western Men' about the brave Cornish patriot, Squire Trelawney. She'd refused at first, until he'd promised to reciprocate with a Bavarian song, and by the time she reached the final chorus he had it off by heart and was joining in lustily:

'Here's twenty thousand Cornish men
Will know the reason why!'

'Very rousing!' he said, punching the air in mock-heroic fashion before admitting that he couldn't actually remember the words to any Bavarian tunes.

'That's not fair! You lied!'

Max laughed. 'If I'd told the truth, you'd never have agreed to sing "Squire Trelawney".'

At last they saw signs for Mengleudh. Liz pulled into the boatyard car park and stopped the engine. Glancing around at the array of vessels, ranging from small canoes and sailing dinghies up to 200-ton schooners, she hoped that Max wouldn't be disappointed. It was clear from the number of staff around and all the machinery and equipment that this was a busy place, where boats were not only stored but also built, serviced, maintained and upgraded. But there was nothing to indicate that it had once been a quarry.

'Shall we have coffee first?' she suggested, pointing to a wooden hut not far off. 'Then we'll go for a wander.'

Thankfully the sun was shining, though the air was cold; Max zipped up his jacket as they strode side by side across the car park, their feet crunching on the stony ground. His head swivelled left and right as he took in his environs and he was noticeably quiet, perhaps trying to imagine his grandfather here all those years ago in big boots and a rolled-up shirt, his face covered in sweat and grime. Franz must have felt a million miles from home but it wasn't such a bad place to be, really, on the edge of a winding river and surrounded by woods and fields. At least he'd have been close to nature and aware of the passing seasons.

Liz had forgotten until they entered the café that there were a couple of black-and-white photographs on the walls of the quarry in its heyday. Max examined them eagerly while she went to the counter to order, then they took their drinks in polystyrene foam cups out again into the yard.

'I like the photo of the men sitting on a wall taking a break,' Max said, sipping his cappuccino. 'They looked quite cheerful. I wonder if they'd just had Cornish pasties for lunch.'

Liz laughed. 'I expect so. Pasties were originally developed for miners with filthy hands, you know. They didn't eat the crusts – they used them as sort of disposable handles. The pasties were packed full of calories and stayed warm for ages. Sometimes the men carved their initials into the dough to make sure they got the right one.'

'I must try one.' Max's smile was infectious. 'Does your husband serve them at his restaurant, A Winkle in Time?'

He'd remembered the name, then; he'd obviously been paying attention, but she shook her head. 'It's mainly fish, to be honest.'

'I love fish.'

She almost suggested she take him there, but recalling her husband's grumpy face, she thought better of it. 'They sell excellent pasties in our local pub. Don't worry, it's on my "To Do" list.'

After circling the boatyard they followed the course of the river, which wound its way through east Cornwall before joining up with the great Tamar. It was a long time since she'd walked that way, through dense woodland and across fields of sheep and cattle. Every now and then they came across an old stone cottage or a quaint converted barn and Max stopped to look, commenting on some aspect of the garden or architecture and asking numerous questions. He had stories of his own to tell, too – mainly his memories of Franz.

'He liked the simple life, I think. It's strange he didn't make time to visit Pat, but I don't remember him travelling anywhere much. He and my grandmother used to go to the lakes outside Munich for the day, but that's about it.

'They took us children a few times, but we weren't allowed to swim so it was rather boring. I think they were worried one of us would drown. Franz was quite a cautious man, as I recall. Perhaps the shock of war never faded; though he was one of the lucky ones, of course.

'He always had a soft spot for England. He used to say the food wasn't nearly as bad as everyone made out, and he liked fish and chips. He still had some words of English and was keen for us grandchildren to learn. He taught me some nursery rhymes – "Twinkle Twinkle Little Star" and "Baa Baa Black Sheep". He told me he'd learned them from Pat, the little girl with red hair.'

'That's so sweet!' Liz struggled to picture Pat as a child; she'd always seemed old, with her snowy-white hair. But she could imagine her interest in the German soldier. She'd been curious about everything, right up to the very end, and she'd had the biggest heart.

When they came to a wooden stile surrounded by brambles, Liz asked if Max wanted to turn back but he said he was enjoying himself too much, and they tramped across the next field, keeping the river on their right, and she plied him for more information about his grandfather. 'Can you remember anything else he said about Pat or her family? Did he spend a lot of time with them?'

'I wish I'd paid more attention,' Max replied, frowning.

But then his face lit up. 'Wait a minute – he told me he had Christmas with them! I'd forgotten about that.'

'Really? What did he say?' Liz's interested was piqued.

In his excitement Max had upped his pace and his legs were longer and stronger than hers, so she had to hurry to keep up.

'I remember he got angry with me one Christmas Day. I must have been about seven or eight. I was a bit shocked because he was normally so gentle; he rarely raised his voice.

'I was behaving badly because I'd wanted an electric train set, and instead my mother had knitted me a woollen sweater. My little brother was really happy with his present – a game, I think – so I kicked and broke it. My grandfather told me Christmas wasn't about what you received, it was what you gave that mattered. Then he told me a story about a Christmas in England when he was invited to join the family of his little friend, Pat.

'I can see his face now as he spoke – he wasn't angry any more; he seemed wistful. He said he wanted to accept the invitation very much, but was sad because he didn't have any money for gifts. Then he had the idea of making them. Luckily he was very handy and he melted down some old metal spoons and made signet rings and carved photo frames out of bits of wood. Ingenious, eh?' Max grinned. 'He said he was worried no one would like them, but they were very happy. They said they were far more precious than something bought because he'd taken the time to make them himself. He then told me my mother had spent hours knitting that sweater, which I claimed I hated. "How do you think that makes her feel?" I felt guilty and apologised to my mother, and he helped me mend my brother's game.'

Liz was charmed by the tale. She could just envisage how thrilled Pat would have been to receive a signet ring or photo frame, however rough and ready they might have looked, and she wondered what the family had given Franz in return.

'You must tell Rosie the story when you see her. I'm always saying I don't want her to spend her precious pocket money on presents for me – I'd much rather she drew a picture or something, but she won't listen.'

Max nodded. 'Mila's the same. She once made this clay dish for me to put my cufflinks in. It's all crooked and funny-looking, and she can't understand why I love it so much.'

The sun had gone in now; it was getting dark and chilly, so they turned around and walked back the way they'd come. Liz had already invited Max for supper, along with Rick, Charlie-the-reporter and her photographer, Rory; but first she reluctantly drove him to Audrey's cottage to settle in and leave his bag.

As she came to a halt outside the door, she could see Audrey through her front room window, pretending to tidy up; but it was obvious that she'd been looking out and listening for them. Liz wished now that she'd invited Max to stay at Bag End. He wouldn't have been any trouble, and at least it would have kept him away from that ghastly woman. She might put him off Tremarnock altogether.

'Shall I tell Rosie to come and collect you?' she asked, but Max insisted that he'd rather find his own way.

'I can't get too lost, can I? Send an emergency party if I'm not with you by 7.15.'

He was about to leave the car when Reg Carter stomped out of his house opposite and climbed in his own vehicle. Liz hadn't yet mentioned Tremarnock Resists, but she did so now, explaining about the proposed development and the villagers' protest.

Max seemed genuinely interested. 'How brave! I hope you win.' He made her promise to show him the encampment, adding with a joke, 'I like the sound of the treehouse. I've always fancied living in one myself.'

It was a good job that Liz had already prepared supper – a big lasagne that just needed warming up in the oven – because by the time she'd collected Lowenna from Jean's, given her a snack and bathed her, it was almost 7 p.m. and Max and the other visitors would be here any minute.

'You look nice! Lovely top!' Rosie commented, when she came downstairs from doing her homework.

'You've seen it before,' Liz replied vaguely, which wasn't true, as she'd worn it only once to a party when Rosie hadn't been around. It was rather unusual: black, with sheer inserts on the arms and around the middle, and she'd teamed it with some black cropped trousers and her favourite mulberry-coloured ankle boots. She rarely bought clothes, and the boots had been a present from Robert, although she'd chosen them herself. They were suede, quite high – for her – and distinctive. They were also the most expensive items in her wardrobe and she was very proud of them.

Charlie and Rory were the first to arrive. Liz showed them to the front room and went to fetch the drinks while Rosie kept an eye on Lowenna, who had been allowed to stay up to meet everyone. Charlie was in jeans, trainers and a fluffy oversized pale blue sweater with white clouds across the front that looked like a pyjama top. Indeed, Liz wouldn't have been surprised if it *was* a pyjama top, because from what Charlie was saying, it seemed she'd scarcely had time to get dressed this morning, and certainly hadn't brushed her tangled red hair. As she gulped down her glass of wine in record time, she explained that she'd had to hurtle in her ancient VW Beetle from one interview to another, finishing up at the Theatre Royal, Plymouth, to meet one of the actors performing in one of their plays.

'I wasn't planning to write the interview up till tomorrow, then I got a call from the office to say they wanted it for the morning paper so I had to dash back and do it before I came here. I've never bashed out a thousand words so fast. God knows what they're like.'

Noticing that Charlie's glass was now empty, Liz hurried back to the kitchen, thinking it was just as well she'd stocked up; she had a feeling this was going to be a very short bottle.

Rory was silent as Charlie gabbled on; only the tips of his impressive ears turned steadily pinker. When Lowenna climbed, uninvited, on to his lap, Liz hoped that she wouldn't make a grab for them, as she had a habit of doing with people's jewellery.

'Leave Rory alone,' she scolded, but Lowenna paid no heed, brandishing bits of coloured Lego in her pudgy hands for him to admire. The poor man looked quite bewildered.

It was a relief when the doorbell rang. Rosie hurried to answer, and Liz listened to the conversation that took place in the hall.

'Well, hello!' It was Max. 'It's so good to meet you at last!'

'Mum said you look a bit like George Clooney,' Rosie replied. 'I didn't believe her, but she's right!'

Liz felt her face heat up; she could have slapped her daughter, she really could. Still, there was no taking the words back and when Max entered the room, she pretended that she hadn't heard.

'This is Charlie from the *Tremarnock Bugle*,' she said, smiling rather primly to disguise her embarrassment. 'And Rory, the photographer.'

At that moment, Lowenna hopped off the young man's knee, toddled over to Max and stood at his feet, gazing up at him with a puzzled expression. He crouched down to her level and shook her hand. 'And this must be Lowenna! Delighted to make your acquaintance.'

She lowered her eyes shyly, making everyone laugh, before running around in show-off circles and falling on her bottom. Max seemed charmed, so she did it again, but this time it was less funny. Fearing the joke would soon wear thin, Liz decided to take her daughter upstairs to bed. In the meantime, she asked Rosie to dig out their old photos of Pat.

'I won't be long, and we'll eat as soon as Rick's here. Everything's ready.'

Supper turned out to be a very jolly affair, with Rosie regaling Max with tales of Pat and her penchant for bad TV detective dramas and chocky bickies. 'When she used to babysit me, she always made me promise not to tell Mum how many biscuits we had. Sometimes we scoffed a whole packet each. She had a secret supply of sweets in her handbag as well.'

Of course Charlie, Rick and Rosie wanted to hear Max's memories of Franz, and Charlie jotted down his words in shorthand in her notebook. Rick, meanwhile, in an open-necked red and white striped shirt with a forest of grey chest hair poking out, produced fresh photocopies of the old newspaper cuttings that his friend, Des, had sent over from the Cornwall Records Office. This time, the words were much clearer and there was a grainy photograph of two men, one young, one older, standing on the shore beside a fishing boat.

Max's eyes misted up as he gazed at the image.

'That's my grandfather?' he asked, pointing to the younger man in a flat cap and rubber boots. Franz was sideways on, one leg resting on the edge of the boat while he smiled at his companion, who had a cigarette between his lips.

Rick nodded. 'The other one's Arthur Kellow, father of Pat. He was a fisherman; a brave chap, by all accounts – went out in the lifeboats. He's buried in the churchyard here in Tremarnock, along with his wife. It's where we had Pat's funeral, too.'

'They look happy, don't they?' It seemed important to Max that everyone should agree. 'I'm so glad my grandfather was sent here, among kind people who took care of him.' He wiped his eyes with the sleeve of his shirt and everyone pretended not to notice.

'This might sound strange, in a way,' he went on, 'but I want to thank you. I'd say it to Pat and her family if I could but they're not here, so I'll have to thank you and the people of Tremarnock instead.'

Liz glanced at the others; they were clearly touched, as she was.

'Can I quote you on that?' Charlie asked suddenly. It seemed inappropriate at such an emotional moment and Liz's skin prickled, but Charlie was only doing her job, and Max didn't appear offended.

'Sure, if you want to. I meant every word; I really am grateful.'

'This has got everything,' Charlie mumbled, scribbling away in her notebook. She clearly knew that she was on to a good story. 'My editor's going to love it.'

Later, Rory took photos of them all around the table with the bottle containing Franz's message as the centrepiece; then they moved back to the front room, where Liz stoked the fire and Rick gave Max a potted history of Tremarnock.

As she looked across the room at her German visitor, stretching out his legs in front of the dove grey sofa, his elbows wide and hands behind his head, she felt a pang of something, like a sharp stab. It should be Robert settled there, she thought, all relaxed and happy, with a tasty meal and plenty of good red wine in his stomach. He was the one who ought to be enjoying his home, the fire, the company of visitors and Rosie – and his wife.

She felt a bitter taste in her mouth and hot coals seemed to burn inside her. Taking a deep breath, she waited for the feelings to subside and as they did so, a different kind of blackness descended.

Max laughed, and she snapped to; she had no idea what he'd just said. She glanced at him in confusion and he must have noticed, because he looked at her oddly.

'Liz, are you all right?' He leaned forward.

She smiled, catching his gaze. 'I'm fine. I was just thinking it's a shame you're only here for such a short time.'

Where had that come from?

Seemingly reassured, he returned her smile, sitting back again and crossing one leg over another. 'I know where you are now. You won't be able to keep me away.'

Their eyes stayed locked and there was a pause, like a heartbeat, when she wondered what he meant.

'Mum, I just heard Lowenna.' Rosie's voice dragged Liz away and she noticed a frown on her daughter's face. 'I heard her cry,' she repeated more urgently, but when Liz got up and opened the door to listen, the house was quiet and still.

Thinking nothing of it, she would have settled down again; but the atmosphere had changed, and Max announced that it was time to go.

'Thank you for a lovely evening,' he said to Liz in the hallway, kissing her lightly on both cheeks. Then he stepped to one side to say goodbye to Rosie, but she hadn't followed; she was halfway up the stairs.

'Good night,' she called behind her.

Liz wondered what had happened to her manners, but if Max thought her rude, he didn't show it. She stood at the gate for a moment, watching him, Charlie, Rory and Rick strolling up the hill, their voices echoing in the velvety stillness. A shadowy figure came out of South Street and headed past them in her direction. For a moment she thought that it might be Robert, but this man was shorter and broader. Besides, Robert would still be at the restaurant. She spun around and went back inside, closing the door firmly behind her.

Chapter Fourteen

SHE WAS STILL half-asleep when her phone pinged. Beside her, Robert stirred and turned over. She had no idea what time he'd come in last night but guessed that it must have been very late. He usually rose with the lark, and now it was almost 8 a.m.

Lowenna was chattering to herself next door, playing with the toys in her cot. Carefully removing the covers so as not to disturb her husband, Liz climbed out of bed and tiptoed downstairs to check the message. It was from Max.

> Good morning! It's a beautiful day. I fancy a walk along the cliffs. Would you and your family like to join me? If not, I'll call when I'm back.

The sun was streaming through the kitchen window and the leaves on the trees glowed red, orange and yellow. On Saturday mornings Liz would normally make a cooked breakfast for the girls and Robert, if he were about, and then they'd loaf around in their pyjamas. Today, though, a walk was hugely tempting. She'd like to show Max their beautiful coastline, and besides, it was good to shake up your routine from time to time. She could always fix breakfast later.

Rosie grumbled when asked to mind Lowenna for a couple of hours, but by then Liz was all dressed and ready to go.

'You can come too, if you hurry. We'll take Lowie in her pushchair.'

Sitting up in bed with a frown on her face, Rosie shook her head. 'Don't feel like it. What shall I say to Robert?'

'Just tell him I'm taking Max along the cliffs, of course. What else would you say?'

Rosie shrugged and picked at a fingernail, refusing to meet her mother's gaze.

'Is anything the matter?'

'Nah.'

She was in a strange mood and Liz was glad to be getting away. Robert could deal with it for once; it was about time he took his turn.

As she stepped out in jeans, walking boots and a warm parka jacket, her hands tucked into the pockets, her heart gave a little skip. The chilly morning air smelled of wood smoke, salty sea and damp, decaying leaves; the clear blue sky overhead was so bright it almost hurt her eyes. Max was right, it really was a beautiful morning.

They'd arranged to meet at the corner of the street where he was staying and she stamped her feet and rubbed her hands together to keep warm while she waited. It wasn't long before he came out of Audrey's garden gate and strode up the road towards her. He was in jeans and walking boots, too, and the same brown leather jacket that he'd worn yesterday, zipped all the way to the neck and with the sheepskin collar turned up.

As he approached, smiling, she noticed that his eyes were puffy, and the slender lines that ran across his forehead and down the sides of his nose and mouth appeared more pronounced. It crossed her mind that he might be older than she'd thought, but for some reason, the creases only seemed to make him more attractive; they were, to her, the comforting signs of wear, evidence of a face fully lived in and a life wholly experienced.

'Did you sleep all right?' she asked when he was close enough and to her consternation, he winced, as if in pain.

'My host – Audrey…' His dismay was palpable. 'She was waiting up when I got in and she made me have a nightcap. She wouldn't take no for an answer. She talked non-stop for two hours and I almost fell asleep on the sofa. I've never known anyone speak so much. She was like a steam train.'

Liz felt sorry for him, she really did, but laughter bubbled up inside, exploding in a giggle. 'She's a nightmare! She's renowned for it. What was she going on about?'

'Honestly, I've no idea.'

Liz roared again and this time, he joined in.

'You should have warned me,' he complained, once they'd calmed down. 'I'd have brought earplugs.'

Market Square was still quiet; only Ryan could be seen through the window of his fish shop, writing something on the board behind the counter. Looking at the village as if through Max's eyes made Liz swell with pride, and when they reached the seafront, she stopped for him to admire the view.

'It's like a film set,' he commented, turning this way and that and taking everything in, from the bobbing boats in the harbour to the crescent-shaped beach and brightly painted shops and houses behind. 'Munich's a great city, but this – well, this is something else.'

'I fell in love with it the first time I came,' Liz confessed. 'I brought Rosie on holiday when she was very little and when

I broke up with her father, I decided to move here. It was the best decision I ever made.'

As they started to follow the winding trail that led out of Tremarnock towards Hermitage Point, Max took up the conversation again.

'It was a good idea to make a fresh start. I couldn't leave Munich when I got divorced because of Mila and my business. I'd have liked to, though. I think it would have helped.'

The path steepened. Liz's breath became shorter, and her coat caught on the prickly brambles that lined the route. The ground was quite dry, save for the odd patch of sticky mud, and they passed some wild ponies munching on the grass. The animals looked up briefly as the strangers approached, but were reassured by their careful movements and low voices and soon lowered their shaggy heads to carry on grazing.

'How long have you been divorced?' Liz wanted to know, but her voice was whipped away on the wind and once they were well beyond the ponies, she repeated herself more loudly.

Max shouted back that it was three years. 'But we'd been separated for quite a while before that. We shouldn't have got married, really; but then we wouldn't have Mila, so I can't regret it.' They paused for a moment in a sheltered area between the trees. 'It's not ideal for her having divorced parents but my ex, Susanne, is a great mum. We both try really hard for Mila's sake and it works – most of the time. It could be a lot worse, anyway.'

On they went and he, in turn, enquired about Liz's relationship with her ex, Greg, and she said that he had a new family now and rarely bothered to contact Rosie.

'Do she and Robert get along?'

'Oh yes, she adores him – when he's around, that is.'

At last they reached the summit and as the path widened out, the hedges disappeared and before them stretched the blue-grey ocean, as smooth and sleek as a seal's back until it smashed against the dark rocks below and burst into seething white foam. A little way off, up a steep rocky slope, stood a tiny derelict stone chapel: nothing more than a rectangular cell, really, with a roof, a door and four small windows, open to the elements. Liz's hair blew this way and that as they scrambled towards it, clinging onto rocks and shrubs as they went.

Max entered first, and Liz heard him whistle under his breath as he gazed through the window at the wild, rocky coastline and vast expanse of restless water beneath them. There was a damp, musty smell and the cold crept into their bones, making them shiver. This felt like the final outpost, the end of the earth; they could have been the very last of their kind, staring into oblivion.

'If I lived here I'd want to come to this place every day,' Max commented, pushing himself up on to the stony windowsill and resting his chin on his knees as he contemplated the view.

'I'm glad you like it. It's my favourite spot in the whole world.'

'Thank you for sharing it with me.'

Something in his tone caught her attention, a wistfulness, perhaps, which made her suspect that despite outward appearances, he might feel that his life was lacking in some way. She was curious to know if he had a girlfriend but didn't like to ask, so she enquired instead about Mila and the types of things they did when she stayed with him at weekends. He seemed very involved in her life, but also mentioned that he worked a lot.

'Like your husband, I suspect. Has he always been in the restaurant trade?'

Liz said that he had and that it was a tough, competitive business with long hours, even more so now that he was launching the Secret Shack.

'You two should come to Munich for a few days. I'd be delighted to show you round. It's a good place for a break.'

It was a kind suggestion, but she shook her head. 'I'd never be able to drag him away.'

'Just bring your girls, then. Mila would love it.'

It sounded appealing, and she wondered what Robert would say. He'd probably encourage her – he was generous like that – but she'd feel guilty going without him. There again, it was the only way she and the girls would have a holiday because sure as hell he wouldn't be leaving Tremarnock any time soon.

'Thank you,' she said, resolving to put it on the back burner. 'Maybe one of these days. I've never been to Germany before.'

Max seemed in no hurry to leave, but Liz said that it was time to turn around. She was conscious of Lowenna back home and also Charlie, who would be at Bag End soon, having arranged yesterday to accompany them on a visit to Pat's friend, Elaine.

Max sighed. 'Charlie's nice, but—'

'A bit pushy, I know. But it's only because of her that we found you, and I can see it's a good scoop. Perhaps she'll land a big job on one of the nationals next; she deserves it. She's like a terrier; once she gets hold of a story, she won't let go.'

They continued to chat as they retraced their steps, and it occurred to Liz that her newfound friend was much easier to talk to than most men she knew; and unfortunately, she would have to include Robert in that.

At the bottom of the hill, she asked Max, he'd like to come for a late breakfast with her and the girls; it seemed the natural thing to do. 'It might be chaotic,' she warned. 'Lowenna's dreadfully messy.'

He didn't seem fazed, but wanted to be certain that Robert wouldn't mind. Liz pointed out that her husband would most likely be out now anyway, which seemed to reassure him, and when they reached Bag End, he insisted on taking charge of the cooking while she laid the table and kept an eye on Lowenna.

Once they'd eaten and cleared away, Liz suggested that they leave immediately for Elaine's house in the nearby town. Before going upstairs to fetch an extra sweater for herself and Lowenna, she asked Rosie if she'd like one, too, but she shook her head.

'I'm not coming.'

Liz started. She must have misheard.

'What did you say?'

'I've got stuff to do.'

No apology. Nothing. Liz's eyes widened. 'What stuff?' It was the first that she'd heard of it. 'Can't it wait?'

Rosie didn't reply; it was obviously just an excuse. Liz glanced at Max, who shuffled slightly uncomfortably in his seat.

'But Rosie, we're only doing this because of *your* bottle. I thought you'd be desperate to hear Elaine's story.'

Rosie shrugged. 'Don't feel like it.'

Liz felt her cheeks redden. She was embarrassed and bemused in equal measure. Perhaps Rosie was miffed that Liz was taking over her project but if so, why hadn't she said so earlier, then Liz could have taken a step back? She was tempted to try to change her daughter's mind, but feared sparking a row in front of their visitor.

'What a shame!' she said instead. 'We'll miss you.'

She tried to disguise her dismay with a smile, before raising her brows at Max in mock exasperation, as if to say – *Daughters! What are they like?*

To her relief, he smiled back sympathetically. Perhaps Mila was tricky sometimes, too.

Rosie disappeared to her room and when they finally set off in the car with Lowenna, Liz was grateful to him for not mentioning what had just taken place. He seemed sensitive like that. Charlie followed them in her battered white Ford Focus with Rory beside her.

Elaine, who was in her late eighties and had known Pat since school, lived on her own in a two-up two-down Victorian terrace house just off the high street, and it was quite a struggle to squeeze everyone in. They just about managed by perching on the arms of her brownish-yellow floral sofa while Lowenna sprawled on the swirly patterned carpet. A tiny bent woman with short white curly hair and twinkling grey eyes, Elaine rarely received visitors these days and had gone to a great deal of trouble to prepare a tray of coffee for the adults, a big plate of biscuits and some juice for the youngest member of the party.

The old woman was clearly thrilled to have an audience and they listened politely as she recounted stories of her and Pat's childhoods. It was quite hot in the room with the door shut and the radiator up full blast; at one point, Liz noticed Max's eyelids drooping, but he perked up when his host finally reached the war years.

'I don't remember being scared when it started. Pat and I were only young; we didn't really understand, and to be honest with you it all seemed quite exciting. When the PoWs arrived, they used to hang around outside the Nissen huts on the cliff, smoking their stinky roll-ups. On the way back from the beach, Pat and I would post our leftover sandwiches through the hedge. They were always very grateful – they must have been hungry.

'Some Americans came to work at the quarry as well, to drive the lorries. On Sunday afternoons, my dad would take us up there to watch them testing the tanks in the river. They were quite reckless; they used to race them. We thought it was great fun, especially when they crashed. I don't think anyone got hurt,' she added quickly.

'After a while, some of the PoWs, the ones who were all right, that is, were allowed into the village. Pat and I would look out for them. They were nice to us – most of them, anyway. This one in particular, Franz he was called, became friendly with our Pat.'

Max leaned forward at this point and listened carefully, his head tilted to one side.

'Good-looking fellow, he was,' Elaine went on. 'Very young, not much more than a boy really. He was so gentle, you couldn't help thinking he shouldn't be a soldier at all; he was still wet behind the ears.'

'How much did you see of him?' Max wanted to know. 'Did he go into Tremarnock often?'

Elaine frowned. 'I'm sorry, I can't remember. Not that often, I don't think, but I'm not certain. He was more Pat's friend, you see; he used to go out in the boat with her dad, Arthur. I know he spent Christmas with them because he gave Pat a photo frame he'd made out of wood. She was so proud of it; she carried it round with her. She even took it to school to show it off.'

Liz caught Max's eye and they both smiled, remembering their conversation about the homemade presents yesterday.

'"He made it for me specially," she said,' Elaine explained, mimicking a little girl's voice. 'The others were quite jealous. I think she had a soft spot for him, truth to tell, but she was only nine or ten at the time and he must have been eighteen or so. She was like a little sister to him, I reckon. She made him laugh, I do remember that.'

Charlie wanted to know if Elaine had any photos, but she shook her head.

'Lord! We didn't have a camera in those days – couldn't afford one. We didn't have much, but we were happy, Pat and I. We could make a game out of a few old sticks and a piece of string. Simple pleasures, that's what we were used to. Not like children today with all their gadgets and new-fangled whatnots.'

She chattered on for a while longer but was beginning to look tired. When it was clear that she had nothing more to add about Franz, Liz urged Rory to take some photographs before they stepped out once more into the sunlight.

'Lunch?' she asked, as they walked towards their cars.

They agreed to rendezvous again at the village pub. Lowenna, who had been as good as gold up to now, decided to throw a tantrum in her pushchair and Max handed her a set of keys to play with.

'It was interesting to hear Elaine's memories,' he said. 'I'm beginning to form a clearer picture of my grandfather's life here. I'm so glad I came.'

The meal was a jolly affair in the Lobster Pot over Cornish pasties and pints of local ale. Barbara, in a low-cut black velvet top, seemed very keen on Max and offered to give him a personal tour of her black-and-white photograph gallery. She was wearing her usual gold earrings and necklace topped off with a full face of makeup, so it was a bit of a surprise when she emerged from behind the bar to reveal a pair of extraordinarily muddy men's jeans, held up with a brown leather belt.

'Oh, these,' she said, glancing down apologetically when she noticed everyone gawping. 'They're Tom's. I was camping last night and spilled coffee all over my own trousers. I've been in such a rush this morning I haven't had time to get changed.' She laughed. 'What must you think of me? I look like a bag lady!'

Amused, Max wanted to know all about the camping arrangements. Meanwhile, beside the fire, Rory and his ears were turning steadily pinker, and Charlie was helping Lowenna in a highchair to eat her pasty in between mouthfuls of her own: 'One for you, two for me,' and so on, an arrangement with which the little girl appeared to be perfectly satisfied.

Only Liz felt oddly disconnected, as if she were high above, looking down on herself and not particularly liking what she saw. She thought that this might have something to do with Robert's absence, or rather his presence, just up the road at A Winkle in Time. He'd be supervising the lunches now, then probably heading over to the Secret Shack.

She told herself that her discomfort made no sense; she hadn't invited him to join them, but then he wouldn't have come anyway, so what would have been the point?

'What's the plan this afternoon?' she heard Charlie ask, jolting her back to the here and now.

Liz tucked a strand of hair behind an ear. 'The old prisoner of war camp,' she replied, before taking a swig of her bitter shandy. 'And after that, Max wants to see the protest site.' She nearly added, 'At least *someone's* showing an interest,' but of course Charlie wouldn't have known what she was talking about, so she didn't bother.

High above Tremarnock and not too far from Polgarry Manor, where once there were rows and rows of large tunnel-shaped Nissen huts, made of corrugated metal and containing wooden bunk beds, only one remained. This had been turned into a café, mainly used by ramblers and dog walkers. It was here that Liz and her party went next, and while it was a beautiful remote spot, you could imagine how bleak it must have seemed to the prisoners on a cold winter's day with nothing about save fields of sheep and the odd derelict barn.

'Shall we go inside?' Liz suggested, after they'd circled the hut and Rory had taken more photographs.

Although the café owners had done their best to make the place welcoming, with plug-in heaters dotted around and colourful paintings, nothing could mask the deathly chill that seemed to seep up from the damp concrete floor and through the thin walls. In fact Liz could swear that it was colder inside than out, though that didn't seem possible; it was certainly less cosy than her tent, which at least drew warmth from the surrounding earth.

It was quite dark, too. It must have seemed to the inhabitants that they were living in a glacier. She could imagine that at night, in particular, they would have been grateful for the proximity of their living, breathing fellow prisoners when the one coke-burning stove in the centre of the room was out, the rain drumming against the metal sheath and the wind whistling through the ill-fitting window frames.

Max paced up and down a few times, his hands clasped behind his back, before chatting to the woman who had bought the building with her husband several years before and turned it into a going concern. She knew little about the prisoner of war camp but had some interesting information about Nissen hut design and their inventor, Major Peter Norman Nissen.

Afterwards, as they walked back to the car, Liz said she hoped Max didn't feel that it had been a wasted journey and he insisted not, although he did express a wish again that his grandfather were still alive to share the experience with him.

'It's strange, but I feel closer to him. I always loved him, but he seemed old to me even when he was in his sixties. I couldn't imagine him as a young man before but I can now.'

'I know what you mean,' Liz replied. 'I'd love to have seen him and Pat together.'

'Perhaps they're up there somewhere, looking down on us and smiling. I'd like to think so.'

Liz was quite prepared for him to ask to be dropped back at his bed and breakfast when they'd finished looking around, but he insisted that he'd rather go straight to the campsite, where they had arranged to meet Rosie.

Lowenna had fallen asleep in the car and woke only when she was bundled back into her pushchair, and when they reached the play park, Liz was surprised to see that the number of tents seemed to have mushroomed in the past couple of days.

She wondered who the newcomers were. Everywhere you looked, folk were brewing cups of tea on wobbly Primus stoves while children tripped over guy ropes and horsed around on the swings. A new TRESPASSERS WILL BE PROSECUTED notice in red letters had appeared on the tree nearest the entrance, but no one was paying the slightest bit of attention.

So packed was the site now that Liz suspected if any more arrived, they'd have to spill out into the surrounding lanes and the car park opposite. She'd love to see Reg Carter's face when he observed the mayhem; he might spontaneously combust.

Rosie was sitting on a swing talking to Rafael. To Liz's relief, she looked happy and was smiling; she must have recovered from her bad mood earlier in the day. Liz would have gone to say hello, but unfortunately Audrey must have spotted the group approaching because she came beetling out of her marquee in a long floral housecoat, waving her arms in greeting.

'Yoo hoo!'

Sensing Max shudder, Liz couldn't resist giving him a nudge. 'Here comes your number-one fan.'

'Save me!' he implored, but there was nothing to be done; Audrey was soon alongside, taking him by the arm and coaxing him, like a spider with a fly, towards her canvas web.

For two pins, she'd probably have zipped him up inside with her, leaving the others out in the cold, but he turned and beckoned frantically so they quickly followed him under the porch and through the door.

'We're besieged!' Audrey said dramatically as soon as they were out of earshot of the other campers, before proceeding to harangue Charlie for doing such an efficient publicity job that folk for miles around had heard about the protest and turned up to offer their support. 'I knew this would happen, I *knew* it,' she went on, glaring accusingly at the reporter. Charlie mouthed 'sorry', though she didn't look it. Then she glanced at Rory, who attempted to hide his smirk with a cough.

'We had a BBC camera crew here earlier,' Audrey went on, undeterred. 'We've become a *cause célèbre*. Tremarnock will never be the same again!'

Liz did her best to calm Audrey's nerves by saying that the newcomers would soon get bored and go home; and in the meantime, it would be good to have reinforcement. But it was no use. The older woman was convinced that now the strangers were here, they'd never leave.

'I spoke to one family who've come from Redruth. REDRUTH!' she exploded, as if it were the back of beyond. 'There are six of them – Mum, Dad, two adult children and Granny and Grandpa. They've already had their ghastly pop music on and Mum is wearing LEGGINGS.' She shuddered. 'She probably bought them in a cheap supermarket.' To add to her long lists of faults, Audrey was a crashing snob. 'They're not like us. They don't understand our way of life. It's an absolute disaster.'

Max, clearly nonplussed, was standing awkwardly in the centre of the marquee, staring hard at the ground. At the word 'disaster', however, he made the mistake of raising his eyes, and Audrey stopped in her tracks.

'Dear me,' she said in a new, simpering tone. 'How rude! I haven't even offered you a drink.'

Without more ado, she grabbed his arm again and half-pushed, half-pulled him onto a dusty pink chaise longue that had once graced the interior of Polgarry Manor, until one foot had fallen off, the stuffing had seeped out of a hole in the back and it had been relegated to an outhouse.

Max, too startled to protest, sat white-faced and ramrod straight, looking as if he feared that at any moment Audrey might hurl herself on top of him and crush him to death beneath the folds of her billowing housecoat.

Fortunately Lowenna came to his rescue by screaming to get out of her pushchair, at which point Liz insisted that they didn't want a drink as they'd only just had lunch. This wasn't strictly true, but it got them off the hook.

Once out in the fresh air again, Max took a deep breath.

'She's, um, she's quite forceful,' he said, which was an understatement. 'I think we're lucky to get out alive.'

'YOU'RE lucky,' Liz replied, laughing.

'I was afraid she might gobble you up,' Charlie added darkly.

Liz was about to show him Jesse's and Loveday's treehouse, but word of their arrival had got around and in no time at all, people were approaching from all directions. Soon a crowd had formed around them, making it impossible to go anywhere, and questions were being fired at Max left, right and centre: 'How did you feel when you realised the message in the bottle was written by your grandfather?'; 'What did he say about Tremarnock? Is it how you imagined?'; 'How long are you staying?'

Max did his best to answer, but could only get halfway through before being hit with a fresh barrage of queries. In the end he gave up and stood open-mouthed, staring wildly around him like an animal in a zoo.

Fortunately Rick appeared and, noticing the foreigner's dismay, proceeded to elbow his way through the throng. 'Give the poor man some space, will you? He can't hear himself think!'

There was a general muttering and grumbling, but some folk did start to back off and wander away. Once Max could breathe again, he, Rick and a few others started chatting about pirates and smuggling tunnels and the local women who concealed bladders of illicit liquor beneath their petticoats.

'Their main problem wasn't customs officers, it was the drunken sailors who thought puncturing the bladders was a great sport,' said Rick.

'Typical men!' added Jean the childminder with a sniff; Tom, beside her, looked quite put out.

All of a sudden, a cry went up from a middle-aged chap with short dyed blond hair, whom Liz didn't recognise. 'What's happened to our manners? We should show the fella some Cornish hospitality!'

'A barbecue!' someone else shouted – a woman this time – and before they knew it, Liz, Max, Lowenna, Charlie and Rory were being ushered over to the row of tables in the middle of the field and being told to sit down, while all around them campers bustled about fetching knives and forks, plates and glasses.

Only Rosie didn't offer to help, perching beside Rafael on the edge of the table as far away from her mother as possible and with her back turned. So she *was* still grumpy with her. Liz pretended not to notice.

There was no time to ask Max if he were content to stay, as his glass was already being filled to the brim with wine, and bowls of crisps and nuts were being plonked in front of him.

'To your good health!' shouted the man with dyed blond hair, before knocking back his own glass of wine.

'*Achtung!*' someone else hollered: a child who thought he was being funny, but should have been old enough to know better. Everyone ignored him, including Max.

'*Prost!*' came Rick's speedy rejoinder. 'It means "Cheers" in German.' He looked around for backup and Liz quickly obliged.

'*Prost!*' she chorused, raising her glass and taking a large gulp.

The effect was almost instant. As the alcohol trickled down her throat and into her stomach, warmth seemed to spread right through her and her cheeks caught on fire. Max, noticing, smiled at her in amusement, mouthing 'Cheers' back and clinking his glass in the air.

Deciding there was nothing for it but to enter into the spirit of it all, Liz took another swig, and then another. Soon Nathan was lighting a giant portable steel fire pit with a grill on top, and between them, the campers managed to rustle up enough burgers, sausages, chicken pieces and corn on the cob to feed everyone.

As the light began to fade and more wine flowed, the noise increased and laughter seemed to fill the sky, which was slowly turning from streaks of orangey red to midnight blue. Tabitha produced her guitar and played 'Squire Trelawney' again, and Max joined in. When she'd finished and some people had started to peel off to their tents, the remainder, including Rosie and Rafael, huddled around the dying embers of the fire, listening to an impassioned speech from Jean about why the new development should not be allowed to go ahead.

'We know there aren't enough houses in Cornwall,' she said hotly, 'but it's local people who need homes, the young especially, and they can't pay those sorts of prices.'

There was no shortage of agreement, although most folk had heard it all before.

'The houses will be snapped up by investors, not people who want to live and work here and raise their families,' she went on, getting into her stride. 'Our villages are turning into ghost towns, it's a crying shame, and why build on a playground? The swings have been here for as long as anyone can remember and the kiddies love them.'

At that moment Lowenna, who was on her mother's lap, banged her spoon on the table and everyone turned to look. She must have understood more than she let on, because she bobbed up and down shouting, 'Swings! Slide!', indicating wildly in their direction.

Everyone laughed and she buried her face in her mother's chest, but she'd made Jean's point better than Jean herself and it hadn't gone unnoticed with Max.

'Maybe I can help,' he said, frowning.

Jean asked what he meant.

'I'm not sure... I need to think about it...'

Liz and Tabitha exchanged glances and Jean, too polite to press further, just said, 'How wonderful!'

They might have left it there but Rosie, who had been quite quiet until now, piped up, 'I don't see what *you* can do when you live in Munich. It's miles away. Anyway, I thought you were a publisher. What do you know about planning stuff?'

There was a sharp intake of breath followed by an awkward silence, but if Max felt slighted, he didn't show it.

'You're right,' he replied, after a few moments. 'I shouldn't have spoken. I was out of turn. I apologise.'

Someone swiftly changed the subject but Liz was too busy glaring at her daughter to notice what they said. Rosie studiously avoided her gaze. Later, though, after saying goodbye to Max outside Bag End, she turned to Rosie in their hallway with blazing eyes.

'How dare you be so rude to our visitor! That's twice you've snubbed him in one day. Unbelievable!'

Rosie feigned ignorance but Liz stood firm, hands on hips. 'Well, what have you got to say for yourself?'

Rosie's face tightened and her lips hardened into a thin line. 'He's full of shit,' she said, turning on her heel and marching upstairs before her mother had a chance to reply.

Liz heard her slam her bedroom door and Lowenna's high-pitched voice drifted up from the pushchair, where she had been sleeping.

'Wosie cross!'

'Yes, and extremely ill-mannered,' Liz replied, more in amazement than anger, for the wind had been taken right out of her sails. 'I can't understand what's got into her.'

Chapter Fifteen

HIS ARM, WARM and heavy, snaked around her waist as she lay in bed, pulling her towards him, and she scarcely dared breathe in case she broke the spell. Shuffling even closer, he nuzzled into her back and slotted his knees in the crooks of her own, like the two missing pieces of a jigsaw puzzle. A painful lump lodged in her throat; it was a long time since her husband had held her like that.

'I love you, Lizzie.' His voice sounded deep and muffled and the vibrations seemed to run up and down her spine.

'I love you, too.'

Turning over beneath the white duvet, she rested a cheek against his bare chest and inhaled the familiar scent of soap and skin. Instinctively her hand crept down to his hip, his thigh, while he drew lazy circles on her upper arm with a finger.

The church bells struck once, twice, six times in the distance and a seagull squawked outside the window. Her hand strayed again and to her pleasure and amusement, he sprang to life like a flower bursting into bloom.

'You've woken the beast,' he joked and she smiled, raising her chin and planting little kisses on his neck, his stubbly cheek, his lips.

The phone rang by his side and he cursed before reaching out to grab it. 'It's Sarah. I'd better answer.'

'Oh, God.' Liz couldn't help it. His sister never rang unless she wanted something. Shuffling away, she squeezed her eyes tight shut, trying – and failing – to blank out the conversation.

'You what? You're kidding?' He paused before letting out a long sigh. 'Thank God you're OK.'

As he rose, pulling his arm from beneath her, she rolled over again to face in the other direction, then listened as he grabbed his dressing gown and stomped downstairs, the phone still glued to his ear.

'What? Yes. Calm down. Hopefully it won't be as bad as you think.'

The dent that he'd left in the bed was still warm and she curled into it, trying to imagine what it was this time. Had Sarah split from Andy, her husband, again? Or lost her job, or failed to settle a bill and had creditors at the door?

Robert adored his sister and at times it was hard to fathom why. She was a liability, though even Liz had to admit that there *was* something lovable about her. She was like a big child: warm-hearted, naïve and needy. She just seemed to lurch from one drama to another, leaving Robert to pick up the pieces. It was no wonder that Loveday, her daughter, was such a handful.

Liz could hear voices outside, a man and a woman, then a dog barked and a car swished by, its engine steady and low-throated. She thought of Max on the other side of the village – was he just waking, too?

Her heart constricted as she remembered that he was going home in just a few short hours, and it dawned on her just how much she minded. What was she thinking? She must have let his good looks, his foreignness and the glamour of the message in a bottle story turn her head; perhaps she'd been living in Cornwall too long.

But there was an affinity between them, an understanding; she couldn't have imagined it, could she? Troubled by the way her thoughts were leading her, she sat up, hugging the pillow to her knees, and tried to focus on her girls, the protest... and Robert, who reappeared now at the bedroom door.

'Sorry, Lizzie. She picks the worst times to call.' He sat on the end of the bed and reached for her hand. 'She's had another smash. She's OK, no one's hurt. She was on her way to the paper shop and hit a van at the roundabout.'

'Jesus! Not again!' Liz had lost count of the number of prangs that Sarah had caused.

'The car's a mess, she says it's undrivable. She's worried the insurance people will write it off. She can't get to work without wheels.' He hesitated. 'I said we'll pay for a hire car while she gets sorted.'

Liz started. 'How much will *that* cost?'

'I don't know. Anyway, she and Andy can't afford it and she can't afford to lose her job, either. I'm happy to help – so long as you don't mind?'

'Of course not.'

He squeezed her hand and she smiled back thinly. What else could she do?

'I said I'd go over now and call the insurance company for her.'

'What?' Sarah lived in Penzance, over an hour and a half away.

'Andy's working. Anyway, he's useless at that sort of thing. Alex can do the lunchtime shift – it's pretty quiet today.'

For some reason Liz felt panicky, though she did her best to hide it. 'I've invited Max over. I was hoping you'd meet him before he goes.'

Robert looked surprised, as if he couldn't recall the name, and all of sudden she felt foolish for focusing on trivia when he was busy keeping the show on the road – quite literally in his sister's case.

'Would you like me to come with you? I can cancel Max if you want.'

'There's no need. Anyway, it's too far to drag Lowenna.'

She watched as he threw his dressing gown on the chair and pulled on pants, jeans, a greyish white T-shirt and his thick navy fisherman's sweater, an old favourite.

'How's it going with your German, anyway?' he asked, glancing in her dressing table mirror as he ran a comb through his messy hair. 'I'm sorry I've been preoccupied.'

She frowned, unsure how to describe the past two whirlwind days. 'I think he's had a good time. I've taken him all over the place.'

'You're a star.'

She felt the warmth and sincerity in her husband's voice like a physical pain.

'What's he like?' he added.

'Nice.' Such a bland, unemotional word! It didn't even begin to describe the crazy traffic running through her brain.

Leaning forward, Robert kissed her lightly on the forehead. 'I'm so proud of you.'

'Why?'

'Because you're kind and sweet and lovely. I hope he appreciates everything you've done for him.'

It was more than she could take. Flinging off the covers, she threw herself into his arms. 'Oh Robert, won't you just stay and say hello? You can go to Sarah's a bit later; it won't make any difference.'

He shook his head before burying his nose in her hair. 'The car rental place might close early and I don't want to get back late. I've got a meeting with the council tomorrow about the alcohol licence for the Secret Shack. I need to be on top form.'

At the bedroom door, he asked the time of Max's flight. 'Maybe he'll come back, now he's seen Tremarnock. He might book a holiday here.'

'I doubt it.' She didn't mention that he'd invited her to Munich – that he'd invited them both, come to that.

A few minutes later, Robert was gone, leaving her with a pit in her stomach. She would have liked to speak to someone about her feelings but whom would she call, when she didn't even understand them herself?

When Max arrived at around 10 a.m. she had difficulty looking him in the eye, as if she might give something away. He had already been for a long walk towards Polgarry Manor and had brought his bag so that they could go straight to the airport.

Like her, he seemed subdued, and for the first time since he'd arrived, there were awkward silences as they sat around the breakfast table. Rosie was no help. She hadn't apologised to her mother for the previous night and by the looks of things, she didn't intend to. Instead, she picked sullenly at her croissant and left as soon as she could, citing 'loads of homework', although she had claimed on Friday that she didn't have much.

Even Lowenna seemed to sense the strained atmosphere and behaved in a most unlovely fashion, grizzling when she wasn't allowed to put her spoon in the jam jar and spilling milk down her front. It was almost a relief when Max suggested one last stroll around the village before they set off for the airport.

'I'd like to see the ocean again. I'm so far from it in Munich.'

Lowenna cheered up when they stepped outside, but they hadn't gone more than a few steps when Esme came down the hill towards them, pushing Caroline in her wheelchair. She explained that they were on their way to Mass. Liz wondered how they'd make it, as the Catholic church at Cardew Heights was some way off at the top of a steep hill.

'It'll be fine – look!' said Caroline.

She hopped out of her chair and hobbled a little distance on her special boot. When everyone clapped, she turned around and grinned, and Liz noticed her pink cheeks and sparkling eyes. She looked ten years younger than when they'd last met. The sea air, along with Esme's careful nursing, must have done her good.

It was the first time that Max had met the women. He asked how the injury had happened and was interested to hear about St Michael's Mount and Caroline's plan to walk the entire length of the Camino Santiago de Compostela.

'I'm not sure I'll manage it now,' she said. 'Though maybe, when my ankle's healed completely—'

'It's a long way,' he interrupted. 'What's your motivation? Is there a spiritual element to it?'

Caroline appeared slightly embarrassed. 'Well, I'm not religious, but... I think everyone's looking for something on the walk; different things, I guess.' She and Esme exchanged glances.

'And have you found it yet – that different thing?' Max looked at Caroline strangely, and his question seemed to hover in the air between them.

She hesitated before smiling, but the smile wasn't for him; it was for Esme. 'Maybe, yes. I think so.'

For some reason Liz felt slightly awkward and she shuffled from one foot to another, but Max only laughed.

'That's great! I'm happy for you. It must soften the blow of the injury, if you see what I mean.'

The women went on their way and once they were out of earshot, he whispered to Liz that he'd never seen two people so much in love. Taken aback, she was about to put him right by insisting that Caroline was married with children while Esme had always seemed incurably single. However, she then remembered the débâcle with Rick, which had never been fully explained; and come to think of it, nor had Caroline's slightly mysterious solo appearance in Cornwall.

It was certainly true that Esme looked happier than ever before. Tony had noticed her glow, too; he'd even dropped the odd hint about the situation to Liz, which she'd chosen to ignore. At that moment, it was as if a veil fell from her eyes and she realised how dumb she'd been, how blinkered.

'Oh my goodness!' she blurted. 'I can't believe I didn't twig!' Her mind started racing ahead, wondering what would happen with Caroline's marriage and how she and Esme would work things out. 'I hope they can find a way to be together – if they really love each other, that is.'

'You're such a romantic.'

She smiled. 'Aren't you?'

'Oh yes. And I don't believe it's right for people to stay together just because they think they should. Life's short; if you're lucky enough to find love, you should grasp it with both hands, however inconvenient it might seem to everyone else.'

His speech troubled her, and she thought for a moment before replying.

'But what about the children?' she said at last. 'Isn't it selfish to put your own happiness before theirs? Caroline's kids might be grown up, but they'd probably be devastated if their parents split. You have to think of them, too.'

'Well, I've not met her kids, so I don't know what they're like. What I do know is it wouldn't have been good for Mila if Susanne and I had stayed together. No kid wants to see their parents miserable and arguing. I'd say that's far more damaging in the long run, wouldn't you?'

Liz felt uneasy, but fortunately they had arrived outside A Winkle in Time, which gave her an excuse to change the subject. Pointing out the restaurant to Max, he put his face up close to the window and peered in, but it was still early and no one was there.

'It looks very cosy. Does it do well?'

'It does,' she replied. 'I just wish it wasn't quite so all-consuming.'

On reaching the seafront, they sat on the bench overlooking the harbour and he mentioned his weekend home on a lake, where he kept a boat. It was the first that Liz had heard of it.

'It's very quiet and peaceful. I go there to do my thinking.'

She wanted to know more and it soon became clear that far from being a modest little place it was, in fact, a rather large chalet with its own mooring and swimming pool, plus easy access to the nearby ski slopes in winter.

'It sounds – extraordinary,' she said, feeling slightly duped; although she'd been able to infer from previous conversations that his business was successful, he had never let on that he was seriously rich.

'I'm very fortunate,' he admitted, sounding almost apologetic. 'It doesn't matter, does it? It doesn't make any difference? I mean, it's only money.'

She wondered why he seemed anxious, but made light of it. 'Don't be silly. Of course not!'

Leaning forward, elbows on knees, he fixed on a point on the horizon before explaining that he'd been thinking he would like to do something here in Tremarnock, in his grandfather's memory.

'Oh?' Imagining that he meant a memorial of some sort, like a statue or a plaque, nothing could have prepared Liz for what came next.

'How much are developers paying for the playground?'

'I don't know. Thousands and thousands. I've no idea.'

'Have they signed the contract yet?'

'The council's definitely said they can have it.'

Max stroked his chin. 'What would you say if I told you I was going to try to buy it?'

Liz inhaled sharply. It felt like a betrayal. She was horrified, she really was. 'We don't want a big new estate in the village, you know that!'

She thought that he might try to argue with her but to her astonishment, he threw back his head and laughed. 'What do you take me for, Liz?'

It soon became clear that he didn't intend to build anything, but would buy the land to ensure that it stayed as a playground.

'My grandfather adored children and he loved Tremarnock; he'd be delighted to know that thanks to him, it had been saved. It would be the perfect way of remembering him, don't you think?'

Liz was so taken aback that for a moment she couldn't speak, but as the information slowly sank in, she found herself thinking that there was a certain, delicious logic to the plan, a kind of neat rounding off of everything that had come before: the protest and encampment, Rosie finding the message in the bottle, their research with Rick, the newspaper follow-ups, the TV report, Max's visit – and now this.

It might just be the best possible outcome, better than she could ever have hoped, but she told herself not to get carried away.

'What can you do?' she asked. 'I mean, how would you even go about it? The developers might put up a big fight. Or maybe the council won't be able to get out of the contract, however much you're able to offer.'

At that moment a small dog tore past them, followed by a red-faced woman in a khaki mac: Jenny.

'Heel!' she shouted. 'Bad dog!'

But Sally took not a blind bit of notice and they watched her scamper onto the beach, stopping briefly to sniff at something interesting before haring off again with her mistress in hot pursuit.

'It's worth a try, anyway,' Max said, refocusing. 'Don't you think?'

'Of course! It would be amazing, but—'

'I'll get onto it as soon as I'm back in Germany. I'll call my lawyer friend. He'll know what to do.'

He turned and looked at Liz earnestly. 'Please don't mention this to anyone yet, in case it doesn't work out. I don't want to raise any hopes. I'll let you know as soon as I have some news.'

It crossed her mind that the plan would not only give a massive boost to Tremarnock Resists, it would also mean that for the time being at least, he would need to remain in touch with her.

'Let me know if I can do anything to help,' she said, warming even more to the idea.

Max smiled. 'For starters, can you email me the name and number of the developer? Also the relevant people at the council and anyone else you can think of. My assistant's great; she'll do the rest.'

Liz didn't feel nearly as gloomy as they strolled home, loaded his bag into the car boot and set off for the airport, because she knew that they'd be speaking again soon. Even so, it was hard to say goodbye, to listen to his polite words of thanks and allow him just to brush one cheek against hers, and then the other, his hand placed lightly on her shoulder. Then he was gone.

Afterwards, she stood by the car and watched him walk towards the terminal, wearing the exact same outfit that he'd arrived in two days before. His visit had gone so fast, yet it seemed to her that everything had changed.

At the entrance, he turned and waved, and bleakness settled on her like a cold blanket. She got into her car and drove off. Switching on the radio, she tried to listen to some music, but the noise hurt her ears so she snapped it off.

Robert rang when she was almost home to say that he'd finished with Sarah and would be back himself in about an hour. 'Let's watch a movie tonight. We haven't done that for ages. I'll pick up some pizza on the way.'

In the past, she'd have jumped at the idea; snuggling up together on the sofa in front of the TV used to be one of their favourite things. Today, though, even the thought of him, her girls, the cat Mitzi, Bag End and a roaring log fire in their cosy front room couldn't seem to lift her mood.

'Lovely,' she told her husband, without conviction. 'See you soon.'

Chapter Sixteen

DREAMY. IF SOMEONE were to ask Esme how her week had been, that was how she would describe it. Seven days since *that* kiss. A lot can happen in seven days. It had gone by in a flash, and yet each precious moment had been one to treasure, like pearls on a string around the neck of a white-throated woman. And although the time had slipped too quickly through her fingers, it was worth more to her than all that had gone before and that might, perhaps, go after. Forget cheap imitations, this had been the genuine article. Seven little days and seven whole nights. A week could be an amazing thing. Dreamy. Dreamlike. Gorgeous. Illusory.

A shadow passed over her and she glanced at Caroline, who was curled up on the sofa with a book, her bad leg resting on the arm. She must have sensed something because she took off her reading glasses and smiled reassuringly.

'Everything all right?'

'Yes.' Esme pretended to go back to her own reading, but her heart was too full, her mind too busy thinking, savouring, fretting.

A rosy pink light filled the room as the setting sun started to slip below the horizon. Until now, she hadn't known such bliss existed: the pure heaven of being with someone, of holding the *only* someone who could fill the aching hole in her soul, whose touch was as light as a feather yet powerful enough to move mountains and cause earthquakes. It was awe-inspiring and frightening. It was *real*.

They'd made no plans; every day had unfolded naturally, depending on the weather and their mood, spreading itself out before them like a sumptuous map. The only choice they'd had to make was which direction to go in. Should they take a stroll to buy the daily newspapers, then stop for fresh coffee and croissants in a café? Or, now that Esme's car had been repaired, drive to an out-of-the-way beauty spot and find a pub with oak beams, a roaring fire and a good ploughman's for lunch?

Caroline's family had gone remarkably quiet, phoning only infrequently, and once she had been able to walk a little further, the options had become much wider; they'd even been to Truro to mooch around the shops and cathedral. With no deadline and nothing to get back to, they'd taken it exactly as they pleased, pausing for cups of tea and cool drinks, or to browse in stores and buy little gifts for themselves and each other: a silk scarf here, a pair of silver earrings there. It had all been quite delightful.

And they'd talked. How they'd talked! About everything under the sun, from books, art and politics to handbags and face cream. And when they'd tired of talking, they'd continued on their way in companionable silence until the next topic of conversation had cropped up. They were never far from each other's sides and had often touched: a shoulder, a hand, the tips of their fingers brushing beneath their overcoats, as if they needed to be sure that the other person hadn't suddenly disappeared in a puff of smoke.

The only subject that they'd avoided was the future. Esme had been too scared to raise it and Caroline... well, it had been hard to tell what Caroline thought about *that*. Best not to project forward, Esme had decided; best to try to enjoy the moment and treasure it, like a perfect pearl.

'What shall we do about supper?'

Caroline's voice snapped her out of her reverie. The light had faded now and it was almost time to switch on the lamps; they must have been sitting there with their books for two hours at least.

'I don't know.' Esme's reply was slightly reluctant, for a meal would mean getting active again. 'What do you feel like? We have plenty of food – chicken, rice, all those vegetables we bought at the farm shop; we could go out or stay in, whatever you fancy.'

Caroline swung her legs off the sofa, arched her back, stretched her arms above her head and yawned.

'Let's stay in,' she said, lowering her arms again. 'I'll make supper tonight – it's definitely my turn.'

Esme started to protest but her friend was having none of it. 'I insist. Don't move. I'll bring you a G and T.'

She started limping towards the kitchen and Esme noticed with a pang that her walking seemed to be improving by the hour now, not just the day. Soon, she'd be out of her boot and wouldn't even need crutches, the ankle was healing so fast.

When she returned with a long slim glass of gin and tonic and a slice of lemon, she must have seen something in Esme's face because she asked again if she was all right and this time, Esme frowned; she couldn't help it.

'What is it?' said Caroline, knitting her own brows.

'I was just...'

'Yes?'

'I was just thinking how much better you are.'

She didn't need to explain herself; Caroline understood. Placing her friend's drink on the table, she beckoned her over to the sofa. They sat side by side, and Caroline rested her head on Esme's shoulder.

'I don't ever want this to end,' she said simply.

'Nor do I.'

Their hands crept towards each other, their fingers interlaced, bead-like, and Caroline took a deep breath.

'I wish it wasn't so complicated.'

'It doesn't have to be.'

'It's easier for you; you don't have so many people to think about.'

'It's never been easy,' Esme replied heavily. 'I'm not sure anything ever is. You have to fight for what you want, don't you think? For what really matters to you.'

There was silence for a moment, then Caroline rose suddenly and paced around the room, as best she could with her injury. 'You're right. I must be brave. The children know Philip and I aren't happy. It'll be a shock, but they're old enough to deal with it. It's not as if I'm abandoning them. We can still see each other often and speak on the phone. The only difference is that I won't be with their father any more. I'll be here – with you.'

The pacing stopped and she stood in the centre of the room, gazing at her friend as if for the very first time. The whites of her eyes were very bright and there was an aura about her, a kind of glow that exerted a pull like that of a flower for a bee. It was as if all of a sudden one of the great mysteries of life had revealed itself to her, as if she realised that she held the keys to the kingdom in the palm of her hand. 'We're meant to be together, aren't we? It's in the stars.'

Esme nodded, her heart so full that she thought it might burst. She opened her arms and Caroline walked in, crouching carefully at her feet, her cheek resting on the other woman's knee.

'Are you sure you won't get bored of me?' whispered Caroline.

'Of course not,' said Esme, stroking her lover's hair.

'The children say I'm quite annoying to live with. I can be a bit picky sometimes.'

'I don't mind.'

'I'll have to bring my stuff over from France.' Caroline raised her head and glanced around. 'Where will we put it? The flat's full already.'

'We'll find room.'

'What if you tire of me?' She was looking for trouble, pushing Esme to change her mind.

'I won't.'

Caroline reached for her topaz necklace, twisting the stone around and running her fingers along the silver chain.

'Then that's all settled.' She glanced up and her smile lit the room, taking Esme's breath away. It was the sun breaking through clouds, it was Monday made Friday, it was a tidal wave that swallowed up a thousand doubts... and most of all, a curve that made the whole world spin and also set it straight.

Later, back in her tent at the campsite, Liz dreamed about Esme and Caroline. They were walking down the aisle together, radiant in big white dresses and frothy veils, clutching bouquets and surrounded by smiling friends and family. They reached the altar and the vicar, in a white surplice, started the marriage ceremony; but before he was halfway through, a voice at the back of the church boomed: 'Stop!'

Liz, who was in one of the pews, turned to look and saw Robert standing at the door, his hair on end, his eyes wild and staring.

'This can't go on,' he cried, his arms flailing. 'It's against the laws of nature!'

There was a general gasp. Caroline shrieked and Liz slumped forward, feeling sick and dizzy. She couldn't understand, because Robert loved Esme and had always supported gay marriage. In her heart, she knew that this wasn't really about the two women – it was about her, and something he thought she'd done.

She wanted to shout that he was wrong, that she was innocent and Esme's marriage should proceed, but she couldn't because it wasn't true.

'Please don't do this!' she cried, weeping, but he marched down the aisle regardless, tearing the veil from Esme's head and hurling it to the ground before doing the same with Caroline's.

Woken by her own sobs, it took a moment or two for Liz to realise that she'd been dreaming. The relief was immense. She opened her eyes, grateful for the daylight, and, taking care not to disturb Lowenna, tucked up beside her, she climbed out of her bag as quietly as she could, crawling on hands and knees to the door before unzipping it and peeping out.

The grass was wet and the air smelled damp; the sky overhead was cold and grey. Now that the leaves had started to wither, Loveday's and Jesse's treehouse was more visible and she could see Jesse's blond head through the window as he moved about inside.

Audrey's marquee was quiet, but a little way behind, Annie, in fuchsia pink Lycra leggings and a black top, was putting mats on the ground ready for an early-morning yoga class. Meanwhile, closer to home, Rick, in his favourite, all-year-round beige cargo shorts and white T-shirt, was boiling a kettle on the stove while inside the tent his lady friend, Marie, was admiring herself in a hand mirror and brushing her hair.

Liz had a slightly stiff neck and shoulder and wondered if she'd nodded off in a weird position. Shivering, she was about to throw on some warm clothes when she noticed a group of officious-looking people heading purposefully across the field towards them.

Leading the way was Rod Halliday, the tall thin man from MegaCrest Homes, and behind him, Eric Bosomworth from Porthcaron District Council. Sgt Kent was also there, and several others whom Liz didn't recognise, while Reg Carter, the smallest and fattest of them all, was having a job keeping up.

Barbara must have seen them, too, because she emerged from her own dwelling in a fluffy white dressing gown and slippers, her blonde hair sticking out in all directions, before proceeding to stomp towards them, her arms wrapped tightly across her impressive chest. She looked quite comic and Liz started to laugh, but her amusement soon faded when the officials stopped and Reg caught up, raising his wretched loudspeaker.

'Attention, please!' he bellowed, while the other suits hung back, looking slightly sheepish.

Liz pulled her coat on over her pyjamas and climbed into her trainers before scooping up a rather surprised and sleepy Lowenna, bundling her into her own coat and hurrying outside to join Barbara. The landlady was a force to be reckoned with, for sure, but no one should have to stand up to Reg on their own, particularly in nothing but a dressing gown and slippers.

Slipping an arm through Barbara's as soon as she was alongside and balancing Lowenna on the opposite hip, Liz watched the other protesters start to make their way over, some muttering and grumbling, deliberately taking their time, others scurrying anxiously.

As soon as he had a big enough audience, Reg cleared his throat and spoke again. 'I have been asked to make an announcement on behalf of Porthcaron District Council,' he said pompously. 'I have here an interim possession order from the court. We have copies which we shall distribute in a moment.'

At this point, he held up a bundle of papers and flapped them under the noses of the crowd. People backed off, as if they were facing a swarm of bees.

'This land belongs to the council,' Reg resumed, 'and as such, you're illegally trespassing. The court has ordered that unless you leave within twenty-four hours, you'll be committing a criminal offence and the police will have the power to arrest you.

'Be warned, this is no idle threat. The time for negotiation is over.' Then he tucked the papers under one arm and raised his fist, looking as smug as a tin-pot dictator with a weapon of mass destruction in his garden shed.

Sgt Kent strode forward now and took the loudspeaker. 'Now listen here, folks. You've made your point, you've had your say and it's time to pack up and go back to your homes.' He was standing very straight, chin raised, shoulders square, but the slight tremor in his voice gave him away. 'Like Mr

Carter says, the court's ordered you to leave and if you don't go, I'll be obliged to come down here with my officers and put you in handcuffs and bundle you in a police van.' He scanned the crowd, picking out the faces one by one. 'We don't want that now, do we? We're reasonable people. I'm sure we can all see sense.'

Glancing around, Liz spotted a lot of uncomfortable expressions – one of which, she knew, was her own. She hadn't heard from Max since he'd emailed on Sunday night saying that he'd arrived home safely, and thanking her again for her hospitality. What if he'd changed his mind and decided not to try to buy the land? What if he'd already heard that he couldn't?

She tried to reassure herself that she was being silly, but then an even more alarming thought popped into her head. Perhaps he was at this very moment pulling out all the stops, but his best efforts would be doomed to failure because it was simply too late. After all, twenty-four hours was nothing and she, for one, had no intention of being arrested. Like most of her companions, she suspected, she'd bail out before that happened, giving the developers carte blanche to move in with the diggers.

There were cries of 'Down with MegaCrest Homes!', 'Get out of our village!' and 'We shall not be moved!', but it all sounded rather half-hearted.

Liz, still arm in arm with Barbara, whispered, 'D'you think they'd really go through with it?'

Barbara shook her head. 'There are too many of us. It would be chaos. They'd be scared of people getting hurt.'

But her words lacked conviction and all of a sudden, she seemed very small and really rather vulnerable in her fluffy white dressing gown and slippers. She would be no match for a gang of burly police officers; they'd have her bundled in their van with the door shut tight before you could bat an eyelid. And unfortunately, the same could be said for most of the protesters.

The MegaCrest Homes man took centre stage now, straightening his tie as he stepped up beside Reg Carter and Sgt Kent. 'On behalf of the company, I want to reassure you all that our aim is to work with you, not against you. Once you've cleared the site, we intend to call a public meeting where we'll listen to your objections once again and make detailed notes. This is your village, and as far as possible, we plan to take your wishes into account. Before the building work starts, we want everyone on board and working towards the same goal.

'I realise that at this point in time, the prospect of the new development is unsettling and a little frightening. We've made some mistakes, I'll grant you that. We should have explained ourselves better earlier on in the process and talked more to you.

'However, I'm confident that once you fully understand our aims and objectives, you'll change your views. You'll realise that we're not here to destroy Tremarnock; we're here to enhance your village and make it a better, more exciting, modern and vibrant place for you and your children and grandchildren. We want other rural communities with similar issues to look to us for inspiration and see us leading the way – a beacon of excellence in the heart of Cornwall.'

It was a good speech; some of the onlookers seemed impressed, nodding enthusiastically in approval. There were rumblings of, 'Now you're talking!', and 'That's the first sensible thing I've heard.'

Others, however, weren't fooled.

'You're only coming over all reasonable to get us out!' shouted Ryan the fishmonger, whose thick caterpillar-like eyebrows danced up and down as if they had a life of their own. 'It's all about profit for you. You don't care about us. As soon as we've cleared off, you'll be back to your original plans.'

The MegaCrest fellow shook his head and said it wasn't true.

Someone cried, 'We should at least give him a chance. They're going to turf us out anyway – maybe if we all sit round the negotiating table, we'll get a better deal.'

'There's no way that lot'll negotiate anything,' hollered the man from Redruth with the dyed hair. 'Smarmy buggers. I wouldn't trust 'em as far as I could throw 'em.'

'Language,' Audrey tutted. 'Can we please keep it clean?'

But everyone ignored her. Rick said he agreed with Ryan, and Liz and Barbara nodded vigorously, at which point the mood seemed to alter and there was a sense that everyone was coming around to the doubters' perspective. Reg Carter must have felt it, too, because his face grew pinker and he jabbed his pudgy finger indiscriminately.

'Let there be no doubt in your minds,' he barked. 'These are no idle threats. The police will be here in exactly twenty-four hours, at which time anyone remaining on this site will be arrested. You need to think very carefully. Do you really want your children to have law-breakers for parents? Have you considered what it will mean to spend a night in the cells and come out with a criminal record? Ponder the wider implications. Is this what you really want for yourselves and your families?'

'Nothing wrong with a bit of porridge!' Liz glanced over her shoulder and saw Nathan-the-postman's head bobbing up.

There were roars of laughter and calls of, 'I'll have honey on mine!' and, 'A bit of salt for me please. Smashing!'

A lady in a bright red scarf got out an accordion and started playing 'Widecombe Fair'. Everyone joined in, including Lowenna. The noise was deafening and it was quite clear that no one was interested in the officials any more; they shuffled uncomfortably, looking like gate-crashers at a ball.

At last, after conferring with each other for a moment or two, the MegaCrest man shrugged his shoulders, nodded at his co-conspirators and they began to move off. There was an ear-splitting cheer, and Liz craned her neck, determined not to miss the sight of Reg Carter glancing over his shoulder as he broke into a trot, perhaps fearing that a rotten egg or a tomato or two might come his way.

The crowd's elation was immense, but it didn't last long; everyone knew that they were only playing for time. Sensing the mood darkening, Barbara swung into action, pushing forward and shouting out about the necessity for a meeting. However, without a loudspeaker it was difficult to hear what she was saying; besides, she was so small that few could see her above the throng. Then Liz spotted Ryan, who was a tall, strong chap, bending down to whisper something in her ear, and the next thing she knew, he was crouching on the ground while the doughty landlady picked up her dressing gown and climbed onto his shoulders.

As he rose slowly, clutching her ankles to keep her from falling, she raised her arms aloft. A magnificent sight with her blonde hair and flowing white candlewick gown, she clapped to get everyone's attention, and the chattering quickly subsided.

'As you can see, we've reached a crunch point in our protest,' she hollered. 'The question now is what to do next.

Do we fight on, risking arrest, fines and imprisonment, or accept defeat and move out?'

She went on to suggest a meeting at midday where they would put it to the vote. 'We'll use Audrey's marquee, as it's the biggest.'

Audrey tried to complain, but no one was interested. The crowd started to disperse, amid much muttering as they began to rehearse their arguments for and against.

Lowenna had been as good as gold while watching the excitement from the safety of her mother's arms, but now let out a shriek, demanding to be put down. Liz obliged, realising too late that the little girl had no shoes on; not that this bothered her in the slightest. As they strolled back to their tent, she had great fun sinking her toes into the squidgy damp ground and marvelling as the mud sprayed up her legs and onto her pyjamas and coat.

It wasn't until they had dressed, cleaned up and tidied away their sleeping bags that Liz was finally able to sit down and send a text to Max.

> They've issued a court order. We have 24 hours to get off land or be arrested. What should we do?

Pressing send, she told herself not to hold out any hopes. Max was only human, after all, and couldn't perform miracles. The chances were that soon, Tremarnock would be filled with expensive new houses and fast cars and there would be absolutely nothing that anybody could do about it.

She and Lowenna would simply have to grit their teeth and find a new play park.

Chapter Seventeen

BEING A FITNESS trainer, Annie was very nippy on her feet and quickly dashed around the village, knocking on people's doors to tell them about the meeting and urging them to come along. Rick was already busy sending texts but everyone agreed that a personal approach was a good idea, too; besides, you couldn't rely on folk checking their phones regularly.

When Esme opened her front door to find Annie on her fire escape, pink cheeked and panting, her immediate thought was that someone had been taken ill. She was relieved to discover that this wasn't the case, but also dismayed at the prospect of a large number of her friends being carted off to the cells the following morning.

Caroline, who was still in her nightclothes, hobbled to the door as well. When she heard about the court order, she insisted that she and Esme must go to the meeting in the marquee to lend their support.

'We'd better leave pronto, because it'll take me a while to get there,' she said over her shoulder, already making her way to the bedroom to dress.

Esme smiled inwardly at the 'we'; she thought she might never get used to it. After so many lonely years on her own, suddenly being part of a couple felt both thrilling and deeply comforting, like climbing into a warm bath at the end of a long cold journey.

It was barely two days since Caroline had agreed to stay, yet Esme was already mentally planning the rest of their lives together. The possibilities seemed delicious and infinite: weekends away and foreign holidays together; dinner parties where she, Esme, would no longer be the only single person around the table, pretending that no one noticed and it didn't matter; Christmases and Easters in each other's company. These occasions had always felt desolate before, despite the fact that friends had made such an effort to include her.

Depending on how things panned out, of course, Caroline would wish to continue to see her children on festive events, just as before. Secretly, Esme hoped that one day she might be invited, too, though she knew that she mustn't run away with herself. After all, it was perfectly possible that Helen and Andrew would never even agree to meet her, let alone accept her enough to want her to join their family gatherings. Only time would tell.

In any case, Caroline hadn't even told them her news yet. She was waiting until her leg was well enough for her to travel before arranging to speak to them and Philip in person. It was a daunting prospect, and Esme had resolved to accompany her friend to France and to be there in the background for moral support. She could scarcely begin to imagine what a shock and how upsetting it was going to be for the entire family, and Caroline would need all the love and understanding on offer.

Once ready, Caroline and Esme set off arm in arm down the hill, passing by Jean's house, Dynnargh, where the garden was covered with dead leaves; Tom was spending almost all his time at the campsite, and had failed to sweep up.

Danny, landlord of the Hole in the Wall pub, was making his way up Fore Street having had a visit from Annie himself, and he took Caroline's other arm as they headed slowly towards the play park, conferring as they went.

'It's no good,' he said, pointing out a pothole before Caroline could put her foot in it, 'we can't beat the council or the developers, not when they've got the law on their side.'

'We could shin up the trees,' Caroline suggested, 'they couldn't cut them down with us in them.'

Danny, who was sporting a handsome ponytail, pointed out that this would be a bit tricky for her with her injured ankle, and besides, many of the other villagers wouldn't be capable of climbing either.

'Plus, most of us have got jobs and families and other commitments. We can't just give up our livelihoods to live in trees indefinitely. We're not Swampy.'

There was an even larger crowd milling around the field now, and there wasn't room for everyone to squeeze in Audrey's marquee, big as it was. It would have made sense to hold the meeting out of doors, but it had started drizzling and it was cold, too. So everyone made sure that the children and elderly were undercover while the rest hovered around the entrance with umbrellas and raincoats.

Fortunately Barbara, now out of her dressing gown, had managed to borrow a wireless karaoke microphone belonging to someone's granddaughter. It was a bit squeaky but did the job all right, and she climbed onto an old chest in the centre of the marquee so that as many people as possible could see her.

Liz, who had managed to find a space just big enough for herself and Lowenna inside the door, checked her phone for a message from Max, but there was nothing. She bit her lip, wondering what he was up to. He'd seen her text, for sure, so why hadn't he responded? Perhaps he was embarrassed to admit that he couldn't really help.

Tucking the phone back in her pocket, she watched Audrey scanning left and right to make sure that no one misbehaved or tried to nick anything. Meanwhile, Rick and Tom resembled a pair of slightly decrepit bodyguards on either side of Barbara, who now cleared her throat to speak.

The choice was clear, she said, when the hubbub had died down. They would either have to adopt more aggressive tactics by chaining themselves to fences, occupying trees and so on, or call it a day. The former would require a great deal of courage and necessitate a lot of inconvenience. The latter, though a dreadful prospect, would at least mean that they could all go back to their homes and lives having made their views clear and without any criminal records or nasty fines.

Beside Liz, Charlie-the-reporter was scribbling in a notebook while Rory tried to take pictures, which wasn't easy when there was scarcely room to swing a cat. Someone had clearly alerted the local TV station, too, because they had sent a small team – hoping, no doubt, that the protest would hot up and there would be lots of lovely, newsworthy conflict.

Opinion seemed to be divided more or less along generational lines, with the older folk favouring a dignified surrender while the hot-headed youngsters wanted to fight on. Loveday, who wasn't that fond of her waitressing job, was especially keen on the idea of tree-squatting, which would mean that she could stay tucked up in her sleeping bag under the boughs for the foreseeable future.

'People who can't climb can be in charge of bringing us food,' she suggested, adding brightly, 'and doing our washing and that sort of thing. We won't be able to wash anything up in a tree, will we?'

'I'm not scrubbing your undergarments,' Audrey replied, wrinkling her nose.

But Caroline piped up that she'd be happy to oblige, and Esme seconded her. 'Neither of us is very agile but we want to do our bit.'

Annie, who could shin up a tree in no time, didn't seem as bothered about the laundry aspect but said that she'd miss exercising dreadfully, until Nathan pointed out that she could still do press-ups and pulls-up in the branches. Besides, she'd have to go to the loo sometimes and could use the opportunity to jog a few times around the field.

He then came up with the idea of having special T-shirts printed with Tremarnock Resists on the front, and the conversation was side-tracked while they discussed colour schemes and matching beanie hats, so they would look as if they meant business. It fell to Barbara to steer them back on course and after another twenty minutes or so of deliberation, she announced that it was time to put it to the vote.

Rick and Tom were to count the show of hands and the room fell silent while Barbara prepared herself, patting her hair and straightening her sparkly black sweater. Liz checked her phone again. Nothing.

'Those in favour of continuing our protest,' Barbara boomed.

A fair number of hands went up, including Loveday's, naturally, and Jesse's, too, because he wouldn't have been allowed to disagree with her even if he'd wanted to; though quite how he proposed to fulfil his sous-chef duties while also being a full-time eco-warrior was anyone's guess.

Others in favour included Ryan, Jesse's and Loveday's friends, Nathan and Annie, the younger members of the Redruth clan and Mr Redruth himself, plus assorted others.

Once they'd all been counted, Barbara tapped her microphone once more. 'Those against,' she said.

This time, a sea of hands rose into the air. Loveday groaned loudly.

Ryan shouted, 'Quitters!' and stormed out of the tent, because there could be no mistaking the result: the surrender vote had won.

That was that, then. Liz's stomach flipped over and her heart seemed to sink into her boots as she felt for her phone, sitting cold and lifeless in her pocket. The villagers had spoken, and a chill seemed to creep into the whole tent. No one uttered a word as Rick and Tom finished totting up.

It was Barbara who finally broke the silence.

'The outcome is decisive,' she announced, as if it wasn't already clear. 'Those against taking further action have won by seventy-three votes. Our protest will come to an end at eight o'clock tomorrow morning.' Rick tugged her sweater and she bent over so that she could hear him properly, straightening up after a couple of moments and nodding. 'It's been suggested that we should go out in style – with a bang, not a whimper. We could have some music, maybe a brass band…' As she glanced around, a few musicians shouted out that they would bring their instruments. 'And some colourful banners. Let's wear bright clothes, too,' she went on, warming to her theme, 'and cheerful smiles. Let's show the world how much we love our village and that whatever happens, whatever misfortunes befall us, the people of Tremarnock will stick together and stand proud!'

There was a loud cheer, but she hadn't quite finished and asked them to quieten down for just a minute more.

'I suggest we all rise at crack of dawn tomorrow to pack up our things. When the officials arrive, we can have our banners and so on ready and process down the hill towards Market Square.'

'I've got plenty of coloured pens and paints and cardboard I can donate,' Esme called, 'I'll fetch them after the meeting.'

'We can make the banners in my tent,' added Felipe. 'I'll think of some good designs.'

Barbara gave a thumbs-up. 'If anyone wants me, I'll be in or around my tent for most of the day or on my phone.' Then, clasping her hands together and raising them high, she cried, 'The people of Tremarnock stand united!'

Tom and Rick helped her down from her podium and the crowd, Liz and Lowenna included, started to stream out of the marquee.

'Well that's that, then,' said Jenny, whose husband, John, had a comforting arm around her shoulder. Liz merely nodded, too upset to speak, and hurried towards her own dwelling, clutching Lowenna in her arms. As soon as they were inside, she threw herself onto her sleeping bag and burst into tears. Max had given her confidence, and she'd dared to hope that he'd be able to pull the rabbit out of the hat and save the day; but she'd been wrong.

On seeing her mother's distress, Lowenna toddled to her side, crouched down and gave her a hug, stroking her cheek as you would a child.

'Mamma sad,' she said anxiously. 'Mamma cry,' which only made Liz feel worse.

'Mamma's OK,' she lied, putting an arm out and drawing her daughter close.

Snuggling into her side like a small animal, the little girl whimpered in sympathy and Liz wept some more. She was thinking that life could be so unfair, though whether her misery had more to do with the failure of Tremarnock Resists or Max's strange and unexpected silence, she wasn't sure, and didn't really care.

Instead of heading back to the flat after the meeting, Esme decided to go straight to her pottery studio in the next village. It was where she kept her pens and cardboard and besides, she needed to check on it after so long away. Caroline wanted to go, too, and Esme was only too happy for her to come along. For years her work had been the most important thing in her life; it seemed extraordinary that her lover was still unfamiliar with the place where she had spent so many long hours, moulding and shaping bits of clay into her many different creations.

The studio was an old converted garage that she rented from an artists' co-operative, complete with tables, shelving, kilns and its own ventilation system, crucial for the safe release of toxic gases. The space was shared by two other ceramicists, each of whom had their own separate corner to work in; but until Caroline arrived, Esme had used it far more than the others who, unlike her, had children and other commitments to attend to.

Two large windows had been inserted into the sides so that there was plenty of natural light, and as they entered, their nostrils were filled with the scent of stone, dust, brick, clay and sweat – a mouldy, organic aroma that was strong, but not unpleasant. Dotted around the place were throwing wheels and buckets filled with murky water and clay scraps, while one wall was lined with cupboards and on the other was a sink and tool shelf.

Despite the fact that the studio was empty, you could almost sense the industry and the presence of people hard at work. Caroline gazed around in amazement; the space was much larger than she'd imagined. She wanted to see all of Esme's pieces, which were sitting where she'd left them some weeks ago on a tall wooden storage shelf unit in the centre of the room.

One by one, Esme took her lover through them, showing her the conventional bowls and vessels that usually sold for a decent price, as well as her asymmetric pieces – the tall, narrow forms that she loved to experiment with and that were her real raison d'être. The ones that dissatisfied her would be broken up and the clay reclaimed for future use, while the others were waiting to be fired and glazed. Caroline particularly liked a large urn, which had been commissioned by a wealthy patron and was already overdue.

'You must finish it!' she gasped, when she heard how much the buyer would be paying. 'It's all my fault it's late. I'm a terrible distraction.'

Esme smiled. 'You are.' She took Caroline's warm, soft hand in hers and gave it a squeeze. 'But I wouldn't have it any other way.'

Next, she showed Caroline the small damp room where she and her colleagues stored pieces that were still moist and needed to be trimmed, perhaps, or have handles applied. Then there were two kilns of different sizes for firing. When they'd seen everything, Caroline wanted to sit in the space that Esme usually occupied, looking out of the window at the quiet, narrow street lined with trees and Victorian terrace houses of the type that exist in almost every British town and city.

'It's got a wonderful feel. I can see why you like coming here,' she said, sighing, while Esme perched beside her. 'It's so peaceful. It must be glorious to have your own dedicated workspace. I'd love to have somewhere like this to paint.'

'Then you must,' Esme replied gently. 'Every woman needs a room of her own. There are lots of empty studios round about and they won't cost much to rent; we'll find you the perfect one. I want you to paint again – it's part of who you are.'

Caroline rested her head on Esme's shoulder and smiled gratefully. 'You're so good to me.'

'Why would I not be?'

'Oh, I don't know. I suppose I feel I've messed you about such a lot with my dithering and doubting. You were always the strong one, weren't you? You always had to look after me, rather than the other way round.'

Esme was silent, reflecting on the truth of this statement as she put an arm around Caroline, pulling her in tight. She felt very small and light; quite fragile, really, like a little bird or a delicate vase, all too easily broken. It was Esme's job to be tough and resilient for her sake, although in reality, if Caroline so much as clicked her fingers, she would fall at her feet. Putty in her hands, that's what she was. A vase and a blob of putty. What a pair! They were going to have to muddle through somehow.

The phone rang in Caroline's bag, making them both jump, and Helen's name flashed up on the screen.

'I'd better answer,' she said, rising and walking over to the other side of the room, where she listened to her daughter, nodding occasionally and responding in a low voice that Esme couldn't catch.

At one point, Caroline pulled a stool from under the bench and sat down, resting her cheek on a knuckle. Esme's heart pitter-pattered, because she could tell that something was up. The strain showed around her lover's mouth and eyes and her brow was furrowed.

Yes, yes, no, no. Her head went up and down and from side to side but still, Esme hadn't a clue what was going on. Watching and trying to interpret was torture, so she rose and went to the small kitchen near the damp room, where she put on the kettle and made two cups of tea, using milk from an open carton in the fridge.

By the time she returned to the studio with the drinks, Caroline had finished her conversation and was standing wide-eyed in the centre of the room, staring at something without seeming to see.

'What is it?' Esme asked, putting down the mugs and hurrying over.

Unable to speak, Caroline remained in Esme's arms for quite a while, stiff and unyielding, as if shock had turned her to ice; and when she finally opened her mouth, she was barely audible.

'Philip's been rushed to hospital. He had another fall.'

'Oh God!' said Esme. 'Is he all right?'

Caroline paused, her head clamped against her lover's chest. 'They don't think he's broken any bones.'

'Thank goodness.' Relief washed over Esme, but it didn't last long. Loosening her arms, she took a step back and stared into Caroline's eyes, which were dull and obscure, all the sparkle gone. 'But...?' she asked, knowing that there was more.

Caroline's face had turned pale and she seemed to shrink into herself, pulling in her shoulders until they almost met in the middle. 'They said he's deteriorating more rapidly than expected. His limbs are very stiff and his balance is bad. They're going to keep him in for a few days for observation. And when he comes out, he's going to need someone with him at all times. They don't think he'll be able to live on his own again.'

Feeling her legs weaken, Esme slumped in a chair. 'So? We'll find him a carer. It doesn't have to be you, Caroline.'

Caroline didn't move. 'Helen says it's my fault.'

Esme knew how much this would hurt. 'It's not true,' she cried. 'And you know it.'

But Caroline shook her head. 'She says it wouldn't have happened if I'd been there. He's missing me so much and it's sent him into a downward spiral. She got a call early this morning and had to rush to the hospital. It must have been terrible for her. She had to cancel work and he's dreadfully upset, too, and not making a lot of sense. She sounds at her wits' end.'

Esme took a deep breath to try to calm herself. She could feel rage bubbling just beneath the surface, but it would get her nowhere. It was the sense of impotence that she couldn't stand, this and the knowledge that in a contest between herself and Helen, Helen would always win. If the young woman had been there in front of her she could have punched her, she really could, but fear, rather than hostility, was the motivating force.

'Did you tell her your foot's still in a boot and you can't get very far?' A querulous, self-pitying quality had crept into her voice, which she hated. 'Surely she and Andrew can cope for a few days? We can find someone to nurse Philip when he comes out of hospital.'

There was a deafening silence that filled Esme's head and made it throb. Caroline was still standing; she'd hardly moved, and when she finally spoke, her words seemed to blast through the atmosphere, shattering everything in their path.

'She's pregnant, Esme. She's expecting her first child.'

As if Esme needed reminding. How, she wondered, could two such small statements carry so much force? Despite having no children herself, she could imagine the strength and intensity of that pull and knew in her heart of hearts that the game was up.

'So what will you do?' she said heavily. 'Will you go back?'

Caroline blinked slowly and gave the slightest nod. Now, a cannonball hit Esme right in the chest while another crashed into her solar plexus, smashing it into little pieces. Her head swam and she felt herself sway on the stool and start to fall. Caroline caught her just in time and the pair tumbled to the ground where they lay in a heap, tangled in each other's arms.

'I'm so sorry,' Caroline was saying, over and over through her tears. 'I just can't do this. I can't abandon Helen – and Philip needs me.'

Esme was weeping too, but at the mention of his name, a red rage descended again. '*He* needs you?' she spat. 'Him? That cheat and bully? What about *me*?'

Caroline didn't reply. She didn't have to. As always, Esme knew that she was going to have to accept and cope as best she could. Helen was Caroline's flesh and blood and of course she loved Philip, her father, too. Families were bound by invisible ties – husbands and wives, children, parents and grandchildren. It was the natural order of things, and who was Esme to try to take on Nature?

She rose slowly, adjusting her clothes and smoothing her hair as if a neat outward appearance would somehow bring her inner turmoil to heel. Not that she really cared. For her, all was lost and the world, which only a short time before had glittered and fizzed with promise, now seemed hollow and hopeless.

'I'll just go for a bit. I'll come back,' Caroline whispered.

But Esme didn't believe her. 'He won't let you, not once you're there again. He'll get Andrew and Helen on his side and use her and the baby against you; he'll do everything in his power to keep you.'

'You make him sound like a monster.'

'Well, isn't he? He lied to you for years.'

'He's still my husband.'

'Then go back to him – go!' Esme raised an arm and pointed at the door. Frightened of her own anger, she made Caroline tremble, too.

'Forgive me,' she beseeched, clasping her hands, prayer-like. Her blue eyes swam with tears and she looked just like the lost young girl who'd arrived at St Hilda's all those years ago.

Esme groaned, a long, low sound like a wounded animal. She knew that she was cornered, done for, and her body seemed to crumple, all her fury gone.

'Of course I forgive you,' she said, holding out her arms again for Caroline, who stumbled in, needing comfort as always, and looking to Esme to be strong.

'I'm going to miss you so much,' she whispered through her tears. 'I'll write every day.'

It wasn't nearly enough, but what could Esme do? 'And I'll always be here, waiting for you,' she replied dully.

Chapter Eighteen

IT WAS HARD to go back to the campsite armed with pens, paints and cardboard and pretend that nothing had happened. Esme's eyes were red and puffy and Caroline was as pale as death. Luckily, however, the place was a hive of activity and no one noticed the peculiar appearance of the two newest arrivals.

It had stopped drizzling and in one corner of the field, folk were tuning up their instruments and practising a repertoire of songs, while Felipe was busy transforming his tent and the surrounding area into an artists' hub. He'd laid out canvas sheets, easels and his own supply of stationery, and there was already a sign above the door saying, BANNER-MAKING HERE!

The children who were too young to be at school were toddling around the place, hunting in bushes, having been charged with the task of finding some long, strong sticks on which to nail the banners. From the evidence on offer, they weren't having much success. The sorry little pile of twigs on one of Felipe's canvas sheets looked more like kindling than suitable sign material, but the kids were having a marvellous time, which was all that really mattered.

Esme and Caroline scarcely exchanged glances as they threw themselves into helping Felipe, because they knew that one or other might so easily burst into tears again. The last thing Esme wanted was to return to her flat right now, which in her mind's eye already felt empty and sad before her lover had even left. Keeping active was her best weapon against despair; in fact she thought that she might have to be frantically busy for the rest of her life.

Liz, too, was trying to take her mind off things, and had by now made two trips back to Bag End with Lowenna, her pushchair laden with carriers containing clothes, toys and some of the many other items that had accumulated in the tent since they'd been sleeping there. She tried to be subtle about it, because no one wanted the council or developers to get wind of the fact that a surrender was imminent; though their spies would be out and about, and the protesters accepted that it would be difficult to keep things under wraps.

After dropping off the second lot of carriers, Liz decided to stroll over to A Winkle in Time to see Robert. He'd no doubt have heard the news from Jesse, who was working that day, and of course he'd be relieved that the protest was coming to an end, but still she hoped that he might be able to give her some comfort; a hug, at least. Instead, an arctic blast hit her as she walked through the door.

'The police have objected to the alcohol licence,' he barked. Instinctively, she took a step back. 'They say it'll encourage rowdiness and bad behaviour and it'll be dangerous for children and families using the beach.' He was red in the face and fuming. You could almost see the smoke billowing from his ears, nose and mouth. 'It's absolute rubbish,' he went on. 'They're just flexing their muscles. The bastards enjoy making it difficult for small businesses like mine – they love the power.'

Helpless in the face of his fury, Liz was temporarily lost for words and when she did ask if he could appeal, he flew at her again.

'It's not a question of appealing! There'll have to be a formal hearing now, which will spin things out even longer. If I'm turned down, I'll challenge it, but we're not there yet. I'll get the licence in the end but it's going to take far longer than necessary. It's extra hassle which I really don't need.'

He was so cross that Liz didn't think there was any point in talking to him about the protest; in fact it would probably only enrage him further. She popped into the kitchen to see Jesse and Alex, who were busy prepping, and even Lowenna's smiley face did little to lighten the subdued atmosphere. Clearly the boss's mood was affecting everyone.

'Does he know about the court order?' Liz asked.

Jesse shrugged. 'I haven't told him, haven't had the chance. He's been too busy ranting and raving; I couldn't get a word in edgeways.'

Liz sighed. Of course the Secret Shack was important and she was sorry that he was upset, but he wasn't the only one with disappointing news, though he was certainly behaving that way.

There was nothing to be gained by hanging about, so after asking her husband if she could do anything to help and being roundly rejected, she and Lowenna headed to the marketplace. At the bakery they bought a selection of hot pasties, cold drinks, bread and milk, which they took back with them to the campsite and distributed among their friends.

She and Lowenna then walked over to Felipe's tent to help with the banner-making, and the little girl had great fun messing around with the paints and crayons. There was quite a crowd, both inside and out, and lots of laughter as people tried to come up with witty slogans, some of which weren't particularly witty at all: '*MegaCrest = MegaBollocks*'; '*Hands off our playground!*'; '*I AM QUITE CROSS!*'; '*I'm so angry I made this sign!*'; '*We're not anti-development, we're AIR BREATHERS!*' And so on.

It was as if the realisation that they'd lost the fight had finally sunk in, and now everyone was determined to make the best of a bad situation. Only Caroline and Esme still seemed downcast and Liz couldn't help wondering if they'd had a row; they were barely communicating. At one point, when Liz and Esme were kneeling side by side on the floor, putting the finishing touches to a multicoloured border with lashings of glitter and gold stars, Liz asked if everything was all right.

'You're very quiet. Is something up?'

Esme looked uncomfortable. 'I'm fine. Just a bit tired, that's all.'

Liz wasn't convinced, but decided to leave it at that.

There was a bit of a party in the field that night with lots of wine and beer. Rosie and Rafael had arrived after school with some friends and erected their own tent to sleep in, so there was an alternative teenage do going on as well. They were rather rowdy but as it was the last evening, the villagers were happy to put up with it. At one point, Liz saw Rosie and Rafael dancing quite close but looked away quickly, not wishing to embarrass them.

When she retired to bed at around 11 p.m., full of crisps and alcohol, she tried not to check her phone yet again for a message from Max, but couldn't resist. She wasn't really expecting anything but still, the empty inbox brought a lump to her throat. Why hadn't he at least dropped her a line to tell her that he couldn't buy the land after all, and wish her luck for tomorrow? She began to type:

> How is Munich? Last night under the stars for me. Strangely enough, I'm going to miss it.

After hovering on 'send', she quickly pressed the delete button instead. It would be humiliating to write again when he hadn't replied to the last text; it might look like begging.

Lowenna snuffled in her sleep and Liz turned off the little lamp before lying there for quite some time, listening to the stillness. After tomorrow, she thought, life would go back to normal. She'd clean the house, water the plants and tick off all the other chores that she'd been avoiding for the past couple of weeks.

Soon, very soon, she might fail to remember that she'd been part of a protest group and that for just a brief window of time, she'd actually believed that victory was at hand. As for the handsome German... she suspected that he was going to take a little longer to forget.

The whole of Tremarnock came out to watch the final march, along with many folk from the surrounding villages and towns. Charlie had put out numerous announcements on varying social media platforms and had managed to generate a lot of excitement. You could feel it in the air.

The campers had timed things carefully, having risen very early to take down their tents, carry them to their homes or cars and clear the field of all debris. When the police turned up on the dot of 8 a.m., along with assorted council officials and Reg Carter, of course, Barbara was already at the playground exit, holding aloft a magnificent technicolour poster which read, '*WE'RE REALLY NOT HAPPY ABOUT THIS!!*'

Behind her in a long orderly line were rows of people, all two abreast and dressed in black and white, the colours of the Cornish flag, because they hadn't been able to get T-shirts and beanies made in time. Most were brandishing cloth or paper banners suspended between two poles, while a few had small children on their shoulders. At the very back stood a brass band complete with trumpets, trombones, tubas, drums and euphoniums, plus cymbals, triangles and bells for the kids. When Barbara turned and gave a rather impressive wolf whistle, they struck up 'When the Saints Go Marching In' and the people started to process slowly out of the field and down Fore Street in the direction of the sea.

It was a sunny morning and the sky was bright blue. Liz, who was pushing the stroller, was amazed to see the narrow roads flanked with well-wishers, who cheered as the protesters streamed past and waved hats and scarves. Rosie was still sulking and walked a few steps behind. She had flatly refused to discuss the argument over Max, which was very unlike her, and she and Liz were barely speaking. Liz was baffled and a bit upset; they'd always been so close in the past. She had decided not to force the issue, however; better to put it on the back burner until the march was over.

Of course everyone knew the words to the song and joined in lustily while the children clashed their cymbals, rattled their maracas and pinged their triangles. They weren't much good at keeping in time, but no one cared. On reaching the seafront, the band switched to a stirring rendition of 'Jerusalem', which was partly drowned out by the noise of crashing waves and screeching seagulls. The banners flapped in the wind while everyone had a damp nose and pink face. All the stores were closed, because the shopkeepers were either on the march or watching from the sidelines; surrounded by flashing cameras, Liz began to feel rather like a film star, waving and smiling so much that her cheeks hurt. No one would ever guess that she was crying inside, and she wanted to keep it that way.

At Rick's shop, Treasure Trove, they turned right and began to climb the fairly steep cobbled slope that was South Street. As she passed A Winkle in Time, Liz peered through the window and was dismayed to spot Robert drying glasses behind the bar. He saw her, too, and nodded before lowering his head again and resuming his task.

She felt ashamed on his behalf, because he must be the only soul in the village at work right now. If he didn't want to join the march, he could at least have bothered to come out and show some solidarity. Stubborn, that's what he was. Stubborn and wrong.

In the marketplace, Barbara stopped by the war memorial while the protesters fanned out around the edge of the square, spilling into the little streets round about to allow the band to remain in the middle.

There was silence for a moment. Then she nodded at the conductor, who stepped forward with his baton, gave a one-two-three and the musicians struck up their grand finale, Rodrigo's *Concierto de Aranjuez*. They performed at their absolute best; it was hauntingly melancholic and beautiful and brought almost everyone to tears. When it finally came to an end, people milled around for a while, muttering and exchanging glances as if waiting for something more to happen, but there was nothing else. Barbara chatted with the conductor while the musicians started to pack up their instruments, ready to go home.

Charlie was still moving about among the crowd, getting some last comments, but even Rory had put down his camera, and the TV crew that Liz had seen earlier had melted away.

So this really was it, she thought miserably. It felt like such an anticlimax. The local council and developers had kept well out of the way today, but she could just picture their jubilation behind the scenes; they were probably rubbing their hands together, the council looking forward to its fat cheque and the MegaCrest Homes lot to bringing in the bulldozers. Already, she imagined, they might be erecting security fences around the playground to prevent further trouble and she didn't think she could ever bear to walk that way again. She'd just have to take an alternative road out of the village from now on.

Momentarily forgetting Rosie's huff, she turned to speak to her.

'Shall we pick up the car and go and get a hot chocolate at the café?'

It was something that they'd always enjoyed doing together. Rosie made a sour face.

'I can't—' she started to say.

But Liz wouldn't take no for an answer and put her in charge of the stroller so that she couldn't wander off.

'C'mon. I need cheering up, even if you don't.'

They were starting to weave their way through the throng when all of a sudden, a jubilant shout stopped them in their tracks.

Spinning around, Liz saw someone run towards Barbara, waving a piece of paper in the air. She couldn't make out the face but she'd know that pompous, nasal voice anywhere: Reg Carter.

By standing on tiptoe, Liz could just about peer over the heads to the memorial, where he stopped and raised his arms.

'I have some good news!' he cried breathlessly. He was without his loudspeaker today, but the crowd had fallen so silent that you could hear a pin drop. 'The playground has been saved!'

Liz let out a gasp, as did everyone around her, and her heart started thumping in her chest.

A woman yelled: 'Is this a joke? Are you having us on?'

Reg shook his head. 'Upon my word, it's the truth. The council has received a better offer for the land, which they've accepted. They've only just finished talking to their lawyers, which is why I'm telling you now. I'm pleased to say,' he went on, puffing out his chest, 'that the new buyer wishes to preserve the area as a children's play park. There will be no housing development after all.'

The crowd let out a thunderous roar and poor Lowenna, in her pushchair, slapped her hands over her ears.

Cries of, 'I can't believe it!' and 'We've won!' filled the air and Liz caught sight of Charlie, nonplussed for once, just standing open mouthed and staring at Reg, her notebook and pen hanging limply by her side.

For a moment, Barbara, too, looked utterly confused, but she quickly patted her blonde hair and composed herself.

'That's wonderful!' she said. Then she added, 'Can you tell us who the new buyer is?'

Reg's reply was too quiet to catch. There was uproar, with yells of, 'We can't hear!' 'Speak up, will you?' and, rather more rudely, 'Where's his megaphone now, the stupid old git?'

Unabashed, Reg repeated himself and Liz strained her ears to no avail. But then, like a game of Chinese whispers, those in front started to turn around and pass the name to the person behind them. By the time it reached her, the mystery saviour had become 'Knox Buyer' but it was enough for her to glean the truth.

Knox Buyer? Max Maier. Her heart swelled to the size of a watermelon. He'd come good. He'd saved the day! She wanted to run around the square screaming and dancing but settled instead for hugs with Lowenna and all those standing close by. She tried to hug Rosie, too, but she backed away, her arms pinned firmly to her sides. It saddened Liz, but she was determined not to let it spoil the joyous moment.

Even Reg dashed around shaking people's hands and slapping them on the back and generally behaving as if the good news was all thanks to him and he was entitled to the credit. It was Jenny Lambert, who was normally quite mild-mannered, who raised her voice to remind him and anyone listening that he'd sided with the enemy and wasn't welcome in the protesters' midst.

Reg's face turned puce. 'I've always done my best for this village,' he spluttered. 'Some people are just ungrateful.' But he didn't hang about any longer, sensing, perhaps, that if he valued his life, it would be wisest to scarper now.

Of course no one wanted to go home or back to work after that, and the suggestion went around that they should repair to Barbara's pub on the seafront to celebrate. Naturally, she thought this was an excellent idea, and led the way back to the Lobster Pot where she announced that the first round was on her.

'I'll get the second,' shouted Rick, who was drunk on the excitement. There were an awful lot of them and Liz hoped that he wouldn't regret his generous offer in the cold light of the next morning.

'And I'll do the third,' Tom piped up before Jean could stop him. They were clearly in for a riotous few hours.

Liz was sitting on the sea wall with a glass of red wine in her hand chatting to Felipe, Nathan, Annie and a few others when Rosie gave her a prod.

'It's your phone,' she said irritably.

Dipping her hand in her pocket, Liz could feel that the mobile was, indeed, vibrating; she'd been talking too much to notice. She pulled it out and on seeing Max's name flash up on the screen, she quickly answered.

'Hey!' he said warmly, 'I was about to leave a message. Has anyone told you what's happened?'

Liz took a few steps away from the group before saying that she thought she could explode with happiness, which made him laugh. She went on to describe the march, the brass band and Reg's timely arrival just as they were all packing up and getting ready to go home, and all the while Max listened quietly, seeming to relish every detail.

When she'd finished at last, he said, 'I'm so glad it's worked out. I hope you all have a great time today – you deserve it.'

He sounded slightly wistful, as if he'd rather like to be there himself; but that was impossible, of course.

'I hope you didn't have to pay too much?' Liz asked, feeling slightly guilty that he wasn't here enjoying himself, too, and he told her not to worry.

'In the end I think the council were relieved to have a reason to pull out of the MegaCrest deal. There was a lot of opposition from all sides.'

'Well, we're all eternally grateful, as I hope you know.' All of a sudden, an idea came into her head and popped out of her mouth before she had time to stop it. 'You must come back for a celebration, so we can say thank you in person. You and Mila, if she likes. We can also talk about a plaque for your grandfather, or whatever you want. I can speak to the others and send some possible dates.' Heat rose to her face and she wondered if she'd said the wrong thing. After all, Max might not want to return to Tremarnock so soon, if at all. He might have saved the playground, but that didn't necessarily mean that he'd wish to become bosom buddies with the villagers. She started to say that perhaps, on the other hand, he would prefer to organise his grandfather's memorial from a distance, but he interrupted.

'I'd love that! I'm sure Mila would, too. I'll ask her mother – I'm sure it'll be OK.'

Liz hung up and felt herself floating away. The others must have noticed because Annie walked over to where she was standing and tugged her arm, as if to anchor her to the ground.

'What's happened?'

'Nothing,' Liz replied, quick as a flash.

Annie clearly wasn't convinced. 'You look like the cat that got the cream.'

Keen to get away, Liz hurried inside the pub to speak to Barbara, who was behind the bar holding forth about some aspect of the day's events, surrounded by a coterie of jovial villagers including Bramble and her partner Matt. When Liz told them about Max's call and the possibility of a thank-you celebration, they clapped their hands in delight.

'Marvellous idea!' said Barbara. 'Let's put our heads together and think what to do. It needs to be pretty special.'

Someone suggested a dinner dance in the Methodist church hall, but that was vetoed because the heating wasn't up to much and the roof leaked.

Then Bramble proposed Polgarry Manor, which was already becoming popular for weddings, music festivals and the like. 'We could put up a marquee in the grounds and have a barbecue and a live band. I wouldn't charge for the venue – that would be my and Matt's contribution – but everyone will have to chip in for the food and drink.'

It was a very generous offer and Barbara thanked her warmly, before arranging for them all to meet for coffee at the manor tomorrow morning to discuss dates and divvy out some of the tasks. 'I think we should have the party soon,' she said. 'If we leave it too long he might go off the boil.'

Bramble agreed. 'How about 5th November – Guy Fawkes night? We can have fireworks and hot dogs and a great big bonfire.'

Everyone loved the idea but there wasn't much time, and Liz would have to check that Max was free. As she left the pub to join the others outside again, it occurred to her that Rosie was probably the only person who wouldn't want him to come. Well, she'd just have to put up with it. Liz had already started composing an email to him in her head. '*Dear Max, in order to show our appreciation...*' She frowned. Too formal. '*Hi Max, I've been talking to the villagers and...*'

Her mind wandered off. What to wear? Jeans and a warm sweater would be the most practical, although she might need a new top to go on underneath, something a bit glamorous, especially if there'd be dancing. She would offer to pick him up from the airport again and could take him somewhere new. Truro perhaps, or Bodmin Moor for a long walk. He'd probably enjoy Jamaica Inn, though it was dreadfully touristy. This time, she thought, she'd insist that he stay at her place rather than Audrey's; if Mila came, they could share the spare room next to her own. She would make a joke of it, telling him that she wouldn't take no for an answer, and promise not to do an Audrey and ply him with drink and keep him up till 2 a.m.

Bag End would need a good clean, and she would sweep the fireplace and buy fresh flowers. She'd want it to look lovely and welcoming, and she could make a big casserole for him in advance. If she prepared everything properly, she'd have more time to enjoy herself when he was here.

Should she put kisses on the end of her email? Maybe just one. And she'd give him a key, so he could come and go as he pleased. If she made it all sound appealing enough, he couldn't possibly refuse, could he? She had better book an appointment with the hairdresser and get her nails done as well. But only once he said yes, of course.

Chapter Nineteen

CAROLINE WAS DUE to return to Paris on Monday. That morning, Esme's despair reached depths that she had never known existed. On awakening, she moved about the flat as if in a trance, checking under chairs and in cupboards to make sure that nothing was left behind. A forgotten item wouldn't have mattered; she could always post it – but she needed to keep performing mechanical tasks just to stop herself from going insane.

The only thing that she couldn't bear to help with was the packing. Watching Caroline fold up and put away her clothes and other possessions would have been torture, so Esme was careful not to stray into the bedroom while the suitcase was still open.

At one point she left Caroline alone to drive to her studio, guessing that no one would be there and hoping to find some peace and solace among her half-finished creations. But she found none. Instead, the place felt sterile and empty, just a room full of dust and rubbish. Once, the mere act of sitting at her bench, dipping her hands in the bucket of murky water beside her and kneading her fingers in the slab of grey clay would have been enough to give her a thrill of pleasure, but not now. She wondered if she would ever feel inspired to work again.

Since making her decision, Caroline had been in practical mode, bustling about doing jobs and refusing to engage in any kind of meaningful conversation. When Esme returned to the flat, however, she sensed that her lover's mood had changed.

Once she had put her suitcase by the door, Caroline took Esme's hand in hers and suggested a last walk along the cliffs. 'Can we go to the place where the shrine of the Lost Lady of Tremarnock is supposed to have been?'

Esme was doubtful. 'I told you, there's nothing to see and it's a fair way from the car park. I'm not even sure you'd manage it with your ankle.'

'Please,' begged Caroline. 'I'd really like to.'

And of course, Esme couldn't refuse. It was the story of her life, really; she was unable to deny Caroline anything.

The flight was at 4.15 p.m., so it made sense to take her suitcase with them and drive on to the airport afterwards. It was only a few short miles out of Tremarnock to their destination, but the road up to the cliffs was steep and narrow and some of it had to be done in first gear.

'I hope we don't roll backwards!' Caroline commented and Esme had to reassure her that she'd done the same journey many times before.

'The woods are one of Jenny Lambert's favourite spots. I used to go there quite often with her and Sally, but not so much recently.'

When they reached the brow of the hill, the road split into three, and Esme turned left down what was little more than a dirt track flanked with hedges. At the very end was an open gate leading to a small car park with a sign at the edge shaped like an arrow that said, TREMANTHIA WOODS ¼ MILE.

'The ground's quite rough and uneven. Are you sure you still want to do it?' Esme asked, stopping the car and turning off the engine, and Caroline said that she did.

After wrapping her bad foot in a plastic bag to keep the boot from getting wet and muddy, they set off together across the wide, empty field in the direction of the trees, following the path of a small stream to their left. The sky was grey and overcast but luckily it wasn't cold, as Caroline had to pause frequently to rest.

On reaching the woods, they plunged into semi-darkness and she marvelled at the wide variety of trees: assorted conifers and broadleaf species such as oak, ash, cherry, chestnut, beech and lime, along with holly bushes that grew all the way along the track. The path soon started to climb in a long incline up a steep bank; it was carpeted with decaying leaves and quite damp and slippery, so Caroline needed Esme's arm for support. At the top they crossed through the stream and took the left fork to a small clearing, where more tracks and paths led off in a bewildering number of directions.

Caroline stopped, confused, but Esme pointed directly ahead, and they continued. Suddenly they came face to face with a large red deer, cleverly camouflaged by vegetation. Caroline jumped and hung onto Esme's arm, but it was more frightened than they were and soon darted back into the bushes.

Before long, the trees thinned out again. A kissing gate led into another field, which they had to walk across before they could climb a stile to get back to the woods. Just a little way beyond stood a large elder tree, with a metal plaque beneath and some writing that had faded and grown indistinct with age. Caroline read the words as best she could, stumbling a little and needing Esme's help:

Elder be ye Lady's tree, burn it not or cursed ye'll be.

Turning to her friend with raised eyebrows, Caroline asked what it meant, and Esme explained that elders are traditionally associated with witchcraft, perhaps because their berries were used in medicines. There used to be lots of superstitions about cutting down or burning them.

'Creepy,' said Caroline. 'I bet there used to be all sorts of ghastly witch rituals round here.'

'Oh yes,' Esme agreed. 'There were lots of trials in the seventeenth century. They were held at the Assize courts in Launceston, and the convicted ones were hanged. Later, though, people became less wary of witches and some were even quite revered. In the 1800s, a Cornish witch called Granny Boswell was famous for being able to cure ringworm in cattle. She used to provide funny old charms and people quite liked her, though you didn't want to get on her wrong side because she could curse as well.'

The woods became dense and dark again quite quickly. When a woodpigeon fluttered out of the undergrowth in front of them, they both started. Soon, they were crossing over the spring once more and Caroline spotted a field with an earthwork through a gap in the trees, which Esme explained was the remains of a Norman motte and bailey castle.

'This is where we start heading back. We'll be going on a different path, though, because we're doing a big circle.'

She was intending to stick to the same, well-worn track that she'd used many times before, but Caroline had other ideas. A few yards further on, she left Esme's side, plunging off the path towards the very centre of the woods, where the vegetation was at its thickest.

There was nothing for it but to follow and in they went, deeper and deeper, stooping beneath low hanging branches and fighting their way through tangled ivy. Their feet crunched on fallen twigs and their coats snared on prickly holly until Esme began to wonder if Caroline had gone quite mad.

'Don't you think we should turn back? We might get lost.'

But Caroline was having none of it. 'Just a little further,' she insisted, hobbling ahead on her bad leg.

To their right, an inquisitive robin perching on a bough fixed them with its beady black eye before ruffling its feathers and swooping off; a squirrel that had just finished burying a nut scampered up a tree.

'It feels so ancient,' Caroline commented over her shoulder.

'No shrine though. I did warn you.'

Esme bent to avoid another branch and scraped her cheek on a bramble. 'Ow!' Instinctively her hand shot up; there was crimson blood on her fingertips. She frowned, angry with herself for agreeing to the detour.

Caroline pulled a tissue from her pocket and was about to pass it over when she stopped short, putting a forefinger to her lips.

'What?' Esme was losing the will to live, but her lover cocked her head to one side and ignored her.

'Can you hear that?' Caroline said at last.

But all Esme could perceive was the sound of her own laboured breath. She was just about to insist that they leave the thicket and find the path again when she fancied that she did catch something – a tinkling, like the sound of running water. It was puzzling, as they'd left the stream some way back.

'There must be a tributary. I didn't know.'

Forgetting all about Esme's scratched cheek, Caroline upped her pace and pushed further inwards, following the sound of water.

After about a hundred yards or so, she stopped abruptly and let out a gasp.

'What is it?' Manoeuvring herself alongside, now, at last, Esme could see what the fuss was about, for there in front of them was a large, smooth, mossy green rock with a strange circular hole in the centre. Through it tumbled a miniature waterfall, like a sort of pixie cascade. At its base was a small round pond and as the water hit, it frothed and sparkled like crystal.

'It's beautiful!' Caroline cried, turning to Esme with glittering eyes. 'This is the site of the shrine. I know it. We've found the Lost Lady of Tremarnock.'

Esme laughed. 'How do you know?' But her laughter soon faded when she realised that her lover was in earnest.

'Don't you remember? In the book it talked about a wood and a rock with a hole in it and a waterfall tumbling through. It can't just be coincidence. I'm certain this is where the legend started and where people came to pray.'

They were silent for a moment, and as Esme continued to gaze at the scene before her, a strange thing happened. Little by little the colours seemed to become more vivid and each object more clearly defined: the deep green moss, the damp grey rock, the gnarled branches of overhanging trees, the sparkling white foamy water and the rich brown earth round about, all seemed to light up like a theatre set to enchant a rapt audience. Surely nothing natural could be quite so intense or carefully drawn?

She only snapped to when Caroline seized her arm. 'Quick! We must douse ourselves in the water!'

It sounded absurd but she was quite serious, bending down at the edge of the pond and dipping in her hands. Esme watched, mesmerised, as she ran her fingers just below the surface, making little rivulets and swirls, her gold wedding ring glinting when it caught the light. She crouched down further and submerged her hands completely while Esme continued to stare, statue-like; she couldn't seem to move. Then all of a sudden, without any warning, Caroline cupped her palms, rose up from the ground and threw a shower of water all over her own head and hair.

'You're crazy!' said Esme, gasping; she hadn't seen it coming. 'It must be freezing!'

But Caroline didn't mind. Down her hands went and up they came again and again, this time splashing her face, her neck and the crown of her head until she was half-soaked.

Giggles bubbled up inside and Esme laughed; she couldn't help it.

'Stop it!' she cried.

But Caroline continued for quite some while before turning to her lover, her blonde hair sticking to her head, her face wet and wreathed in smiles. 'Come on, it's your turn now!'

Esme hesitated for just a moment before squatting down, but her knees creaked and she felt foolish and uncertain. 'What do I do now?'

She watched with a mixture of fascination and horror as Caroline submerged her hands again, this time tossing a shower of water over Esme's lower half, before rising up and dousing her brow and the crown of her head as a vicar would a child at its baptism.

'Be gone, all our troubles,' she said sonorously, and Esme laughed again, despite the ice-cold liquid trickling down her cheeks and neck.

'May we be reborn!' she replied with mock solemnity, crossing herself like a priest.

She would have got up then, assuming that the fun, if that was how you would describe it, was over, but Caroline knelt at her side, wrapping an arm around her shoulders and pulling her in tight.

'Close your eyes,' she commanded and once again, Esme did as she was told.

'Dear Tremanthia,' Caroline whispered, 'thank you for leading us to your holy spring and to the site of your shrine. Thank you for showing us your secret waterfall. You promised all those years ago to help the women and girls of Cornwall, especially in matters of love. Well, Esme and I love each other very much. Please help us find a way to be together for ever. And in the meantime, support us when we have to be apart. Amen.' After she'd finished, she turned to Esme, her eyes moist with tears. 'It hasn't all been in vain, you know. Not for me, anyway.'

'Hasn't it? All those lost years...'

Caroline shook her head. 'Don't you see? Your love has sustained me. It's only thanks to you that I've been able to keep going, to raise my children and support Philip's important work. Helen and Andrew are decent people and Philip's done a lot of good in the world, too. Whatever else he is, that has to count for something.'

A painful lump lodged in Esme's throat and it was all she could do not to cry. Caroline leaned over and planted a trembling kiss on her cheek and murmured in her ear, 'We must be brave, my darling. Tremanthia will help us.'

The whole silly ceremony seemed like superstitious claptrap to Esme, but she didn't say so. With nothing else to cling to and no other comfort on offer, she decided she had better go with it.

'Please help me cope when Caroline leaves,' she mumbled, not knowing to whom she was talking or indeed, if anyone was listening. 'Take away my loneliness and give me hope that one day, we'll never have to be parted again.'

The wind whistled through the branches, and something rustled in the bushes; a small animal, perhaps. Then everything was as it had been before. Esme took a deep breath and inwardly cursed herself. She felt annoyed with Caroline for making her go through the pointless ritual, and angry with herself for failing to stop it.

They were both silent as they rose. Only Caroline nodded goodbye to the rock and waterfall before they began to pick their way through the thicket in the direction of what they hoped would be the path. It took a while to get back on course, but they managed it somehow, and it wasn't until the trees started to thin out and they could once more see clear sky that they finally spoke again.

'What an amazing experience!' Caroline said. 'Did we imagine it?'

'There was a rock with a hole and a waterfall all right,' Esme replied dryly. 'I'm still not convinced about the shrine bit, though.'

But as they walked slowly back across the field towards the car park, she couldn't help noticing a new quickness in her step, and a lightness of spirit that hadn't been there before. It might just have been coincidence, but for the first time since Caroline had booked her return flight to Paris, Esme was struck with the feeling that this wasn't the end, and that somehow or other, everything was going to be all right.

The women had already agreed not to prolong their farewell. When they reached the airport, Caroline switched back into practical mode, piling her things on the trolley and refusing to meet Esme's gaze.

'That's everything then,' she said crisply, when she was ready to make her way towards the airport entrance. An inattentive observer might have drawn the conclusion that she'd had enough of Cornwall and was keen to be off, but Esme saw how tightly she gripped the handle of the cart, her knuckles white, and knew better.

'Goodbye my darling,' Caroline whispered. Their lips brushed and she made a strange choking sound before turning on her heel and pushing her trolley as swiftly as she could over the zebra crossing and across the car park. She'd already warned Esme not to help her with this bit; she couldn't bear it.

'Go quickly,' she'd commanded. 'Drive away and don't look back.'

It nearly broke Esme's heart, but she did as she was told, climbing back in the car, switching on the engine and peering through the windscreen blurred by her tears as she accelerated away.

It was just as well that she didn't see her lover, small and frail, stagger at the edge of the crossing and need assistance from a passer-by. Nor did she know that in the departures lounge, someone had to summon a security guard because a slight blonde woman with a sprained ankle was distraught and weeping and could barely stand up.

As soon as Esme was away from the airport, she pulled into a layby and wept until her head throbbed, her cheeks burned, her eyes stung and she could weep no more. It was a relief, really, because in the past few days it had taken all her strength to hold back. Now, at last, she didn't have to fight any more.

A white van went past and the man in the passenger seat turned to stare, but she pretended not to notice. Let him look, she thought. He'd cry too if he knew grief like mine. Suddenly, misery gave way to fury and she banged the wheel and screamed, 'I CAN'T LIVE WITHOUT HER! IT'S MORE THAN I CAN BEAR!'

The sound seemed to ricochet around the walls of the interior and come right back at twice the original volume. She flinched before hollering again, 'I CAN'T DO IT! DON'T MAKE ME! I'D RATHER DIE!'

Pausing, she listened for the echo; only this time, it sounded strangely different. Her eyes opened wide with surprise and she thought that she must have misheard; but then the voice came again, loud and clear, stopping all other thought in its tracks: 'HAVE FAITH! BE PATIENT! YOUR WISHES WILL COME TRUE!'

As she breathed in and out deeply, a sense of calm started to flow through her veins, replacing the panic of before; and out of her mouth came a quick, whispered prayer of thanks. Cars continued to whizz past and she feared that soon, someone might report a distressed woman in a layby and call the police. Reaching into the glove compartment for some tissues, her hands trembled slightly as she wiped her eyes and blew her nose; but she managed it, and even found a comb in her bag to straighten out her hair.

When at last she was done, she turned the engine back on and pulled out of the layby, checking carefully in the mirror. She was thinking all the while that although she had left her religious beliefs behind long ago, a crisis was a crisis; and if life chose to throw her something strange and really rather spiritual, it was probably a good idea to seize it, as a drowning man would a lifebelt, and not to ask too many questions.

Chapter Twenty

GUY FAWKES NIGHT had been a big deal when Liz was a child. She could still remember the excitement of waiting for her father to return from work, bringing with him a small selection of fireworks that he'd picked up at the corner shop: rockets, sparklers, Catherine wheels and so on. After supper, he'd put on his Wellington boots, thick coat and funny old hat and head down to the bottom of their small London garden clutching his crucial equipment, including jam jars, matches, a hammer and nails.

Liz would watch with her mother from their sitting room window, her nose pressed to the glass as he'd nail the Catherine wheels to some rickety trellis and place the rockets carefully in their pots. She'd thought him terribly brave. After finishing the preparations, he'd stand back and do a thumbs-up and she and her mother would squeal with pleasure.

'Is it time now?' Liz would cry, and her mother would nod and put a protective arm around her shoulders and say she hoped that Daddy would be careful, which made Liz shiver but also added to the thrill. A slight sense of danger was part of the fun, after all. She'd known from a very early age that the reason they celebrated the date was because a man had tried to blow up Parliament and that he'd come to a very sticky end. To her young mind, the grisly details, heavily edited by her parents of course, had seemed quite delightful.

Back then, 5th November had been a red-letter day that everyone looked forward to. By the time Rosie had come along, however, people had started celebrating Halloween more, and although there were still public fireworks displays in most towns and cities, fewer had parties and gatherings at home.

So when the evening of the grand Guy Fawkes night do at Polgarry Manor arrived, Liz felt obliged to explain again to her eldest daughter why the festival had once meant such a lot and why it was a good idea to be reviving the tradition. Swept up in the excitement of the party plans, Rosie had stopped being morose and seemed to have got over her huff at last. She hadn't said why she'd been so rude to Max, but Liz had decided to let the matter rest. She tried not to mention his name, though, as it seemed to annoy Rosie.

'When I was little, boys and girls used to make their own models of Guy Fawkes out of papier mâché and things,' Liz said, as they tidied away their late lunch and wiped the kitchen table. 'They'd wait outside train stations and shops, crying, "Penny for the Guy!", and people would give them money.'

'That's begging!' observed Rosie.

Liz laughed. 'I suppose so, but it didn't seem like it. After all, they weren't asking for something for nothing; people admired the Guys and gave more for the best ones. Sometimes you'd see a scrappy old thing that had probably taken five minutes to throw together and my mother – your granny – would scoff about it, but she'd always chuck a few coins in the hat. She had a big heart.'

'I wish she was still alive,' said Rosie wistfully, bending down to pick up Lowenna's dirty spoon from the floor. She'd never met Katharine, who had died when Liz was just sixteen, but she'd heard so much about her.

Liz took the spoon and put it in the dishwasher, then gave Rosie a hug. 'She'd be so proud of you.' Not wanting to be left out, Lowenna tugged on the legs of their jeans so Liz scooped her up, too, and they all had a cuddle.

'Right,' she said, breaking away at last and putting her youngest down again. 'We'd better go and get ready. Lots of warm clothes, remember. It'll be cold later on. And don't forget your toothbrush.'

Rosie had arranged a sleepover with her school friend, Mandy, or rather a wake-over, as they'd most likely be up chatting for most of the night, which meant that the following day would be a write-off.

They all headed up the stairs, but when halfway up Rosie asked, 'Can I borrow your hat, Mum – the one with the furry bobble?'

Liz frowned, because she was rather fond of it and had hoped to wear it herself.

'Pleeeease?' Rosie wheedled, clasping her hands in mock supplication.

Liz sighed. 'All right, but you're not to lose it. It was a present from Tabitha, remember?'

Rosie's eyebrows shot up, as if this was the fussiest, most unreasonable comment she'd ever heard. She seemed to have a mental blank about the fact that she quite often lost her mother's things, though strangely she managed to take perfectly good care of her own. Liz's most expensive makeup had a mysterious habit of finding its way into Rosie's drawers, too, and she'd once found her favourite silk blouse lying worn and crumpled under Rosie's bed. It was infuriating, but also par for the course when you had a teenage daughter, she supposed. At least Rosie always owned up and apologised, though it didn't stop her repeating her misdemeanours.

She disappeared into the bathroom, locking the door behind her, and Liz heard the shower go on. Guessing that she'd take ages, she decided to pack Lowenna's small bag and walk her around to Ruby and Victor Dodd's house, where the little girl was to spend the night. The Dodds, both in their sixties, lived near the seafront and had opted to forgo the party, as Victor was currently only semi-mobile while he waited for a hip replacement. In any case, they said, they didn't much like fireworks but adored Lowenna; the feeling was entirely mutual, so it was a win-win situation.

Of course Lowenna wanted to pack several teddies and all her favourite toys and it took some while to negotiate. Eventually she settled on one ted and a fluffy owl, plus three books and her pink plastic tea-party set, which fortunately came in its own handy case that could be carried separately.

The Dodds already had a single bed with safety rails that they used for visiting grandchildren, along with plastic plates, cups and cutlery, so Liz didn't have to take those, and she popped a big box of Ruby's favourite chocolates in the bag as a thank-you present.

'I'm taking Lowenna now. Hurry up! I won't be long!' she called through the bathroom door on her way downstairs again, but the shower was still running and there was no reply.

'Whatever does she *do* in there?' she muttered.

Lowenna pulled a cross face just like her mother's, which made Liz smile. 'Naughty Wosie. Bad girl.'

'I bet you'll be just as much of a nightmare when you're her age,' Liz commented wryly, but it went right over the little girl's head.

When they reached the Dodds' cottage, Liz picked her up so that she could ring the bell. While they waited, she became quite clingy and Liz hoped this didn't mean that she'd gone off the whole sleepover idea and would kick up a terrible fuss when left. As soon as Ruby's grey head appeared around the door, Lowenna broke into a wide smile and before long the pair were walking hand in hand down the hallway, chatting like old friends. Liz hadn't even kissed her daughter goodbye.

'I'll be back tomorrow at about nine,' she called after them, eager to return to Bag End to shower and dress. 'Ring if you need me. Hope you have a lovely time!'

There were spots of rain as she hurried home and she found herself thinking it was a good job that she hadn't already put on her makeup, as it might have been spoiled. Of course if the rain didn't stop, the fireworks display might be ruined, too, but right now that didn't seem as important.

Max wasn't due to arrive until around 8 p.m.; he'd arranged for a taxi to take him from Plymouth station straight to Polgarry Manor. He'd been in London during the day attending to some business, and was catching the train from Paddington. He was coming alone, because his daughter had school tests next week and needed to revise, so her mother had vetoed the trip. Liz had thought that Rosie might be disappointed, but she hadn't seemed it.

'She's younger than me and anyway, she lives miles away. We couldn't exactly be friends,' she'd said loftily.

Tremarnock had been abuzz with talk of the party ever since the date had been fixed, and almost everyone had a job to do: Bramble and her fiancé, Matt, were quite used to organising big events and had arranged a whip-round to pay for the larger items, including the hire of a marquee, tables and chairs for those who wanted to sit down to eat and, most importantly, the fireworks.

Tabitha's boyfriend Danny was in charge of the music line-up, which he was good at as he often staged gigs at his pub and had plenty of favours to call in from friends in the music business. Barbara and a team of helpers were on catering duty, while Rick and some of the other men were responsible for building and manning the bonfire as well as lighting the fireworks. A class of local primary schoolchildren had been asked to make a huge Guy, the biggest they could manage, and everyone was bringing food: hot dogs, burgers, salads, bread rolls, puddings, dips and so on.

To the villagers' amusement, Reg Carter had made a generous donation towards the drinks. No one was fooled; it was obvious that he was trying curry favour and win back support, not least because fresh parish council elections were to be held in the New Year.

Jean the childminder was still so incensed by his treachery that she'd wanted to reject the cash, but she'd been shouted down by Audrey, who'd made the point that money was money and that she, for one, couldn't afford to chip in any more than she already had.

'Besides,' she'd added, 'a hole in his bank balance might make him think twice before getting in cahoots with the wrong people again.'

She had a point; and as Reg was notoriously tight-fisted, always last at the bar and slow to settle his bills, folk had agreed that hitting him where it hurt was too delicious an opportunity to miss.

Liz herself had made two giant pots of chilli con carne and rice and Barbara was lending an industrial-sized hotplate to keep them warm. Luckily Bramble already had generators, plus lights to put in the trees and around the grounds. The manor house itself would be open all night so that people could pop in and use one of the many bathrooms. It wasn't as if any strangers would be coming; they were all friends and there would be plenty of beady-eyed adults to keep an eye on things and make sure the youngsters, in particular, behaved.

Only Robert had steered clear of party talk, although he had donated cash and agreed to hire temporary restaurant staff for the night so that Alex, Jesse and Loveday could have the evening off. He himself, of course, would be working as usual, and for once Liz hadn't tried to dissuade him. What would be the point? He'd taken little interest in the message in the bottle, his head was still filled with the Secret Shack and he hadn't even met Max.

Rosie had at last vacated the bathroom when Liz returned, slightly damp from her walk, and she darted in quickly and locked the door. It was after 6 p.m. when the pair finally met up again in her bedroom and Rosie looked her mother up and down.

'What are you *wearing*?'

Liz glanced down at her new plum-coloured shirt and fiddled with the buttons and hem. 'Don't you like it?' she asked, blushing. 'I bought it last week.'

'I like the top,' Rosie replied, rather nastily. 'But what are those *trousers*?'

They were quite racy: tight, black and shiny, with little silver zips at the ankles.

'They're not real leather,' Liz said hastily, wishing that her daughter would stop scrutinising and go away and leave her alone. 'They're reasonably thick material, so they should be warm. The girl in the shop said they're very fashionable.'

Rosie frowned. She herself was in skinny jeans and a cream sweater, but the look wasn't entirely casual; behind her pale blue glasses she had on glittery gold eyeshadow and heaps of black mascara, and her thick fair hair had been carefully moussed, scrunched and tousled.

'Aren't they a bit young for you?' she persisted.

Liz squirmed. 'Oh dear! Do you think so?'

Rosie's eyes narrowed and she tilted her head, staring at her mother in an odd sort of way. 'Did you buy them for Max?'

The cheek of it! If Liz hadn't felt so cornered, she might have laughed. 'Of course not! I bought them for me. I like them, or at least I thought I did.'

'You act weird around him,' her daughter said suddenly. 'And he flirts with you like mad. I think he's a creep.'

Liz's mouth went dry and her heart missed a beat. 'Nonsense!' Her reply was a little too quick. 'He's just a nice guy, really friendly. You're the one who acts weird around him and I wish you'd stop. It's embarrassing.'

There was an uneasy pause and Liz feared that Rosie would argue back, but she seemed to think better of it and shrugged instead.

'Whatever.'

Relieved, Liz asked if she should put on something different all the same. 'I don't mind, honestly, if you'd prefer it?' Whatever it took to keep her daughter quiet.

'No. I mean, you look great. You've got a lovely figure and everything and they're cool. Wear what you want. It's just that I've never seen you in anything like that before.' She gave herself a generous squirt of her mother's perfume, then sauntered from the room.

Liz gazed for the umpteenth time in her long mirror. It was true; she normally wore jeans and sweaters just like her daughter, though she did have a couple of quite glamorous dresses for nights out. Robert used to say that he loved her best with no makeup and, preferably, nothing else on either, but he hadn't made that joke for a while. She'd wanted to wear something a bit different for what was, after all, a very special occasion; but maybe her daughter was right, and the fake leather was too much?

Resolving to try one more thing before discarding the trousers, she slipped on her black ankle boots and the transformation was dramatic. Suddenly she looked sexy and sophisticated and not at all as if she were trying too hard. The old grey socks had been the culprits, and what she'd needed was a pair of heels to set off the ensemble. They wouldn't exactly be practical, but at least it had stopped raining now; if the ground became too muddy, she could probably borrow a pair of Bramble's Wellington boots.

She decided that Rosie was just being a bit silly and immature about Max; she'd got a bee in her bonnet. It was, of course, the reason why she was so odd about him, but Liz wouldn't listen to her. Why should she? She was still only a child, after all, and Liz could be friends with whomever she liked.

Buoyed with fresh confidence, she headed downstairs to find her coat and bag before she and her daughter set off for the manor, carrying the heavy pots of chilli and rice to load in the boot of the car. It was dark now but fairly mild, and there was a scent of wood smoke in the air. Rosie had pulled down Liz's cream bobble hat over her forehead, teased out a few wisps of hair and looked lovely.

Polgarry was about four miles out of Tremarnock, at the top of a long, twisty country road lined with tall hedgerows that seemed to zigzag for miles. At the end was a set of handsome iron gates, which Bramble and Matt had only recently installed. Liz drove through them onto the gravel drive with fields on either side, coming to a halt in the circular area in front of the manor where quite a few other vehicles were already parked.

It was a large, imposing building with grey walls and mock battlements. When Lord Penrose, Bramble's grandfather, had lived here he'd allowed it to fall half-derelict, but Bramble had put a lot of money and effort into its restoration. It was no longer gloomy or forbidding; quite the opposite, in fact – lights shone from the windows and little lanterns guided you through the terraced garden all the way up to the oak front door.

'We should probably go round the back with the food,' Liz said.

They could hear sounds of electric guitars being tuned and microphones tested as they staggered across the grass. She could feel her heels sinking into the mud and was already regretting her choice of footwear, but it was too late now. It served her right for being vain, she thought. The ankle boots might have to go in the bin tomorrow.

Rosie oohed and aahed when she caught sight of the large pink marquee, lit up against the night sky and with a stage at the back peopled with musicians and technical folk. In front, various men were putting the finishing touches to a giant bonfire with a grotesque grinning man-sized Guy on top. He had a beard and a black wig with a tall brown hat perched on top; on his body, stuffed with newspaper, was a white shirt, brown belt and waistcoat, while down below he wore black trousers and lace-up shoes. He looked horribly lifelike.

Tables and chairs were dotted all around, and long trestle tables were covered with dishes of food wrapped in plastic film. Glancing to her left, Liz saw a flat area for the fireworks display, cordoned off with rope. Some men and women were nailing Catherine wheels to a frame while others were lining up small items in front and putting bigger ones at the back, furthest from where the audience was to stand. Rick, Tony, Felipe and the rest had put a lot of thought into planning the display and taken plenty of safety advice. Still, Liz hoped that nothing would go wrong; every year there were reports of accidents, some even fatal, usually because someone hadn't followed instructions.

Barbara, in a green Barbour jacket and red scarf, spotted Liz and Rosie with the chilli and rice and hurried over to help.

'I've set up the hotplate over there,' she said, pointing to a space to the right of the marquee, and relieving Rosie of her heavy dish. 'People have been bringing food all afternoon – there's going to be masses. We won't go hungry, that's for sure.'

As Liz followed her friend, she was aware of more folk arriving behind her and soon the trickle turned into a wave. By 7.30 p.m. the grounds were heaving with mums and dads, grannies and grandpas, children and even a couple of babes in arms, all in brightly coloured woollen hats and scarves, gloves and thick jackets.

Rosie had long since disappeared with her mates. Everyone else seemed to be busy, and Liz felt a bit silly on her own in her fake leather and heels. She wished that she could change – what had she been thinking? At least the trousers were mostly hidden by her parka. She was relieved to spot Esme by one of the trestle tables stacked with food, making herself useful by removing the plastic film and putting serving spoons in the dishes. Liz's pleasure soon turned to concern, however, when she noticed her friend's long face.

'Where's Caroline?' she asked, glancing around for her.

She realised that she hadn't seen either woman for several days, but had assumed that everything was all right. They'd certainly seemed to recover from what she'd guessed had been a row before the final protest march, when they'd been so frosty with each other.

The next thing Esme said, however, brought Liz up short.

'She's gone back to Paris.'

'What?' Liz thought she must have misheard, but then she noticed Esme's eyes fill up, she put a hand over her nose and mouth and abruptly turned away.

'I'm sorry.' Liz felt Esme's pain and would have given her a hug, but she backed off and shook her head. 'I'll be fine, really. It's been a shock, that's all. I'd rather not talk about it, if you don't mind.'

She was a private person and Liz knew better than to push it. 'Well, you know I'm here if you want me. You just need to ask.'

She was still thinking about the exchange and wondering why Caroline had left when the first band started playing – a group of local lads and a female vocalist called Hettie Shiner, who used to do the odd waitressing shift for Robert while still at college. About halfway through the first set, she announced over the microphone that it was time to light the bonfire. Everyone started to gather around in a big circle, waiting for the poor Guy to go up in flames.

Liz had hoped they'd hang on for Max; this whole event was in his honour, after all. But Barbara, sounding rather officious, insisted that it was getting chilly and they needed the fire for warmth. There was enough extra wood stacked nearby to keep it going all night if they wanted.

The primary schoolchildren who had made the Guy were instructed to form an orderly line and lead the counting from ten backwards while the onlookers joined in.

'Ten! Nine! Eight! Seven...'

And there was Max. Liz spotted him, walking around the side of the house in his brown leather jacket with the sheepskin collar. He had a bag slung over his shoulder and looked a bit lost, which wasn't surprising as he'd never been to the manor before. She stood on tiptoe and waved; when he failed to notice, she left the crowd and hurried towards him, hoping that she'd get the chance to explain about the Guy's symbolism before he was incinerated.

On catching sight of her at last, his face lit up. Slinging his bag on the ground, he raised his arms in greeting. He looked so friendly and familiar that without thinking, she almost ran into them, stopping herself only just in time.

'You got here!' she said, overcome with shyness all of a sudden.

He seemed a bit shy, too, and they kissed awkwardly on both cheeks.

'Yes, but I nearly missed the best bit. Look!'

She spun around and at that moment, Rick held a giant taper to the base of the bonfire and it burst into yellow and orange flames. The crowd gasped as they licked and crackled around the edges before gaining strength and shooting upwards. Soon they reached the Guy's feet, then his legs and torso; finally his head, hair and hat caught fire and swiftly disintegrated. The last image Liz had was of his face, complete with ghastly grin, contorting and shrivelling in the heat while his tall hat toppled sideways before being consumed.

There was silence for a moment while the audience absorbed the spectacle, followed by loud applause. A few small children burst into tears and had to be comforted.

'That was horrible!' said Max, laughing, and Liz had to agree.

'I know, it's pretty gruesome. Come on, let's go and dump your bag and find you a drink. You must be tired after your journey.'

They began to make their way towards the back entrance of the manor but didn't get far; Max, of course, was the star of the show and as soon as folk recognised him, they wanted to shake his hand or slap him on the back and thank him for saving the playground.

Before long Barbara arrived, too, wanting to spirit him away to the marquee, where Tony was to make a speech and presentation in his honour. Hot on her heels was Audrey, in a turquoise fake fur coat and matching hat that couldn't be missed, and behind her, Bramble, who was to explain the order of events.

Audrey and Barbara took an arm each and Max could hardly refuse to go along. Looking over his shoulder as he was led away, he raised his eyebrows in mock horror, mouthing, 'See you later.'

Liz, left holding his bag, managed to smile back, but in truth she felt rather miffed. They'd hardly exchanged a word, and now it seemed likely that he'd be monopolised by admirers and she wouldn't see much of him at all. Disconsolate, she headed over to the manor on her own to leave his things before going in search of a drink. Soon she heard someone announce that Tony was to 'say a few words' and, glass in hand, she too went to the marquee to watch.

Max looked quite uncomfortable up on the stage beside Tony, in a navy jacket and canary yellow scarf, and he was even more ill at ease when Tony gave a rather florid address that made him sound like the Lord Our Saviour.

'Thank you very much for your extremely kind words,' Max said, when Tony had finished waxing lyrical and passed the microphone across. 'I would just like to point out, however, that my name is Max Maier, not Jesus Christ, and I can assure you I have many, many faults. Sometimes I even pick my nose.'

Everyone tittered.

'But seriously,' he went on, when they'd quietened down again, 'my grandfather would be so glad to know that the playground has been preserved for the children of the village. Perhaps one day I'll be able to bring my own grandchildren here and tell them about Tremarnock Resists and how you all became eco-warriors, bravely fighting the authorities and sleeping in tents and trees.' He paused a second time for more laughs. 'Thank you for putting on this wonderful event. I'm very happy to be here once again, and thanks most of all to a young lady called Rosie who found a bottle washed up on the beach with a letter from my grandfather that he'd written more than seventy years ago.'

It was a delightful, unscripted speech delivered in his perfect, strongly accented English, and everyone was charmed. The clapping went on for quite some time, during which Liz scanned the faces around her. She saw Rosie a little way off to the left, standing beside Rafael, whose hair was sculpted into a splendid purple Mohican.

'I'd now like to ask the young lady in question onto the stage to present Max with a gift,' Tony boomed.

Liz started. She hadn't been expecting this. Nor, as far as she knew, had Rosie, who looked flustered as she limped towards the steps.

Liz was grateful to Bramble, in a red jumper and matching pompom, for standing behind Rosie as she went up on stage to make sure that she didn't stumble. Once there, Bramble leaned down to whisper something to her before motioning to a woman at the back, who handed over a fairly large square brown paper package with a big purple bow wrapped around the middle.

'It's for you,' Rosie said, thrusting the parcel unceremoniously into Max's hands. Few could hear what she'd said because she hadn't got the microphone, so Tony leaned over and held it to her lips.

'I said, it's for you,' she repeated, quite crossly.

The microphone squeaked, the onlookers laughed and there was an expectant pause while they waited for something more, but nothing came.

Liz felt herself cringe and wished for a moment that the ground would swallow her up. 'For goodness' sake, say something nice,' she hissed under her breath.

She watched with dismay as Tony reclaimed the microphone and made a joke about teenagers liking to keep things 'short and sweet', while Rosie stalked off. If Max were offended, he covered it up well, ripping open his present and passing the wrapping to Bramble. All eyes fell on him as the gift was revealed: a medium-sized black-and-white sketch in a white frame.

'It's by a local artist, Fergus Wall,' Bramble explained. 'He's quite well known. He used to live in a cottage on the grounds but he's moved to Spain now. He drew this when he was here. It's a view of the sea and sky from his former studio. I hope you like it.'

'It's wonderful,' said Max, holding the picture up so that everyone could see. 'Thank you so much. I'll treasure it always. I think I'll hang it in my office so I can look at it every day.'

After that, he and Tony got down from the stage and a folk band began to set up. Some people started to leave the marquee and make their way towards the drinks and food before the fireworks, which were due to begin at nine. Others – mostly the young – hung around, perhaps to dance.

Liz noticed Max talking to Barbara, Bramble, Matt and the ever-present Audrey, and decided not to get in the way. Meanwhile Rosie was back with her gaggle of friends, including Rafael, talking and laughing in the corner. Liz would be having words with her later, she thought grimly. Her silly, surly behaviour in front of the audience had been way out of order, particularly after their exchange about Max in the bedroom earlier when Liz had had to put her right.

Jean, in a black hat with a thick strip of silvery fur around the edges, approached with Tom. They picked up more drinks and went with Liz for something to eat. There was so much choice that she was unsure what to have, and finally settled on some of her own chilli with a spoonful of green salad and some French bread. Jean, meanwhile, had a hot jacket potato with beans and sausages, served by Jesse in a white chef's hat, while Tom opted for a burger.

'It's a shame Robert's not here,' Jean commented as she stood munching on a forkful of beans. It was quite hard to eat with bendy paper plates and plastic cutlery, but she managed it somehow.

Liz shrugged. 'He's always working.'

Noticing Esme hovering on her own behind a large bowl of tomato salad, pretending to be busy, she beckoned her over.

'Have you eaten?' she asked.

Esme said she had, but Liz wasn't sure that she believed her. The older woman's shoulders drooped and despite her tall, broad stature she looked fragile and shrunken, as if someone had come along, pulled her apart and done a poor job of putting her together again. Her long multicoloured coat still fitted, but seemed to hang badly, and her trademark bun was falling to bits. Unusually, she wasn't wearing any of her statement jewellery, either.

'What are you working on at the moment?' Liz asked, trying not to show her concern. 'Any interesting commissions?'

Esme shook her head. 'I was so busy with...' She paused and swallowed. 'With Caroline, you know. I need to get back into it...' Her voice trailed off and she stared hard at the ground.

'Shall we have coffee soon?' Liz suggested quickly. 'Maybe Monday or Tuesday, before you go to the studio?'

'That would be nice.' Esme managed a half-smile. 'Thank you.'

The air felt cold away from the bonfire. Tom went off to fetch more drinks and by the time the fireworks started, Liz had lost count of the number of glasses of wine that she'd had; she was feeling a bit tipsy. She hadn't seen Max again but as she strolled towards the rope cordon, he was standing with Nathan and Annie behind a group of children waving sparklers.

'I lost you!' he said, breaking away. 'I was looking for you everywhere!'

'Sorry. I thought you were occupied with Barbara and Audrey. You're so popular tonight – everyone wants a piece of you.'

He was about to reply, but the band had stopped playing and before they knew it, the team in charge of fireworks had let off two big smoke balls and a string of noisy firecrackers, followed by a line of fountains that fizzed and sizzled before launching multicoloured sparks into the sky. The crowd whooped then gasped at some subsequent loud bangs, raising their eyes heavenward as a volley of bottle rockets exploded, followed by roman candles that popped and spluttered before shooting off rainbow balls of light.

Liz watched, mesmerised, until she became aware of Max fidgeting by her side.

'Are you all right?' she asked, glancing at him.

He bent down and whispered in her ear. 'To be honest, I don't much like fireworks.'

She laughed, thinking he was joking, but then saw from his expression that he was serious.

'It's the bangs and explosions,' he explained apologetically. 'I've never been much good with loud noises.'

'Oh gosh!' Liz pulled a face. 'Why didn't you say before? We would have planned something different.'

Max shrugged. 'You sounded so excited. I didn't want to spoil it for you.'

There was another loud bang followed by a series of whizzes and he flinched before flashing a contrite smile. 'I'm just a great big baby, really. Mila thinks it's hilarious. Don't tell anyone!'

Liz was amused, but also dismayed that what was supposed to be a thank-you party was turning out not to be such a treat for him after all. So far, the delay between fireworks had been minimal, but now there was a brief pause while Rick and his team prepared to light the Catherine wheels.

Without thinking, she seized Max's wrist. 'Come on! Let's go somewhere quiet till they're over.'

He didn't resist and she started to pull him away from the crowd, past the bonfire and the food tables. Loveday, in a big pink coat, the two fat buns on either side of her head sprayed scarlet and gold, was standing by the drinks stand with a pint of something in her hand. She opened her mouth to speak but Liz wasn't stopping.

'We're in a rush, sorry!'

On noticing that she had hold of Max's wrist, the girl's jaw dropped and her kohl-rimmed eyes opened wide, but Liz ignored her. She saw Max grab a bottle of wine in his free hand before she hurried him beyond the marquee and around the rear of the house, where soft lights shone through a set of big French doors.

They were some way from the hubbub here, and it was a relief to escape the crowds. Liz was planning to take Max on to the terrace when she stopped suddenly, thinking that she could hear whispering. A tall, thin silver birch to their left gleamed in the darkness and behind it, a clump of dark green bushes stirred as if something – or someone – were behind.

Curious, she let go of Max and tiptoed a little way towards the disturbance before turning to him with a finger pressed to her lips.

'Did you hear that?'

The leaves rustled again and he nodded.

Leaning sideways and craning her neck, Liz could just about see, through a gap in the branches, something woollen and cream coloured; but it wasn't until the boughs shook that it became clear it was a person's back.

The cream sweater was very familiar, as was the hat with a furry bobble. Liz suppressed a gasp. She'd know that hat anywhere – it was hers! What's more, it was now apparent that the girl, for this is what she was, was in a passionate clinch with a boy with an outlandish Mohican hairdo; and from the looks of it, they were enjoying themselves very much.

Rosie! And with Rafael, too! Liz would have called out, but Max tugged her sleeve.

'Leave them be,' he said, sotto voce.

'But—'

'You were that age once, weren't you? I bet you disappeared into the bushes with boys sometimes, didn't you?'

An image flashed through her mind of her younger self, aged about fifteen, making out in the woods behind the park with a blond boy named Jacob. It had been her very first kiss, the one you never forget.

'Maybe,' she admitted.

Max laughed quietly. 'Of course you did! It's normal! Don't embarrass her.'

He was right; and although Liz hadn't yet forgiven her daughter for behaving badly on stage, she couldn't help feeling chuffed. As far as she knew, this was Rosie's first kiss, too. How special! Liz used to worry that her daughter's disabilities would put boys off, but here was living proof that this wasn't the case. And Rafael, though a bit wild for her liking, was quite a catch.

'We'd better not leave them too long,' she said, giggling under her breath as they sneaked away. 'I'll have to come back soon and flush them out.'

They climbed over a low wall onto the deserted terrace and stood side by side for a while, staring at the velvety blackness that lay beyond the manor's boundaries. The odd burst of fireworks in the distance didn't spoil the moment and when they looked up, the sky was filled with myriad twinkling stars.

'That's the Plough,' said Max, pointing. 'Leading to the North Star.'

'I used to like star-bathing when I was a child,' Liz replied. 'On a warm, clear summer's night, I'd get a cushion and lie on my back and let the stars sort of soak through me.'

'Were you happy – as a child, I mean?'

The question caught her by surprise. 'Yes, until my mother died. After that, I was miserable for a very long time.'

'But you're happy again now?' he asked softly.

She thought about it for a moment. 'I guess so.'

'You don't sound too sure.'

'Well, most of the time anyway,' she added, fidgeting with the zip of her coat and giving a nervous laugh. She was keen to change the subject. 'Would you like to see the mermaid fountain?'

'What's that?'

'It's not far. Come on, I'll show you.'

Liz knew Polgarry very well, having been here often to visit Bramble and Matt. Beyond the terrace there were steps down to two separate gardens, and in the centre of one was a rectangular pond with a broken fountain that she'd grown to love.

Max tucked the bottle that he'd been holding under an arm, before thinking better of it and taking it out again. 'Shall we have some wine first?'

'But we haven't any glasses! I'll go—'

'Wait.' Setting the bottle down on the ground, he shoved his hands in his jacket and she wondered what he would do next. 'Abracadabra!' he cried with a flourish, producing a glass from each pocket. 'See? I'm not as stupid as I look! I picked them up after I'd made my speech. I was trying to find you.'

'Magic!' Liz's laugh sounded like running water, tinkling and mischievous until it turned into a hiccup. She put a hand over her mouth to try to stop herself; she really was quite drunk. Swaying slightly, she watched him pour the white wine before passing her a glass and chinking his own against hers.

'To us!' he said, momentarily catching her eye.

Robert's face swam into her vision but she batted it away.

'Cheers!' she replied, putting her lips to the brim and taking a sip, which seemed to loosen her tongue. 'I'm glad you've come back to Tremarnock. I wish you were here to stay.'

Chapter Twenty-One

How could she have said that? What was she thinking?
She was plastered, that was the problem. She'd better go
home before she made even more of a fool of herself.

'I, um…'

She staggered, trapping her heel in the edge of a flagstone,
and almost fell, but Max caught her.

'Whoa!' he cried, staggering too before managing to steady
them both.

He was strong and muscular and his arms seemed to
swallow her up. She closed her eyes and the world spun for a
moment; but pinned against his chest, she felt safe.

'You OK?' he mumbled, and it was only then she realised
that she had spilled her wine down his front, making them
both damp.

'Sorry!' She attempted to wipe his jacket with the corner
of a sleeve but only rubbed the stain in more. She stopped,
staring at the mess she'd made. 'I've ruined your nice coat!'
To her surprise, there was a wobble in her voice and she felt
like bursting into tears.

'Hey, it's not a problem,' Max said softly. 'I can get it dry-
cleaned. Come here! There must be something else. What's
the matter?'

She didn't really know, or she would have told him; but suddenly everything seemed too much: the party, Rosie's attitude to Max, Rosie and Rafael, Robert not being here, sad Esme, Max himself, the Secret Shack...

'I think I've overdone the wine,' she confessed. 'I feel a bit dizzy.'

Max took her hand and his own felt warm, comforting and a little strange. 'Do you want to sit down?'

It sounded very appealing, but she didn't fancy going inside where she might bump into someone she knew – not in this state, anyway; she'd rather sober up first.

'Let's go to the fountain. There's a bench there.'

He put an arm around her as they made their way down the uneven stone steps onto a gravel path that led to some rusty metal railings. The gate squeaked open, and he followed her across a wide patch of grass flanked with flowerbeds towards the remains of a brick gazebo, which was covered in ivy and missing its roof.

It was very dark away from the bright lights of the manor, and they almost walked straight into a longish rectangular pond, well camouflaged by the dark green weed that trailed across its surface.

'Stop!' cried Liz. 'There she is!'

She gestured to a stone fountain in the middle of the water that was shaped like a voluptuous mermaid, missing her head. Made of pale stone, she shone in the moonlight and seemed to preside over her surroundings, including the ancient bare trees and unkempt bushes and the plants that rambled over the crumbling seat nearby.

'She's very curvy.' Max seemed amused. 'I wonder what happened to her head.'

'Maybe someone stole it, or perhaps whoever put her here bought it like that. Bramble doesn't want to replace it. I'm glad. I like her as she is.'

Walking over to the bench and plonking down, she was relieved to take the weight off her feet; she hadn't realised how much they were hurting. Still carrying the wine, Max sat beside her and took a swig straight from the bottle before offering it to her.

She shook her head. 'I'd better not.'

'Sure?' He took another swallow. He must be a bit tipsy now, too, but didn't seem it.

They were just a few feet from the water and there was a plop, perhaps a fish breaking the surface. Stretching her legs out, Liz glanced idly at her feet, tipping the boots from side to side.

'They're caked in mud,' she pointed out unnecessarily, because he'd followed her gaze.

'Mine too, but they're old, so it doesn't matter. Do you want me to try to clean them up?'

'It's all right, thanks.'

He didn't appear to have noticed her trousers before, but he commented on them now. 'Are they leather?' He seemed quite surprised.

'Fake,' she replied, apologetically. 'I'm not too sure about them, to be honest. Rosie was horrified.'

This made him laugh. It was a lovely noise: deep, infectious and unrestrained. 'What would she prefer you to wear? A nice sensible skirt and cardigan?'

'Probably.'

'Well, I like them.' There was a pause. 'In fact, I like everything about you.'

It came out of the blue and she felt herself start as the

blood rushed to her cheeks. She was pleased and dismayed in equal measure.

'I like you, too.' Did that sound tacky?

There was another pause and the silence made her head throb.

Then Max spoke. 'Did you mean what you said back there?'

'What?' She was feigning innocence. Really, she knew exactly what he was talking about.

'About not wanting me to leave.'

It was a good job that it was so dark or he might have noticed her squirm. Anxious about the direction in which the conversation was going, she attempted to backtrack clumsily. 'It's lovely to have you as a friend.'

'Is that all we are – friends?' His deep voice was teasing, yet heavily laden with meaning; he was playing with fire. They both were.

She glanced at him, frightened, and his intense blue eyes seemed to penetrate hers, boring deep down in search of the truth. Her heart banged in her chest and she wanted to get up and leave, but felt rooted to the spot.

'I must say, you're very pretty, Ms Hart.'

Polite yet playful, the compliment, delivered in his sexy foreign accent, completely floored her. Already feeling like Judas and Jezebel rolled into one, she should have stopped him there and then; but the next thing she knew, his lips were on hers and his strong arms were reaching around her back, pulling her close. Her body seemed to liquefy as his tongue sought out her own and she couldn't help but respond, all her resistance gone.

Sweet, sweet kisses, he gave her: urgent, hot and passionate. He seemed like a man possessed. Burning up with desire herself, she tried to make a pact with the devil: *let me do this just once and get away with it. I'll never be unfaithful again.*

Still locked in an embrace, he hoisted her on to his lap, pushing one hand up under her coat and easing the other slowly but surely between her legs. She wriggled with pleasure. Soon, very soon, there might be no going back.

'Don't!' she blurted.

He stopped at once and took his hand away. She burst into tears and clung to him, the source of both her comfort and her pain.

'Are you OK?' he whispered, holding her tight and absorbing the sobs until she managed to calm down.

She shook her head miserably. 'I'm sorry. It's all right for you – you're not married.'

'I understand,' he said heavily, before wiping away her tears with a thumb. 'I have strong feelings for you, Liz. Maybe it's wrong, but I can't help it.'

'Robert would be so hurt if he knew. How could I do this to him?'

Max didn't reply.

Everything that had gone on between her and her husband these past few months seemed to descend on her now like a great weight: his absences, her resentments, their lack of communication, the lack of sex, the fact that they didn't have fun together any more and could no longer seem to see eye to eye.

But didn't all marriages go through bad patches? It was probably just a phase, and he hadn't actually done anything bad. He didn't gamble, drink or womanise; he wasn't violent and he only ever wanted what was best for her and the children.

'I have to go,' she said, rising abruptly. 'This mustn't ever happen again.'

They were silent as they made their way back across the grass, her stomping several paces ahead while he trailed behind. It was a relief to see the light coming through the French doors again and to hear the sounds of music. The fireworks must have long since finished.

Liz had temporarily forgotten about Rosie, so it was a shock to find her waiting with Rafael on the terrace.

'Where were you?' she said accusingly. 'I've been searching for you everywhere.'

All of a sudden, an image of her daughter with Rafael in the bushes flashed through Liz's mind and she thought how different two kisses could be – all fresh and new in Rosie's case, while Liz's own, though thrilling, had been steeped in betrayal. Esme and Caroline had probably embraced, too. Had it been glorious or terrifying? Both, probably. Three kisses, all with such different meanings and implications.

Realising that her mother was miles away, Rosie repeated her question, more insistently this time. 'Where *were* you?'

Liz felt if she had GUILT stamped on her forehead in bright red letters and couldn't even look at her daughter; she stared at the ground instead.

'Max wanted to see the mermaid fountain,' she replied, as steadily as she could.

It sounded innocent enough, but when she finally peeked at Rosie's face, it told a different story. Glancing from her mother to Max and back again, a strange, suspicious glint came into her eye.

'Where's Robert?' she asked suddenly, and Liz's stomach lurched. It was more of a reproach than a question – and, perhaps, a warning. Rosie knew full well that her stepfather was working.

'Have the fireworks finished?' Max's comment came at just the right moment, puncturing the awkwardness, and Rafael confirmed that they had. If he, too, had picked up on the uncomfortable atmosphere he didn't show it.

'Do you want to dance?' he asked Rosie but she said no, she was tired.

Full of dread and confusion and not knowing what else to do, Liz followed her daughter stiffly back to the marquee area. The crowds had thinned out now, because the younger children and their parents had gone home; but the bonfire continued to burn brightly and there were still plenty of people.

Liz's mind was racing. She was desperate to go home, too, and bury her head under the pillow, but she'd promised to help with the clearing up. Besides, it was Max's do, really, and she could hardly leave before him when he was to stay with her at Bag End. How she wished that she'd never offered him a room! Tomorrow, perhaps, he could go to Audrey's or even fly back to Munich, but it was too late to rearrange things now. It was a relief to spot Tony and Felipe near the drinks table. She left the others and hurried over to say hello.

'Are you all right, darling?' Tony peered at her oddly. 'You look as if you've seen a ghost.'

She tried to disguise her unease with a laugh. 'I'm fine. What a great event!'

The incident with Max seemed to have sobered her up and she no longer felt drunk, only confused and miserable. Keen to shift the spotlight from herself, she asked if they'd spoken to Esme. 'I'm a bit worried about her, to be honest. She seems quite down.'

354

Tony, who was much shorter than Felipe, nodded, adjusting the yellow scarf around his neck and sticking his hands in his jacket pockets. 'She's devastated,' he said, lowering his voice. 'She's just lost the love of her life.'

'Oh!' Liz's heart went out to her friend. 'How terrible for her! Why has Caroline gone? Do you know?'

Tony explained that he and Felipe had seen Esme earlier; she'd been about to leave but they'd persuaded her to stay and they'd had a long chat.

'I'm glad to say she opened up a bit. It's difficult for her, you know.' Tony scratched his nose thoughtfully. 'She's from a different generation, very bigoted and backward. She wasn't allowed to be gay when she was growing up and she was made to feel a lot of shame, poor darling. Caroline, too. They hid their love for all these years and Caroline only got married to please her parents and fit in. She was all set to leave her husband at last when he became very ill, and her daughter pressured her into going back.'

'That's so tragic.' Liz felt tearful again. Filled with sudden self-pity as well as sympathy for the women, she was tempted for a moment to compare their situation with her own. But then she thought of all the years of suffering those two had endured and how, just when they thought they'd finally found happiness, it had been snatched from them. Beside all that, her present predicament was as nothing.

'Maybe Caroline will change her mind?' she blurted. 'It's just plain wrong for them not to be together when they love each other so much.'

'It is,' Felipe added gravely. 'Life is short. It is not a performance.'

'I think you mean rehearsal, darling,' Tony said patiently. 'Life's not a rehearsal.'

They all agreed to rally around Esme, who would need lots of support in the coming days, weeks and months.

'She mustn't be on her own too much,' said Tony. 'I've persuaded her to come for supper tomorrow night and we're going to take her to the theatre next weekend.'

Liz mentioned that she and Esme would be having coffee soon, too. 'Thank God she's told you what's going on. At least we know, and can help her more.'

It seemed as if Tony was now on a mission to bring her out of her shell. 'Can you believe she's still worried what people will think? I told her there'll always be prejudice, but it's probably easier to be gay now than at any other point in history – and thank God, the law's on our side. It's time to be rid of all that crippling shame. It's a totally wasted emotion.'

'Here here!' Liz wanted to go and look for her friend, but Felipe informed her that she had already departed.

'We saw her into a cab five or ten minutes ago. She seemed all right, better after our talk, I think. She's a strong lady, Esme. I think she will get through this. Maybe even something good will come of it. You never know.'

So absorbed had she been in the conversation that Liz had temporarily forgotten about Max, but she remembered him now and felt the blood rush to her cheeks all over again. What on earth had possessed her? She must have been mad. But there was no denying that he was gorgeous – and that kiss! Just thinking about it made her head swim. Glancing over Tony's shoulder, she looked for him among the crowd but he was nowhere to be seen. A strange sort of push-pull sensation made her insides wobble. She wanted to go and find him, she couldn't bear him out of her sight; yet at the same time, she wished him far away.

Felipe was also scanning the crowd for someone: his younger brother. 'I wonder where Rafael is. I haven't spotted him for ages.'

Liz wondered whether to mention seeing him in the bushes with Rosie, but decided against it. It was good gossip and Tony, especially, would probably love it; but Rosie would never forgive her for telling, and relations between them were sticky enough as it was. It wasn't clear if the kiss had been a one-off or if Rosie and Rafael were dating now. Whatever the outcome, Liz hoped that neither would get hurt, for their own sakes as well as for her future relations with Tony and Felipe.

There was a pause while all this raced through her mind, then Tony checked his watch before pronouncing with a gasp that it was almost midnight.

'It's past my bedtime. I need my beauty sleep, you know!'

Noticing a black bin bag on one of the tables, Liz went to fetch it and started gathering up the empty cups and plates strewn around. The bands, she knew, were due to finish at half-past twelve, and it would be no bad thing to try to speed things up. Tony offered to help but he was clearly ready to leave, so she refused. After kissing both men goodbye, she resumed her task, wondering what on earth she would say to Max when she saw him next. How could she act normally around him and in front of her family after what had happened between them? It was an impossible ask.

Cold, tired, achy, wired up and distressed all at once, all she wanted was to go to sleep and pretend none of this had taken place. And why had Rosie looked so suspicious back there on the terrace? Had she guessed or, worse, seen what had happened by the mermaid fountain? But how? Paranoia set in and anxiety gnawed at her insides.

She was bending down to pick up a bowl from the ground when she felt a tap on her shoulder. She jumped up, startled. 'Oh!' Her nerves were in tatters.

She raised her eyes, which met those of her very tall husband whose warm, wide smile made her heart and lungs contract so that she could scarcely breathe.

'Hello, gorgeous!'

'Robert! What are you doing here?'

It wasn't exactly friendly, but he ignored the slight. 'I wanted to catch the end of the party, but most of all I wanted to see *you*. I left the temporary guy to shut up shop.'

'Does he know what to do?' She sounded sharp and disapproving, but really she was upset with herself.

'Don't look so worried! He'll be fine.'

'It's almost over here now, anyway.' She cast around for more rubbish and shook her bin bag to make the contents settle. 'I promised Bramble I'd help clear up and then I want to go. I'm exhausted.'

'Come here, you!' Robert said gently, taking the bag from her and putting it on the grass. He opened his arms and she walked in – she could hardly refuse – and he held her tight. 'Don't be cross.'

Squeezed against his chest, she inhaled the familiar scent of her husband's clothes, his aftershave, and was shocked to think that only a short time before, she had been just as intimate with a different man entirely; rather more so, in fact.

Sensing her stiffness, Robert tried to win her over. 'I'm sorry I've been such a horrible husband. I heard on the grapevine that the council have changed their minds. They're going to give us the alcohol licence after all. It's a huge relief. Once the Secret Shack is up and running, I'll be able to take much more of a back seat. The end's in sight, I promise. Thank you for being so patient.'

Liz's throat hurt when she swallowed. 'I know you, you'll still be just as busy when it's open. You're incapable of delegating.'

He bent down and kissed the top of her head before resting his cheek there. 'It's not true. And anyway, I'm going to take on a top-rate manager. As soon as he or she's in place, my aim is to have as little to do with the Shack as possible. I'll have so much time on my hands, you and the girls will get bored of me. You'll be desperate to get me out of the house.'

Before, his words would have delighted her. It was what she'd wanted so badly, after all. Now, though, they just made her feel sick.

'I'll believe it when it happens,' she muttered unpleasantly, before breaking away and leaving a chilly space between them.

She imagined that she would have annoyed him, which was what she wanted, really, because his kindness was killing her. Instead, though, he took her face in his hands and pressed his lips to her forehead.

'Trust me,' he whispered.

Her insides flipped and a little voice inside her head whispered – *don't trust ME.*

'I'm going to book us all a week's holiday,' he went on. 'Maybe in February half term, before the summer season starts. Anywhere you fancy. France, maybe, or Italy?'

She didn't reply and he was about to kiss her again when he noticed her glance to the right.

'Who's that?' he asked, following her gaze.

Behind the marquee, in front of some bushes a little way off, was the shadowy figure of a man, standing very straight and still and staring at them intently. Liz's heart started thumping so loudly that she thought Robert would hear: Max.

Realising that they'd noticed him, he spun around and walked rapidly in the other direction, but not before Robert had commented, 'Strange fellow, I wonder what he's up to.' He turned back to his wife, eyebrows raised. 'Do you know him?'

'It's Max, the German,' Liz replied. Her mouth had gone dry. 'I can't believe you haven't met him yet.'

'I will tonight, because he's staying with us, isn't he? Odd that he didn't say hello.'

'It's so dark, he probably doesn't recognise me.' The lie that slipped out was as smooth as melted butter and as soft as warm, falling rain.

The music stopped for a moment and the place seemed to turn quiet, as if those left at the party, suddenly embarrassed by the sounds of their own voices, had clamped their lips together. Deep in the woods beyond the manor, an owl hooted, and a log on the bonfire dropped with a thud onto the burning embers where it crackled and spat.

Robert picked up the bin bag again and held it open for Liz while she threw in more litter. They worked together for quite some time in seemingly companionable silence. And all the while she was thinking of Max in the moonlight by the mermaid fountain, of his hot kisses, ardent words and eager hands – and of that strange, suspicious glint in her daughter Rosie's eye that she had never seen before.

Chapter Twenty-Two

WHEN THEY'D FINISHED filling three giant bin bags and knotted the tops, and the area around them was clear of rubbish, Robert suggested strolling over to the marquee.

'I'd like to catch the last few minutes of the band. Coming?'

Liz shook her head. 'I need to speak to Bramble first. I think I saw her go indoors.'

It wasn't true, but she wanted some time to marshal her thoughts. She decided to avoid the terrace where she and Max had been confronted by Rosie, and instead made her way past the dying bonfire towards the front entrance of the manor.

People were busy packing up tables and chairs and carting the catering equipment towards their vehicles. The fireworks area had been tidied and was no longer cordoned off. It was strange to think that by tomorrow, once the marquee had gone, too, you'd probably never know that there had been an event here at all.

Still, it would be the talk of the village for days to come, and there would no doubt be numerous tales to tell. Perhaps she, Liz, would be the only guest anxious not to indulge in post-party gossip, but that in itself might appear odd and raise suspicions just when she needed to draw attention away from herself. She found herself wishing that she could confide in Tabitha, her closest confidante now that Pat was gone, but rejected the idea; it would place too much of a burden on her. After all, Tabitha adored Robert and vice versa, and although her loyalty to Liz was probably greater, it wouldn't be fair or wise, perhaps, to put it to the test.

No, Liz thought, feeling her heels sinking into the mud with each step and cursing, yet again, her stupid choice of footwear, this was something that she was going to have to deal with on her own.

As she rounded the corner of the house and entered the car parking area, she was met with an array of glaring headlamps which made her blink. A car door slammed, making her jump, and then the driver reversed out of the bay, his wheels crunching on the gravel.

'Liz?'

A voice behind her made her start again. When she spun around, she was dismayed to see Max striding towards her, his collar turned up against the cold and his hands firmly in his pockets. It was impossible to see his expression.

'Oh!' she stuttered. 'I didn't realise it was you.' As he drew closer, she tried to thaw the ice with small talk: 'What a lovely party! Everyone's gone to so much trouble. Such delicious food!' She was babbling, she knew.

Max ignored it all. Taking her gently but firmly by the arm, he started to lead her across the grass and up the manor steps to the heavy oak front door, which he pushed open as if it weighed nothing.

'Where are we going?' she asked, but he didn't reply.

Glancing around before they went inside, she wondered if anyone were watching, but folk were far too busy going about their own business. The wide, marble hallway, lit with flickering candles, smelled of must and furniture polish; strange, crusty-looking gentlemen on horseback and crinoline-clad ladies peered at them from the heavy gold-framed oil paintings hanging on the walls. In the centre of the room, resting on a large round wooden table, was a weighty bronze statuette of a naked youth playing a pipe. He seemed to wink and glimmer mischievously, while at the far end, an imposing staircase, covered in a faded burgundy carpet, led to the galleried first floor.

All was quiet and still. Then, to their left, a door creaked and there was the sound of retreating footsteps. Liz guessed that they belonged to Maria, Bramble's stern but loyal housekeeper, whose quarters were in that part of the house. Maria had looked after Lord Penrose for many years and although too elderly to be of much help nowadays, Bramble had become fond of her and couldn't bear to let her go.

'She's like part of the furniture,' she once told Liz. 'She can be a bit fierce, but she and Polgarry belong together and I'd never ask her to leave. This is her home.'

Max stopped for a moment and scanned his surroundings before whispering, 'I need to talk in private. Where's best?'

As all the activity was taking place at the back of the house, they could, perhaps, have retreated to a corner and stayed where they were. But wanting to leave nothing to chance, Liz picked a door to the right and led the way down a long, dimly lit corridor to a hexagonal room in the east wing, where she knew that Bramble and Matt sometimes ate breakfast in the morning sunshine.

There was little furniture in there, save a round table, two upright chairs and a desk on one side with an ancient Bakelite telephone. The curtains were open and moonlight filtered through the leaded windowpanes, casting strange shadows on walls and floor.

Having closed the door softly behind them, Max turned to Liz with a troubled look.

Her pulse, which was already raised, started to beat even faster. 'I'm sorry about what happened back there,' she blurted, before he'd had a chance to open his mouth. 'I shouldn't have—'

'I'm staying here tonight,' he interrupted. 'Don't worry, Bramble says it's fine. It would be totally wrong to come back to your house under the circumstances.'

His last three words seemed to ripple outwards in ever-expanding circles and a vivid picture of their passionate clinch lodged itself like a pebble in the deep crevasses of her brain. It would be a great relief if he didn't come home with her, but it wouldn't stop her feeling guilty for her part in this sudden, rather desperate change of plan. After all, she couldn't pretend that she hadn't wanted that kiss, could she? She could have pushed him away.

'I'm sorry...' she said again, but he shook his head to stop her.

'When I saw you with your husband back there...' He paused, as if needing to gather his thoughts. 'I didn't realise. I thought from what you said that you weren't happy together. Clearly I was wrong.'

He sounded hurt and a little angry with her, too, which made her miserable and defensive. She hadn't misled him, had she? Not deliberately, anyway.

'We weren't, we aren't getting on,' she replied. 'At least, I think we might be all right now.' She took a tissue from her pocket and blew her nose. 'It's complicated. Things haven't been good between us for a while, but he's promised me he's going to change.' Determined to do the right thing at last, she mustered all her courage and forced herself to look Max in the eye. 'I want to believe we can make it work. I have to, for the sake of our girls as well as for me and him. You understand, don't you? You have a daughter. Please tell me you do.'

He nodded, but he looked so sad that her heart hurt and it was all she could do not to reach out to him and try to comfort them both. She hated herself for causing him pain and cursed herself even more for the suffering that Robert would endure if he ever discovered what had happened. That kiss, so hotheaded and urgent, wasn't supposed to have meant anything, was it? Yet somehow it seemed that it had.

Her bottom lip trembled and she swallowed hard, anxious to hold it together at least until she was alone.

'I can't stand seeing you unhappy.' Max's voice cracked and suddenly she herself could stand it no longer. Taking a step forward, she gave him what she hoped would be a consolation hug; but instead, his whole body caught on fire again, just as it had back there in the garden. Pulling her in closer, he held on tight as if his life depended on it and she could feel him trembling, his sorrow and desire mixing together to form a dangerous, potent cocktail.

They'd only met on a few occasions and yet she felt so strongly connected to him, not just physically but in a deeper, more cerebral way, too. It didn't seem to matter that she'd never seen his home or family or even been to Germany. She felt that she understood something of the essence of him, the true, important part, and the rest was merely detail. But she was married and that link, real or imagined, would have to be severed.

'I'll ring you when I get back to Munich.'

His words rattled her insides and she jerked her head away from where it had been resting on his chest and pulled back, alarmed. 'Don't! You mustn't!'

'Not even just to see how you are?' he asked with a groan.

'No! Not for any reason at all.'

'Are you saying you never want to hear from me again, Liz?'

She bit her lip. It sounded so final, but it was the only way.

Pulling back her shoulders, she took a deep breath. 'We have to say goodbye,' she replied as firmly as she could. 'Robert's waiting for me outside. Thank you for everything. I've enjoyed knowing you, even though it's been so brief. I hope you have a safe journey home.'

Leaving him no time to protest, she reached up and pecked him on the cheek before walking past him to the door. Her footsteps echoed on the wooden floor as she retraced her route, but she didn't hear him follow; he must have decided to wait until she'd gone.

Back outside in the cold night air, she felt sad but also strangely liberated, like a deep-sea diver gratefully breathing in her first gulps of fresh, clean oxygen on the surface. She told herself that having said farewell to Max, the worst, most difficult part was over; it was incumbent on her now to repair her relationship with her husband and get on with her life. Bruised feelings there might be, but thank God, no one had been permanently damaged.

She couldn't have been gone long, but the music had finished now; the crowds had dwindled even further and a trickle of people were making their way in her direction towards the car park. It took her a few minutes to locate Robert, standing just outside the marquee chatting to Rosie and her friend, Mandy, and her parents, and he smiled as she approached and held out his hand, which she took.

'I was wondering where you were. Shall we go now?'

'Yes,' she said thankfully, interlacing her fingers with his own.

It wasn't difficult to explain that Max wouldn't be staying with them after all. 'Bramble offered him a room and he accepted. I don't blame him; it's a pretty special place to spend the night. He's going home tomorrow, so I don't think we'll see him again.'

Rosie said nothing but she looked pleased; she was heading back shortly with Mandy and her parents. Robert didn't seem surprised or put out, either. 'I guess I'll have to meet him another time, then. I expect he'll be over again at some point.'

'You OK?' Liz whispered, as she leant over to give her daughter a goodbye kiss.

She half expected a rejection but to her surprise and delight, Rosie hugged her back.

'Love you, Mum.' It was the first time she'd said *that* for a while. 'See you tomorrow.'

Liz felt warmed through. Rosie couldn't have seen her and Max at the mermaid fountain; she just mistrusted him and now he was gone. Everything was going to be all right after all.

As Liz and Robert strolled towards their car, she realised that she hadn't thanked Bramble or Matt for hosting the party, but it didn't matter; she'd write them a note tomorrow.

The moon hung low in the sky as they drove down the narrow, winding country lanes towards Tremarnock. When at last the village came into view, nestling at the foot of the cliff, Robert stopped the engine for a moment so that they could gaze out at the glassy sea, laced with silver ripples and shimmering swirls and spreading out before them like a bride's veil.

'Aren't we lucky to live here?' he said, sighing.

His deep voice, and the purr of the engine as he started it up again, made Liz feel safe and sleepy.

'Mm,' she murmured, searching for his leg beside her and resting her hand on his warm knee.

They continued in silence for a few more minutes before pulling up outside their cottage where Mitzi, the cat, was waiting for them on her usual perch by the front gate. The window boxes, once filled with colourful geraniums, were now bare apart from dark green ivy that still trailed down the terracotta sides like a leafy curtain.

'Just us tonight,' Robert commented, applying the handbrake. 'That makes a change.'

There was an edge to his tone, an echo from their past that made Liz smile, and when he suggested a nightcap, she wasn't surprised. Tired though she was, she said yes without a murmur.

After taking off their coats and boots, they went into the sitting room, which smelled of wood smoke mingled with the scent of white lilies, which were in a vase on the mantelpiece. Liz turned on the table lamps, creating a warm, cosy glow.

'Shall I light the fire?' said Robert, kneeling on the rug in front of the grate and pulling some kindling from the nearby basket. 'There's no rush up in the morning, is there? We can have a lie-in.'

He struck a match and the flames started to lick and splutter before dancing up the chimney. She fetched his whisky and an Amaretto for herself, and as the sweet liquid trickled down her throat, she remembered how, in a previous life, they had done this sort of thing together all the time.

Patting the cushions on the sofa, she beckoned him to join her and he sat down, glass in hand, while she ran her fingers through his thick brown hair. And all the while they chatted in low voices about this and that: the party, their girls and a possible holiday together, but it was obvious that both their minds were on something else.

Pulling up her feet, she curled against him and he wound an arm around her shoulders. She could feel the rise and fall of his breath and when he took a sip of his own drink, his stomach gurgled in reply.

'Are you hungry?' she asked, turning her head to look at him. 'Would you like me to make you a sandwich?'

He said no, at least, he wasn't hungry in the way that she meant, and although he sounded dead-pan, the corners of his mouth curled suggestively.

It was her cue. Swivelling herself around to face him, she wrapped one leg over his and arched up, planting little kisses on his chin, his jaw, his nose, the dent that appeared on his right cheek when he was trying to hide a smile, and finally, his full, soft lips.

Before long, his hands began to explore, and he slowly removed her clothes – deftly peeling off her sweater, shirt and bra, her fake leather trousers splattered with dry mud and finally, her socks and lacy knickers, until all that remained, resting in the groove of her collarbone, was the thin gold necklace with a heart-shaped locket on the end that he had given her for her birthday.

With the curtains drawn and the door closed, suddenly the room felt hot and sticky with anticipation and she licked her lips as he lowered her onto her back and knelt beside her, gently biting her neck before moving down to her breasts, her navel, the jutting bones of her hips.

Now that she was fully exposed, she guessed that he would linger for quite a while as he always used to do, enjoying her white limbs and naked vulnerability, stroking and teasing with skilful fingers and tongue until she'd have to beg him to stop. But tonight she had no time for such games; she wanted to seal the deal.

'Hurry!' she said, reaching for his belt, his flies, yanking down his trousers and pants and noticing in passing how the flaps of his shirt, still buttoned to his chest, rose magnificently, like a sail in the wind.

He half-pulled and she half-wriggled off the seat and onto the carpet where she lay spread-eagled, curving her back and pushing up slightly as he eased his familiar weight onto her.

'I want to really feel you,' she commanded, running her hands over his tight stomach, which was as hard as a board, and his backside powered up as the muscles began to perform their fluid gymnastics.

He moved slowly and carefully at first but soon, a potent rhythm took over and she cried out in grateful recognition, remembering and not remembering the distinctive pattern of his movements and that particular, delicious tango that their two bodies had always managed to create.

'Come in me,' she urged. She wanted him to fill her up there and then till there was nothing left of her, no black thoughts or guilty memories, until he'd washed her completely clean.

He didn't argue, and she watched his face intently all the time, noticing the focus in his eyes, the ridiculously long lashes that flicked at the ends like a girl's, the mouth stretched tight, the beads of sweat forming on his forehead and she thought – *aren't I lucky? He's mine!*

He climaxed with a strange, grateful cry, like a primal howl, and she felt humbled by the trust that he had placed in her and awed by the sweet simplicity of his pleasure. Their sex had never been selfish but always like a gift to each other, an act of giving and receiving. How could she have forgotten? How could she have treated it so carelessly?

Tears pricked in the corners of her eyes, which she tried to disguise by turning her face away. At first he didn't notice, but then, when his breathing began to slow, he half-sat up, propping himself on an elbow, and examined her anxiously.

'What's the matter?' He was trying hard to read her expression, searching for clues. 'Did I do something wrong?'

'No,' she replied truthfully. 'You were wonderful. That was the best. It's just that it's been so long.'

She imagined the quiet street outside, the countless souls tucked up in their beds sound asleep and Max, perhaps, staring up at the high, corniced ceiling of his temporary abode, going over and over what had taken place between them.

'I wish we could do this more often,' she said.

He nodded, as if she'd stolen his exact same thought and made it all her own. He kissed her eyelids, the tip of her nose and finally her mouth, before lying down again beside her, his head curiously childlike against her pale breast, his hand on her thigh.

'I love you, Lizzie,' he whispered, and her answering sigh was like the wind rustling through the falling autumn leaves outside the window and the fretful, tossing Cornish sea.

'I love you, too, my darling,' she replied, meaning every word. 'If only the world would go away and we could stay like this for ever.'

Acknowledgements

With many thanks to my agent, Heather Holden-Brown, my editor, Rosie de Courcy, and all at Head of Zeus. Also to Orla Meehan, Associate Solicitor, Clintons, for her legal advice, and, as ever, to my husband, Kevin, for his love and support.

A letter from the publisher

We hope you enjoyed this book. We are an independent publisher dedicated to discovering brilliant books, new authors and great storytelling. If you want to hear more, why not join our community of book-lovers at:

www.headofzeus.com

We'll keep you up-to-date with our latest books, author blogs, tempting offers, chances to win signed editions, events across the UK and much more.

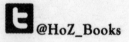 @HoZ_Books

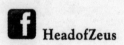 HeadofZeus

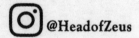 @HeadofZeus

HEAD of ZEUS